THE BEGINNING WOODS

Malcolm McNeill

Sky Pony Press
New York

Library of Congress Cataloging-in-Publication Data available on file.

ISBN: 978-1-5107-2290-3
eBook ISBN 978-1-5107-2291-0

Cover design by Sammy Yuen
Cover art credit Emily Coggins

Printed in the United States of America

Interior layout: Joshua Barnaby

Us.

The crisis took place in every country. It was compared to a plague that knew no boundaries, or a fire that ravaged a forest. But scientists were able to cure the plague, and the secret of putting out fires had been discovered long ago.

There was no stopping the Vanishings.

When they first began, nobody realized what was going on. Crumpled piles of clothes were discovered at the bottom of gardens or in cupboards under stairs, but that was no reason to suppose someone had been Whisked Away Into Nothing, that they had Ceased To Exist, that they had been Cancelled Out.

Such things were unheard of, after all.

Then the Vanishings began to spread. Before long thousands were Vanishing every day, and it became clear something unusual was going on—especially from a scientific point of view.

Of course, whenever a great problem threatens the world all enemies put down their swords and work together to find a solution. This was the case with the Vanishings. Scientists came from far and wide to form an International Symposium in Paris, and a special fund was set up to provide them with everything they needed to carry out their research.

It was decided to house the Symposium in the Trocadéro Palace, an old museum filled with ancient artifacts, archaeological treasures, paintings, sculptures, and fossils. Artists and inventors had gathered at the Trocadéro in 1878 to mark

PROLOGUE

There was a time, not so long ago, when a strange phenomenon swept the world, baffling scientists and defying explanation.

It had nothing to do with gravity or electricity.

It altered no weather patterns, sea levels, or average temperatures.

The migration of beasts across the globe did not change, and plants continued to grow, bloom, and die in their proper seasons.

Even the biochemical reactions that sustain life went on with unceasing vigor, as they had for millions of years, propelling organisms down myriad paths of development, just as the continents drifted apart, moved by the massive forces generated in the bowels of the earth.

Almost the entirety of creation was ignored by the new phenomenon, which concerned itself with one thing alone.

Contents

For my parents

their achievements at an International Exposition, so there was a pleasing historical precedent, but since then, the palace had fallen into disrepair, and an immense effort was required to renovate it in time for the Grand Opening.

Overnight, a skeleton of scaffolding sprang up against the walls. Beneath the flapping plastic that cocooned the building, a team of sand-blasters went to work on the decades of grime and soot that had blackened the granite and limestone. Hundreds of workers with wheelbarrows poured into the museum and carted off the many treasures to L'Hôtel des Invalides, where they were wrapped up and placed in storage. An army of engineers burrowed deep beneath its foundations, installing laboratories, generators, wires, and computers, while gardeners dug their fingers into the barren slopes leading down to the Seine, planting trees and shrubs, decorating them with fountains and pools of water. Finally, stonemasons laid a terrace of granite flagstones in front of the palace, and erected golden statues around it to lend the old building the grandeur it deserved.

The opening ceremony of the International Symposium for the Prevention and Cure of the Vanishings was a great day for the human race: a day of hope and purpose. The palace gleamed like a hero's smile, proudly bearing its pennants and flags as medallions of trust and responsibility. Below, the doctors and professors processed through the gardens, their chins tucked solemnly into their necks, their whole manner imparting gravity, wisdom, and, most of all, determination.

When they reached the terrace, a band struck up and the crowds of people cheered. They were the champions of humanity, proclaimed the trumpets and the drums. They were going to pit the might of science against the mysterious disappearances that threatened to devour the human race.

After speeches, applause, music, and cheering, the Seekers, as the scientists came to be known, filed into the Trocadéro, where they immediately went to work on a buffet lunch provided by the Mayor of Paris. The people remained out-side watching the windows, expecting a triumphant shout to go up at any moment, but the palace only settled into the evening gloom, like an old man in a deck chair fold-ing a newspaper across his face. As darkness fell, the crowd began to disperse. Flags, no longer needed for waving, were dropped onto pavements, banners were stuffed into bins, and the cafés and bars began to fill up once more.

How long would it take the Seekers to stop the Vanishings? That was the question on everyone's lips. Six weeks? Six months? A year?

"We do not know the length of the road ahead of us," the Chief Researcher said in his speech. "We do not know if it will be easy or difficult. We must be patient. We must be cautious with our hopes."

So the world held its breath and waited for the first findings.

Meanwhile, the Vanishings continued unabated. In every country, people Vanished without warning. Seeming to sense they were about to be consumed, they took themselves off somewhere secret, like dying elephants. Because of this, most of the Vanishings went unwitnessed—until the telltale puddle of clothing was found there was no reason to suppose a Vanishing had happened at all. But now and again, people would find themselves trapped in crowded train compartments, or in business meetings, where it was not possible to escape the public eye. Some Vanishings even occurred live on television. Elenia Diakou, the Olympic champion figure skater, Vanished in front of six million viewers while singing the Canadian national anthem on the gold winner's podium; Paul Herbert, the French financier, unintentionally set the record for the highest-altitude Vanishing when he disappeared from beneath his parachute at 57,000 feet; and Edwin Wong, the virtuoso pianist, Vanished while laying down the final chords of Rachmaninov's *Prelude in B minor*, which the judges deemed so in keeping with the nature of the piece they awarded him the Queen Elisabeth of Belgium prize, even though he was not there to receive it. It goes without saying that there was no shortage of wild theories to account for the Vanishings—but nobody paid them any attention. Everyone was waiting for the Seekers to crack it. Only they could come up with the answer.

But the days turned into weeks, the weeks into months, and the Symposium doors remained closed. In this vacuum of information, a new, frightening idea took hold—that the Vanishings could not be stopped, that they would continue until nobody remained.

Only one thing gave cause for hope, a little quirk in the behavior of the Vanishings that soon became obvious.

Children did not Vanish.

There was something about children the Vanishings did not like, or could not touch.

But nobody could say what this was.

After two long years of evidence-gathering and fruitless speculation, the Chief Researcher was forced to admit that the Symposium was no closer to understanding the Vanishings than before. In the storm that followed this confession, a new man took over—an unknown scientist called Professor Courtz.

His inaugural address on the steps of the Trocadéro inspired fresh confidence in the hearts of those who were afraid. They took comfort in his military-style mustache, his gray hair slicked back with tonic, and most of all, in his astonishing blue eyes, which sparkled with intelligence. There was something solid and reliable about him, something well thought out and structured, like a judge's closing remarks or a balanced equation.

He ended his speech with an appeal for privacy to study the Vanishings undisturbed. All future contact, he announced, would be made through subordinates at monthly press conferences. Those watching barely registered the significance of these words. But that public appearance was indeed his last, and afterward he disappeared from view.

At first this odd conduct was tolerated and even appreciated. The new Chief Researcher was a serious man who did not seek celebrity. Well and good! But after some time, his reclusive behavior lost its appeal. Nobody believed the bland reassurances of the Symposium bulletins, and an idea gathered force that the Professor himself had Vanished, that he—even he!—had succumbed.

It was around this time that the light appeared, glinting and twinkling in the highest window of the Trocadéro. Nobody knew who spotted it first, but there it was, shining through the night when all others had been extinguished. This tiny beacon was all the troubled citizens of the world needed to regain the faith they had lost. When the children of Paris woke from nightmares of empty houses, their parents would carry them to a window and point across the rooftops.

There he sits, they would say. There he sits, working away. One day he's bound to solve the Vanishings.

One day soon!

PART ONE

THE VANISHINGS

There are many ways of disappearing besides Vanishing.

Some people fall into the sea and are marooned on desert islands. Others climb into the mountains, where they shiver and make clothes out of yak fur. There are even those who leave their lives behind and take to the open road, where they get sore feet and a magnificent suntan.

People have always disappeared; it's nothing new. It's something people just do.

Doctor Boris Peshkov,
Reflections on the Vanishings

1

In A Bad Light

Boris tapped the desk lamp that had just flickered and died, then unscrewed the bulb and examined the faintly glowing filament, his worn engineer's fingers unflinching on the hot glass.

So that was it, he thought. At long last.

When he'd left the Symposium, he'd made himself a peculiar promise: he would continue his struggle to solve the Vanishings until all the bulbs in his apartment had blown. Only when he sat in total darkness would he allow himself to admit defeat.

For days now, he'd been carrying this last lamp from room to room—to the kitchen to prepare pots of coffee, or the bathroom to stare at his hollow-eyed reflection—trailing the extension cord around the towers of boxes and stacks of files that were his only companions.

And tonight his time had run out.

He sat in the darkness, overcome with relief. For so long now, he had wanted to surrender and let it all go. He had done all he could, and more. It was time to stop.

Except . . .

He picked up a screwdriver and pushed himself to his feet. An hour later, the refrigerator lay in pieces and he had built a new lamp from its dismantled parts. But instead of turning it on and resuming his work, he placed his chair by the window and stared out at the lights of Paris and the streets they half revealed.

In the distance, across the rooftops, the many windows of the ISPCV were dark—all except one, where his old mentor, Professor Courtz, wrestled with the same mystery. He gave Courtz's light only a momentary glance, and fell instead to watching the late-night loners of Montmartre, meandering around below as though trapped in a labyrinth from which there was no escape; the drunks, the *flâneurs*, and the entangled; the eaters of opium; the criminals. One day soon, he knew, he would join them—when his struggle against the Vanishings had driven him mad.

What hope did he have, after all? He was no longer a top Symposium Seeker, with access to laboratories and state-of-the-art equipment. Now, he was nothing more than an unknown Russian scientist sitting alone by the window of a tiny Montmartre apartment. He had his pencils, his notebooks, and his brain, and that was all.

But maybe that would be enough.

Of all the scientists in the world, Boris was the closest to unlocking the secret of the Vanishings.

But he did not know this.

If someone had told him—if, one day as he sat at his desk, a peculiar little man had crept out of the cupboard behind him and whispered softly in his ear: "You nearly have it, my lad, keep going!" he would not have believed him for a moment, even if the little man had then disappeared in a flash of blue light. Sometimes, he thought the Vanishings were a mystery he would never understand.

Nevertheless, even Courtz and the Seekers were far behind Boris in the quest to solve the Vanishings. Boris had something they did not, something worth more than Symposiums and funding and hi-tech equipment.

He found the Vanishings beautiful.

Every night, on his own, he studied his files and reports, his photographs and videotapes, trying to find some kind of common cause or link between each case. Over and over in his head, he saw the films he had gathered of people fading from the world. The Vanishings were *sad*, it was true. But were they *surprising*? He did not leap to this conclusion like everyone else. The Vanishings were certainly strange, but strange in a way that made him tremble with longing, a longing to understand them and put an end to them, and maybe even a longing to Vanish himself—something he was quite prepared to do, if it meant discovering a solution.

Answers, he knew, would not be coming from the Symposium.

Courtz and the Seekers treated the Vanishings like a problem of science. Boris felt a different approach was necessary. He reacted to the Vanishings not as a scientist trying to analyze a new phenomenon, but as a complete individual, a living, breathing, feeling soul.

The Vanishings, he had argued again and again, had nothing to do with science. They came from something else, something human, something *poetic*. They had sprung from a place where science had no authority: the human condition itself. They had been started not by a change in scientific law, but by an alteration in human nature, possibly even a tiny alteration—a single turn of a single screw in a machine of a million parts.

Perhaps this change had been brewing for centuries in the processes of history, like a potion in a Witch's cauldron.

Perhaps it had struck like a bolt of lightning in recent years.

But it had come.

He lit a cigarette and continued to stare out of the window at the streets below.

As far as he could tell there was only one chink in the Vanishings' defenses, a tiny window through which he hoped to force entry. Again and again, he came back to this clue, but he could not see what it meant.

Children did not Vanish.

Children had always been the choicest prize of the Wolf, and here was the Wolf, leaving them be. Not because it wanted to; not out of kindness. Whenever he saw a child pass in the streets below his window, he thought he heard the Vanishings snarling in the air—held at bay, somehow, by a lollipop. And this puzzled him.

"Perhaps it is children who will stop the Vanishings," he muttered, scratching at his beard. "Not men like me."

Thoughts like these, dispiriting to others, only aroused his determination. He switched on his improvised light and opened his notebook to look back through his thoughts. Doing so, could set off a new association. But tonight he got no farther than the very first entry—a short question, written the moment he'd learned of the Vanishings. He'd erased it at once, but the letters were still visible, the indentation still there under his fingers. Now it looked more ridiculous than ever, no better than the wild guesses put forward by the celebrity scientists on television.

He snapped the notebook shut and threw it away from him, then fell once more to staring out of the window. This time, there were no thoughts, no ideas, no memories—only a deep sadness that captivated him, and seemed to speak more truly of the Vanishings than words ever could.

He did not stir again until his watch beeped. It was nearly time for the meeting.

Heaving himself to his feet, he slung on his rumpled black jacket, thrust some coins, keys, matches, cigarettes, pencils, and paper into his pockets and left the apartment, his heavy tread booming on the stairs that would take him out into the electric glow of the Paris night.

The question remained, faint in his notebook, faint in the back of his mind:

What if it's all got something to do with the Woods?

Ten minutes later, he slid onto a stool in a tiny café hidden along the rue Jacquemont. It was two in the morning, and as usual, he was the only customer. Ghostly white sleeves hovered in the gloom behind the bar; with a clink, a candle, and a coffee materialized in front of him.

He lit a cigarette and waited. In the mirror above the bar, his reflection watched him from behind dimly glinting bottles, his pale face drawn with exhaustion.

If I solve the Vanishings, will I be able to sleep and enjoy life, the way other people sleep and enjoy life?

It seemed an impossible fantasy, but a pleasing one, and he was beginning to dream of a simple garden, of potatoes and cherry trees, when a movement in the mirror caught his attention. He was being observed, he saw, by a tall figure standing in the shadows near the door. If it was the woman he had come to meet, she had entered so quietly neither he nor the bartender had heard.

"Mrs. Jeffers?"

"Who else would it be, this time of night?" She moved forward a little, enough for him to see long, wrinkled hands arranging the folds of a golf umbrella. "Get him to turn off the lights, will you?"

"Lights?" He glanced around. "You mean the candles?"

"You don't *turn off* candles, Doctor Peshkov. It's the cigarette machine. The beer fridges. And that absurd Eiffel Tower lamp beside the register."

"But why?"

"You know why."

"I do?"

"Look—have him light more candles if the dark frightens you."

But the bartender was already making the necessary adjustments. "*Pas de problème,*" he murmured. "*Pas de problème.*"

"Pierre, *merci,*" said Boris, as candles appeared one by one in bottles along the bar.

"Lovely," the old woman said approvingly. "Now we can get down to business."

She left the shadows, and Boris watched in the mirror as she organized her limbs on the stool beside him. She was about as old as he'd expected from the antiquated handwriting of her letter. Her dark-gray hair was twisted into a serpentine tower, held in position—magically, it seemed—by a single silver pin, long as a knitting needle, thrust diagonally downward. Ornate silver earrings hung from her ears, which drooped under their weight. Her face was long and bony, and covered in an elderly fuzz of white hair, while her close-set, penetrating eyes reminded him of a bird—a heron, or a crane.

It was all typical of the cultured, eccentric sort he'd expected. So why, as he studied her, did he feel a creeping unease? From the moment he'd seen her appear in the shadows by the door, a small balloon of fear had been inflating in his throat.

"I don't remember the last time I was up so late," she complained, propping her umbrella against her stool. "I suppose you adore nighttimes in cities. Wandering the streets. Collar up. Frowning like a murderer."

"You've been following me?"

"At night? Not likely. As far as I'm concerned there's nothing worse than a city at night."

"And yet, here you are."

"This is a special occasion. Speaking of which. Monsieur! *Puis-je une* WHISKY!" She rapped on the bar, making a loud clacking sound, and he noticed several silver rings glinting on her fingers. "It's not past your bedtime though, is it?"

"What? No. Actually, yes," he said. "It's been past my bedtime for two days."

"What's keeping you awake? Monsters under the bed?"

"There are no monsters under the bed."

"Are you sure?"

"Quite sure," he said. "I've checked."

"You had to check? I like that, *hehheh*, that's good. *Merci*, dear boy." The bartender retreated with a hushed *de rien*, and she sipped her whisky. "So what is it, if it's not monsters?"

Boris crushed his cigarette into an ashtray and imagined telling her what happened when he tried to sleep.

How he'd lie down and close his eyes.

How one of the Vanished would appear in his mind.

How he'd think about this person—who they were, where they lived, who they'd left behind—and how he'd find something had slipped from his memory, their age or some other detail. How this would torture him so much, he'd have to get up and go through his files until he found the missing information. And then he'd be trapped. He'd have to look at them all, one by one. Because the thought that terrified him more than any other was that one had been forgotten—that not only a name, or an age, or a birthplace, but an entire life had slipped from existence forever.

The café door banged—a stack of freshly printed newspapers hit the floor. He blinked and came out of himself. From the old woman's face, he saw that he hadn't just imagined telling her—he'd actually spoken his thoughts out loud.

"I thought you'd be like this," she said, touching his arm. "And seeing you now, and listening to you, I understand so much about you. You're a kind man, and you've taken the Vanishings to heart, that's all."

Boris felt his eyes, absurdly, filling with tears. His rough fingertips fumbled them away. If the old woman saw she pretended not to.

"So," he said. "Why were you so determined to meet *me*? Why not one of the Seekers?"

"Oh, my little story isn't something you want regular scientists getting their hands on," she said, with a quiet smile. "It's for someone a bit more . . . from both worlds, if you know what I mean."

"There's only one world."

"Have you checked that, too?"

"I don't need to. I'm sure."

She clicked her tongue. "Don't say that. It doesn't come from you, from your heart. Professor Courtz might say it. But not you."

The sudden mention of Courtz took Boris by surprise. "He's a recluse. How do you know what he'd say?"

"It's plain what kind of man he is. All circuit boards and equations. He'd rather words were numbers and ideas were formulas. You're different. There's something of the cauldron about you. Something Witch-made. It's a mind like yours that'll solve the Vanishings, not a mind like his. Don't you know that?"

"I know Courtz." He gave her a grudging look. "Perhaps you know people you don't know quite well."

"You'd be surprised, dear boy, what I know, you really would."

"Do you know how to stop the Vanishings?"

"I know how they started."

"That's nothing. Even Pierre knows that. *Pierre, les Disparitions, c'a commencé comment?*"

"*Par les Anglais,*" mumbled the bartender from behind a newspaper.

"You see?" said Boris. "It was the English. Everyone has an opinion. What's so special about yours?"

"Who's talking about opinions? This isn't something I thought up. It's something I saw."

"We have to correctly interpret what we see."

"And if there's only one possible interpretation?"

"Then there is no need to seek out mine."

"I didn't come here for your opinion. I came here for your help."

"My help?"

"Your help," she said again, nodding. "I *would* say your help alone, but we never really are alone, are we, Doctor Peshkov? Even the most solitary traveler is pursued by demons. Or *Wolves.*"

"Wolves?" He glanced at his reflection. The other Boris was there, no surprises. "What do you mean?"

"First things first. I'll tell you what I saw, then we can get down to business. Are you ready?"

He nodded, and she leaned in close to whisper in his ear. It was only a short sentence—having said it, she leaned back and sat waiting for his response.

He scratched the side of his face to hide his disappointment. Why did he bother with these meetings? They always turned out the same way. Some wild story. Some strange fantasy cooked up by a lonely soul. Over the years he'd heard hundreds of theories. And this one beat the lot.

"A *baby* started the Vanishings?" He was unable to conceal his disbelief. "That's what you wanted to tell me?"

"That's it, yes," she nodded, before adding hastily: "I'm not saying he did it on purpose. He can't have known what he was doing—I mean, he's only just learned to walk."

"I'm sorry," he said. "I've never heard anything more ridiculous."

"There's that fellow Courtz again. Why do you keep trying to be someone you're not?"

"Whatever our differences, we are both scientists. We share certain basic standards. By those basic standards, it's absurd."

"Is it? What have you discovered about the Vanishings that makes you so sure?"

This was a good point, he thought, but he was unwilling to waste any more time. He reached into his pockets for some coins and was about to leave when a late-night taxi turned on the road outside. Twin shafts of light swept through the bar, catching the old woman side-on.

"Dratted stuff," she muttered, flinching slightly. "Just no escape, is there?"

The moment was over in a second, but he saw it. Pain flickered in her eyes, and the skin around her nose and mouth tightened. Even her hair changed, the iron-gray gleaming white as the light passed over it.

Somehow he managed to conceal his first reaction. Then panic was galloping up on him. He fumbled for a cigarette, and snapped one match after another trying to light it. Giving up, he reached for a candle—but that stopped him dead.

The candles . . .

All that fuss about the lights . . .

The cigarette tumbled from between his nerveless fingers. Somewhere a thousand miles away, the old woman was speaking. Was he feeling all right? He'd gone all pale. And he was pale enough to begin with!

"I'm fine. I just . . . I thought I saw . . . Please, go on . . ."

He put his palms flat on the bar. Lowering his head, he forced himself to breathe steadily. Deeply.

And then he saw her umbrella, propped against her stool. Her *neatly folded* umbrella.

His body went weak.

She'd been folding it when she came in. That meant she'd had it open. But it hadn't been raining. She'd been walking around on a clear night under an open umbrella. Why?

You know why.

He felt himself collapsing. He did know. He'd just refused to admit it. And now the question was rising in his mind, no longer faint, no longer a whisper—but a roar.

What if it's all got something to do with the Woods?

Tensing his shoulders, he held himself together with sheer force of will.

It couldn't be that. It was impossible. He would prove it.

He caught Pierre's eye. "*Lumière*," he mouthed.

Bizarrely unconcerned, the bartender sidled toward the switch that would ignite the chandelier glittering darkly above them. The old woman had noticed nothing and was still talking, but now he couldn't understand a single one of the words she was saying.

. . . *Beschreibung deß Lebens eines seltzamen Vaganten, genant Melchior Sternfels von Fuchshaim, wo und welcher gestalt er nemlich in diese Welt kommen—*

German.

Why was she talking German all of a sudden?

Panic drove him to his feet. She stopped and stared in astonishment as he stepped away from her. She saw the guilty flicker of his eyes toward Pierre, whose hand was lifting toward the tiny brass switch.

"Oh, you merry fools," she muttered.

Her hand snapped down for her umbrella. The chandelier lit up in a blaze of light.

She jerked like a bomb had gone off, her arms coming up to cover her head. A second later, she went for her umbrella again, bending down, but this time she keeled forward, toppling off her stool. He threw his arms around her.

"You idiot!" she got out. "Turn it off!"

He stared in horror at her upturned face. Her eyes were bulging out of their sockets, white as hard-boiled eggs.

She was blind.

He'd blinded her.

And her hair! The gray tower of tightly bound coils was falling apart, crumbling like ash from a cigarette.

He ripped off his jacket and threw it over her. "PIERRE!" he screamed. "*Vite! Vite!*"

The bartender was pressed back against the wall, shaking his head from side to side.

"*Vite? Comment-ça, vite?*"

"*La lumière, pour l'amour de Dieu! Éteins!*" Pierre's hand flapped up.

click

Nothing.

clickclickclickclickclick

"PIERRE!"

"*Ça ne marche plus! Ça ne marche plus!*"

Boris vaulted the bar and struck the brass plate a terrible blow with his fist. It disappeared into the wall with a puff of dust—the light flickered but did not go out.

He spun back around.

The old woman was pulling herself along the bar, knocking over stools and bottles. His jacket had fallen from her head, and now the light was really going to work, turning her from a tall old woman to a hunched, shriveling creature. Her spine arched into a question-mark curve, the vertebrae popping one by one. Her face drew against her skull like a sock pulled too tight. She lifted her hands to shield herself—they crisped and crackled into blackened claws.

He vaulted back over the bar and snatched up her umbrella. Pressed the catch and pushed.

It jammed.

clickclickclickclick

Howling, he smashed it to pieces against the bar.

The old woman sagged against a table. Candles and bottles went flying.

"Idiot . . . scientist," she got out. Teeth dropped from her mouth and rattled across the table like dice. Then she slid onto the floor, a tangle of skin and bones—curling up, smaller and smaller. Above her the chandelier rattled with malevolent energy, every one of its crystals shivering with delight as it punished the old woman for daring to intrude where she did not belong.

Boris cast around, snatched up a stool, and sent it spinning upward.

With a violent crash the bar was plunged into gloom.

Swiftly, he was on his knees beside her. Her breath was coming in shallow gasps. She was saying something.

What was it?

Again!

Candle . . .

There were many scattered around. He relit one and held it next to her, anxiously touching her shoulders, not knowing what to do, how to help.

A twitch of her fingers motioned him away.

He jammed the candle in a bottle and slumped back against the bar. He watched that light as it worked its ancient magic, stroking her with the gentlest of touches, a painter at a work of restoration.

He'd nearly killed her.

He'd nearly killed one of the Forest Folk.

He pressed his trembling hands to either side of his head. Now he knew two things he hadn't known before.

Why the old woman had come to him.

And that it all very definitely had something to do with the Woods.

2

THE ORPANAB KOBOLD

Babies come in all shapes and sizes.

A baby might be beautiful or ugly, fat or thin, it will make no difference. Whatever its appearance, the baby will be loved, and will enjoy the nurturing consequences of that devotion.

The one thing a baby absolutely must not be is spooky. A spooky baby will struggle to kindle love.

"Is this thing before me really, truly, in actual fact . . . a baby?" That is the terrible doubt in the minds of those who behold a spooky baby. "Might it not be *something else?*"

The baby who started the Vanishings was one such spooky baby.

In those early days, the Vanishings had not yet begun. He had set them in motion, and they were still to make their grand debut, but even so—right from the morning of his arrival at the Surbiton Center for Orphaned and Abandoned Babies, he made himself known as an oddity.

Nobody knew where he'd come from. The ORPANAB nurses only knew he'd been found in a bookshop, and this lack of information was, in itself, spook-worthy. Babies arriving into their care usually came with some token from their previous lives. A tear-stained note. A snot-streaked blanket. This one had the nerve to arrive empty-handed. And what was even more extraordinary, what boggled the minds of the nurses, was that he'd been found entirely naked, without even a sheet of newspaper to wrap him in.

But it was no surprise he was unwanted, the nurses thought. He was just *so spooky*.

Instead of the plump little arms and legs of conventional newborns, he had hard, animal limbs more suited to leaping and burrowing. He had a way of staring, too, of staring and staring—and it was such an adult stare! He seemed to know things beyond his age, as though he might open his mouth and start reciting Shakespeare, or make a comment about recent political developments.

Indeed, when he did open his mouth for the first time, on the occasion of a yawn, his spookiest feature was revealed: his teeth. Not the partially visible buds sometimes found in newborns, but ten shining little pearls, perfectly formed and hard as barnacles.

He was only, at the most, a few days old. And already he was snapping the ends off pencils.

Spooky!

Things got spookier still when he was brought to the main dormitory. On an average day, this was the noisiest room in England. Noisier than the stock market or Parliament or the Monkey House in London Zoo. A hundred babies, all screaming at once, as though making up for those tedious months of floating in amniotic fluids, unable to make a single squeak. Day in, day out, a roar of confusion, interrupted only by stunned, milky stupor.

But on his arrival, the clamor fell silent. One by one, as the startled nurse passed between the cribs with the newcomer in her arms, the babies rolled over to stare at the eyes glittering darkly from the crook of her neck.

They knew What This Was that had arrived among them. They knew he did not belong.

The newcomer seemed to agree. That same afternoon, the nurses caught him scuttling across the nursery, heading for the exit—the first of many determined attempts to escape. Again and again, he had to be hooked down from a windowsill, where he would sit with his face pressed against the glass, longingly looking out at the world below. One week he disappeared entirely, sparking a manhunt and a newspaper article—he was on the rooftop, clambering among the Victorian chimney pots.

Measures were taken. Procedures put in place. None worked.

They tethered him to the bars of his crib. The tether was undone.

They added a lock. The lock was never seen again.

In the end, the exasperated nurses bolted a lid onto the crib. From within this hutch, he glared back at his captors, plotting his next move. On the third day, the crib was empty. Three of its bars had been chewed through, as though by a wild animal. That afternoon a police helicopter spotted the baby racing across the common.

The nurses were perturbed.

None of them had seen anything like it.

None, that is, except Frau Winkler, an ancient German from the forests of Bavaria. The rooftop escape had brought back a memory of a picture in a book of fairy tales she'd read as a child. It showed a moonlit, magical scene—a farmhouse encrusted with snow; perched by the chimney stack, a Kobold, his nose lifted to the delicious odors wafting up from the oven below.

Er will den Stollen stehlen, the inscription had read. He wants to steal the Stollen.

Seventy years this memory had slept in her mind, but when she saw the baby among the chimney pots, it came back to her once more.

The Kobold had escaped the story book, had he, and tracked her down at the end of her days?

She would keep a close eye on his activities!

Every afternoon at three o'clock sharp a bell would ring, and visitors would file into the dormitory with a view to helping themselves to one of the babies on display.

The moment he heard the bell, the Kobold would roll onto his front and examine these Maybe Parents, his jet-black eyes staring fixedly. The couples would move around the room, bending now and again to coo at the bawling infants. Sooner or later, they'd be drawn to the Kobold's corner, sensing that something dwelled there, that it was a lair of some sort. By now, the Kobold would be sitting up, his oddly squashed head held perfectly still, his long fingers curled around the bars of his cage. It seemed to Frau Winkler that of all the babies, only the Kobold knew what was at stake. When the Maybe Parents were close enough, he would stretch his arms through the bars of his prison. Smiling uneasily, they would bend closer to get a better look, and then—he could not help it—the Kobold would smile back, revealing his teeth.

The brave would shudder and turn away. The faint-hearted would scream.

The Kobold would shrink back into darkness.

Later in the afternoon, nurses would enter and remove several of the lucky babies, passing the Kobold with a look of admonishment.

What did you expect?

Why would anyone want a thing like YOU?

And the Kobold would roll onto his side and face the wall, and not look around for some time.

The Balloon and the Moldy Corner

This wall the Kobold faced whenever he rolled away from the world was not blank plaster like the other walls in the ORPANAB Center. It was decorated with a mural, painted years before when the ORPANAB Center had been a government asylum.

The artists had been the inmates, themselves. Under the supervision of a local entertainer named Boppo the Color Clown, they had been permitted to express their innermost feelings upon the wall of their canteen. Though the canteen was now a dormitory, and Boppo the Color Clown was long in his grave, their masterpiece remained.

If the ORPANAB babies had taken the mural to be a representation of the outside world, which most had never seen, they would have understood that the Taj Mahal, the Alps, a main street, and a jungle all stood together in close proximity, and that the world was populated by braying, bucking donkeys pursued by police officers with red faces and stomping black boots.

Most of the Maybe Parents found it a comical piece of work, but some sensitive souls couldn't look at it without thinking the donkeys were too bewildered and the officers, too menacing. These people (like the Kobold) found themselves drawn to an almost invisible detail, added by a patient with an old soul, perhaps, who had stood at the top of a ladder while the others splashed around below, pouring pent-up longing and sadness into an image of heart-stopping beauty: a Hot-Air Balloon, hanging high and away on the upper edge of the mural and therefore the world, about to drift free of the sky into some other unknown region.

The Kobold spent hours gazing up at this Balloon and the two indistinct pilots in its basket. They never turned away like the Maybe Parents, never scowled like the nurses, or held him upside down by the ankles and rudely wiped his bottom. They looked right back, smiling and waving. Before long, the Kobold lost all interest in the Maybe Parents and never once turned to examine them when they entered in the afternoons. Instead, he gazed longingly at the Hot-Air Balloon and the smiling faces—longingly and hopefully, then fearfully and anxiously, for the Hot-Air Balloon was heading directly for the Moldy Corner.

This sinister patch of ceiling was never reached by the sunlight that streamed in through the sash windows of the old asylum. It remained always in shadow, and there the damp, vaporous breath of the babies gathered and became mold—dark, swampy mold. There was something about this Moldy Corner that was truly monstrous, and the Kobold watched its growth in terror. Each day, it crept closer to the Balloon, and its occupants only smiled and waved, unaware of the horror bearing down on them.

Did they not see?

Was there no way to warn them?

There was not, and the Kobold was forced to watch as the mold passed over them with the slow certainty of an eclipse.

And then they were gone.

Only Frau Winkler noticed these obsessions. She wondered if the mold was a portal the Kobold used to escape the ORPANAB after dark. When she was alone on night duty, she would check his crib at regular intervals. Finding him asleep, she would stare at him mistrustfully. "Who are you?" she would whisper on those occasions. "Where do you come from?"

Those questions were the only words ever addressed to the Kobold during his stay at the ORPANAB Center. No kootchy-koos, no words of affection, no bedtime stories. Instead: "Who are you?" and "Where do you come from?" over and over again, repeated a thousand times and always in the deepest part of the night, when the soul is ruptured by sleep, when cracks appear, emitting dreams, but through which in the other direction outside impressions may also creep, becoming stowaways in the soul. At that time, at that soft, vulnerable time, who knows how those questions influenced the Kobold's developing mind.

Perhaps all our lives have been shaped by a strange old woman hunched over us in the night, and what she whispers. . . .

LIFTED, HELD, HOOKED, AND PICKED

The next words the Kobold heard were: "Time to go!" and "Come on then!" and "Up with you!" Not Winkler's words, but those of Mr. Linklater, the ORPANAB director, and not whispered, but said in a business-like way with impatient clicks of a pen.

Three months the Kobold had sat in his hutch. His official status had been downgraded from Unwanted to Unwantable, and it was high time he was shipped to the long-term depository in the countryside.

So here was Mr. Linklater saying, "Let's have none of this nonsense!" and "What the Devil's he playing at?" and "Get me an aspirin, will you, Mrs. Winkler." The transfer forms had been completed, but it seemed the Kobold no longer wished to leave, and had fastened himself to a bar of the crib by means of biting it.

Tickling, nipping, and prodding proving ineffective, Mr. Linklater thrust his pen between the locked jaws, pried them apart and snatched the Kobold up. The hidden consequence of this action was to break the Kobold's view of the Hot-Air Balloon. He at once began to make a most unusual noise—a low, threatening growl like the snarling of a woodland creature. Frau Winkler and the other nurses, who had never heard the Kobold make a sound, hunched their shoulders in surprise, and all the babies burst into a chorus of screaming.

"Um . . ." said Mr. Linklater, undergoing the sensations people undergo when they are snarled at by small creatures.

"Do not worry, he does not bite," said Frau Winkler, knowing full well the Kobold very definitely did bite, and would at any moment. But she had a nurse's courage and took the Kobold from Mr. Linklater's outstretched arms.

"You frightened him, that is all," she said. "He had settled in here so nicely he does not want to leave."

Holding the Kobold in front of her like a ticking bomb, she marched him out of the dormitory and down the corridor, Mr. Linklater hurrying behind. But it was visiting hour, and the would-be parents were waiting in a long line for admission to the dormitory. Held out like this, the Kobold was presented to them for one last series of rejections, as if he had not quite absorbed his lesson and needed a reminder. One by one, the visitors shrank back in horror, and each time the Kobold screamed louder.

"You see?" Frau Winkler kept saying in her no-nonsense way. "*Nobody* wants you! *Nobody*! It's for your own good!"

But then, just as she got to the end of the line, a bearded mountain of a man stepped out, blocking her path.

"I'm Forbes!" he boomed, brandishing a prosthetic hook under her nose. "Hand him over!"

Frau Winkler screamed. The big black beard, the making-demands-and-introducing-yourself-at-the-same-time, the merry twinkle in the man's eyes and, most of all, the *hook* could mean only one thing: he was a pirate. In her astonishment, she loosened her grip and the Kobold, sensing freedom, made a break for it.

A falling baby is no laughing matter, especially one doing so head-first toward a tiled floor. Mr. Linklater immediately dropped his clipboard, which was a good start—it showed a gentlemanly sympathy and freed up his hands. But the sight of the clipboard falling next to the Kobold caused the word "Galileo" to flash into his mind, so for vital milliseconds, he was trapped in a state of flop-mouthed speculation: Which one would hit the ground first? Baby or clipboard? As for Frau Winkler, she was frozen by a Witch trial instinct: Now we'll see! If he really is the Kobold he will land on all fours. If not, he will smash his head open and that will be that!

Fortunately, the Kobold did not reach the ground to provide the hoped-for proof. With lightning speed, the pirate lunged forward, his hook flashing down.

"ARRGGGHH!" screamed Mr. Linklater, thinking in a moment of pure terror the baby had been impaled and he would lose his job. But all was well; the pirate flipped the Kobold and caught him in the palm of his hand—he'd hooked him by his diaper.

"*Guter! Gott!*" gasped Frau Winkler.

"I think he likes you, Forbes," said a quiet voice, and for the first time it became apparent that another person was there, a small, thin woman with wispy hair.

"Alice, I think he does," said Forbes, because the Kobold had gone quiet, and was studying him seriously. Forbes gave the Kobold's ear a nip with his hook, causing a giggle, the first noise of pleasure the Kobold had ever produced. "What's his name, nursie?"

"Kobold!" Frau Winkler blurted out.

"Kobold?" said Alice, her light eyes turning sharp and hard. "What sort of name is that?"

Frau Winkler drew herself up and assumed a dignified expression. "It is not a name. There was a chimney in a book

and he was sniffing it. He was trying to steal the Stollen!"
she finished, unable to believe that none of these idiots
understood.

There was a silence, then the click of a pen.

"Wait for me in my office, Mrs. Winkler," said Mr. Linklater.
Frau Winkler departed, Forbes and Alice remained, and Mr.
Linklater apologized, apologized, apologized: stress, pressure, staff shortages—no ORPANAB babies were given
names until placed with a family.

"And are you such a family?" he asked, bending sideways,
for some reason, with an insinuating grin. "Have you come
to view our collection? We have a great many."

They were not a family, at least not yet; they were a couple. And no, they didn't want to look at any other babies; this
one would do.

Mr. Linklater bent in the other direction. Ah, but this particular infant was due to be shipped, the cogs of bureaucracy
had been set in motion by certain forms he'd filled in, he'd
have to fill in others to stop them. Why this one, he wanted
to know, when there were so many others?

Oh, no special reason. Maybe because the little mite had
gone quiet on Forbes's shoulder and was nuzzling his ear-
lobe. Or maybe it was the allure of the propitious rescue, of
being there at the right moment with a quick hook. Fate had
spoken, it was meant to be, etc.

So after the necessary documents were completed, the
baby who had started the Vanishings was placed in the care

of Forbes and Alice Mulgan, and henceforth disappeared into their arms, into their car, and into their home—a natural progression, having already entered their hearts.

Later that afternoon, the family Mulgan assembled itself on the living-room sofa.

"He's a funny little fella," Forbes said, bouncing the Kobold on his knee.

"I wonder what his parents looked like," Alice said.

"Doesn't matter," said Forbes. "We're his parents now."

"Yes," said Alice. "We are." She snuggled up so Forbes could get his arm around them both. "What'll we call him?" she asked, fondling the Kobold's rather sharply-pointed ear.

"He's only a little thing. Let's give him a little name. But with a bit of bite. Like what he's got."

"What about . . . Max?"

"Max Mulgan," said Forbes, trying it out. "I like it!"

"I like it, too."

"That's it then!" Forbes tapped the Kobold once on each shoulder. "I name you King Max of Bickerstaffes Road!"

That evening King Max was shown his domain—a converted storeroom upstairs. As kingdoms go, it was sparsely populated. There was a crib Alice had seen in the window of a thrift shop and repainted. There was a set of drawers Forbes had found in the street and fixed up. On a shelf sat a magic lantern which, when lit at night and given a touch to set it turning, cast silhouettes against the wall—the shadows of birds, flying around and around and around.

Best of all, by some miracle or coincidence, Alice had decorated the wall opposite the bed with a mural. The one in the ORPANAB Center had been an amateurish effort, but this was a work of talent. It represented a country fair. There was a bouncy castle, a Merry-Go-Round, a ring toss, a petting zoo, a rummage sale, a bakery stand, a cotton candy caravan, and a donut wagon. With a touch of sinister genius, Alice had painted a Wolf standing unnoticed on its hind legs among the playing children. But Max hardly noticed this masterstroke. Something else caught his attention, something far more important.

In the background, between the prize vegetable competition and the pet dogs obstacle course, a Hot-Air Balloon was going up, trailing ropes that drooped toward the ground. It was bigger than the Balloon at the ORPANAB Center, big enough so the people in the wicker basket could be clearly made out. A thin man with round glasses. A woman with auburn hair. Still waving, and still smiling.

He smiled right back at them.

They had escaped the Moldy Corner. They were getting closer.

3

THE DARK MAN

A few months after Max's arrival at Bickerstaffes Road the Vanishings began. Even as the Mulgans watched the hullabaloo unfold over the following years, they had no idea the small boy they packed off to school each day with sandwiches and a carton of milk was the cause of it all.

Under the gentle strokes of their affection, he had shed some of his Koboldry. His ears were a little pointed, his skin stubbornly pale, and he ripped open bananas with his teeth—but the monstrous beginnings that spoke of spooky origins had faded with each passing year, until he was only a boy—small and quick as a thorn, with eyes that made the teachers falter in their lessons, but a boy nonetheless.

The first annual Symposium press conference came and went. The second, the third, the fourth, the fifth. None meant much to Max, or to any other eight-year-old. The Vanishings had always been around. There were educational puppet shows at nursery schools, cartoons on TV, projects at school, and Symposium speakers at morning assembly, who told you what to do if Mommy or Daddy "took off all their clothes and went away."

1.   Find a safe person.

2.   Dial 000.

But there were the same speakers, cartoons, and puppet shows for Crossing the Road, Not Talking To Strangers, and Not Playing With Matches. The Vanishings were just part of all that.

People Vanished.

It was something people just did.

So the Vanishings were a bit like the Dark Man. They were always there, and always had been.

Max saw the Dark Man almost every day. When Alice drove him to school in the morning, the Dark Man would be outside the gates. When Forbes took him to their local library, the Dark Man would be moving among the bookshelves. When they went on vacation to a campground in the mountains of Wales, the Dark Man was sitting in a corner of the local pub, warming his hands before the fire. Lying in bed at night, Max imagined that if he got up and peeked through the curtains, he would see the Dark Man under a street lamp, staring up at him.

And once he did.

And he was.

Even when the Dark Man wasn't around, he probably was, really. He had a clever way of going from plain sight to nowhere in the twinkling of a moment. All he had to do was step back into the shadows and he was gone—and shadows were always close by him. In his rumpled black suit, with his jet-black hair and beard, he was half made of them already. Only his pale face, shining like the surface of the moon, and his eyes, burning with curiosity, weren't so well camouflaged for darkness. And often that was all Max could see: the face, the eyes, and the curiosity.

He never confronted the Dark Man, or told anyone about him. The Dark Man was like the Squonk, a creature in one of his favorite library books—W. T. Cox's *Fearsome Creatures of the Lumberwoods*. Squonks lived in the forests of northern Pennsylvania, hiding themselves away on account of their ugly, baggy skin.

> Mr. J. P. Wentling, formerly of Pennsylvania, but now at St. Anthony Park, Minnesota, had a disappointing experience with a squonk near Mount Alto. He made a clever capture by mimicking the squonk and inducing it to hop into a sack, in which he was carrying it home, when suddenly the burden lightened and the weeping ceased. Wentling unslung the sack and looked in. There was nothing but tears and bubbles.

If he questioned the Dark Man, or told anyone about him, he would melt away in bubbles and tears. And he didn't want the Dark Man to go. The Dark Man was somewhere between a shadow and a friend.

As it turned out, though, the Dark Man was the one with questions.

The first time Max heard them, he was ten years old. He was in the supermarket with Alice, tagging along behind her, eating the chips she'd passed down. Near the bottom, he stopped to tilt the good crumbs into his mouth, and when he lowered the bag, Alice and the shopping cart had disappeared and the Dark Man was there like a clap of thunder, ten times close and a hundred times big.

He didn't introduce himself or explain what he wanted. He just asked two questions. Before Max had a chance to answer there was a clatter and a shout, and a snake of shopping carts rolled between them.

When it passed, the Dark Man was nowhere to be seen. Only his questions remained.

Who are you?

Where do you come from?

These questions seemed easy, and at first, Max believed he knew the answers. But the more he thought about it, the more he began to wonder.

If he'd answered the Dark Man with, "I'm Max Mulgan, I come from Bickerstaffes Road," somehow he knew the Dark Man would have replied, "No, you aren't," and "No, you don't." So the questions lodged in his mind, and other questions piled up behind them.

Where did I come from?

Where did where I come from come from?

Where did the where where the where where I came from come from?

Nobody except the Dark Man seemed interested in these questions. They weren't in the end-of-term tests at school. They weren't on quiz shows on TV. Nobody talked about them.

Nobody mentioned them.

This made him feel different. And that made him feel alone.

And that bound him to the Dark Man more than ever.

THE BOGGY CLUMP

But sometimes it was good to be alone.

Near Bickerstaffes Road was a park called Newton Fields, a wide, open place with a play area, a duck pond, and a resident Wind that blew with unending breaths across the grass, collecting and delivering birds and snapping the pages of newspapers. In the middle rose a hill where people gathered for picnics in summer, Bonfire Night in autumn, sledding in winter, and Easter-Egg-rolling in spring. Standing on its crest, Max could see all the way across the park to a row of stately houses whose wide windows were partly concealed by poplar trees. As he watched the slender trees swaying with pleasure in the Wind, he liked to wonder who lived behind those distant, glinting windows.

His favorite spot was a corner of the park where a stream ran. He could sit there all afternoon on a hummock of grass, unseen except by roving dogs and the fetchers of kicked-too-far soccer balls.

The stream was interesting. Minnows darted around above the orange mud. Birds dropped from the trees and dipped their beaks into the water.

Once he saw a kingfisher.

There was always something different.

At the park's edge, the stream passed through a metal grill and into a concrete tunnel, vanishing underground with a swirl of its cloak. He liked to watch the water gurgle through the bars and disappear into the darkness while he thought about the Dark Man's questions.

One day, a large branch floated down the stream and clunked against the metal bars. Twigs got caught in the branch, then leaves got caught in the twigs, and soon a Boggy Clump had formed. The bigger it got, the faster it got bigger, and after a few more days the grill was snarled with muddy junk—a doll, a pair of shoes tied together at the laces, a broken umbrella, a telephone. By the next weekend the roar of water that had echoed up from the concrete tunnel had fallen silent, and the stream had spread into a shallow, still pool.

This pool was terrifying to behold. Dead insects floated on its surface, trapped in a film of green algae, and a yellowy froth gathered around the edges. Alice called this froth Witch Spittle, a name that gave Max nightmares about what happened when he wasn't there. Even so, the pond was dreadfully fascinating, and each day he would run from school to succumb to its evil power. The pond was generating something deep in the depths of its foulness. As he stood there one day, staring hard at the still water, a cheap plastic soccer ball bobbed with a bubbly glug to the surface—a mutated eyeball to stare back at him.

Screaming, he ran home and told Forbes the pond was watching him. Forbes nodded solemnly, pulled on his rainboots, and off they went to the park. One look was all Forbes needed. He strode into the water, took hold of the branch—still sticking out of the Boggy Clump—and gave it a heave. Watching from the edge, Max experienced a deep, satisfying thrill as the Boggy Clump crumbled apart, and all the built-up water, the algae, the dead insects, and the Witch Spittle drained away.

But Forbes wasn't done. With skillful swings of his hook, he flung the bits of trash and junk onto the bank, and in a matter of moments he'd cleared the grill. As final proof of his mastery, he hoofed the soccer ball toward the center of the park. An hour later, the stream was rushing on its underground journey just as before, and there was a line of black bags next to the park trash cans.

For the rest of the day, Max stayed close to Forbes, admiring things he'd never noticed before, like how he could butter his toast with one stroke of his knife, or drain a mug of scalding-hot tea in one gulp. Everything was simple with Forbes and he was afraid of nothing, not even Pond Eyeballs and Witch Spittle.

Forbes knew the answer to everything. Maybe even the Dark Man's questions.

Max decided to ask him. He waited until bedtime, when he was sitting on the end of the Mulgans' bed. He sat there every night, to tell Forbes and Alice a story.

Mostly, his stories were about what he'd learned at school. The night before, it had been about snow.

"We found out about snowflakes today," he'd told them. "How they're shaped like a star, with all these patterns and diamonds. Mr. Chandra told us that's how water crystals form when they freeze."

"That's right," said Forbes. "And did you learn how they all have eight arms? Like an octopus?"

"Six," said Alice, giving him an elbow. "It's six, isn't it Max?"

"Yes," said Max. "But Mr. Chandra is wrong. It doesn't have anything to do with how water freezes. It's the Starmakers."

"Oh-ho!" said Forbes, wriggling with pleasure. "Who are the Starmakers?"

"Don't you know?" Max had been surprised at this, because Mr. Chandra hadn't known either. "If you look even closer at a snowflake, if you look much more closer than ever, you see tiny chisel marks on the snowflake. Tiny chisel marks made by tiny silver chisels."

"Is that so?" Forbes said, winking at Alice.

"The chisels belong to the Starmakers," Max explained. "Snowflakes are stars that weren't good enough. Each Starmaker makes thousands of stars a year, and they throw most of them away because of little mistakes. But now and again, once every million years, one of the Starmakers looks up from his anvil. And all the other Starmakers look up as well and put down their chisels, because they know what's happened—finally there's a star perfect enough to go in the sky. The proud Starmaker takes his star out into the Hall of Stars and hangs it up for everyone to see. Then, for a long time, there's silence and no more stars are made and no more snow falls, because the Starmakers are resting and admiring the new star."

On other nights, the Mulgans learned that Wind was the breath of Giants, and the sky was blue because it had been painted that way. Neither had anything to do with the warming of the land and sea at different speeds, or the particular way light was scattered by air molecules. The cleverest thing about these stories, the Mulgans felt, was that Max put on such a great show of believing them to be true. And poor Mr. Chandra—he had to be reassured at parent evenings that it was all just a private family joke.

Except it wasn't a joke.

As far as Max was concerned, they weren't stories at all. They were *explanations*.

They were simply there in his mind, as though from a book he couldn't remember reading.

But he had no answers to the Dark Man's questions. And when he asked Forbes and Alice, he could tell they were questions unlike all others, because something in the room changed—maybe even everything.

"Where do you *come* from?" Forbes repeated, glancing at Alice. "Uh . . . you mean . . . where do babies—?"

"No! I mean, who *am* I?"

"Oh." For a moment Forbes looked relieved, then he adopted a careful expression Max had never seen before.

"You're Max Mulgan," he said. "You're from Bickerstaffes Road. You live here with me and Alice. We're your parents and this is your home. Isn't that right, Alice?"

"That's right."

But Max wasn't going to be fooled by those Mr. Chandra answers.

"I don't mean that," he said. "I mean who am I *really*?"

"That *is* who you are really," said Alice, her voice tightening. "Who *else* could you be?"

Forbes glanced at Alice, then leaned over, kissed her on the cheek, and turned back the duvet.

"Come on lad," he said, getting himself up and holding out his hook. "Time for bed."

Max clung onto the hook, and Forbes slung him over his shoulder in the way that he did, and carried him into his kingdom. After tucking him in, Forbes sat on the end of the bed. "It's my turn to tell a story," he said. "Except this isn't a story. It's real."

"Like my stories?"

"Eh . . . yes. And . . . no matter how strange it is at first, just remember—it's got a happy ending. So . . . there's nothing to worry about. Okay?"

"Okay."

"Our story begins in a magical land on the outskirts of London called Surbiton." Forbes scratched his beard. "Actually, it's not really a *land*. It's more of a . . . commuter town."

"But something magical happened there?"

"The most magical thing ever," Forbes said. "We met *you*." And so Max learned that he was adopted, and he learned what that meant. He heard about Mr. Linklater and the ORPANAB, and how he'd been found in a bookshop.

"And now you live with Alice and me," Forbes said when he'd finished. "You're Max Mulgan. We're your parents and this is your home."

"What happened to my real parents?" Max asked at once.

"Your birth parents? Nobody knows."

"Did they Vanish?"

"Not then, no. The Vanishings hadn't started then."

"So where are they? Why haven't they come back for me?"

"Nobody knows."

"Maybe they have Vanished."

"It's possible. Nobody knows that either."

"Nobody?"

"Nobody apart from them."

"They're dead, aren't they?" Max asked, and without knowing he was about to, he began to cry for his poor, dead parents.

"Nobody knows," Forbes murmured, putting his great comfy arms around him and rocking him. "Nobody apart from them."

After a cuddle, Max felt himself being lowered back onto his pillow. Then Forbes was tucking the blankets under his chin. His face, smiling with planetary kindness, loomed close.

"Nobody knows who your parents were, Max," he said. "You can choose who they were *then*. And who they are *now*. You can choose."

He bent over to kiss Max on the forehead. "Good night, Max."

"Good night, Forbes."

The night-light clicked and its yellow glow sprang up against the wall. Max rolled onto his side to face the wall. With a quiet, mechanical whirr the flock of birds swept around the room.

I get to decide who they are. And nobody can tell me I'm wrong.

From the Hot-Air Balloon, the man and woman stared back at him.

His birth parents? No . . .

His *Forever Parents*.

The black silhouettes moved across the wall with agitated, flapping wings—a never-ending flight that went around and around.

dead they're
dead they're
dead they're
dead they're

His eyes closed. He was inside a flock of honking birds, high up in the sky, and they were flying with whirring, beating wings.

His parents . . .

The birds . . .

The Balloon . . .

A wicker basket creaked . . .

He heard voices . . .

Laughter . . .

Someone was singing quietly . . .

Sunlight glinted on eye glasses . . .

Auburn hair shined in the sun . . .

A flame roared. The basket swayed. His Forever Father played a tin whistle. His Forever Mother sang in a low voice.

He was with them in the Balloon and they were together, and because they were together they were happy.

Then a hook gave the sky a touch, and in a dark corner of the dream a shadow was set in motion with a mechanical whirr. On the horizon a black smudge appeared, there was a beating of wings, an approaching flurry: a flock of birds, of Canada geese!

One cannoned past. Another. Then hundreds. They thundered around the Balloon, blotting out the light, a storm of honking and a hammering of wings. But, just as suddenly, the Balloon was free. They had passed through and the sky was silent and bright and blue again.

Only, there was a new sound. A low, sinister hiss.

The Canada geese had made a hole. They were losing height!

His Forever Parents leapt into action. Bedding. Books. Luggage. Armchairs. The writing desk. The tin whistle. All of it went overboard, tumbling toward the waves where the sharks were already circling, arguing about who was to get what.

And for a while it worked. Land appeared. Hopes rose. So did the Balloon.

Then the hole tore wider. They began to sink again, faster than before.

His Forever Parents took stock. Land was still far off. They weren't going to make it.

Something else had to go. They cast around.

There was nothing. There was something.

His Forever Mother hopped over the side and dropped out of sight.

Gone!

That bought a few extra minutes, but not enough, not nearly enough! His Forever Father gave him a blessing, a hug, and instructions for how to grow up and be good—then flung himself into the cold, shark-filled waters.

And . . . that was it . . . they were gone . . . and the Wind blew, and the shore came, and the dream broke into many parts that went skittering around and became a thousand other dreams, many dream children with one Mother—the Balloon dream, his favorite. It returned to him many times, always filling him with a deep, heart-wrenching love for his Forever Parents, who had sacrificed themselves so the Balloon could carry him to land. When he woke his eyes would be bright with tears, and he would lie in his bed filled with the sad happiness of leaving a wonderful dream behind.

The Ocean

Max wasn't the only one with dreams.

As a boy, Forbes had dreamed of becoming a great scientist, an engineer who would build rockets, spaceships, and factories of shining steel, or a famous doctor who would cure disgusting diseases like the Mumbles or Grout.

But somewhere along the line, something went horribly wrong and he ended up cleaning the meat grinder at Chumley Slaughterhouse.

For twenty years, he stood beside the grinder holding a long pole with a hook on the end. When a piece of meat or gristle got caught in the grinder's teeth he would scrape it out and flip it into a bucket marked BEEFBURGERS. And while he hooked and scratched, scraped and fished, he dreamed his dreams and was happy.

As the years went on, though, his dreams began to leave him. One by one, they dropped from his pockets and rolled into the grinder, where they were mashed up with hundreds of sheep heads. In time, only one dream remained, and because it was the last, it tugged sadly at his soul. Seeing it go, he lunged after it, lost his balance—and his right hand was whipped off so fast he hardly noticed it had gone.

Six months later, he returned to the slaughterhouse with a prosthetic hook. It was useful for scratching out the smaller pieces of bone that couldn't be reached by the long, clumsy pole—but although he worked twice as fast as anyone else, and the meat grinder was the cleanest in the country, whenever he looked at it, he thought about the rockets and dreams that had been crushed in its mechanical jaws.

To replace his lost dreams, he went to the racetrack to bet on the dogs. Now and again, he came home with a bundle of ten-pound notes, but mostly he returned empty-handed, and then Alice would shout at him until she was blue in the face. Forbes would shout back, getting red in the face, and they would storm off to separate parts of the house: Forbes to the television set and a can of lager, Alice to the greenhouse at the bottom of the garden where she kept a bottle of pale cream sherry, and there they would sit in obstinate silence wondering when it was all going to end.

But it did not end. It went on and on, and slowly Alice lost her dreams as well.

They crawled into the grime under the fridge.

They were silenced by the bank manager's frowns.

They seeped out of her so slowly, she did not notice they were going, until one day she woke up, looked in the mirror, and did not recognize her own face.

It was then they decided to foster a child.

They wanted someone who was full of dreams. Someone who could bring dreams back into their lives. They chose Max, and for a while, the racetrack and the shed at the bottom of the garden went unvisited. He told them their bedtime stories, and it all went according to plan.

But as Max grew up, the Mulgans came to realize his dreams were of the wrong sort. They were dreams about his birth parents. He kept these dreams close to him. He held them tightly in his fist like a bunch of balloons he would not share. Before long, they were looking up at a boy who was high in the sky, floating through the blue, while they remained below, drowning in the ocean.

4

SOMEONE PORTERHOLSE
PORTERHOLSE SOMEONE

Wh18at's that you're writing?" Alice asked.

Max curled his arm around the paper. "Just a story," he said, without looking up.

They were in the backyard. Alice was sitting in a deck-chair, eating tinned peaches. Max was lying on the picnic blanket with his tongue in the corner of his mouth.

"What's it about?"

"Dragons."

"Ooh. I love Dragons."

"No you don't."

"I don't?"

"You love *pretend* Dragons. These are real *actual* Dragons."

"Oh." Alice sucked some of the syrup from her fork. "I didn't realize there were real *actual* Dragons."

"That's because nobody writes stories about them. They're all about these weird Dragons that talk and are clever and live in mountains and things. How could a Dragon talk?"

"Well, why don't you read me your story so I'll know about them."

Max put down his pencil. He didn't need to read the story. It was all in his head. He was only writing it down because the Dark Man had asked him to.

There's a loose stone at the bottom of your garden. It's been there for years. Put the stories under it.

Why do you want to read my stories?

I think your stories would be different from everyone else's.

And it was funny the Dark Man had said that. Because the stories *were* different.

"At the start, there's a bunny rabbit," he said. "The bunny is hopping through the forest, looking for a home. And he goes into a hole. And the hole is really warm and comfy. He thinks he'll be happy there, so he starts to dig around, to make some extra room. Then the whole place begins to shake. A great big blast of Wind comes down the tunnel and he whizzes out into the air. *Splat!* The bunny hits a tree and he's dead."

"Yikes."

"It's sad, but it happens a lot. Bunny rabbits can't tell the difference between tunnels and the nostril of a Dragon. They get confused."

"The nostril of a Dragon?"

"Yes. The Dragon is underground, see—"

"Wait—what's it doing underground?"

"It's sleeping. That's all they do most of the time. They're very lazy."

"Dragons don't sleep underground."

"Real ones do. Then they wake up and go crashing around looking for trees."

"Trees?"

"That's what they eat. Not any trees. Just special ones."

"No . . . no, Max. Dragons eat people and . . . horses and things."

"Those are pretend Dragons. They're just make-believe. These are real Dragons."

"Oh, yes. I forgot."

"Real Dragons are herbivores. They're stupid and slow. And definitely can't talk."

"What about fire? They don't breathe fire then?"

"Sometimes. But only because of the hunters. Usually the fire is just inside them, in their stomachs, to burn up the trees they eat."

"That doesn't sound very likely."

"That's what Mr. Chandra said. But we have acid in our stomachs. Why shouldn't Dragons have fire?"

"That's true, I suppose. Who are the hunters?"

"I'm getting to them," said Max. "So after he's had a good sneeze, the Dragon goes back to sleep, and the forest goes quiet, and after a little while along comes a hunter. And when he sees the dead rabbit all covered in gooey snot, he knows there's a Dragon nearby. So he starts jabbing this long pole into the ground."

"He wants to wake up the Dragon?"

"Right."

"Isn't that dangerous?"

"The hunters know what they're doing. He jabs his stick into a hummock, which is really the Dragon's eyelid, and the ground breaks apart and this Dragon roars up. Earth and stones and bugs and things are raining down, but the hunter is ready, and he sticks the pole into the Dragon's mouth, right into its gums."

"Ouch! Why the gums?"

"It's the only soft part of the Dragon. He wants to really hurt the Dragon. To make the Dragon angry."

"That doesn't sound very nice."

"It's the whole point. See, when the Dragon gets angry it breathes fire."

"It doesn't sound very clever, either!"

"It's what the hunter wants. Because there's a story in the Dragon Fire. That's what he's been after all along."

"There's a story in the Dragon Fire?"

"Yes."

"I like that idea. What does he do with the story?"

"I . . . haven't got that far yet."

"So why aren't you writing it in your homework notebook?"

"My notebook?"

"It's for school, isn't it?"

"No. It's just." Max bit his lip. "Just because."

"Because . . . ?"

"For fun." He was writing for the Dark Man as well, of course. But it was fun.

"Where did you get the paper from?"

"Mr. Chandra let me have it." And that was true.

"I thought you didn't like Mr. Chandra?"

"He said I could write as many stories as I wanted," Max said. "He said he'd be interested to read them." That was true as well, just so long as *he* meant the Dark Man, not Mr. Chandra.

"That reminds me," Alice said. She took a crumpled flyer out of her pocket and handed it to him. "Someone stuck it through our front door this morning. Interested?"

It was printed on an ordinary piece of paper—but Max stared at it in surprise. There right in front of him, in big letters, were the very questions the Dark Man wanted answered:

Who are you?
Where do you come from?

"Why our front door?" he asked.

"Sorry?"

"Why did they put it through our front door?"

"Oh, not just ours, silly. Everyone's. So they'll know about it and come and see."

"Know about what?"

"Read the other side," Alice said. She returned to her peaches. "It all sounds a little weird to me."

Max flipped it over:

*Unable to fathom the mysteries of existence?
Lost in a labyrinth of puzzling questions?
Feel like you're being followed by someone
you don't know?*

Read books!

*For centuries, great minds have stored
their wisdom in literature.*

*I, Porterholse, invite you, dear neighbors,
to the grand opening of The Book House, 8
Newton Fields Road, this coming Saturday
at one o'clock. Every story ever written,**
*under one roof! Read in the comfort of
someone else's home! Refreshments provided!*

Fondly yours,
Porterholse, esq.
* figuratively speaking

"Where is it?" Max asked.

"Only across the park," Alice said. "Like to go?"

He nodded happily. Maybe he could get the answers the Dark Man was looking for. Besides, if everyone had got the leaflet, that meant his Forever Parents had, too. They were sure to come.

For now, though, he had to finish the story, so he took it inside where he could finish it in secret, up in his bedroom.

Later that afternoon he put the story in an envelope and left it under the loose stone on the garden path, just as the Dark Man had instructed.

The following morning, it was gone.

He spent the next week dreaming about his Forever Parents and their reunion.

He would enter a room lined with bookshelves and decorated with stuffed animals—weasels, Canada geese, and armadillos. His Father would be at a workbench, gutting a salamander, and behind his glinting glasses there would be a sad look in his eyes. His Mother would be kneeling before the fire, tossing coals one by one into the flames, on the carpet beside her a book face-down and a cat belly-up, purring beneath her hand. She would be the first to see him, and the sharp turn of her head would alert his Father. He would lift the salamander guts onto a tray, and his glasses would clink down beside them. The cat would flop over and, for a moment, they would all simply look at him, not daring to believe—because he might disappear, their long-lost child, he might fade into nothing; they'd seen such apparitions before. But he wouldn't disappear, not this time, and then . . . then they would say it, they would say a name, and it would be his name, the name they had given him, not Max, that was only a pretend name . . . they would say something else . . .

his real name . . . his Forever name . . . who he really was . . .

When the day of the grand opening finally arrived, he dragged Alice out of the house, along the road, into the park, past the swings, around the pond, and all the way to that distant land he had often glimpsed from the hilltop, the Newton Fields Road mentioned in the flyer. The park's resident Wind surged at their backs to hurry them along, and the poplar trees swayed with happy abandon, as though they had been waiting for his arrival.

Why haven't you come sooner?

This way . . .

This way . . .

Number eight was easy to spot. A banner hung flapping from the garden wall and bunches of balloons jiggled against each other, tied to gateposts. With a final *WHOOSH*, the Wind deposited them outside the house, then left them, snatching up a bunch of balloons and making off into the sky.

The banner turned out to be a bed sheet, and the letters were a patchwork of cut-up Argyle socks:

GRAND
OPENING
TODAY

The house, though, seemed in two minds about guests. The windows on the top floor were hidden behind heavy shutters, but those on the ground floor had been flung open.

Guests had already begun to arrive, and people could be seen moving around in the high-ceilinged rooms.

Max pulled away from Alice and ran toward the front door, which had been propped open by an umbrella stand. He'd recognize his Forever Parents at once, he was sure of it, and they would recognize him, so he rushed from room to room, checking only the faces, seeing nothing of the house, itself.

But there must have been a delay. They weren't here yet.

There wasn't a hint of auburn hair. And of course, there were glasses, but none glinted in that special way.

Disappointed, he returned to the hallway to check upstairs, but found his way blocked by a group talking in hushed tones. Alice was there, too, and he squirmed his way in to stand next to her.

Nobody had come to meet them either. Where was this Porterholse person?

Nobody knew.

Nobody had ever met him. Or seen him. Or heard of him.

The man was a mystery. And was he a man?

What kind of name was Porterholse anyway? Was it Someone Porterholse, or Porterholse Someone?

The house, according to neighbors, had been empty until about eight years ago, when it had been bought by an old woman, an eccentric, standoffish sort called Suffrenia Jeffers who spent most of her time away (on Caribbean cruises, she'd told them). She had been spotted on occasion by late-night joggers and dog walkers moving around the park with a golf umbrella and an antique lantern, as if she had once buried treasure there, only forgotten the spot. Several of those lanterns were on display in the house—tall, glass-funneled brass relics that showed signs of recent and regular use. The woman herself had been seen preparing the house in the morning, but now she was nowhere to be found.

Unless she was upstairs . . .

The whole upper floor was barricaded behind a door at the top of the only staircase. There was even an obscure warning on the door:

Where the Wind comes from
Do NOT open

Max understood: the Wind lived up there, and if anyone opened the door, there would be a gigantic gust that would send all these people flying out of the front door and spinning up into the clouds. But nobody else seemed to think like that. They even stood around watching while a man walked up the stairs, tried to open the door (it was locked), knocked, and called: "Hello! Is anyone home?" For a few seconds there was no response, then there was an exasperated huffing and puffing, followed by a stomping and thudding, as of a large animal moving back and forth.

Huff!

Puff!

THUD THUD THUD!

Everyone apart from Max looked astonished. Perhaps it was simply a Someone Another or Another Someone, they decided, who rented the upper floor as a separate apartment, was angry with the intrusion, and wished to be left alone.

At any rate, the front door had been found wide open and welcoming. The banner and balloons had been put out. There was even a cast-iron piggy bank stationed on a low table inside the front door, its flanks divided by etched lines into butchery regions such as hock, jowl, and loin. *If you take what you like and pay what you can, the pig will not object* said a sign around the pig's neck. Deciding the place was meant to operate on a self-service basis, the guests began to explore—turning their attention, at last, to the books.

Max had never seen so many. Apart from the kitchen, three large rooms were entirely given over to shelves, stacked floor to ceiling and wall-to-wall, the books pressed together without a wafer of space between them. A single extra syllable in a single book, Max figured, would have brought the whole structure crashing down. Selecting one at random, he pulled it free from the tight embrace of its neighbors, which instantly snapped together, as if another book, farther along the shelf, had appeared out of nowhere to take its place. The television cabinet was minus a television and plus a hundred or so hardcovers. The fireplace was stuffed with a pile of books that disappeared up the chimney and overflowed, perhaps, onto the roof. A book had even found its way into an aquarium in the hallway—the goldfish, solitary beside its underwater castle, floated over the sodden pages, seeking a way to turn them with its gently flapping fins. Footstools and stepladders had been provided so the upper reaches of the shelves could be explored, and the whole place was chock-a-block with armchairs, sofas, and beanbags.

The infinity of books was equaled only by the riches found in the kitchen at the back of the house. As promised, the cupboards were crammed with boxes of tea, jars of coffee, and varieties of cookies, some of the common sort—fruit shortbreads, chocolate chips, jammy dodgers, Viennese swirls, digestives, teacakes, macaroons, bourbons, ginger nuts, custard creams, Abernethies, Rocky Roads, party rings, and Garibaldis—as well as rarities such as Cornish fairings, paprenjaks, oat crisps, Bath Olivers, koulourakia, snickerdoodles, Russian tea cakes, stroopwafels, and vanillekipferls. The cookie eternity was in turn matched by the sandwiches and cakes stashed away in the cold, white forever of the fridge—the tuna and cucumber triangles, shrimp salad baguettes, chicken and mayonnaise baps, bacon and egg butties, porchetta tramezzinos, roast beef grinders, and Philadelphia zeps, all individually wrapped in tinfoil, while the cakes were folded in greaseproof paper and stacked in patisserie boxes—Black Forest gateau, ginger and treacle tart, Bakewell tart, carrot cake, strawberry flan, Bundt cake, crumb cake, Dundee cake, angel cake, madeira cake, Boston cream pie, punschkrapfen, tarte tatin, tiramisu, Christmas cake, date and walnut loaf, Battenberg, galettes, fat rascals, lamingtons, cannoli, chocolate fudge cake, pineapple upside-down cake, croquignoles, and Prinzregententorte, with jugs of whipped cream, double cream, clotted cream, vanilla cream, cherry sauce, chocolate sauce, maple syrup, caramel syrup, treacle, and brandy butter, all chilled and ready to be spooned or spread or tested with a guilty suck on a dipped pinkie.

These riches provided the guests with definitive proof of welcome, and banished the last traces of uneasiness. Tea was brewed, cookies chosen, cakes sliced, cream poured, books selected, and armchairs settled into. Before long, the only sounds to be heard were the whispers of turning pages, the clink of cutlery, the occasional delicate, embarrassed nibble, and the huffing and thudding from upstairs, which repeated itself throughout the afternoon.

Only Max settled down without a book.

He'd come for parents, not stories, and there wasn't a single Mother or Father to be found. Slipping away from Alice, he hoisted himself onto the windowsill in the front room and pulled the curtain across to create a shell of glass and cloth. If his Forever Parents came up the garden path they'd see him there, unhappy and alone. They'd understand how much he'd missed them, and they'd never abandon him again.

It began to rain.

The Wind upstairs huffed and puffed. The poplar trees swayed with pleasure.

His forehead dunked sadly against the glass.

Maybe they had died.

Maybe the sharks ate them after all.

The curtain rasped and Alice was there. "What are you hiding here for?" she asked.

Max shrugged and stared out at the rain. "I couldn't find anything."

"You can't have looked very far," she said, holding up a book. "There's a whole series of these. It's called"—she glanced at the cover—"*A Pocket of Ghosts & Goblins*. See?"

Max breathed on the window and drew an outline of a Balloon in the mist. He didn't want Alice around when his Forever Parents showed up. That would be . . . awkward.

"Reading's boring," he said, without looking around. That'd make her go.

And it did. She placed the book beside him, and in the window's reflection he saw her leave. As if he'd been waiting just for this moment, a man sitting in an armchair got to his feet. Max watched as the man crossed the room and came to stand directly behind him—so close he could see the man's eyes in the window, staring right at him.

He turned around.

The man was standing with a cup of tea raised high against his chest, holding the saucer and the cup very precisely in delicate hands. He had thin, fair hair and a long, frizzly beard. Tiny muscles all over his pale, sickly face were twitching and trembling. His brown eyes, though, were alive with a spark that was fierce and kind at the same time.

"Reading's boring?" he said, peering at Max. "Is that *really* what you think?"

Max shrugged, but somehow he couldn't look away from the man's eyes, which seemed to see straight through him.

"Personally, I think reading is the most important thing there is," the man continued. "Or one of them—we mustn't get carried away. There are diamonds, but there are flowers, too!"

He spoke with a peculiar accent Max recognized. Wherever the Dark Man came from, this man came from the same place—except, maybe from a different time. He wore a dark coat reaching almost to his knees, a white shirt tucked into high-fitting trousers, and a black waistcoat with a watch chain. He looked like he'd stepped out of a history book.

"These writers, after all," the man went on quietly, "these poor Devils sit thinking for a horrible length of time, hours and hours every day, for years on end—their entire existence! While you're watching television and playing computer games, staring at a screen with your brain in the grip of a machine, they're wrestling with the secrets of the universe! And when at last they do find something their work has only begun, because then they have to write it all down, they spend their last drop of blood capturing it with the utmost precision, sweating over every word so others will be able to understand their feelings and thoughts, all this for one purpose, and one purpose only—the transmission of the human condition through time! Now," he said, raising his finger, "that's not for everyone, I'll admit. Each must live in their own way—the flowers and diamonds again! But even so, even so, let me ask: How long do YOU sit still and wrestle with the secrets of existence, in the course of a day? Two hours? One hour?" His eyes narrowed. "Not one minute! Not one minute do you spend! Yet, here it all is, all that work, all that thinking, ready and waiting. The greatest story of them all—the story of human life—here on these very shelves, all thanks to those writers who toiled like the most wretched of slaves with next to zero hope of reward. And how do you repay them? What epitaph do you chisel out on their tombstones? Reading. Is. Boring. I think you haven't thought it through, have you? Otherwise"—his eyes narrowed even further—"you wouldn't come out with anything so stupid."

He reached this insulting conclusion staring right at Max, right into his eyes, with such penetration that Max suddenly got the impression the speech was only a distraction, something to pass the time while he got on with this staring of his. He even felt a prickling in his brain, as if the man was rummaging around in there with his long fingers to see what he could find. Even as he thought this, the man took a step closer and the brain prickling intensified.

"*When you read,*" the man whispered, "*you discover who you really are. You find traces of yourself, little pieces you didn't know were there.*"

He held Max's eyes a moment longer. Then, with a dramatic flourish, he pulled the curtain across. Seconds later the front door banged, and Max turned in time to see the man striding down the garden path, scribbling into a notebook with feverish energy. Somehow, he was not surprised to see the Dark Man outside the gate. The pair of them shook hands, then disappeared together, conferring closely.

When you read you discover who you really are.

Max picked up the book Alice had left him and looked at the back:

A Pocket
of
Ghosts *&* Goblins

Discover the ways and habits of Sprites and Shades, Gremlins, Ghasts, Brouhahas, Frights, Bloodguddlers, Brownies, Urchens, Hellwaines, Imps, Trollots, and Kobolds in these fairy tales gathered from twenty-three countries around the world.

When Alice came back to check on him he was up to the Brouhahas.

Want to go?

Not yet.

Okay.

A plate clunked down beside him. A sandwich. A cake. He looked down a few pages later and the plate was empty, his fingers sticky with chocolate.

The sun went down. Imps and Hellwaines skittered about in the garden. Trollots pressed their noses against the windowpane.

The street lamps came on. The curtain opened.

Time to go. No!

But it *really was* time to go, and Alice was dragging him back across the park, getting him out of the Book House only by purchasing not just *A Pocket of Ghosts & Goblins*, but *A Sackful of Monsters*, *A Chalice of Devils & Demons*, *A Cauldron of Witches & Wizards*, and *A Barrel of Giants*, too.

His Forever Parents didn't show up in the Book House that day, or the next.

But he no longer expected them to.

They'd been there all along, frozen on a page among all the millions of pages.

He wasn't supposed to wait for them. He had to find them.

He read on the windowsill, with the curtain drawn to hide him from the other people. In this secret nook, he tramped over mountains, wandered through forests, struggled across deserts, and delved into caves. He sailed oceans to far-flung continents, lost himself in the crowds of foreign towns, and poked his nose into the dungeons of ogres. He explored the ethereal citadels of Wizards and Genies, and even crossed the boundaries of time to visit distant eras, past and future—all in his search for his Forever Parents.

But it wasn't long before he began to suspect there was something wrong with his approach. There were, after all, so many books. It took months just to get along one shelf.

Deciding he needed help, he wrote Someone Porterholse Porterholse Someone a letter.

Dear Someone Porterholse Porterholse Someone,

I'm looking for my Forever Parents in your books and I can't find them because there are so many and I want to know if maybe you saw them once there did you? When you saw them, they might have been in a Balloon. If it is true, please write to me. My name is Max Mulgan, 37 Bickerstaffes Road, and tell them to watch out for the geese. I'm on the windowsill most days.

Thank you very much

Max Mulgan

P.S. I hope you get this letter soon.

P.P.S. The iron pig is nearly full.

P.P.P.S. Please tell the Wind upstairs to stop making so much noise.

He left the letter by the pig, hoping the Wind wouldn't sweep downstairs and blow it away.

The very next morning he got his reply.

THE STORYBOOK

It was left on the window ledge—a pale cream envelope with a silky, luxurious feel. When he tore it open, he found no note inside, only a small iron key that tumbled out onto his hand. On the underside of the envelope flap was a short message:

The Cupboard Under the Stairs

He was there in a flash, testing the handle in surprise.

It hadn't been locked before. He'd opened it once to have a peek, but there hadn't been anything special—just some raincoats hanging from a rack, a pair of rainboots, a vacuum cleaner with a bloated dust bag, and a couple of those odd lanterns. All the usual under-the-stairs stuff.

Nothing odd.

Nothing secret.

So why was it locked now?

The key turned easily. He looked left, looked right, then slipped in and closed the door before anyone saw.

Inside, it was stone-dark.

The closet had one of those string light switches, he remembered. Groping forward, he snapped it down. The bulb screwed into the underside of the stairs came on.

Coats, vacuum cleaner, boots, lanterns—it was all gone, and the cupboard had been transformed into a cozy reading room. A rug now covered the drafty floorboards and the bric-a-brac had been cleared to make space for a low table and an armchair. On the table were a woolen blanket and a pair of fingerless gloves.

On the armchair, sinking into a cushion, was a huge black Book.

No book like it had been on the shelves outside, or anywhere. He got down on his knees. Reaching out, he placed his hands on the Book's cover, afraid they might slide into that inky surface as into a pool of water. Instead, they encountered polished wood. Sturdy brass hinges held the cover in place, while the spine was a thick strap of leather, dotted with the heads of tiny nails. There were no markings—no title, no author's name, no publisher's logo. There was only the smooth surface, cool and mysterious beneath his fingers. At first glance it was black, but when he bent closer he saw purples, deep greens, and browns, all swirling around in whirls and loops. The Book had retained the mark of its origin—a tree somewhere in a forest—and so it seemed wild and alive.

Like it hadn't just been made.

Like it had *grown*.

Heavy footsteps passed in the corridor outside, startling him. Looking around, he saw a bolt, shiny and new, screwed into the door frame. He slid it across, then lifted the book with a grunt, wriggled under it, and sat in the armchair with the Book in his lap. Leaning back as though opening a trap-door, he heaved the cover up, over, and down.

click

A mechanism in the hinges snapped into place, turning the cover into a rigid board, allowing him to rest the Book across the arms of the chair. It seemed to float in front of him, suspended in the air, weightless despite its size.

The first page was blank. Even so, his fingers trembled across the grainy paper, sensing the Book's surprise at his touch. A pungent smell rose from its pages like the startled emission of a squid—the tang of forests, of pinecones and rotting leaves, of gleaming moss, stagnant ponds, frogspawn, sap, bark, and fungus. It was nothing like the Forest Fresh air freshener Alice sprayed over the house to get rid of the smell of her cigarettes. It was the real thing. It boiled up through his nostrils, filling his brain, and he turned eagerly to the next page, anxious to discover what kind of stories could be found in a book such as this.

They began on the following page, written in dark ink by the same hand that had scribbled the message on the envelope:

The Beginning Woods is bigger than the best of dreamers could ever imagine, darker than they could ever fear, full of more wonders than they could ever desire.

As soon as he read these words, he knew: it was in the Beginning Woods that he would learn the truth about his Forever Parents.

THE WOODS AND THE WITCH

At first, the Storybook frightened him—it gave off such a thick warning, like a tome of black magic. *I know more about you than you know about me*, it seemed to whisper. There was something unrevealed about the Storybook, as if it held secrets as well as stories—secrets it was unwilling to share.

But this uneasiness soon passed. Often, he sat in the cupboard, cradling the unopened Book on his lap, running his fingertips over the cover, murmuring incantations and words of invitation—a summoning spell for his Forever Parents. During school, he would think of where he had left off, and when afternoon came he would rush to the Book House, sneak into the cupboard, and plunge into the story once more. Every page he turned he expected to come face to face with his Forever Parents. With every story, he took another step toward them. When he reached the end of that Storybook, another appeared to take its place. Then another. They were as limitless as the world they described: a magical forest, where the chaos and tangledness of trees ruled with total power.

The Beginning Woods was like the World, minus science and plus magic. In each story, something familiar became twisted and strange. London was in the Woods, but it was a London of long ago, of top hats and horses, cobblestones and candles. It came as no surprise that in the Beginning Woods the Wind came from Giants, and the sky had been painted blue. Dragons, too, were just as he'd imagined—slow and stupid, foraging for trees and pursued for their stories by the Dragon Hunters.

His favorite tales were about a creature of absolute evil called the Wasp Witch. She cropped up in several stories, sometimes taking a major role, sometimes only passing through to lay a curse or cause some other malevolent circumstance. She wasn't the only Witch in the Beginning Woods; there were hundreds—they were a kind of breed—but they were rather more significant than riders of broomsticks and owners of cauldrons. To be a Witch in the Beginning Woods was to occupy a particular place in the order of nature, to be fundamental to the workings of the universe. They spent their time inventing nasty things, such as cockroaches, quicksand, and *ceratocystis ulmi*. A Witch always came into being as a man or a woman because they needed fingers and thumbs for inventing things and wielding their tools. This particular Witch had sprouted from the darkness beneath a rotting log like a growth of Old Man's Beard, and shared with that fungus the habit of spreading herself around and popping up where she was least wanted.

As a Witch, she had been responsible for the creation of Stinging and Sucking Creatures such as Wasps, Visps, Hornets, Mosquitoes, Fleas, Midges, Horseflies, Scuttlebugs, Vampire Moths, Redbottles, Bloodflies, Squirmers, Catnippers, Gnats, Ticks, Pokklers, Anklejabbers, Tree Lice, Merchant Bugs, Ivy Eaters, Ghoulwhips, Scorpionflies, Goldenback Murderers, and their ilk. Not only did she invent them, but she marshaled their forces and governed their actions. Having created a new batch of Wasps, she would set them loose on picnics in great swarms, or blow them singly through a straw into a classroom, and in this way she fulfilled her witchery functions and took part in the processes of nature.

Because of these practices, she was known as the Wasp Witch. But it was not in the creation of Mudflies and Cooters that she made a name for herself in the history of evil; these were, after all, relatively lowly nuisances—they hardly compared to the Volcanoes and *Yersinia pestis* thought up by renowned Witches of terrible power and authority. She had another talent, for which she could be freely condemned as a villain of the highest order.

She stole color.

Wherever she went, she kept an eye out for anything colorful. If she saw an apple radiant with the splendor of summer, she would take it in her hands, polish it against her sleeve, then send her tongue into it—a highly specialized tongue she had crafted herself, snipping off her own useless tongue with a pair of pruning shears and stitching this new one in its place.

She craved the colors of living things most of all; they were more fulsome, their flavors subtler, complex and delicate. It really was horrible the way she stole the gold from a Golden Eagle, or the glittering beauty from a Rainbow Trout. Afterward, the stricken beast would be completely translucent, like a jellyfish. As for her, she didn't give a hoot; she would march off to find her next victim without a backward glance.

Such a creature was the Wasp Witch.

But it wasn't because of her that Max returned to these stories again and again. There was another character attached to the Witch, who always appeared at her side.

This was the boy, Kaspar Hauser.

He lived with the Witch in her cottage. She had kidnapped Kaspar from his parents when he was a baby and raised him in a box, in such a way that the wretch actually believed she was his Mother, and never for one second considered that his real parents might be elsewhere, praying for his safe return. Armed with a brush and pan, he spent his days cleaning her workshop and cottage, collecting all the leftover parts of Stinging Insects—the jointed legs, wings, abdomens, feelers, eyes, suckers, antennae, mandibles, and so on—and reordering them into labeled bundles. He would make Frankenstein insects out of these parts, many-legged, inside-out, and upside-down beasts, like Quantipedes and Lurchers. Because the Witch was always busy with her experiments, his life was very hard: nothing but work, work, work, from the moment he woke to the moment he fell, groaning with exhaustion, back into his narrow box.

Naturally enough, by the time he was ten years old Kaspar was thin and tired, hardly a boy at all, and more like an insect himself, with ribs you could rattle a stick against and eyes as large as plates. One day, he was so exhausted he could not get out of his box and lay under his blankets sobbing and apologizing. The Witch howled and spun, and sprinkled Earwigs into his bedclothes, but there was nothing to be done; he was too weak to even move, and at last she relented.

She had worked him too hard.

He needed help.

Would he like a companion?

Yes, he would, very much! Kaspar bounded up, flung his little arms around his Mother's neck and kissed her happily. A playfellow? Marvelous!

So that afternoon the Witch took Kaspar into her workshop and cut him in two, into two boys who were identical in every way.

She divided his name as well. One half she called Kaspar, and the other Hauser.

In the first few weeks after the operation, the boys rejoiced in each other's company. The day's work, burdensome for one, became a pleasure for two. They chattered, they sang, they laughed. Time flew by, and if they were still exhausted at bedtime, then at least they felt it was down to the capering, jumping, and somersaults, and not the sweeping, dusting, and scrubbing. The Witch watched this jubilation with alarm. She didn't like it. She missed the good old days of groveling and cringing. So she devised a plan, a diabolical, monstrous plan that only a real genius of evil could have conceived.

One morning, she took Kaspar aside and said: "Listen up, Snotnose—we're running low on Wasp parts. Go into the Woods and fetch me some Buttercups, Nettles, and Tree Sap." Then she added, as if as an afterthought: "Get Kaspar to help you."

"You mean Hauser," Kaspar said at once.

"I mean what I mean, Mr. Smartypants," the Witch shot back. "Do you think your own Mother can't tell you apart?"

Now, right from his fingertips to his toes Kaspar felt like Kaspar, and was more certain of being Kaspar than of anything else in the universe. Nevertheless, this was his Mother he was talking to!

"But . . . I really am Kaspar," he said, running his little fingers all down his body to be sure.

"*Tsk tsk,*" said the Witch. "Who knows best?"

"Mother does," said Kaspar automatically (because he actually did believe this to be true).

"That's right. And who loves you with a most perfect love?"

"Mother does."

"And does a most perfect love mix things up and get them back to front?"

"No."

"Well, then," said the Witch. "Who are you?"

"Hauser," said Kaspar firmly, glad to have it all sorted out and cleared up.

The only trouble was, she told Hauser he was Hauser as well, and naturally he completely agreed, so later on there was a fist-fight over who was the proper Hauser. Called in to referee, the Witch declared that Hauser was Kaspar and Kaspar Hauser. Kaspar was covered in glory—at last he was proved to be who he wasn't: Hauser, and none other than Hauser! But his triumph lasted only a few short hours—later that afternoon the Witch dropped a bomb by asking him to "fetch Hauser from the woodshed." By the time the twins went to bed they were half-mad with confusion, and when they woke the next morning, they had no idea who was who. Terrified, they ran to their Mother's boudoir.

"Which one's which?" they screamed. "Which one's which?"

"Good morning, Mommy," the Witch growled from under her blankets, where she was sucking her fingers with delight. "We're sorry for making noise and waking you."

"Good morning, Mommy," they recited obediently. "We're sorry for making noise and waking you." Then: "Which one's which? Which one's which?"

"Who loves you more than anything?"

"Mother does!"

"With a perfect love?"

"With the most perfect love!"

"Can a perfect love get by without sleep? Can it get by without rest?"

A perfect love could not. Nor could it get by without scrambled eggs, two slices of hot, buttered toast, a cup of coffee, a spotless parlor, freshly washed linen, and a weeded garden. Only when the perfect love was installed in a deck-chair with a glass of chilled Madeira and a bowl of violet creams were its needs satisfied. By this time the twins were beside themselves, charging back and forth in a frenzy.

"You're Kaspar, aren't you?"

"Are you sure? I thought you were!"

"Oh no, ha-ha, that's right, I am, ha-ha! Or am I?"

"Ha-ha! Oh, Mommy . . . ARRGH!"

"ARRGH!"

"WHICH ONE'S WHICH?"

"WHICH ONE'S WHICH?"

To which the Witch returned: "What did I tell you yesterday?"

"We don't know!"

"We can't remember!"

"What do you feel? What do you feel deep down inside your own hearts?"

"When I woke up I was sure I was Kaspar," said Kaspar.

"When I woke up I was sure I was Hauser," said Hauser.

"W-R-O-N-G!" mocked the Witch, roaring with laughter. "You've got it all topsy-turvy. Just as well I'm here to sort you out, eh? What would you do without your old Mom?"

In this way, she removed their power of deciding anything for themselves. Every morning, she switched their names. And woe betide the twins if they contradicted her authority. If they did: Thunderbolts, Hand Grenades, and Crocodiles.

The twins, of course, did doubt their Mother's opinion. They doubted her horribly. Which was awful, awful; she was their Mother, after all, and the psychological ramifications of Not Trusting One's Own Mother, of Criticizing A Perfect Love—well, they were rather troublesome. So they tried to ignore their nasty, disgusting, ungrateful little doubts, they pushed them downward, but the harder they pushed, the stronger the doubts became. One day, the doubts became so strong their heads began to spin. They joined hands to keep themselves steady, but only found themselves spinning faster. The faster they spun the more they doubted, the more they doubted the faster they spun, and when they fell apart they found they had doubted their own identities so much they had changed into two little girls.

The Witch was delighted with this new ability, and put it down to her own bio-mechanical engineering skills. As for the twins, they got into the habit of changing shape all the time, searching for forms that felt like home. The little girls weren't right, so what about old men with crooked teeth?

Or maidens in green dresses? Or lanky seafaring gentlemen? No, no, and triple no. To make matters worse, the more they changed, the harder it became to find their way back. Eventually, they forgot their original appearances altogether and simply hopped from one disguise to another.

In that unhappy state they relied on their Mother more than ever.

How did this tragedy end?

How did the Witch receive her comeuppance?

Greed.

The one color the Witch longed for more than any other was blue. She had a weakness for it, perhaps because it was rare in nature and she could never get enough to satisfy her. Bluebells and forget-me-nots, of course, were beautifully blue, but they were so slight it was hardly worth bothering; even a meadow of bluebells hardly constituted a square meal. The one real source of blue in nature was the sky, and it was torture, torture to the Witch to have this infinity of her only desire sliding about over her head every day. She had tried everything in her power to get at it. She had constructed towers, she had hauled herself up mountains, she had built enormously long wooden spoons, she had flung herself from elasticated contraptions—all to no avail and sometimes even with humiliating consequences.

Then she discovered a curious and most interesting piece of information relating to Gertrude Farby-Himmel, the Wizard* responsible for inventing the particular shade of blue used to paint the heavens.

This Wizard was a woman of great foresight. She had understood that the friction of soggy clouds against the sky would eventually cause blank patches, so she had created a reserve stock of paint, which she had stored in a creature called the Bluebird. When the sky needed a second coat, all she needed to do was take the Bluebird, crush it in a pestle and mortar, and dissolve it in a tub of ethyl acetate. Then she could get out her mops and rollers and paint the sky all over again.

The existence of this Bluebird came as a great surprise to the Wasp Witch, and of course she became eager to locate it. She sent out her spies, and they discovered almost at once that Ms. Farby-Himmel had left it in the keeping of a Woodcutter.

This was a disappointment and a setback. It meant there was an axe to think of.

Axes were the only thing in the Woods that really scared the Wasp Witch. You couldn't do much to an axe, but it could do things to you! For every dream she had about the Bluebird, she had a nightmare about the axe. If she even came near the Woodcutter, she knew he would swing his axe

---

* Just as Witches are responsible for inventing sources of misery and evil, Wizards spend their days discovering ways to improve creation.

and that would be it—because there's nothing a Woodcutter hates more than a Witch.

As luck would have it, the twins solved the problem themselves. They wanted to pay their Mother back for all her many kindnesses, so they waited until one of her birthdays, then transformed themselves into two little girls and went skipping off to the Woodcutter's cottage. They charmed him with their lively chatter and gay laughter, and *ooh*-ed and *aah*-ed over the Bluebird, and sobbed so much when they had to leave that the kind old dunderhead decided it would do the little creature no harm to have a change of scene for a day or two.

In short, the twins succeeded and returned to their Mother in triumph, with the Bluebird in shackles. What scenes there were then! Domestic bliss! She almost fainted with delight, and after "ladling" them each a few times for doing something independently of her orders, she turned to the matter in hand and sent out her tongue. With a wet *splat* it fastened onto the Bluebird, and with slow pulsing movements began to draw out the color.

But how the bird was twittering! Would the Woodcutter hear? He would! He'd put on his Seven League Boots and come running! Quick, quick, get the color out, every last drop!

But the color kept coming. No matter how she sucked, the Bluebird did not fade even the tiniest bit, and carried on tweeting just as loudly as ever. There was enough blue to cover the entire sky, after all, and a sky of blue was simply too much, even for the Witch. And now the Woodcutter was striding with fantastic leaps and then: BANG! There he was! Right in front of her!

Run? From a pair of Seven League Boots? Just you try it! The Witch tried to skedaddle, but managed only two ungainly steps before she tripped and fell, rather conveniently, to her knees.

So much the easier, thought the Woodcutter, rolling up his sleeves.

SWISH!

Off went her head, bouncing into the juniper bushes.

Rather dismayed by this turn of events, the Witch stood up and began running in circles. But the valiant Woodcutter didn't stop there. Knowing Witches to be resilient creatures, he spat on his palms, lifted his axe, and chopped her into little bits. Then he tossed the bits into a barrel and spun it around so fast that all the colors she had ever stolen leaked out of the side and found their way back to their original owners.

And that was the end of the Wasp Witch, and the end of her story.

As for Kaspar and Hauser—did they ever find their true forms, let alone their parents?

Max read his way through Storybook after Storybook, eager to discover the fate of the unfortunate boy(s), but no further mention came of him/them.

This disappointed him, because it was on account of the boy split in two that he had loved those stories so much. Sometimes, he had even found himself whispering angrily at the pages, over and over again:

"She can't make you do that!"

"SHE'S NOT YOUR REAL MOTHER!"

5

SLAM!

Forbes?"

"Yup?"

"Where are we going?"

"Where are we going? Where do you think we're going?"

"Are we going to school?"

"Where else would we be going?"

"Why are we walking though?"

"What's wrong with walking?"

"Why isn't Alice taking me in the car?"

"Do you want the adult answer or the kiddie answer?"

"Can I have the adult one?"

"Do you want to press the button?"

"No thanks."

"Okay. Hold hands while we cross. It's like this. The trucking company that delivers livestock to Chumley's has changed its schedules, which means they're coming in the evening instead of the morning, which means I'm working nights, which means I have to sleep during the day, which means the only time we've got to see each other is in the mornings for these twenty minutes. And a bit before bedtime. Which isn't much."

"What about the weekend?"

"I don't know. What about the weekend?"

"Aren't you going to be around?"

"Not on Sunday. That's double pay. I'll be around on Saturday, but you spend the whole day at the Book House. So . . ."

"So we're going to do this every morning?"

"Rain or shine."

"The car's better."

"Who wants to sit in the car? We've got the sun, the sky, the life of the town. What more do you want?"

"I get to read in the car."

"So I hear."

"And I can't read at school. Only at break and lunch."

"You read at lunch?"

"There's nothing else to do."

"You never play football?"

"Football's stupid."

"You've got to do something to join in."

"Why?"

"People don't like people who don't join in. Look—invite some of your classmates around on Saturday and we can have a barbecue up in Newton Fields. We don't have to play football. There's British Bulldogs, or Kick the Can. Together stuff."

"We don't have a barbecue."

"We can improvise! Alice can make anything from anything—you watch. She'll get that grill out of the oven and put it over some bricks. I can pinch some chops from Chumley's."

"I don't want to. Saturdays are for the Book House."

"You spend the whole day at that place! What's so great about it?"

But Max couldn't tell Forbes what went on in the Book House. The Storybooks, the Beginning Woods, his Forever Parents—all that was a different world, a million miles away from Bickerstaffes Road and the Mulgans.

They stopped at another crossing. Forbes was still holding his hand, but it felt odd; Forbes was holding onto him, but he wasn't holding onto Forbes. With his free hand he reached around Forbes to jab the button, hoping the awkward movement would make him let go. It didn't, and they crossed the road in silence. Forbes soon began talking again, about Joining In, Getting Pals, and When He Was A Lad. Max didn't want to listen to any of that, so he went deep inside himself until Forbes became a distant thing with no meaning. The next time they stopped they were at the school gates.

"How many have you got on you? Three? Four?" Forbes was asking, and Max stared up at him, not understanding. After a moment, he realized Forbes was talking about books.

"Just the usual." He had three in his bag and two in the pockets of his duffel coat.

A car pulled up next to them and a girl bounced out. She stopped on the pavement to adjust her bag on her shoulders, waved at the driver, then ran off through the gates, her pigtails twirling, while her Mother drove away, throwing a curious glance at Forbes and Max, who were still holding hands and saying nothing, it seemed.

But a lot was being said—maybe everything.

Max knew that if he pulled his hand free it would all come out, it would be obvious, he may as well tell Forbes there and then about his Forever Parents and the Beginning Woods. He tried, as a secret experiment, to pull the tiniest amount, just a little, to see if he could work his hand free. Forbes held on, and tightened his grip by the same tiny amount—so Max gave up, looked at the pavement and let his arm go limp; if Forbes wanted his hand, he could have it. It was stupid of Forbes to think holding his hand meant anything.

The school bell rang among the buildings. But Forbes didn't even react. He didn't even seem to hear.

It was five to nine.

Now, Mr. Chandra would be reaching for the attendance register.

Now, he'd be saying "Max Mulgan," and there wouldn't be any answer, because he was stuck out here. And when school finished, he'd still be here, glued to Forbes, who showed no sign of moving.

What was he thinking?

Was he about to say something?

Why didn't he just *let go* and *go home?*

He pictured Forbes wandering up the road on his own and felt sorry for him. But this moment of pity transformed at once into sizzling anger. He wished Forbes wasn't there. He wished him away.

Go on.

Go!

Why don't you just Vanish!

Forbes spoke then, quietly and hopelessly: "You've got to start living in the real world, Max. With us. With me and Alice. Or it's not going to work. It's just not going to."

Max couldn't bear it—he tore his hand free and screamed at Forbes like he was flinging rocks—Once! Twice! Then he ran off through the school gate, throwing it shut behind him just to be sure Forbes wouldn't follow.

It was only later, shaking and shuddering in a stall in the bathroom, that he realized what he'd done—the rocks he'd flung—the words he'd yelled.

"You can't make me!"

"YOU'RE NOT MY REAL DAD!"

From that day on, Max kept his hands in his pockets when they went into school. He walked like that wherever he went, without realizing why.

Forbes, though, understood perfectly.

When Max flung those rocks at him he hadn't even blinked. They hurt, they hurt . . . but children say mean things all the time. They hate their parents and say so. They storm off. They slam the door.

A door would have been okay.

But this was a *gate*, and when it swung shut, it gave a metallic clang. Then Forbes not only flinched—he was felled by a killing blow.

It was the clang of the grinder.

It had gotten hold of his last dream after all.

From that day on, whenever he saw Max with his hands in his pockets, he remembered those words, "You're not my real dad!" and heard again the SLAM of steel jaws. Whenever he was at the grinder and the jaws went SLAM SLAM SLAM, he remembered how Max had torn his hand away and shouted, "You're not my real Dad!"

And that from then on was the life of Forbes: no dreams left, "You're not my real Dad!" and SLAM SLAM SLAM.

SLAM
SLAM
SLAM

Bonfire Night

During this time, a darkness spread through the house, a mold came down from a corner, a shadow expanded. It was invisible but it was there.

The meetings at bedtime ended. Forbes was away at work and Alice stayed up late, so those stories about the Wind, the stars, the snow, the sky, the Giants and Dragons, and those quiet rituals of Tucking In and Turning Off The Lights, were all reduced to a single word. Max would call "Good night!" down the stairs, and Alice would reply "G'night!" Even that single word was difficult to say. Sometimes he stood for whole minutes in the darkness on the landing, his throat working, unable to get it out.

The walks to school ended, too. Forbes was too tired. He would come back from the slaughterhouse night shift and crash straight into bed.

Max didn't mind. It meant he could walk to school alone.

Alice offered to drive him again—no thanks!

You don't want to read in the car?

No thanks!

He began to get up early, make his own breakfast, and leave before Forbes got back and Alice woke up. When he got to school, more than an hour before class, he would sit alone in the library and read while the cleaner polished the tables around him. Sometimes, he read books from the Book

House, sometimes the library's own books. His favorite was an old geography textbook. In it, he'd found a series of maps entitled CONTINENTAL DRIFT.

The first showed Pangaea, the huge land mass that existed before the tectonic plates slid apart to form the continents. The series of illustrations showed the great territory splitting up into Australia, Antarctica, the Americas, Eurasia. Max thought it looked like a photograph torn into pieces.

The Beginning Woods, he decided, was like Pangaea—the world as it ought to be, perfect and together, before something went wrong and it all broke apart, making the world as it was.

Circling Pangaea was a single ocean, its name written out in swirling script:

The Panthalassa Ocean

The name of this ocean captivated him.

What a name it was, a beckoning, magical name!

One night, staring at his Forever Parents in the mural, he decided it was the ocean they had been trying to cross in their Balloon.

They had discovered it.

It had been named after them! Was that his name?

Max Panthalassa?

He kept all of this secret from the Mulgans—even his reading. If they saw him with a book there would be a complaint, or a cutting remark, and then there would be a Talk, which would turn into an Argument, and then a Fight.

So he sneaked books back home and read them out of sight, in his room. If he heard Forbes or Alice moving around outside the door, he would jam the book under his pillow. Then he'd get angry, and imagine what would happen if they came in.

"You have to start living in the real world," they'd say, and he would shout back at them: "You can't make me! YOU'RE NOT MY REAL PARENTS!"

They never did come into his room, and never said, "You have to start living in the real world." But that didn't matter. He imagined they did, and got angry as if they had, and in this way he built up a store of resentment against them for something they had never done.

Eventually, he retreated into the attic. Among the dead wasps and carpet cuttings, discarded toys, and boxed-up Christmas decorations, he could read in peace. Sitting with his back against the mysterious stillness of the water tank, he would open his book, and the story would take him like a tornado takes a house, spinning and twisting to another land—far from Forbes and Alice and Bickerstaffes Road.

He was up there one Sunday, reading in the quietness of the attic, when Forbes came back from the slaughterhouse early. And suddenly the house was full of noise. The front door slamming. Footsteps booming on the stairs.

Forbes calling out, "Just hopping in the shower."

Alice shouting back, "They're about to start!"

He put down his book, scooted over to the hatch, and edged it open to peep down. Forbes was in and out of the bathroom in a flash and passed underneath in a dressing gown, toweling his hair dry.

Usually, he washed at the slaughterhouse. He must have left in a hurry. And someone must have given him a lift.

What was going on?

Max lowered the ladder and went downstairs to the kitchen, slowing as he passed the living room. Forbes and Alice were standing in front of the TV. An old man with gray hair and a bushy beard was talking into a microphone outside a museum-ish kind of building.

> *I must apologize for my long absence. Sometimes, one must go into the wilderness to discover the truth . . .*

He went into the kitchen, made himself a jam sandwich, and poured a glass of milk. The rich tones of the man's voice filled the house.

> *. . . in coordination with international lawyers and heads of state, I have drawn up a series of emergency measures to be enacted universally and in every country signatory to . . .*

When he passed the living room, Forbes and Alice hadn't moved. The cigarette in Alice's hand was turning into a long droop of ash. He got back into the attic, arranged his milk and sandwich within easy reach, and settled down again for a good afternoon's read.

"MAX! MAX GET DOWN HERE!"

Forbes's voice was like the crack of a whip.

Max froze, then slipped his book under the water tank and crawled over to the hatch. Forbes was thudding up the stairs again, his beefy legs flashing out beneath his dressing gown.

"Give it here! Quick! No arguments!"

Max drew back slightly. He knew he meant the book. "Give what?"

But Forbes went straight past without stopping and disappeared into his bedroom. After a bit of banging around, he reappeared and clattered down the stairs.

His arms were full of books.

Max didn't even use the ladder. He dropped through the hatch, landed on all fours and sprang at Forbes.

"They're mine!" he screamed, hauling on Forbes's elbow. "Give them back!"

He managed to make him drop one in the hall, but Forbes just kicked it toward Alice, who was standing by the cupboard under the stairs, holding the door open—she snatched it up and tossed it into the darkness. Forbes bent in after it, his broad back blocking the entire door as he wriggled around in the narrow space.

Max whirled on Alice. "It's for your own good," she said, cutting him off. "Go into the kitchen. I'll be in to make lunch in a minute."

Lunch? How could she talk about lunch? "It isn't fair! They're mine!"

She wasn't interested. "Do as I say."

There was nothing else for it: he stormed through the door and slammed it, jamming a foot against it.

Let them come! Let them try!

They stayed in the hall, talking quietly. He pressed his ear to the door.

"Did you check his schoolbag?"

"I'll do it in a minute. I want to hear the rest of this."

"What are we supposed to do with them all? We can't keep them here."

"They'll tell us I guess."

"Don't forget the ones in the attic. He hides them under the water tank."

"It's coming back on. I'll get them later."

Their voices got fainter as they returned to the living room. But the TV got louder. Max squeezed his head against the door and held his breath. This time it sounded like two reporters:

Astonishing news today in Paris—nobody expected anything like this. The repercussions are going to be quite simply unimaginable. Appeals for calm are likely to fall on deaf ears.

*That's right, Terry, it's going to be the biggest cul-
tural upheaval the world has ever seen. The long-term
consequences are unforeseeable.*

*For those of you just joining, there seems to have
been another delay. We were expecting to hear from the
Prime Minister, but now it seems there's, yes, there's no
word yet of any . . . no sign of any movement at the
Trocadéro . . .*

"I'd better go check on him. Shout if anything happens."

"He's not going to be happy about this."

"He'll just have to get used to it, won't he?"

"Grab me a couple of cookies, will you? I haven't had a
chance to eat."

Max leapt away from the door and sat at the table before
Alice came in. She stood opposite him, her arms folded.

Was he hungry?

What did he want for lunch? Anything special?

She'd fix him a Welsh Rarebit if he wanted.

He looked right past her like she didn't exist. He swore
he'd never look at her again. He couldn't believe she thought
a *Welsh Rarebit* was a fair exchange for his books.

She waited, staring at him as hard as he wasn't staring at
her. He knew Alice could wait for a long time; she would
want to get back to whatever was happening on the TV. Sure
enough, she soon unfolded her arms and put her hands on
her hips.

Wasn't he hungry? Okay. He could come and get her when he was ready. He'd need her when he was hungry, wouldn't he? And he *would* get hungry. He couldn't sit there *forever*.

Couldn't he?

That's what she thought!

She left, and he sat exulting in his victory, which was multiplied by a billion when she had to come back for the cookies she'd forgotten. On her way past him again, though, she put a couple down in front of him, a masterstroke that turned his victory on its head.

Then he was alone again.

For two hours, he didn't move. He stared at Alice's ashtray, overflowing with cigarettes. He stared at Forbes's blood-stained overalls crumpled up in the washing machine. He stared at the cookies. He got bored of being angry and began to daydream.

It was time to run away, into London, into the world. Into the Woods.

To find his Forever Parents.

Why hadn't he thought of this before?

He would leave a note. He began to compose it in his head.

I've gone to find my Forever Parents because nobody is interested in them apart from me. Don't come looking for me because that will be a waste of time

and you won't find me. Anyway, I know
you don't really want to find me and I
would be better off dead as far as you
are concerned.

He spent some time adding bits and moving things around. Then he wondered why he was leaving a note at all.

Forget the note.

Just go.

Wouldn't it be amazing to *actually go*?

But first—couldn't he eat one of the cookies? They were the crumbly, buttery kind with nuggets of spicy, crystallized ginger.

There was no denying it: he was getting hungry.

He started thinking about the Welsh Rarebit, about whether it would have bacon or not, and this made him hate Alice more than ever, because she was trying to trick him into not leaving—if he stayed and ate the Welsh Rarebit it would be like a trap, he wouldn't be able to leave ever, and pretty soon, he'd be like the fat rabbit in the playground at school that everyone had fed through the wire mesh. It must have realized it never had to budge an inch, because it just sat and ate and got fatter and fatter, until one day it just died.

No. He wasn't going to be like the fat rarebit. Rarebit?

Rabbit.

Welsh Rabbit.

Did they have rabbits in Wales? Whales.

Whales Rabbit.

He fought back the urge to scream. His stomach gurgled and his mouth filled with saliva at the thought of hot, melted cheese sprinkled with salt. He groaned and put his head down on the table, next to the cookies. An inch away from his eyes, they appeared the size of spaceships. He pawed at them. A few crumbs were scattered on the tablecloth, big as rocks. He collected them on the tip of a finger and sucked them off greedily.

Any minute now, he would get up and actually go. Any minute.

He'd break into the Book House and live there, that's what he'd do. During the day, he'd sit in the cupboard under the stairs and read the Storybooks, and at night he'd sneak out and feast on cakes and sandwiches and write stories wherever he wanted. He'd read the Storybooks until he found out how to go to the Beginning Woods, and if Forbes and Alice came to get him he'd tell them to GET LOST. I get to decide who my parents are, he'd say. That's what you told me. And I've decided—they're not you! They're ANYONE but YOU!

The kitchen door banged and he jerked in surprise, and then Alice was there, like she'd heard it all, and when she saw him still sitting at the table, when she saw that even the cookies were untouched, she got angry, which was great because it meant he had won—but then she started shouting that Forbes had gotten rid of the books, that there would be No More Stories, No More Fairy Tales they were DANGEROUS they made people VANISH So it was finished It was over Which Was Good because they Had A Bad Effect On Him ANYWAY and who did he think he WAS treating the PLACE LIKE A HOTEL?

CRASH!

Max snatched up her ashtray and hurled it through the window above the sink. Bits of ash swirled between them.

"SNOWFLAKES!" he yelled at the top of his voice.

Then Forbes was there with a WHAT'S GOING ON IN HERE? that smashed the room to splinters, and with a duck and a dive Max was gone, out of the house and along the street, and suddenly he was doing it, he was running away and it was the best feeling ever!

At last!

It was over, and he was free!

He would never see the Mulgans again! Haha! The Book House was closed on Sundays, but that didn't matter. Someone Porterholse Porterholse Someone had helped before and he'd help again—especially when he heard what Forbes and Alice had done to the books.

But . . . what was this?

Mr. Nesbitt, the owner of the newspaper shop up the road, was also out, and also running.

This was odd, because normally Mr. Nesbitt was only ever behind racks of chewing gum in his shop, listening to his transistor radio and doing crosswords. Now he was struggling along the pavement on the other side of the road with three shopping bags in each hand—three shopping bags absolutely bursting with books.

What was he doing?

Had he run away from his parents, too?

His bags were so heavy every step cost him all the breath he had, and he refilled his lungs with high-pitched yawps. Farther up the road, someone else was running in the same berserk fashion, lugging a box on one shoulder. Whoever it was veered across the road and disappeared into the turning that led to Newton Fields.

Mr. Nesbitt took the same route. Slowing down a bit, Max followed them.

This new road—known as The Approach—was a long, narrow avenue that led to the park's main entrance. Usually, it was a sleepy place with rustling trees and neatly kept gardens, but today some kind of mass evacuation was under way. All along the road men, women, and children were leaving their houses, every last one carrying a bag, dragging a suitcase, or lugging a box.

Just like Mr. Nesbitt, they all headed for the park. Max went that way, too.

What. Was. Happening?

More people joined the rush at every corner, streaming in from other parts of the neighborhood. There was such a confusing clamor of shrieks, of parents shouting instructions and children demanding explanations, of OUT THE WAYs and

MIND YOUR BACKs and GIVE US A HANDs and JUST COME ONs, that Max could hardly make out a word of it.

Bewildered, he was caught in the stampede and swept toward the park gates, where the crowd was funneled into a tight pack. For a moment, he was trapped in a crush of jostling bodies and jabbing elbows. Then, with a roar and a sudden acceleration, they were through, surging across the grass and up the hill to swell the ranks of an even bigger crowd that had already arrived.

"PASS THEM TO THE FRONT!"

"GIVE THEM HERE!"

The suitcases and bags, backpacks, and boxes passed over the crowd, carried by arms that rippled up with the precision of centipede legs until they reached the crest of the hill, where they were hurled onto a growing pile.

"Watch out, boy!" Max hopped aside.

An old man barged past with a wheelbarrow. Tottering a little, he turned to haul his barrow backward up the hill. It toppled onto its side, spilling books across the grass. Max stooped to help him—but then stopped and stood there with a book in each hand.

Books.

It was books.

Everyone was getting rid of their books.

"Come on!" the old man snapped, holding out a trembling hand. "Those things are *dangerous!*"

Max handed them over without saying a word.

He looked up at the massive pile of suitcases and boxes. No!

Nononono!

He turned and ran for the Book House.

Even from a distance, he could see the angry mob. The police cordon. The bottles and clods of earth exploding against the shutters.

Even from a distance he could hear the roar of the crowd. THE BOOKS! HAND OVER THE BOOKS!

He ran faster. Ploughed straight into the back of the crowd. "You can't take them!" he screamed, forcing himself forward. "They're mine!"

Kicking and wriggling, he reached the front and tried to duck under the linked arms of two constables. But just then, the police line broke and the crowd surged around him. Someone pushed him from behind. He fell to his knees, and before he could get up again, he was knocked forward, flat out. Feet pounded down, crushing his legs, his arms, his hands. He tried to curl into a ball. A body fell on top of him, squeezing him into the ground.

So heavy!

He couldn't move at all! He couldn't even breathe!

Then abruptly, the weight lifted. He gasped and rolled over, sucking in air. A hand grabbed his arm and yanked him roughly to his feet. The Dark Man's face bent close.

"Get out of here!" he growled. "Go home! There's nothing you can do!"

"They're MINE!" Max shouted, ripping his arm free.

Before the Dark Man could react, he darted between two policemen and vaulted over the wall. But his feet caught on the gatepost, and he tumbled into the garden.

CRACK

His head whapped off a flagstone, and the world went black. Then white.

Then came back with no sound attached.

Dazed, rolling from side to side, he looked up at the faces and bodies moving back and forth in a blur.

Everything had doubled. Two garden gates were sliding across each other. Two walls were rising and sinking. Two-headed policemen were everywhere. Even the Dark Man had multiplied. One Dark Man was wrestling with a man holding a large brick. Shoulders surging, he planted a hand on the man's chest and pressed him backward over the wall with pneumatic force. Another Dark Man was trying to get through the gate, dragging two policemen along with him.

Impossible!

Blood trickled into his eyes. He blinked. Drew his sleeve across his face.

Struggled to his feet.

Took a few tottering steps toward the Book House.

Get inside.

Get the Storybooks.

Get the—

Halfway up the path, he stopped and blinked again, shaking his head hard.

The shutters on one of the top floor windows.

They were open. They were never open.

They were open. And a man was there, looking down from the shadows.

A man of impossible size. Gigantic.

Stooping forward. Too big for the room.

And growing—his face, huge, pale, and white. Porterholse!

A bottle slammed into the wall near the window, and suddenly the man was gone, pulling on a rod to close the shutter.

Max staggered up to the front door: Locked! He pounded his fist against it. Again. Again. Again.

"Let me in!" he shouted. "Porterholse!"

Another bottle hit the wall above him, showering him with glass.

"MAX!"

He put his back to the door. The Dark Man was free of the policemen, racing up the path. Men were streaming over the wall, their faces ugly and furious. Pelting the house with bottles and stones.

Pain flared in his shoulder. The impact twisted him, and he cried out. A rock!

Then something came looping toward his face, spinning and winking and growing larger and larger and larger.

A bottle.

Then darkness and down.

And then there were stars.

Proper, nice, glittery stars. Up in the night sky.

Confused, he blinked and smacked his lips. He was lying on his back. Grass was under his fingers, cold and slightly damp. He sat up, groaning as his head throbbed. He was in Newton Fields near the swings. A familiar presence moved out of the shadows, and the Dark Man knelt beside him, his normally pale face reflecting a flickering, reddish glow. He said nothing, and only looked past Max toward the hill in the center of the park.

Max followed the direction of his gaze. Then he got to his feet.

On the hilltop crackled a mountain of fire, its long flames surging upward as though trying to escape their bindings. Silhouettes of people were moving around it, their shadows cast long and flat all the way across the park.

He left the Dark Man and approached the bottom of the hill. The bonfire shook and trembled above him. Orange, glowing shards lifted and curled into the night sky, cooling as they went, bright at first, then cold and invisible, disappearing like shooting stars in reverse.

"We didn't find the answers," the Dark Man said behind him. "Now it's too late."

Max looked at him wordlessly, then went back across the park to the Book House. A fire engine was there, blue lights flashing out and around, mingling with the orange glow of the street lamps. A fireman was directing an arc of water into the building through the space where the roof had been.

"It's the same all over London," a bystander was saying.

"All over London?" another said. "All over the world, more like."

Max watched the Book House collapse inward with a roar, and his tears vaporized in the heat.

Sharks and fires.

He'd lost his Forever Parents again.

And this time, he knew, it was for good.

THE BETTER CHOCOLATE

School was cancelled all that week and all the next.

Max stayed in his bedroom for two days after the bonfire in Newton Fields, refusing to come out or talk to anyone. Alice kept sitting with him and saying things about changes and figuring things out. He would have to try not to miss the stories, she said. He would have to concentrate on what was real, on what was right in front of him.

The trouble was he didn't like what was real and what was in front of him.

Everything was going to be better now, Forbes kept saying. Nobody needed to worry about the Vanishings anymore. As long as you stuck to the new guidelines, you'd be safe. All thanks to the Seekers and Professor Courtz.

This name was suddenly everywhere. On the news. In the classrooms. In the morning assembly. Courtz. Courtz.

Courtz. He hated even the sound of it. At night, he had nightmares that a hand was pressing stones against his window, rubbing them up and down against the glass.

crrrtttzzz

crrrrtttzzzzzz

crrrrrrrrrrrrrttzzzzzzz

One day, a garbage truck drove along Bickerstaffes Road, followed by workers in fluorescent jackets, who picked up boxes people had left outside their houses and heaved them into the back of the truck—the remaining books. Max watched from his window as they collected the boxes Forbes had left outside. These were his books, the books he'd read to tatters, the books he'd bought—*A Sackful of Monsters, A Chalice of Devils & Demons, A Pocket of Ghosts & Goblins, A Cauldron of Witches & Wizards*, and all the others. They went into the back of the garbage truck, and the crusher came down, and the Ghosts & Goblins, Witches & Wizards, Monsters, Giants, Devils, & Demons were pounded to a pulp and driven off to be incinerated in the huge Volcano furnaces that were under construction all over the world. Professor Courtz had condemned spontaneous book-burning. It had to be done in the proper fashion. It had to be organized. Methodical. Thorough.

A single story was enough, he said, to trigger a Vanishing. Not one could be allowed to slip through the net.

Over the following weeks the Censorship tightened its grip. Strange scenes began to appear on the news: huge, violent crowds surging back and forth; protestors being chased down streets; the sinister pall of smoke that rose above Greenwich when the Volcano furnaces were ignited. At first, it was just stories that fed the flames. Soon it was other things, too.

Paintings.

Drawings.

Poems.

Movies.

Music.

Cartoons.

A list was published of Censored Products, Systems, and Activities. Its official name was CEPSA, but it came to be known as Courtz's List. It was so long it had to be alphabetized, and there was a copy of it up in every classroom, post office, and supermarket. Max memorized it, wondering about all these weird-sounding things that were disappearing from the world. As he walked home from school, he would mutter it under his breath: " . . . plays, poetry, prayer, predestination, priesthoods, propaganda, prophecy, proverbs, puns, puppetry . . ."

All these things, he was told, encouraged dreaming, and dreaming was the cause of the Vanishings. Anything that encouraged dreaming had to be stamped out. A Symposium official went around all the houses on the street, to make sure everyone complied with the new rules. The mural in Max's bedroom had to go, she said. So Alice scrubbed it away, and put up wallpaper covered with tiny hexagons. One day, a Symposium education officer visited the school. He was energetic and friendly and bounced around with a big grin on his face.

"Imagine a chocolate bar," he said to the assembled children. "It's all right, go ahead. Just this once won't hurt. Imagine the biggest, tastiest, most expensive chocolate bar in the world. Close your eyes. I want you to picture it. Really picture exactly how good it is."

Max imagined a giant cockroach tearing the roof off the school, crushing the man in its jaws and flinging bits of his body all over the room.

"Do you see the chocolate bar in your minds? Are you imagining it?"

"YES!" the children screamed.

"When I say NOW," the man went on, "I want you to open your eyes. And then you'll see a chocolate bar that's a billion times better than the one you're imagining, a chocolate bar that makes yours look like a cardboard cut-out. Ready?"

"Ready!"

"Remember, this chocolate bar I've got here is going to be a hundred billion trillion times better than yours, I guarantee it. Do you believe me?"

"NO!"

"Well, we'll see. Open your eyes . . . NOW!"

They opened their eyes. He was holding a cheap bar of chocolate, the kind you could buy in any shop and eat in a second.

"Now, which one's better?" asked the man. "This one, or the one in your heads?"

"In our heads! The one in our heads!"

"Really?"

"REALLY!" all the children howled—then they fell silent and watched as the man began to eat his chocolate.

"Mm-MM," said the man, cramming one hunk of chocolate into his mouth after another. "This is really good. This is delicious. You know what? I love chocolate! Chocolate is the best. How are you enjoying yours? Taste good?"

They looked back at him.

"What's up?" he asked, polishing off the last cube. "Something wrong with your chocolate bar all of a sudden?"

And then his smile disappeared. He took the microphone and came to the very front row of children, where the smallest and youngest were sitting.

"It doesn't matter how fantastic something is in your head—if you can't make it real, it's nothing. The tiniest cell of the human body is more amazing than the biggest Dragon! Why bother with the imaginary world at all? The real one is so much better. And now there's this extra-special danger to dreaming that wasn't there before, a DEADLY DANGER that makes it really important for us to GET RID OF THE IMAGINARY WORLD COMPLETELY. People who prefer dreams to reality Vanish and never come back. The world they dream about doesn't exist, but they spend their whole lives in that world. And they stop existing. The imaginary world is just imaginary! It's WORTH nothing because it IS nothing! We don't need it anymore. We don't want it." He crumpled up the wrapper of his chocolate bar and tossed it into a wastepaper basket he had ready on stage. "So let's chuck it, yeah?"

"YEAH!" screamed the children, because the man had produced a box of real, straight-from-the-fridge chocolate bars and was flinging them over their heads.

YEAH! YEAH! YEAH!

They all got the message. Avoid dreams.

Avoid anything that encouraged dreams. And avoid Vanishing.

This was advice Max couldn't follow. If he stopped dreaming he would lose what was most precious: his Forever Parents. He'd never met them, he'd never seen them, yet everywhere he went, he felt them. And only because of his dreams.

During this time, a dull ache began to grow inside him, as though something in the center of his being was withering up, like the seaweed on the nature table at the back of his classroom.

For his twelfth birthday, he received a second-hand bicycle Forbes had found and repaired.

It was too large, so he had to mount it from the curb, but once he was on, he could travel at enormous speeds.

He spent that autumn racing along the Thames, through the city, and out into the countryside, where he would roam the fields, jumping over streams, turning over rocks and rotten logs, braving the onslaught of nettles and farmers' dogs. If he came to trees, he would stare at them sleepily, wondering what secrets they might contain, and wander for hours beneath their branches, led this way and that by the rustling of the leaves, hoping to stumble on a way to the Beginning Woods and be reunited with his Forever Parents. Then, in the evening, he would return, his bike decorated with ribbons made from twisted grasses, his face glowing with the heat of the long journey, and his shoes dusty from the country paths.

But in the winter months, he wrapped himself up in an old navy sweater, a coat, and a scarf, and roamed the labyrinthine streets of London, peering in at the windows he passed and staring into every stranger's face.

Sometimes he would go to the bridge in St. James's Park and feed the Canada geese that gathered there.

Sometimes he would skim stones by the Thames.

Sometimes he would perch on the sundial in Kensington Gardens and watch the lonely old men in black overcoats pass by, like the shadows of grandfather clocks set loose from the hallways of empty houses.

And when it was too cold, he would stay indoors and peel away strips of wallpaper in his bedroom, trying to get to the country fair that wasn't there, and the Hot-Air Balloon that had departed long ago. He would make faces out of the strips, faces with frowning eyebrows and heavy, sorrowful mouths. Then he would scatter the pieces and begin again. Many sad faces were made and scattered before spring that year, and each night, there was less of the hexagon wallpaper and more of the blank, gray plaster that lay underneath.

Sometimes, lying in bed, he would stare sleepily at the patches of plaster, made luminous by the moon, and imagine they were maps of a far-off land where people possessed the strange yet necessary power of remaining where they were, not dying or Vanishing, not being dreams or becoming ghosts. Just being *there*, forever.

Such a world seemed fantastic beyond all other worlds, and he often wondered if that was the world his Forever Parents had been trying to reach in their Hot-Air Balloon.

6

INTO THE MOLD

Max's life with the Mulgans was ended, quite unintentionally, by a man called Reginald "Chopper" Chumley.

Reginald "Chopper" Chumley was the enormously fat and friendly owner of Chumley Slaughterhouse. His family had owned the slaughterhouse for generations and it was "Chopper" Chumley's pride and joy. Every day, thousands of cows and sheep would go in, the blades would whizz and chop, and out the other end would come all sorts of wonderful things like giblets and tripe, glistening in the afternoon sun.

During the day, he ran the slaughterhouse gift shop, selling pencils and key rings and extolling the virtues of mechanized meat retrieval. But despite his enthusiasm, he was a poor businessman. After investing millions of pounds on miniature replicas of the Chumley decapitator, he was declared bankrupt, and a firm of accountants took over the slaughterhouse. In their calculation, grinder cleaners with one hand did not figure as worthwhile.

"We can get crows to do it for free," they decided, and with a flick of a pen, Forbes was given the boot.

So that afternoon, he scraped the grinder one last time, took his severance check, and walked with slow, determined steps to the racetrack.

Over the next few months, things at Bickerstaffes Road took a sharp turn for the worse.

Alice hardly moved from the kitchen. When Max left for school, she was sitting at the breakfast table, and when he came back she was still there, in her dressing gown, smoking endless cigarettes.

She watched his every movement, her gray eyes light and hard.

Meanwhile, Forbes would spend the day out in London, looking for work. In the evening, he would return red-faced and sweating, clutching a plastic bag heavy with beer cans. Those cans, and the potion they contained, exerted a fearful influence over him. Under their spell, he transformed into a hunched ogre with gnarled eyes and fiery breath. Max took to hiding in the attic again, in his old place behind the water tank among the dead wasps and rolled-up bits of carpet cuttings. In this little nook, he would stare out of the skylight at the stars, which were always so cold and far away, lonely and surrounded by darkness. Sometimes, he thought, or knew, that he heard a soft music pouring in through the window-pane, a high-up, faraway, melancholy trembling that seemed as soundless as the whisper of snowflakes across glass. But those were isolated moments of comfort. When he came down from the attic, the real world was always there, ready and waiting with its iron hook and fiery breath.

As the months went on, Max saw the Mulgans less often. He was old enough now to go where he wanted in London's vast labyrinth, and fast enough to steal sandwiches from supermarkets. Forbes and Alice didn't seem to care what he did, where he was, or when he came home. They didn't even check his report cards, and just signed without looking at his grades. By the time he was thirteen, he was coming home long after the street lamps had blinked into life. Forbes would be watching the sports round-up after the news. Alice would be in the kitchen. Max would go straight upstairs to his bedroom and close the door. They had become entirely separate entities; they passed each other as silently as space-ships, and there was nothing but cold between them.

THE GETTING BIGGER DARKNESS

Max couldn't sleep.

Forbes had dropped off downstairs with the TV turned up. That was where he slept now, in the living room, and each night a different sound kept Max awake.

Tonight, it was another history program. One about war. Helicopters thundered above the house, tanks roared up and down the street, and artillery blew craters in the garden. He thrashed around, longing for midnight when Alice would go down to turn the TV off.

But midnight came and went. Why didn't she go? Somehow, he knew that she was lying in bed waiting for him to do it, just as he was waiting for her.

Well, he wouldn't. He wouldn't.

Never!

He got out of bed.

Groped his way downstairs into the darkness of the hallway.

A wedge of shifting television light angled out under the door. Was Forbes awake? He crept closer and peered through the gap between the hinges. No, he was slumped in his armchair with his head flopped back, cocooned to the waist in a purple sleeping bag. In the flickering light, it looked like he was being slowly devoured by an enormous worm that had risen out of the floor.

Max slipped through the door, tiptoed to the television and turned it off, then stood looking out of the window.

It was snowing.

The first, fat snowflakes of winter were doffing against the glass, floating down out of an impenetrable darkness.

This darkness, he'd been told at school, extended for billions of light years in every direction. The strangest thing about this darkness, he remembered, was that despite its size, which was already impossible for anyone to imagine, it continued to get bigger, not smaller—that the amount of darkness in the universe was increasing, while not a single atom was being added to the amount of anything else.

Maybe Forbes wasn't watching television at all.

Maybe he was watching the Getting Bigger Darkness get bigger, and that was why he had the television up loud, so he could drown out whatever high-pitched noise the Getting Bigger Darkness made as it moved against itself.

The armchair creaked behind him, and he turned to find Forbes staring at him. The sudden silence had woken him.

"It was really loud," Max whispered. Forbes only stared at him, his face empty. So he added, "Good night."

"You hate me, don't you," Forbes said then.

"Yes," Max replied at once, simply, without any effort.

The room split and a gulf opened up between them. On the far side, Forbes floated in his armchair, indistinct and meaningless, and Max finally understood, as he stood on the edge of this abyss, that his life at Bickerstaffes Road had come to an end. He got out of the living room. The TV came on behind him. At the far end of the hall, the front door waited like a portal to another world.

He moved toward it and took the cold metal latch in his hand. A thin, freezing stream of air came in through the keyhole, whispering against his fingertips.

It was time.

There was no use pretending.

He opened the door and cold air washed around him. Beyond the car and the driveway, he felt a presence passing in the darkness, something vast and invisible—and he seemed to hear, far off in the night, the distant call of the Woods.

"You're letting all the heat out."

He hung his head and slowly closed the door. Then he turned around, keeping his eyes down.

Alice was there, standing at the foot of the stairs. She was in her dressing gown; a golden box of cigarettes was glinting in her hand. He didn't need to see her. He just knew.

"You're so distant," she said. "You won't even look at me. Why won't you look at me?"

It was too much. He pushed past her and fled up the stairs.

For a long time afterward, he sat on the edge of his bed in the dark, waiting. And when Alice had gone back to bed and the house had fallen silent and still, he stood up, turned on the light, and began stuffing his schoolbag with clothes. When he was dressed and his shoelaces were good and tight he stood facing the door.

He should have gone long ago. Goodbye hexagons!

But then the stairs were creaking under heavy footsteps, coming nearer, coming nearer. He held his breath. A key rattled in the door. The footsteps retreated.

He waited a moment, then tried the handle. Locked.

He was trapped.

His shoulders began to shake, and he cried bitterly.

Later, he stood at the window, staring out at the flurrying snow. He thought about all the people Vanishing at that moment. Apparently, one person disappeared every four seconds.

Couldn't he be one of them?

Wasn't it possible for children to Vanish?

He hugged his thin body and squeezed as hard as he could, trying to pour himself into the darkness, to cast himself into nothingness.

"Me next!" he whispered. "Me next!"

But the night made no reply and suddenly, instead of Vanishing, he was in his room more than ever, the walls closing in on him like bullies. His chest tightened and his head began to spin. No air came into his lungs. He flung open the window. Wind surrounded him, swirling snow against his face, bringing with it a soft, musical whisper that calmed his mind. Slowly, the panic subsided, leaving him peaceful and a little sad—how he'd felt, sometimes, at the end of a story.

He stayed in that position for many minutes, grateful for the nighttime breezes that played around him. Then—footsteps again. On the landing. They stopped outside his bedroom. The doorknob rattled.

He scrambled into bed. In moments, he was beneath the covers, tugging the blankets under his body so they covered him like a shell. But the door did not open, and the footsteps moved away, and the lonely, painful sobs that wracked his body softened and broadened and rocked him to sleep.

GOING . . . GOING . . . GONE!

He woke in a tangle of blankets.

Sunshine was bursting through the curtains, filling his room with light. He blinked and stretched, then tensed as the events of the night before came back to him.

He lay still, listening for clues to the mood of the house. Sometimes, there would be arguing, and he would stay in his room until things calmed down. But today, not one sound could be heard. Not even the distant hum of the refrigerator or the gurgle of hot water in the pipes.

He sat up, his palms pressing into the bed and the hairs prickling on the back of his neck.

He was in the middle of a deadly and sinister silence.

He slipped out of bed and checked the landing, realizing as he did so that his door had been unlocked. *Their* bedroom door was open, too. He tiptoed up to it, waited a moment, then quickly looked in. Empty. Nobody was in the bathroom, either.

He sneaked downstairs. Maybe they'd gone out.

He opened the front door, squinting in the bright, glancing light. The car was there, under a white curve of snow. A single track of footprints led up to and away from the morning milk bottle.

They were still in the house.

He picked up the milk and walked through the hallway, turning his head as he passed the living room. The sleeping bag lay in a crumpled heap at the foot of the armchair.

That left the kitchen.

He put his ear to the door and stood there for what seemed like an age, waiting for a clink of cutlery, a drawer opening, the rustle of a newspaper, a word, a whisper, a breath.

Silence.

Maybe they had gone out and another fall of snow had covered their footprints. That had to be it—they'd left for some reason, and unlocked his door. Maybe they'd even run away, beating him to it, and he'd been abandoned again. So much the better, he thought, shoving the door open with the tip of his foot. It cleared the way for his Forever Parents.

The swing of the door revealed Forbes first, then Alice.

They were sitting at the table in their pajamas, still and unmoving, like waxwork models.

The milk bottle slipped from his fingers. Feeling it go, he looked down and watched it fall toward the tiles, where it exploded with a sharp detonation. Ice-cold milk splashed his feet—he jumped back from the spreading pool.

Forbes and Alice didn't react at all.

He crouched and started collecting the broken glass, his eyes flicking up at them, until his hand was full of clicking shards. "Put the glass on the table," Alice said suddenly, in a voice he could barely hear.

He did as he was told, then stepped back. They were both looking at him now, like they'd only just noticed he was there.

And something in their eyes told him: the stillness and silence was not coming from the snow or from anything else, but from the kitchen, and what was going on in it.

"You've cut your hand," Forbes said. "Run it under the tap." Sure enough, blood was trickling down his fingers from a thin cut on his palm. He hurried past them to the sink, glad to get out from under their eyes.

"Don't look around," Alice whispered. "Only look around when we tell you to."

So he stayed at the sink and did not look around.

He stared at the cups and plates piled up on the draining board. He watched a tiny spider make its way across the windowpane. He held his hand under the tap until he could hardly feel it.

And after a while, he began to cry, because he knew without looking that the room behind him was empty.

PART TWO

THE BEGINNING WOODS

The disappeared do not think of themselves as disappeared. They know where they are. It is the people left holding the photographs who do the wondering. A disappearance is something observed rather than experienced.

But what if that were to change?

What if the Vanishings are the first true and proper disappearances? Not just a disappearance from the world, but also a disappearance from your own self?

Doctor Boris Peshkov,
Reflections on the Vanishings

1

THE PASSING SPARKLE CHANCE

He turned off the tap.

The room was quiet. Just the steady drip of water in the sink.

Then even that was gone.

He wiped his wet hand against his trousers. In the silence, he sensed the Vanishing was still in the room, sitting behind him at the breakfast table, its legs crossed, its long fingers steepled under its chin as it watched him, waiting for him to make his move.

"Children don't Vanish," he whispered to himself. "Children don't Vanish."

He closed his eyes and felt his way toward the door, sticking to the left wall. As he maneuvered around the fridge, near where Forbes had been sitting, he stepped on something small and hard. It embedded itself in his foot, making him limp. When he made it to the hallway he closed the kitchen door, then stooped to remove it.

It was a tiny metal nugget, twisted like a small piece of chewing gum.

One of Forbes's fillings.

He dropped it. Ran upstairs to his bedroom. Slammed the door. Put his back against it. He stayed there, his heart throbbing, waiting for the sound of the Vanishings on the stairs.

The Vanishings on the stairs?

Stupid!

He opened the door.

Peeped out onto the landing.

The house was so empty it boomed.

He closed the door again and sat on his bed, looking at the hexagons and the peeled patches of wallpaper.

They really had Vanished.

He picked up his schoolbag, which was still stuffed with clothes, and made a phone call to the Vanishing Response Unit. A minute after he gave the address, he was pedaling down Bickerstaffes Road on his bicycle.

First he went to the site where the Book House had once stood. Now nothing more than a weedy wasteland, it was fenced off from the other houses. The poplar trees that had always welcomed him did not seem to know he was there. Stripped of leaves by the freezing winter, they were motionless under the leaden sky. Even the gusty Wind had gone.

He gave the place a quiet goodbye, then headed into London, cycling slowly through the slush. On his way, he stopped at a café and bought breakfast with the last of his pocket money. A bacon and egg roll, a Styrofoam cup of tea, and a chocolate bar—he ate them leaning against a wall, watching the traffic rumble by.

By the time he got to Kensington Gardens, it was afternoon. He chained his bike to a fence, and walked through the park. He had expected a quiet, snowbound landscape—instead he found a riot of laughter and happiness. It seemed every family in London had come out to enjoy the snow. Missiles swirled in the chilly air; hands packed and threw; faces twisted into grimaces.

He watched from the path, wondering why it had to be so different for him. A snowball struck him above the knee and he hopped back. A girl waved and laughed, her eyes sparkling; he found himself about to duck, swipe together some snow, and join in.

Instead he kept his hands in his pockets, turned away and followed the path to his solitary destination.

He'd come to Kensington Gardens to summon his Forever Parents. The altar for this ceremony was a sundial hidden behind trees and bushes near the Serpentine River. Little more than a block of concrete, it was so high you had to climb the metal rungs on its side to tell the time, and so ugly even the birds avoided it. He would stand on it, stretching his arms up to the sky. Once or twice, he had felt a rush of air against his fingertips, which in a moment of pure exhilaration he'd imagined to be the Hot-Air Balloon, swooping low. But it had only ever been the Wind.

Today was different, though.

Today it would work.

He would just dream harder.

He pulled the sleeves of his coat over his fingers and climbed the freezing rungs. The dial, a metal disc bolted into the top, showed no time under the cloudy sky. Standing astride it, his breath puffing in the air, he closed his eyes, and lifted his arms.

It was important to stretch as high as possible. If he didn't, he might miss the rope ladder when it came swinging down. Tottering a little, he forced himself onto tiptoe and reached up, his fingers groping for what had never been there, but would certainly be there today.

Now.

They would come . . . NOW!

They didn't come.

He drew in a breath, steadied his balance, and stretched up higher than before.

They would come in ten seconds.

He counted them off.

Eight. Nine. TEN!

Nothing.

He'd gone too quickly. He started again, slower this time. Flying a Balloon was difficult and you had to account for the Wind.

Five . . .

Six . . .

Seven . . .

Eight . . .

Nine . . .

Nine-and-a-half . . .

crunch

crunch crunch

Footsteps!

Their footsteps, coming across the snow!

crunch crunch crunch

They'd landed the Balloon in the wide fields of Kensington Gardens, and now they were *right here* at the foot of the sundial.

He didn't dare look!

This was it!

They were about to speak!

"You up there! You! Boy! Care to hurry it along?"

He opened his eyes.

Something had gone very wrong. Instead of a Hot-Air Balloon, he'd gotten an old granny with a golf umbrella.

But what a granny!

Not his Forever Parents, but she'd stepped out of a dream for sure.

Old age had twisted her body into a sharp stoop, so that her head, looking up at him, was almost upside-down, as if she were peering at the underside of a table. Her black overcoat and matching dress were embroidered with shimmering thread, and a purple tie was fastened in a hard knot around the collar of a spotless white shirt. Rings, silver bracelets, necklaces, and earrings glittered on her bony fingers, around her narrow wrists, and from her drooping earlobes, while a long silver pin held her snow-white hair in a twisted tower of gleaming coils.

"Would you mind getting down from there?" she asked. "I've work to do."

"I was here first," he said uneasily, not sure if those rules applied to strange old women.

Instead of arguing, she flipped a backpack off her back and took out a heavy-duty battery-powered drill and a pair of aviator's goggles—those leathery ones that pilots wore in the first days of flying.

"Suit yourself," she said, snapping the goggles over her eyes. "Don't blame me if the cops show up."

She revved the drill into a whine and pressed it into the side of the sundial, setting her whole body against it, as if she might suddenly start spinning herself, being so tiny.

grrrrrrrrrrrrrrrrrrrrrrrrrrrrrrrrrrrrrtz.

grrrrtz

grrrrrrrrrrrrrtz

In a matter of moments, she'd made four holes, and not even carefully, just by jamming the drill in any old how.

The noise was ear-splitting.

grrrrrrrrrrrrrrrrrrrrrrrrrrrrrrrrrrtz

grrrrrrrtz

grrrrrrrrrrrrrrrrrtz

She showed no sign of stopping. She seemed to have forgotten he was there and carried on tirelessly.

He looked up at the sky. It was getting late. How could his Forever Parents spot him from the Balloon if it was dark?

He had to get rid of her.

He squatted and shouted down: "WHAT ARE YOU DOING?"

She lowered the drill. "I'm making breathing holes," she said, as if nothing were more obvious. "What does it look like?"

"Breathing holes?" he said. "That doesn't make sense."

"Is that so?"

She leaned in again.

grrrrrrrrrtzzzzz

"IS IT GOING TO TAKE LONG?"

She rested the drill on her shoulder. "I'd say a good few hours at least. I'm an old sort, after all. And old women are slow! Oh, we're slow!" Her face assumed a crafty look. "Now, if there was a young boy around, he would have the job done in a jiffy. Especially, now my poor fingers are seizing up, and my back's giving in. I made a fast start, maybe too fast. I ought to pace myself. Slow and steady wins the race!"

"Okay! Okay!" he said. "I'll do it!"

He climbed down. The moment his feet touched the ground she thrust the drill into his hands, pulled the goggles over his head, and scampered up the ladder. When she got to the top, she made a visor with her hand and scanned the Gardens.

"Coast's clear!" she called down. "We'll need about fifty, I reckon. You'd better work fast, though—I have to be away before dark."

He didn't hear. He was examining the holes she'd made. By chance or design, they were arranged in a perfect hexagon.

Hexagons . . .

He lifted the drill.

He didn't like hexagons.

grrrrrrrrtz

He'd had enough of them.

grrtz

grrrrrrrrrrrrrtz

grrrrrrrrrrrrrrrrrrrrrrrrrrrrrrrrrrrrrrrrrtz

And then the sundial wasn't a sundial anymore.

It was Forbes and Alice.

Bickerstaffes Road.

The Censorship.

The world.

Everything.

Goodbye!

grrrrrrrrtz grrrrrrrrtz

grrrrrrrrtz

grrrrrrrrtz grrrrrrrrtz grrrrrrrrtz

grrrrrrrrtz grrrrrrrrtz

grrrrrrrrtz   grrrrrrrrtz   grrrrrrrrtz   grrrrrrrrtz   grrrrrrrrtz
grrrrrrrrtz grrrrrrrrtz grrrrrrrrtz

SCRREEEEEEEEEEEEEEEEEEEECH

The drill jerked and sparks flew over his shoulder. He fell back, his hands fuzzy with vibration. Concrete chunks lay at his feet, and wide cracks split the sundial.

"What was that?" the old woman demanded. "What have you done? Speak!"

"Nothing. I just hit something."

He prodded the drill into one of the cracks—it clunked against metal. The next moment, the old woman was elbowing him aside.

"Breathing holes I said! What do you call this? Road works?"

He pulled off the goggles. "Something's under there."

"Don't play innocent with me, Sonny Jim. We all know what's under here."

A screwdriver appeared in her hands. She forced it into the crack and strained against the damp concrete, jimmying the screwdriver back and forth until another chunk fell away.

They both bent close.

"You see?" she whispered. "Like I said. Breathing holes." There was a girl under the concrete.

A tiny girl made of bronze.

Her face stared sadly back at them—the rest of her body was still encased. A few more digs of the screwdriver revealed her narrow shoulders and a pair of wings.

She was a fairy.

"I'll clear her airways," the old woman said. "You dig for other survivors."

She produced a leather wallet from the inside pocket of her jacket and opened it to reveal a gleaming set of dentist's tools—probes, hooks, and chisels. Selecting one, she began picking grit from the fairy's nostrils and mouth. Max revved the drill and burrowed into the sundial, eager to uncover more. Chunks of concrete tumbled one after another at his feet. He found a rabbit. Another fairy. A family of tiny mice. All gathered in the nooks and crevices of a mound or tree stump.

"The Symposium did this," the old woman explained as they worked. "They came in the middle of the night with a crane and lowered an iron cylinder around it and backed up a truck that went BEEP BEEP BEEP THIS VEHICLE IS REVERSING and slobbed a load of concrete into it. I was watching from the bushes."

Max brushed the concrete dust from his sleeves. "They don't need breathing holes, though, do they?" he asked. "If it's a statue."

The old woman stared at him. "Oh, yes they do. Yes, they absolutely do."

"Why?"

"Because it's my fancy, that's why! If I want to play at something, if I want to imagine, then by golly gosh I'll play at it, no matter what the ISPCBonkers has to say." She thrust her arms at the obelisk. "Will you just LOOK at it? The very IDEA of such a thing! A statue, and *this* statue above all others, drowned in concrete? I won't have it. This is more than just a sundial we're dealing with. It's an emblem. A symbol. *This right here is the Censorship.* So I say, out with that idea and in with another. I SAY THIS STATUE NEEDS BREATHING HOLES! This isn't just WHIMSY! This is WAR! This is—"

She stopped with her fists in the air.

The clouds had parted and the last light of day was shimmering over the Serpentine in a thousand glittering sparkles.

"My word," she murmured. "What a light! What a lovely chance!"

She made a lifting movement with her hands. "Come on, then!" she said briskly. "Up with you! Over here!"

Max felt the drill drop from his grip. He staggered backward.

Slipped. Fell on his bottom in the snow.

The sparkles *obeyed* her.

They lifted off the water and swarmed toward her. Then, all the jewelry she wore was shimmering with light as the sparkles leapt from ring to necklace to earring.

Crooking a finger, she made kissing noises at a particularly bright sparkle that alighted on one of her rings.

"Hello, my darling!" she cooed. "What a beautiful little Lord you are! I've a job for you, if you've a mind to help, your Eminence."

The sparkle winked and turned somersaults of joy. It seemed delighted to meet the old woman.

"It's not often Old Light shows itself in the World," she said. "These days, New Light is all the rage. You know the sort— that boisterous, electric-neon, fluorescent light bulb sort of trash. All it's good for is advertising and seeing up noses."

She turned back toward the sundial and lifted her finger. The King Sparkle seemed to frown at the concrete obelisk. It began to *glint* instead of *sparkle*, its joyous spinning becoming harder and more determined. The other sparkles flung themselves into it, and the King Sparkle grew until it was fat as the Koh-i-Noor diamond, twirling on its axis at the end of her finger, throwing off angry spikes.

Then, with slow, effortful steps, walking against a hidden force, the old woman moved toward the sundial.

"Stand clear!" she instructed. "She's about to blow!"

As he got up and moved back, Max felt a voltage building, a humming in the air, as if a pipe organ was emitting a low, distant note.

"In the Olden Days, Old Light was everywhere," the old woman said, pushing herself forward step by step. "A fire in a hearth. A candle by a bed. A twinkle in an eye. A spark of courage. Now, those lights have gone out, and Old Light is barely to be found."

Max clenched his teeth and dug his nails into his palms. The hairs all over his body prickled. The soles of his feet tingled. He felt like he was about to fly apart.

Still, the old woman drove herself closer and closer to the sundial.

"New Light . . . destroys the imaginary," she went on, gritting her teeth, turning her head sideways. "It . . . shines *onto* things. It only shows you the surface. Old Light shines *into* them. It shows you . . . what's underneath!"

She jabbed her hand forward.

The King Sparkle trembled and gave a leap. There was a blinding flash—a release that buckled Max at the knees— and a deafening detonation that reverberated across the park.

The old woman staggered backward.

A blast of grit spattered Max's goggles.

The sundial had been vaporized. In its place was a statue of a boy. He stood tall on a mound, a flute to his lips, his audience a gathering of mice, rabbits, and fairies. The Old Light rushed over the statue's surface, giving it a final polish, before glancing off and skittering back across the water.

Max tore the goggles from his head. "How'd you DO that?" he breathed.

The old woman, herself, seemed amazed. "Who knows? Even I shouldn't be able to manipulate Old Light in the

World, and I invented the stuff. We're not in the Woods, after all."

In his shock, he didn't realize what she'd said. Then his mind doubled back.

"The Woods? You mean . . . the Beginning Woods?"

She turned slowly to face him.

"Name it so if you like!" she exclaimed. Then she drew nearer, her long, withered finger spiraling in a spell-like motion toward his eyes. "It's had more names than you've had dreams. They called it the Never Land last time it drifted close and this boy broke through—but it was the Woods they meant. Now it's happened again. Only this time, the Woods and the World haven't just drifted close. They've collided. Head-on. We've a car crash on our hands!"

She stopped abruptly and looked past Max, her mouth tightening in alarm. He turned around. Nothing was there, only a damp glow coming from one of the park lamps.

Her hand came down on his shoulder and he jerked in surprise. "You know, my boy," she whispered. "All those years you World Ones thought the monsters come out at night. But that's what we wanted you to think. It's during the day we walk among you!"

BOOM!

Her umbrella opened with an explosion of color. "At night—we run for cover!"

Then she was off, galloping along the path, leaving her drill and everything else behind.

He stared after her, dumbfounded.

She was from the Beginning Woods.

She had to be.

Flinging the goggles into the bushes, he gave chase.

The old woman ran at a kind of hyper-drive. Fortunately, the umbrella slowed her down a little, and he managed to keep her in sight.

She was on her way to the Woods.

She would lead him to his Forever Parents.

He pursued her east through Kensington Gardens, all the way to Marble Arch. When she reached the busy junction of Oxford Street and Park Lane, she slowed down to weave between the headlights, twirling the umbrella from side to side like a shield against the oncoming traffic. Cars hooted and pedestrians pointed at the peculiar figure, but she escaped the commotion by disappearing into the narrow streets of Mayfair. There, she hugged the buildings and looped the street lamps, keeping to the shadows. She seemed to imagine herself under attack, because she continued to fling up her umbrella against unseen assailants.

By the time they crossed New Bond Street, the sky was prickling with stars. Max fell back in the deserted street; if she turned, she'd spot him at once. But she seemed unaware she was being followed, and headed deeper into the gloom of Soho. The Vanishings had been busy here, and the buildings stood dark and derelict, the once bustling shops and cafés, pubs, and theaters now abandoned. Drifts of litter clogged empty doorways, and FOR SALE signs, their fastenings rotted away, lay along the pavements. He stepped carefully around them to avoid their booming surfaces, taking his eyes off the old woman only for the tiniest moments.

The road ended at a corrugated iron barrier, nine or ten feet high, reaching from wall to wall. Trees pressed up against it from the other side, as though to break it down and escape into the city. Their roots snaked under the metal panels, coiling and twisting around one another, before burrowing into the pavement and curling down the drains. Their branches crackled against the sky.

Nothing else could be seen of what lay beyond.

He hid in a darkened doorway and watched the old woman go up to a trash can and push her arm deep inside. After feeling around, she took out an object that glinted in the moonlight. It was a lantern, one of those antique ones with a brass handle and a glass chimney.

Just like the ones in the Book House, Max realized.

She snapped her fingers—a magnesium flare glared out, blinding him. When he could see again, the lantern was lit, and she was hunting along the barrier. Cat-quick, Max darted up to the trash can and ducked behind it. The old woman's fingers skittered along one of the metal panels—pulled it back—and she slipped through.

He crept up to the narrow gap she'd left behind. A tree had twisted the panel out of shape, snapping the bolts that held it in place.

Despite everything, he hesitated.

She'd really done it.

She'd broken into a No Zone.

THE NO ZONE

"Don't go into the No Zones," parents were always telling their children, "or the Vanishings will get you!"

They were places of peril where the forces that drove the Vanishings were said to linger in the air like radioactivity.

Some No Zones were nothing more than a single building—a theater, church, or gallery. Others were whole networks of streets, chunks of cities that had been sectioned off and left to decay. The Charing Cross No Zone was one of the largest in the world. Now and again, he had come up against it on his wanderings through the city. He'd never tried to sneak in, though. He'd been looking for his Forever Parents. That meant being among people. There weren't any people in the No Zones.

Just trees.

Steeling himself, he pulled back the loose panel and squeezed through, just in time to see long shadows leap against the buildings—thrown by the old woman's lantern as it lit up the trees. They stood in the road and on the pavement, their roots crumbling cement and asphalt, their branches cracking masonry and smashing windowpanes. It had only been a few years since the Censorship, Max remembered—not long enough for trees this size. Something had pulled them out of the ground, some force had drawn them upward, like beanstalks growing overnight.

Was it the work of the Woods?

He hurried after the old woman. As he went, he found himself passing over huge letters stenciled across the road in traffic paint:

KNOW WE HOW LONG THE PRESENT MUST ENDURE?

And then it became clear the old woman was not the only person breaking into the No Zone.

Everywhere he looked were words. Words written on every surface. Painted, drawn, chiseled, inked, burned, chalked, and even laid out in stone. Entire stories were scratched onto walls, hacked into trees with knives, and painted on doors. There were riddles and jokes, religious-sounding phrases and quotations, long texts crushed into small spaces with tiny handwriting, and sentences expressing mysterious, philosophical ideas. His eyes darted from one to the other, catching at those the moon lit up for him.

157

The so-called living force, the vital sense of existence, without which no society can live and no land endure, is vanishing away, God knows where.

What would the world be, once bereft
Of wet and of wildness? Let them be left,
O let them be left, wildness and wet;
Long live the weeds and the wilderness yet.

. . . nsvergessenheitseinsvergessen
heitseinsvergessenheit
seinsverge . . .

. . . ON THE SCARCELY BREATHING EARTH
A KILLING WIND FELL FROM THE NORTH,
BUT STILL WITHIN THE ELDER TREE
THE STRONG SAP ROSE, THOUGH NONE COULD SEE.

And it wasn't just words. There were sketches and paintings, too. Road signs had been altered to show silhouettes of gryphons instead of pedestrians and cars. Zombies clawed their way up from manholes. Tentacles slithered out of drains. In the window of one building, a girl sat reading a book with her knees tucked under her chin—the whole scene a painting on a steel sheet. He passed a long wall painted to look like a shelf of books. Underneath someone had written with a stub of charcoal:

BURN THIS!

Down one side street, he glimpsed a puppet of monstrous size held up by a street lamp, a sixteen-foot-tall giant, its arms and head hanging loose. In the middle of another road was the oblong shadow of a Punch and Judy show, its curtains closed, a cluster of knee-high elementary school chairs waiting for the audience. Max passed a sign with a schedule of the evening's performances:

MIDNIGHT SHOWING!!!!

**PUNCH VS SANTA !!!!
THE CROCODILE'S REVENGE!!!!
POLICEMAN IN A PICKLE!!!!
JUDY DROPS THE BABY!!!!
THE DEVIL AND THE SAUSAGES!!!!
& SING-A-LONG OPERA WITH SPIKE THE DOG!!!!**

By now, they were far from the boundary of the No Zone. Candles, flickering yellow, appeared in the windows and music floated out into the night—a sailor's jig on a violin, the honk and bray of a saxophone. There was a rattle and a sound of wheels—Max ducked into the shadows just as a man on a bicycle shot past, a long, Dragon-shaped kite flapping in the air behind him, his face alight with glee as he weaved between the trees.

"RUN!" screamed the man. "THE DRAGON IS COMING!" Setting off again, he was almost knocked over by a person with an donkey's head who burst out of a doorway and galloped off, a lantern swinging in one fist. The spectral figure was pursued by a tall, queenly woman in a silk dressing gown. She was howling, her face distorted with fury: "OUT OF THIS WOOD DO NOT DESIRE TO GO: THOU SHALT REMAIN HERE, WHETHER THOU WILT OR NO! FOR I DO LOVE THEEEEEEEE!"

Then they were gone, around a corner and away.

The old woman moved through this world as if she, herself, had created it. On she went, on and on, deeper into the No Zone, moving closer and closer to the very heart of London—the long curve of Charing Cross Road that bent toward what had once been Trafalgar Square. Here there were no more people, no more words, and no more pictures. The music tangled around itself and faded away, and the shouting became distant and full of echoes, merging with the creak and rattle of the trees.

Ahead, the pale shadow of the abandoned National Gallery rose up against the night sky.

Moving aside the branches that blocked her path, the old woman stopped before a dilapidated bookshop. Its name was still visible in peeling letters on the shop window:

ARGAND BOOKS,
ESTD. 1887.

Near the entrance was an oil drum filled with burning wooden boards. The light from its flames flickered over three armchairs, which had been dragged, Max guessed, from an empty hotel or pub. He hid himself behind a tree and watched as the old woman looked around and glanced at her watch. She muttered something, lifted a folded woolen blanket from one of the chairs, wrapped herself in it, then sat before the fire, shooing away the sparks that leapt out at her in eager greeting.

A few minutes later, a man carrying a crowbar and a bundle of floorboards emerged from a doorway farther up the street. He greeted the old woman, stuffed the planks into the fire, then turned and beckoned to Max.

Somehow, unsurprised, Max nodded at the Dark Man, came out from the shadows, and took his seat before the fire.

"I'm sorry about the Mulgans," the old woman began. "It's always a sadness when the Vanishings claim another victim. Isn't it, Boris?"

"It is," said the Dark Man, not taking his eyes off Max for a second.

"But now that they have Vanished," the old woman went on, "we find an opportunity presents itself. To discover how the Vanishings started, and maybe even stop them for good."

Max looked from one to the other. It was strange enough to hear the old woman suddenly talking about the Mulgans as if she knew all about them. It was stranger still to learn the Dark Man had a name. But what did the Vanishings have to do with anything?

The Dark Man noticed his confusion and began to speak. He was a scientist from Western Siberia, he said. He'd met Mrs. Jeffers twelve years ago in Paris. He was studying the Vanishings, and she was investigating a mystery of her own. They'd "joined forces" because of "certain connections."

"Did the Mulgans ever speak to you?" the old woman interrupted suddenly. "About your real parents?"

Max didn't move or even blink, but quite suddenly his heart was beating faster. This was it. He was about the learn the truth!

"They said I'd been abandoned. It wasn't true, though. Was it?"

"They didn't lie," the Dark Man said, glancing at the old woman. "What they told you was . . . the official version of events. But you weren't abandoned. Something else happened. Something . . . strange."

He took a battered packet of cigarettes out of his pocket and lit one restlessly.

"The thing is, Max—we're not sure you have any parents."

There was a dreadful pause that seemed to go on for hours.

Max felt something like a snake uncoiling in his stomach. "You mean . . . you think they're dead?"

"No. I mean—maybe you never had any. That's why nobody knows who they are. That's why, after twelve years of searching, we haven't been able to find them. Maybe you never had parents in the first place."

Max was about to smile, because that was just silly. But then Boris looked at him, and his expression was so serious the smile didn't even get started.

"I must have had parents at some point," he said. "Nobody just appears out of nowhere."

"But what if that's what did happen?"

"What do you mean?"

"What if you Appeared?" the Dark Man asked, his eyes glowing. "Suddenly. Out of nowhere."

2

THE BOOKSHELF BOY

It was a busy day in Argand Books when it happened.

Busy because Charing Cross Road was not yet a No Zone. Busy because the terrible danger of dreams was yet to be proclaimed by Professor Courtz. Busy because the Vanishings had not yet begun.

But they were about to.

The unsuspecting customers—many of whom in a few years would be little more than puffs of smoke, or wisps of ether, or ghosts, or sub-atomic particles, or nothing at all, depending which theory was accepted—stood innocently browsing the shelves, happy to be sheltering from the sudden April shower lashing the asphalt, and blissfully unaware that reality was about to be torn apart and reinvented in such a way as to usher in, like a vaudeville act onto a Victorian stage, the Vanishings.

Argand Books was popular because of its eccentricity, which those coming in off the street attempted to emulate. Otherwise normal types would scuttle crab-like through the door, muttering under their breath and scratching their foreheads—something they would never do in the supermarket, at a bus stop, or at work, because in those places all kinds of strangeness are expressly forbidden, whereas in a bookshop they are positively encouraged. Most of all, they tried to think up obscure titles that would force the notoriously foul-tempered owner to treat them as equals, as true scholars—which is how everyone wants to be treated in a bookshop: not only as a reader of books, but as a proper Nietzsche, someone with unique ideas that can set the world alight. This owner, a serpent-haired old woman, possessed the supernatural ability to point out the exact location of any book without a second's hesitation. Among the Argand regulars, it had become a sport to request a book the haughty owner could not spot. A pot of cash accrued through a sweepstake awaited the genius who could request a book that was not in stock. To date, their efforts had been unsuccessful, and the prize-fund continued to swell. No matter how obscure the title, Argand Books came up with the goods.

It was the candles and lanterns, though, that made the bookshop truly bizarre. They marked the principal eccentricity of the proprietor—her avowed antipathy to electric light. Electrically generated light, began a manifesto in the shop window, is damaging not only to books but to the

principle of reading itself. This text was long and in excep-
tionally small print, so few had actually read it. The gist was
that the omnipresence of artificial light in modern life was
a nuisance. A society had been formed. Subscriptions were
welcome. Inquire within.

Nobody ever did.

Why light was damaging was not explained. But the result
was a dimly lit interior that had customers huddling around
the lanterns, which hung on long chains from the ceiling or
from brackets on the wall, their stubby funnels emitting a
foul smell of burning oil. The cantankerous old woman was
fond of explaining that the engineering innovation involved
in the invention of this individual lantern, the Argand
burner, had been "the biggest leap forward in Natural Light
Production Technology in thousands if not MILLIONS of
years!" For proof she would point to a poster delineating
the history of the world's greatest inventions. The year of
the Argand burner's creation (1784, by the Swiss scientist
François Pierre Ami Argand) was listed next to the great
strides in aviation technology that had first allowed a sheep,
a rooster, and a duck aloft in a Hot-Air Balloon—followed,
on the safe return of the pioneering beasts, by Jean-François
Pilâtre de Rozier, and François Laurent, Marquis d'Arlandes,
who were the first human beings in history to see Paris from
the perspective of a not-very-high-up God—though they
had in fact been beaten to it by the sheep, who had chewed
a peephole in the bottom of the wicker basket (and then

refused to budge to allow the duck and the rooster a peek).

This ancient misanthrope spent her days sitting ramrod-straight on a tall stool in a corner of the bookshop. The only event in the cosmos that could force her from her perch was when a book was asked for that was tucked away in an obscure corner and could not be pointed at. Most of the time, it was in plain sight, and she could simply roll her eyes, tut, and jab her finger in its direction. But because of the layout of the bookshop, certain corners were around other corners and thus out of finger-shot. If books lived in these provincial areas, there was nothing for it: she had to move.

On that showery day in April when the Vanishings were set in motion, she was asked for a book that happened to dwell in such an un-pointable-at region. Some young fellow was after it, some twerp of a student; she'd been watching him inch closer and closer for a good twenty minutes, obviously convinced he had a real poser of a title for her, one the bookshop could not possibly stock, and that the jackpot was certainly his, that come evening he would be thousands of pounds richer, drinking champagne and gobbling caviar. Everyone in the bookshop knew what was about to happen and was watching furtively. She, too, knew exactly what all these rascals were up to, and glared at the presumptuous wretch as he opened his mouth, noticing with distaste the congealed, lardy remains of a chocolate muffin embedded in his molars: "I was wondering," he brayed, tossing his head back so the whole bookshop could hear, "if you might have a copy of *Der abenteuerliche Simplicissimus Teutsch: Das ist, Die Beschreibung deß Lebens eines seltzamen Vaganten, genant Melchior Sternfels von Fuchshaim, wo und welcher gestalt er nemlich in diese Welt kommen, was er darinn gesehen, gelernet, erfahren und außgestanden, auch warumb er solche wieder freywillig quittirt—Überauß lustig, und männiglich nutzlich zu lesen,* by Hans Jakob Christoffel von Grimmelshausen." He drew breath, then plunged on. "An English translation would suffice, in which case the title would be—"

"*Simplicissimus the Vagabond*," the old woman said breezily. "That is, the life of a strange adventurer named Melchior Sternfels von Fuchshaim: Namely where and in what manner he came into this world, what he saw, learned, experienced, and endured therein: Also why he again left it of his own free will. Exceedingly droll and very advantageous to read. Or, if you'd like it in Arabic—"

"Er . . . no," the student said, crushed beneath the bookshop's remarkable inventory. "The English or German would do."

"We have both," the old woman announced, shriveling him up with a look which, despite her antipathy to light of that kind, could only be likened to the blasts of laser cannons.

Compensation came, however, when it transpired she had to move to fetch the tome in question. Unfolding her limbs, she shuffled toward Seventeenth-Century Europe, a dusky, primeval region of literature where ever fewer ventured to go. Once there, she reached up to find the thick volume . . . felt for it with her fingertips . . . felt for its rough, basilisk-skin spine . . .

Now.

Little did the unfortunate student know that he had uttered, with that long and obscure title, a summoning spell that called out to a certain potential waiting to happen. The effect was like opening an umbrella in a thunderstorm. In the churning vault of heaven, electricity has gathered in the clouds, gathered and built, until all that is needed is a suitable moment—a hint, a word of encouragement, a suggestion, a weathervane, a clock tower, the title of a book—for the electricity to be unleashed. As the tall old woman stood with her arm stretched up, her eyes came level with a certain gap on the shelves. This space existed because a mold had infected the shelf—she herself had detected the smell several days ago and removed the books in order to dry out the wood. The mold had not shifted, she noticed, and if anything had spread itself. Resolving to tackle it again that afternoon, she tugged *Simplicissimus the Vagabond* free from his mooring and was about to turn away from the shelves when, without any sign or warning to prepare her for the shock, the potential was unleashed, the lightning struck, and a naked baby winked into existence right before her eyes, right there in the moldy space and not inches from her nose.

The baby was not large but exceedingly long, as some babies are. It immediately began to cry, either because it had kicked out and stubbed its toe in its rather confined space between books, or because this was its first moment in life—traditionally an occasion for sorrow among infants, who are unable to see the attractions of this world in the first moments of entering it, on account of their perverse and cynical natures.

In her shock, the old woman dropped *Simplicissimus*. At precisely the same moment, the baby rolled onto its side and, in doing so, tumbled clean off the shelf. In short, it too began to fall, meeting *Simplicissimus* on its way down and giving it an appreciative glance, no doubt recognizing a fellow traveler, a kindred spirit, a brother-in-arms.

It is in moments of surprise, precisely because surprise prohibits thought, that acts of extraordinary dexterity become possible. With a professional ordering of priorities, the old woman rescued the book first, grabbing it neatly with one hand, and allowed the baby to drop a little farther before breaking its fall by catching it in the crook of her foot.

A few moments later, she was surrounded by customers, who were first attracted by the baby's screams, then repelled by its dark eyes, its spidery limbs, and its SNAP SNAP SNAPPING teeth.

Snap snap snap! they went.

SNAP!

SNAP!

SNAP!

EISTEDDFOD

Max dragged his sleeve across the laminated plastic, wiping away the dirt that had built up over the years:

NOTICE OF LIQUIDATION

Under Section 1.1 of International Law, The Vanishings Act, para. 59; notice is given of closure and termination of all properties containing or relating to the dispersal of printed or recorded matter deemed inappropriate by the ISPCV Council and its Ministers. This property:

Argand Books,
3 St. Martin's Lane,
London WC1H 7TT

is to cease trading until such time when it can be secured in the interests of public safety.

WESTMINSTER COUNCIL

He took a step back and looked up at the weather-beaten façade and boarded windows.

Was this *really* where he'd come from?

After all those dreams about far-off lands, it was a ruined bookshop in central London? Only a few miles away from Bickerstaffes Road? In a No Zone he'd passed a hundred times?

"Watch out."

Mrs. Jeffers shuffled past, unlocked the door and gave it a shove. He'd learned a lot more about her in the long conversation before the fire.

Name?

Suffrenia Jeffers.

Age?

Lost track.

Occupation?

Wizard. Responsible for the invention of, and later modifications to, Old Light.

"As you go in, bear left," she said. "Look for Russian and German literature. You Appeared on the ninth shelf up."

The Dark Man handed him a lantern. "If you remember anything," he said, "even just a feeling or a sensation, take note of it."

Max nodded, throwing his old companion a confused look. He'd learned a lot about the Dark Man, too. He was an actual person, a scientist called Boris Peshkov who had worked for the Symposium. So he wasn't a ghost at all. He was solid and real.

It was like he'd gone through a Vanishing in reverse.

Like I did, Max wondered, as he made his way into the building, his sneakers crunching on grit and broken glass. Like I did when I started all this off.

He found himself in a room filled with tall bookcases. He made his way between them, the light casting deep shadows between their empty ribs, until he found the notice, smeared with dust and mold:

RUSSIAN & GERMAN LITERATURE

Lifting his lantern, he entered the niche and counted up to the ninth shelf. He placed the lantern on the floor, then scrambled up and managed a quick look to the left and to the right: nothing but crumbs of plaster, dust, and cobwebs.

He jumped down.

For a long time he stood still, allowing the distant memories of the place to tug at his imagination, just as the Dark Man had suggested. There was nothing. Not the tiniest reminder or hint of his Forever Parents.

He hunkered down beside the glow of the lantern.

How could he remember?

He'd only been a baby.

The Dark Man had discovered something strange about his memories. From the stories he'd written. It had been the Dark Man's idea, that the scribblings of a small boy might reveal a clue about the Vanishings. But he'd gotten something else instead, something unexpected.

Nothing about the Vanishings.

And everything about the Woods.

Accurate descriptions, one after another.

This had been their first big breakthrough. It was like Max remembered the Woods, without ever having been to the Woods. They wanted to expose him to the Woods more directly. They couldn't take him there, so they did the next best thing: they brought the Woods to him, in the Storybooks.

But before the experiment yielded results, the Censorship came along.

Since then, they had struggled to find a way forward. They had scoured the Woods. They had gone through every lead and every record the World had to offer. They had come up with nothing. Now, with no more clues, there was only one option. One way to reveal the truth about the Appearance. One last experiment.

He shuddered at the thought of what they were asking him to do.

It sounded impossibly dangerous, this plan of theirs. But it didn't seem like he had any choice. He had nowhere else to go. And there didn't seem to be any other way to find out where he came from.

Or maybe there was.

His dreams about the Woods had been true, they'd told him. Surely that meant his other dreams, about his Forever Parents, were also true. He didn't believe the Dark Man's theory that he had no parents. He didn't believe that for a second. He just needed to find them. *They* would be able to explain the Appearance.

And then he wouldn't have to do it. This idea of theirs. This crazy, certain-death idea.

But he still had to get to the Woods.

He would learn nothing here.

Not in the World.

Not in this empty bookshop.

He got to his feet and picked up the lantern, swinging it around for one last look at the place. The light fell across a corner he'd missed. He saw shoes and trousers. Someone was lying there on the floor, asleep.

He edged closer.

No.

The shadows had tricked him. It was just a pile of clothes.

The shirt inside the sweater.

The sweater inside the jacket.

The tie neatly knotted.

The shoes laced.

The socks tucked inside.

The lantern jangled as his hand began to shake. These clothes hadn't been taken off.

They'd been *emptied*.

Above them, carved into the plaster of the wall in tiny letters, were three simple words:

I WAS HERE

And it was as if he hadn't understood the Vanishings, until now.

Into the Woods

When he emerged from the bookshop Boris and Mrs. Jeffers were sitting around the fire, talking quietly.

"Well?" asked the Dark Man, breaking off and standing up. "Anything?"

Max came over and stood behind the empty armchair. He shook his head, and they glanced at each other.

"You weren't really *expecting* him to remember, were you?" Mrs. Jeffers asked a little snappily.

"It was worth a try," the Dark Man muttered, sighing and rubbing his hair. "Considering the alternative, it was worth a try." He glanced at Max apprehensively. "Are you sure you want to go ahead with this? If you want to change your mind, you must say so now."

"No, it's okay," said Max. "I'll come to the Woods." He was about to go on, to tell them about his Forever Parents, but before he could, Boris was already placing a hand on his shoulder and staring deep into his eyes.

"I knew you would," he said quietly. "I always knew you would. But we must go quickly. We do not have much time."

He turned away, and began rapidly shoveling handfuls of snow into the brazier. Mrs. Jeffers lit the lanterns.

"This one is for you," she said. "Take it. Whatever you do, don't let it go out."

"Why not?"

"You'll need it to find your way to the Woods. Boris will explain."

"Aren't you coming?"

"I'll be making the crossing here. You're inexperienced. We've arranged for you to do it somewhere quieter."

"Where?"

"Look," she said. "There are only two questions you need to worry about. Who are you? Where did you come from? If we get those answers, this friend of ours might even be able to stop the Vanishings. Now, do you want to get on with that or not?"

"I guess."

"Then take this and get going. See you in London!"

With that, the old woman turned and disappeared into the trees.

He left the No Zone with the Dark Man.

When they reached the barrier, they ducked into an abandoned restaurant and threaded through the tables to the kitchen.

"We'll be passing back into the streets," Boris said, stopping at a service entrance. He glanced at Max. "Empty your schoolbag."

"Why? My clothes are in here."

"We'll get you replacements."

Max pulled out all his clothes and left them on the floor. The Dark Man extinguished the lanterns, wrapped them in two of Max's sweaters, and stowed them carefully.

"Now, come." He set his shoulder against a delivery door, and thrust it open with a short burst of strength. Then they were out of the No Zone and back among the late-night crowds of Oxford Street.

They went silently, side-by-side for the first time. Now and again, Max glanced at the grim-faced figure, who seemed just by the force of his presence to move people out of his way. It was hard to believe Boris was a normal person like everyone else.

"Are you really a scientist?" he asked. "You're not a Wizard like Mrs. Jeffers?"

Boris gave his shoulders an easy shrug. "You know, in a way the Wizards are scientists. The scientists of the Woods, if you like."

"Do all scientists know about the Woods? Or just you?"

"A good many people know in one way or another. To some the Woods are an idea or a feeling, and will never be more than that. To others they are home."

"How long have you known about them?"

"Since I was a boy." The Dark Man's eyes darkened. "But I do not wish to speak about that. This way!"

A bus roared past, its engines gusting heat. They darted out behind it, crossed Oxford Street and cut up toward Marylebone. They were suddenly alone in a darkened street, their footfalls echoing against the silent buildings.

"We're going into another No Zone, aren't we?" Max asked.

The Dark Man nodded. "We need to go a little more north. I want to get as close as possible to the actual destination. Mrs. Jeffers is right—the first time you cross can be tricky."

They came to another barrier, but instead of approaching it Boris went straight to the door of a derelict basement apartment, the closest to the barrier. He took a key from his pocket, opened the door, and stepped inside.

"Okay," he said. "Lanterns. Dump your bag—you won't need it."

Boris seemed to know exactly where he was going. Lanterns lit once more, he led Max through the empty home, into the kitchen, then the living room, and then hammered on the back of a boarded-over window. The wooden panel fell outward with a booming sound, and they clambered out onto the pavement. They were on the No Zone side of the barrier, in a deserted square of unoccupied town-houses. Here, too, the trees were taking over. There was a small private garden in the center of the square—that was where they'd started off, Max figured.

And now they were on the rampage.

Boris secured the panel back on the window, then turned to face the square.

"You need three things to get to the Woods," he said. "First, it needs to be nighttime. Crossing during the day, I believe, is impossible. Second, you need some form of Old Light—a flame, a candle, a lantern. The third thing you need," he said, pointing toward the center of the square, "is trees."

Max followed him toward the park. The Dark Man stopped at the gate, and peered into the trees. They had taken over the place—the lawns, the flowerbeds, none of it remained.

"It's hardly there anymore," Boris muttered. "I hadn't expected that."

"What's not there?" Max asked.

"The path," said Boris.

He pointed down, and moved his finger forward. Only the barest trace remained. It snaked away and disappeared into the darkness.

"The Beginning Woods is in here?" Max asked doubtfully.

"The Beginning Woods is never exactly anywhere. It drifts. Sometimes it's close, and other times it's far. In a No Zone at night, we're halfway there already."

"Why does night make a difference?"

"Because to get to the Woods, you have to make the World"—Boris gestured around at the buildings—"disappear."

"How are we going to do that?"

"That's what the lanterns are for. Keep your eyes on the flame. The Old Light will do the rest. And whatever you do, don't leave the path."

"How can I watch the path if I have to watch the flame?"

"I never said it was easy," muttered Boris. "Now come on. Just try to feel it with your feet."

He set off through the gates, Max keeping close behind. It was hard to believe the Beginning Woods was anywhere near, not with the silhouettes of chimneys and rooftops looming through the branches and an entire city beyond, with its cars, buses, shops, and hotels, its cement and plastic and metal.

The Dark Man's voice drifted back. "The flame. Keep your eyes on the flame."

"I won't be able to see anything!"

"That's the idea . . ."

He held the lantern more in front of him and stared into the glow. It expanded into his eyeballs, destroying his night vision, sweeping away the rooftops, the chimneys, and the No Zone. Soon all he could see was a burning globe, and trees flickering darkly around its edge. He began to feel the trembling, uncertain presence of a forest, one that extended a thousand miles in every direction. And then he began to imagine it, to see it in his mind's eye—a primitive place of absolute stillness, of boulders dissolving under mossy shrouds, and clearings where nothing had stirred for hundreds of years. He tried to hold onto this fragile image and found himself murmuring over again, as a kind of incantation:

> *Bigger than the best of dreamers could ever imagine.*
> *Darker than they could ever fear.*
> *Full of more wonder than they could ever imagine.*

The more his mind worked on it, the more sure he became that the forest was there around him—and then it was the city that was trembling and uncertain, and impossible to imagine.

His eyes slipped away from the light.

His lantern came up with a jangle of brass.

The Dark Man had been only a few steps in front.

Now, not a trace of him remained.

Gone! Boris had crossed over without him. Leaving him behind. Could you be left behind?

He had to catch up.

He broke into a run. "Wait for me!" he shouted. "I'm coming!" Light swung from side to side. The trees grew and shrank, grew and shrank. He tried to keep his eyes on the lantern, but it was impossible. And . . . where was the end of the park? It had been so small. He should have come to the fence. Or the houses.

He slowed down and stopped. Took a few steps forward. Stopped again. Looked up through the treetops.

The buildings. They'd gone. All of them. All he could see through the branches was the moon and the stars.

This wasn't London.

This was the Woods.

He slowly lowered his lantern. The trees around him quivered, seeming to awaken as a tremor of fear pulsed through his body.

Nighttime.

And he was alone.

Whatever you do, don't leave the path. He looked down quickly. He'd edged off it. He edged back, slowly, one step at a time, trying not to disturb the trees.

Then.

A slight noise.

Crackled above him.

Moving his head very slowly, he looked up. And . . . what was that? Was it . . . could it be . . . that the trees . . . were spelling it out . . .

M a X

He fled.

The path pitched and dived under his feet. But now there was something devious about it, something malevolent and treacherous—and sure enough, suddenly it melted away with a snicker and a wink: Good luck!

He kept going. Branches swung down out of the darkness, blocking his way. He forced his way through them.

Stopped.

Stood still, catching his breath, fighting back panic.

He needed to get on the path again. He tried to retrace his steps, but the trees had closed in behind him. Soon he was squeezing his way sideways between their trunks.

Darkness grew around him.

The shadows thickened.

It was the lantern. Running out of fuel, the flame inside dwindling down. Soon, it was little more than a candle, a faint glow behind glass. He held it up to his face. Don't go out! Stay with me! Just a bit longer!

tap tap tap taptap taptap

He jerked around.

What was that?

He strained his ears. It was a light, rhythmical tapping. Something like metal on stone. Coming from far off to his left.

taptaptap

Only one thing was capable of making that noise.

People!

He ran toward it. The Woods threw obstacles in his way— brambles, roots, and boulders. He staggered through them, over them, around them.

tap tap tap taptap taptap

It grew louder. But quickly it divided in the air, splitting into separate sounds that came at him from all sides.

tap tap tap

tap taptaptaptap

taptaptap

If it was people, they were everywhere. He just couldn't see them. Where were they?

CRACK!

He fell forward, pain lancing up his shins. He squeezed his eyes shut and curled into a ball. He'd tripped on something hard sticking out of the ground.

taptaptaptaptap

Right beside him! In a flash, he was up and scrambling for the lantern. It had fallen against a low, curved headstone. Its light flickered gently against the inscription:

ONE DAY

YOU CAUGHT

A FISH

AND LET ME PRETEND

I HAD

What?

He looked behind.

There was another. That's what he'd tripped on. A headstone, just like the first, low and carved with strange words:

WHEN
I WAS
HOT IN THE
FIELDS, YOU
BROUGHT
WATER

A man was kneeling beside the headstone. He was totally gray from head-to-toe, even his clothes. In his hands, he held a hammer and a chisel. He peered at Max with an amused expression, then stood, bowed, doffed his cap . . . then sank out of sight, vanishing, the hammer and chisel thudding onto the ground behind him.

But already Max had seen the others. They were all looking right at him.

Very carefully and slowly, he stood up.

People?

No.

Ghosts!

Ghosts in a graveyard!

They had to be ghosts. They were all that same peculiar drained gray color. There were dozens of them—men, women, and children of all ages. Each was kneeling before their own headstone. The nearest, a grandfather with his beard tucked into his belt, nodded at him solemnly, then bent close to his stone and delivered one final blow with his hammer and chisel.

tap

He blew the dust from the stone, wiped it carefully with his cap—and melted into the ground with a sigh, his tools dropping behind him. The others returned to their work. The strange tapping rang out once more.

Max edged closer to read the grandfather's words:

I

PUSHED

YOU IN

THE NETTLES

BROTHER

FURGIVE ME

"You shouldn't be here yet," said a voice.

He jerked around, his fright coming out in a startled yelp. A light, gray girl was watching him. She was perched on one of the stones, her skinny knees almost up around her ears. She had a strand of her long hair curled around a finger, and was nibbling at the springy tuft as she watched him curiously.

"You're one of the Warm Ones," she said matter-of-factly. "You're not supposed to read the messages until morning."

Even though she was a ghost like the others, it was impossible to be scared of someone his own age. So for a moment, he watched her back, with a curiosity of his own.

It wasn't that she was pretty . . . he wouldn't have said that, or, at least, he wouldn't have admitted it. But gray was . . . definitely . . . the wrong color for her. And looking at her, right then, he very much wanted to know what her real colors were.

The thought of them, the thought of what those colors were . . . *that* was pretty.

"What messages?" he asked. "Wh-what are you talking about?"

She took the hair out of her mouth and peered at him, her pinched face amused and curious. "Don't you know?"

He came a little nearer. "I'm not from here. I'm from London."

Her arm, thin as a candlestick, pointed into the trees. "London's that way." She hopped off the gravestone and walked up to him boldly. She was barefoot and only wore a thin woolen dress. The cold didn't seem to bother her.

"You're a World One, aren't you?" she said, looking him up and down.

"A what?"

"You're from the World. You must be here for the Eisteddfod Competition. Are you?"

"Yes," Max said. "Well, sort of."

"That's nice. Can I have your shoes before you get killed?"

"Before I . . . what?"

"I know," she said. "Everyone thinks they're going to be the one that survives. Which is strange, because about two hundred World Ones enter it every year, and there's only ever the one survivor."

"Only ever . . . one?"

"Sometimes two. I think once, ages ago, there were three. But that didn't count because they found out after, the third one, he was a big fat cheat. The Dragon Hunters didn't like that at all. It's pretty stupid trying to fool the Dragon Hunters."

"You're just trying to scare me."

"You should be scared. I don't know why anyone would want to enter that stupid competition. Who'd want to become a Dragon Hunter? They're so surly and mean. All they ever do is stride around in the Deep Woods digging up Dragons."

"I'm not trying to become a Dragon Hunter," Max said. "I'm doing it for . . . never mind what."

She seemed surprised at that. "Why else would you enter Eisteddfod? It's so dangerous. You shouldn't ever even go near a Dragon, let alone—"

"I'm sorry," Max interrupted her. He didn't want to talk about Dragons anymore. It just reminded him of the Dark Man's plan. "But . . . are you . . . are you a ghost?"

"A ghost! No!" She reached forward and pinched him, hard. "Can ghosts do that? Of course not! Anyway, ghosts are make-believe. Who believes in ghosts?"

"I just saw an old man. He sank into the ground. He was here. Right here. How did he—?"

"When we're back, we're back. When we go, we go. That's all. Are you going to give me your shoes or not?"

Max looked down at his ratty old sneakers. "Why do you keep talking about my shoes?"

"They're for my brother. He'll be your size soon. They're here tonight on a visit—my Father, my Mother, my brother. My whole family!"

"To see you?"

"Yes!" she said. "Well, they don't get to *see* me. They get to read the message. But I know they're here, and they know I'm here. It's nice." She followed his gaze to the stone she'd been sitting on, which was still blank. It was older than the other stones, too—covered in moss and white lichen, while all the others were new. "I just haven't done mine yet," she added, her eyes flicking toward him. "I'm still thinking what to say."

Max was about to ask how long she'd been in the graveyard when a thin voice rang out in the night air. An old man in a dressing gown was coming through the trees, holding a lantern high.

"That's it! Time for bed! How are your visitors supposed to sleep with all this *taptaptapping* going on? You should've finished by now. You've had all year to think about it! Hammers down! Chop-chop!"

He seemed to possess authority over the spirits. As he passed they melted into the ground, their hammers and chisels thudding onto the grass. He soon spotted Max's lantern and came hobbling up to them, his bright eyes gleaming.

"*There* you are!" He prodded Max in the chest with a bony finger. "We've been looking for you, young man, and here you are right where you're supposed to be! Appearing out of nowhere all over again. You like that sort of game, eh?"

He winked knowingly, and was about to say something more when the girl bounded toward him.

"He's NOT supposed to be here, Father Furthingale. It's too early to read the messages. Kill him and take his shoes! He'll be dead soon anyway!"

"Dead?" the old man exclaimed. "Why will he be dead, child?"

"He's entering Eisteddfod! He's going to get burned to a crisp like all the others."

"Oh, you silly girl, haha!" The old man laughed nervously and glanced at Max. "He won't get . . . burned to a . . . no. No no no. We're quite sure of that. Quite sure."

"How are you sure?" asked the girl.

"Never you mind," the old man said. "You know the rules. Time to sleep for another year."

She pouted and wormed her way under his arm. "Why should I care about rules?" she asked unhappily. "Nobody else does."

He sighed and gave her a comforting squeeze. "I know, my dear. Today of all days, they should be here. It's a long way from your home and the Paths aren't as safe as they used to be. I'm sure they'll make it next year."

The girl darted a guilty look at Max, then buried her face in the old man's chest. "I don't care if they come or not! I don't!"

"You don't mean that," the Father said. "Now come along, it's time to sleep."

Her face appeared, streaked with tears. "No, Father! I'm staying up to count the stars, remember?"

"What in the Woods gave you that idea?"

"Every year they haven't come you let me. That means it's a rule!"

The old man sighed. "Well, yes, I suppose it does. But only the stars to the left of the spire. Don't start in on the ones to the right."

He kissed the top of her head fondly. She spun away, suddenly gleeful, and leapt back onto her gravestone.

"One," she said, pointing up at the sky. Then, after careful selection and a long pause: "Two."

The old man shook his head, smiling, then beckoned to Max. "That goes for you, too, young sir. Bedtime! Our friend Doctor Peshkov is out on the Paths looking for you. When he returns, I want you nicely tucked up safe and sound!"

Max followed the old man through the trees. As they went, he looked back at the gray girl, perched once again on her gravestone.

She wasn't counting the stars at all.

She wasn't even looking at the moon.

She was nibbling her hair, watching him.

The Marylebone Dormitory

"You crossed over almost at once," the Father said as they made their way through the graves. "Doctor Peshkov wasn't expecting that. Normally, it takes longer for the Woods to materialize, especially for first-timers. You got here well ahead of him."

Max kept breaking into a trot to keep up with the old man, who seemed eager to escape the wintery chill.

"Where is here?" he asked.

"Why, Marylebone village of course. Same as where you crossed over."

"Marylebone? In north London?"

"North of London."

"But . . . Marylebone is *in* London."

"Not here it isn't," the old man said. "You'll see."

They soon emerged from the graveyard. The white stone walls of a church rose up ahead, gleaming in the bright moon. It stood on a small country lane that cut its way into the distance between open fields. There were no other buildings in sight.

"London lies a few miles south," said the Father, pointing as they scrunched across the courtyard. "North leads to Marylebone village. Beyond that and you're in the Woods, so it's stick to the Path or face the consequences! Go farther still, and you'll be in the Deep Woods. Dragon territory," he added. "Only the Dragon Hunters go there."

"I read lots of stories about the Beginning Woods," Max said as they went up the steps of the building. "I didn't read anything about churches."

The Father smiled. "How many books would I have to read before I knew everything about the World?"

"Lots, I guess."

"And in this particular case, you didn't know there were churches in the Woods because *there aren't*. You're probably supposing I'm a priest as well. But I'm not!"

"So who are you?"

"I'm . . . a person of welcome, shall we say."

"But this really looks like a church."

"Well, it's like many things in the Woods," the Father replied. "It's different on the inside."

He set his shoulder against the oak door and gave it a shove. They moved through a shadowy hallway.

"This doesn't look so different," Max said. But then the Father pushed open another door, and they passed into the main building.

"Welcome to the Marylebone Dormitory," the Father whispered. "The best night's sleep in the Woods."

The "church" was full of beds. Bunk beds, double beds, king-size beds, cots and hammocks, roll-up mattresses and mounds of cushions, even simple piles of straw in the corners. All the beds were occupied, sometimes with a solitary sleeper, sometimes with three or four. In one bed, an entire family was lined up like soldiers—Mother, Father, and four little children tucked between them. Lanterns glowing on walls and bedside lockers filled the Dormitory with a soft light.

The Father bent close to Max's ear. "Every year before Eisteddfod, the Forest Folk gather in Dormitories all over the Woods to read messages left by the Cold Ones. They bring new gravestones, and take the old ones away as keepsakes."

Max was about to ask the old man about the girl in the graveyard when something blurred across his vision, a misty splotch of purple, there and gone in a second. Frowning, he rubbed his eyes—but almost at once another one appeared, suspended in the light of his lantern. It was a blotchy mix of purples and reds. Its octopus-like body pulsated slowly, and wispy tentacles undulated in the air, reaching out toward him.

"Not him, not him!" the Father muttered, flapping his hands. "He's awake, you silly creature! Shoo! Shoo!"

The blob changed color slightly, then floated off, disappearing from sight.

"Don't be alarmed, it's just the Dream Harvesters," the old man said. "An invention of the Wizards. You can only see them in Old Light. Look! There's one!"

He held his lantern over a sleeping figure. One of the Harvesters had just enveloped the man's head. Its tentacles were sliding into his ears, and small suckers had been placed over his eyes. For a time, it simply lay there, pulsing against his face. Then it detached itself and lifted up into the air, melting away again as it left the Old Light.

"They're quite harmless," the Father said. "Once they've collected enough dreams they go out through the chimney. See?"

At the far end of the building, a fireplace held the dying embers of a collapsed log. A slow stream of Dream Harvesters was drifting up the flue, illuminated by a row of candles on the mantelpiece.

"Where are they going?" Max asked in a hushed voice.

"Some go to another Dormitory to collect more dreams. Those that are full rise into the atmosphere and dissolve in the clouds. The rain falls and the dreams are absorbed into the soil. They become the nutrients that feed the Briarbacks."

"The trees the Dragons eat . . ."

"Precisely! But come now, let's get you to your bed. You're lucky to have one at such short notice. It's our busiest night of the year."

He led Max to a corner farthest from the entrance, where a small cot was pushed against the wall. He took Max's lantern, which had now died out, and hung it from a hook on the wall.

"There's a nightshirt under the pillow," he said, gesturing absently. "In the morning, wrap those World clothes up in your blanket, leave them under the bed, and put on the clothes you find there. Doctor Peshkov will meet you in the morning, but if you want something to eat or drink before then, just go through that door. There's a kitchen to the left, a washroom to the right. Now, good night! And don't worry about the Harvesters. You won't feel a thing, I promise."

With that the old man turned away and disappeared through a curtain.

Max sat on the bed and looked around.

Now that he had a moment to stop and think, it was actually sinking in.

He was in the Beginning Woods.

So much of it was already strange and startling. Warm Ones and Cold Ones. The Dormitories and Dream Harvesters. The girl on the gravestone. He'd expected it to be familiar, like snuggling under the stairs in the Book House and opening another Storybook.

But being here was different.

There were so many things he didn't know.

A boy was sleeping nearby. Obviously, being in the Woods was normal for him. Maybe he was dreaming about going to the World, with its trains and hamburgers and spaceships. Hardly breathing, he watched a Dream Harvester attach itself to the boy's head with undulating movements of its slow tentacles. Its colors darkened, becoming inky with dreams. Eventually, it floated off, pulsing with blues and greens, until it left the nimbus of light and faded into invisibility.

What dream of mine would the Harvester collect? he wondered.

Whatever it was, that dream would dissolve in the clouds, then fall on the Woods as rain. It would be absorbed into the soil so the Briarback trees could grow—the food of the Dragons, the fuel for their fire. Then one day, a Dragon Hunter would feel that fire on his skin, and hear the mingled dreams of the Forest Folk. And the Dragon Hunter would take this treasure . . . where?

What happened then?

What did the Dragon Hunters do with all these stories?

He changed into his nightshirt and hopped into bed. It was freezing cold. He cocooned himself under the blankets, until it all warmed up. When he was ready, he stuck his head out onto the pillow.

Above him, the Dream Harvesters were already gathering.

Okay, he thought, with a shiver of pleasure.

Come and get it.

The Fingernail Escape

The dream was about a Dragon.

It wasn't buried under the soil in the forest like it was meant to be. Somehow, it had gotten lost and ended up in a multi-story parking garage. It was there right in front of him—a foresty Dragon with a tail as green and rich as a jungle river, a mossy giant covered in lichen and tufts of grass like a shipwreck was covered in seaweed and barnacles. If it had been lying crocodile-still in a forest, its body would have been mistaken for a hillock, its knobbly joints for boulders, and its long snout for the rotting trunk of a fallen tree.

Because of the low, concrete ceiling, its head was pressed down and its neck was stretched out, so close to Max that he could almost touch it. It was sleeping, which made sense, because that was what Dragons did mostly. The lidded eyes were shut. The claws with their thick, crusted nails rested motionless on the concrete. The tail was so long it stretched under a row of cars and snaked all the way down the exit ramp.

As for the mouth, it was closed, safely closed . . . or almost closed. It was possible to make out the gleam of teeth behind the Dragon's lips. Nevertheless, the mouth was closed.

Or was it?

Had that gleam of white been there before? Or had it appeared in the last second or two?

And was it getting bigger?

It was. Now he could clearly see the triangular fangs, and behind them the flat, fleshy tongue heaving around.

Little by little, in secret so he wouldn't notice, the Dragon was opening its mouth.

The moment he realized this, he became rooted to the spot and couldn't move. The Dragon rose up, and from the murky cavern of its throat, redness rushed forth, a gorgeous lava exploding from the molten core of the earth, flooding over him, burning him away—

He woke with a start and a shudder.

A mist was before his eyes—he rubbed them and something fuzzy and slightly warm pulsed against his hand.

"Get off," he mumbled, shaking his head. A Dream Harvester slid past his bedside lantern. Then he jerked back against his pillow.

The girl from the graveyard was sitting cross-legged at the end of his bed.

"You were having a nightmare," she whispered. "I'm sorry I didn't wake you, but the Harvesters like nightmares. And it was funny. You were going all—" She screwed up her face into a twisted mash of eyes and nose and mouth. "What was it about? You kept saying *I won't I won't I won't*."

Max sat up, rubbing his ears. They tingled slightly from the Harvester's tendrils.

"There's something I have to do here . . ." he said, still foggy with sleep.

"You mean confront a Dragon and stand in its fire? I know all that. I'd be having nightmares about it, too, if I were you."

He'd forgotten she'd guessed about Eisteddfod.

"But you don't want to become an Apprentice Dragon Hunter," she went on. "So why are you doing it?"

"It doesn't matter. Why are you here? What time is it?"

"Shh! We have to be quiet. Quieter than everything, or the Father will hear and send me back."

"Send you back?"

She waved her hand towards the graveyard.

"Oh." Max nodded. "Right."

"Only, if I go back this time, it might be for good. It might be forever."

Max squinted at her. Even in the lantern light she remained that strange gray color.

"What happened to you? How did you . . . I mean . . . end up there?"

"I drowned in the millpond," she said. "It wasn't my fault. It's all because of those stupid weeds. They wouldn't let go. They did it on purpose, I know they did. I never knew weeds could be so mean."

Max pulled the blankets around him to keep in the warmth of the bed. He knew what weeds could be like; he'd swum in a river once and felt them touching his belly.

"Do you still want my shoes? You can have them if you want. I'm supposed to get rid of them anyway."

"Your shoes? No . . . I don't want them."

"What about your brother?"

"Why should he get them? He doesn't come to visit me. Nobody's ever come to visit me! I don't know why. All the others get visitors."

"The other dead people?"

"We're not dead!" she said, sitting up straight. "We're just Cold. We're the Cold Ones. Being dead doesn't happen till later, till we're forgotten."

"Where I come from it's different."

"Well, obviously we don't die like World Ones. We go slowly. If nobody remembers us or visits our graves, we fade away. Then we die."

"We just go straight to that last part."

"When you die, that's it, there's just a big Nothing," the girl said, her eyes wide. "And guess what? An old woman in my village said there's not even a Nothing, because it's not possible for a Nothing to exist. So I wonder what there is? If there's not even a big Nothing?"

"There's probably everything as usual," Max said. "You just can't see it because you're dead."

They sat and thought about that. It was good to sit in the candlelight, trying to imagine what it was like to be dead.

"We have the Vanishings as well now, on top of death," Max said after a while. Then he was about to tell her about the Appearance, and why Boris wanted him to enter Eisteddfod, but instead he asked: "Do people Vanish in the Woods?"

She shook her head. "No, never."

"How do you know about them, then?"

"We hear things. People cross over all the time, though not as many as before. Sometimes, accidentally. Sometimes, on business. Then there are the ones who enter Eisteddfod. Some of these Forest Folk right here could have been from the World originally. You never know."

"There's lots of them."

"It's because Eisteddfod is coming up. All the Dormitories all over the Woods will be full tonight. You can come to the graves whenever you want, but today is the special day when you're REALLY supposed to come without any excuses, because WE come out and carve messages, and if they don't bring the hammers and chisels and the fresh gravestones, what are we going to carve with? And nobody has EVER come for me, and I've NEVER had my hammer and chisel, and my gravestone is the same old one I've had from the start and it's just BLANK and there's so much I want to say to them!" Her fists bunched on the blankets, screwing it up. She leaned forward, her eyes intent. "But that's not the worst thing. The worst thing is when nobody comes to visit, it means you're being Forgotten, and when you're Forgotten, you don't bother coming back! Why would you? So you just GO and that's it forever and you're DEAD and it's OVER. And I can tell it's coming soon! SOON! It's not supposed to come SOON! You're supposed to get YEARS!" She gathered up the hem of her dress and pressed her face into it— she was crying. "Why don't I get any years? I hardly had any at all when I was Warm. Now, I hardly get any again!"

Max didn't know what to do or say. He reached out and touched the bed in front of her.

"What's that supposed to be?" she said, looking down at his hand. "You're supposed to hug me now."

"Okay," Max said, and he hugged her. Her body was freezing cold, but he didn't mind that.

After a bit, she sat back. "Thank you," she said. "That was nice."

"Next year, I'll come," he promised. "I'll bring you a hammer and chisel if you tell me where to get them."

She sniffed and shook her head. "Next year will be too late."

"I'll bring them tomorrow. There must be some lying around somewhere."

"What do I care about you?" she said, suddenly angry. "I want my parents! THEY'RE the ones who are supposed to remember me! Not YOU!"

Max nodded. He understood that for sure.

"So what's it like?" he asked after a moment. "When you're dead—Cold, I mean."

She looked up at the moon that shined through a high window. It gleamed on her throat, and Max swallowed nervously.

"It's strange," she said. "There's a thing like a Merry-Go-Round. But it's not a normal Merry-Go-Round. It's so big I can't see all of it at once. And I'm not allowed to ride on it, I can only watch it turn. It has all these beautiful Lions and Unicorns and Elephants. But there are horrible things, too, monsters with block-shaped heads. Scorpions and Minotaurs and other things. When they come around I cover my eyes like this. Yuck!" She laughed, but her eyes were darker than before. "I know where they come from, that's the worst thing. They may look like Scorpions and Minotaurs, but really they're—" She stopped and looked at him. "You won't hate me if I tell you?"

"No, I promise."

"Promises mean nothing! Do you swear?"

"I swear."

"What do you swear on? It has to be something proper."

"Okay." He tried to think of something proper. "I swear on my Forever Parents."

"Who are they?"

"They're . . . my parents."

"So why have you got a funny name for them?"

"Look, I swear! What are the Minotaurs and Scorpions?"

"They're the Bad Things You Do In Life!" she whispered. "Like when I locked my brother in the cellar because he was scared of the dark and I wanted to make him get used to it and I held the trapdoor shut and ENJOYED IT. He was crying and everything and deep down inside I enjoyed it! And now it's a Scorpion on the Merry-Go-Round. Oh, I can hardly look! But it's not all bad," she added quickly. "There's this Unicorn, and I love whenever it comes around because it's when my brother had a nightmare and was crying, and I crept down into his bed and cuddled him until he fell asleep. It's so nice to look at because I remember . . . I remember just what it felt like when it happened. It felt like something special . . . like neither of us would ever forget it. And now, maybe he has. Maybe he has! Maybe he only remembers the Scorpions and that's why he doesn't come!"

Max flinched and stopped breathing—she had reached out and taken his hand. Now she was watching him inquiringly.

"Nobody's ever held your hand before, have they?" she whispered.

"Not like this," he whispered back. It was impossible to believe the hand he held belonged to a ghost. It felt so alive, even more alive than the sparrow he'd picked up in the school playground after it had flown into the windows.

She nodded, as if this confession was just what she'd wanted. "What's your name?" she asked.

"Max. What's yours?"

"Martha."

She relaxed her hand a little, as a test, inviting him to let go: he didn't. And then it became something else—he was holding her hand. And she was letting him.

His breath quickened.

"Do you want to play a game?" she asked then. "It's not the kind you can play with just anyone. But I've decided right now I want to play it with you."

"What kind of game?"

"In the game I'm a Queen and you're my Knight. You have to do anything for me. Even if it means you have to die for me, then you do it. But when the game finishes, I'm yours forever."

Max shivered at the thought of such a game. "What do I have to do?"

"The man in the bed over there has a knife in his bag. It's got a bone handle. You can feel it in the side pocket. I want you to steal it."

"What for?"

She sternly withdrew her hand. "You're not allowed to ask questions. Just do it!"

Max slipped out of bed, his heart pounding. The knife was easy to find. He was back in a few moments.

"What next?"

"Kneel so you're facing me. So you're close. Like this." She pulled him toward her so their knees were touching.

"I don't want to die yet," she said. "I don't want to be Forgotten. I know it happens to everyone someday, but I've only had three years. It's like I never mattered! I want to find out why my parents haven't come. And I can't leave the graveyard without your help."

"Tell me what to do, and I'll do it."

"You need to make a hole under your fingernail. I can get into that hole and hide there. Father Furthingale won't be able to find me, no matter how hard he looks."

"Then what?"

"When I get into your finger, I'll be away from my gravestone. The gravestone stops us dying for a while, even without anyone remembering us. It's like an anchor. But I won't have it anymore. So you'll have to be my gravestone."

"You'll be inside me?"

"Something like that."

"Will I be able to talk to you?"

"Yes. Just think about me and I'll come from the Merry-Go-Round. Sometimes, I'll come without being asked, and sometimes I might not hear you."

"Why won't you be able to hear me?"

"It's the Merry-Go-Round. Sometimes, it's like I can't look away or hear anything else. When that happens, you'll have to call me as loudly as you can, with all your strength. I'll even be able to appear outside you like I am now—but only at night."

"How do I be a gravestone, though?"

"You have to do what gravestones do. Think of me. Remember I'm here."

"What happens if I forget?"

"Then I won't be here anymore. Or anywhere."

Max looked at the knife. The tip was sharp and slightly oily. He wiped it against the blanket, then slowly slid the cool metal under his fingernail. He felt a bit sorry for his finger—it had never done anything to him.

"It doesn't have to be a big hole, does it?"

She tossed her head back. "Are you afraid, my Knight?"

He looked into her eyes and made a movement. There was a stab of pain, and she gasped. The knife fell onto the bed—red blood sprang up in a crescent.

"I'm yours forever!" Martha whispered. She seized his finger and pulled it into her mouth—her other hand touched his cheek.

Immediately, the pain was gone. And so was she.

He quickly sat up on his knees and examined his finger under the lantern light.

"Are you in there?" he whispered. "What's it like?"

She didn't reply.

How would she reply anyway?

He tried calling to her with his thoughts instead.

Did it work?

It felt wrong, as if he were only on the surface, when he was meant to go deep. He needed to concentrate. So he took the bone-handled knife back to the bag, then snuggled up under the covers and closed his eyes.

Are you there?

Can you hear me?

He dived down into his own mind, seeking her out, passing memories and random thoughts. The deeper he went, the more he became those broken pieces, his mind falling apart into scattered fragments that took advantage of their new freedom, and began to flit around, reforming into surprising patterns . . .

In short—he fell asleep.

Asleep in the Woods

Hello.

Hello.

I'm dreaming, aren't I?

No! I'm not one of your weird dreams! I had to shove them out of the way! That's how we can talk.

It feels like a dream. I mean, we're underwater for starters. That's pretty like a dream.

This is the bottom of the millpond. This is where I spend most of my time.

It's nice you have these armchairs.

They're yours. You brought them.

Oh. So this is what it's like under the gravestone?

I'm afraid so.

It's murky.

I know.

It's very hard to reach you.

I think it'll be easier next time now that we know how.

What are those lights over there? Is there a car driving around?

That's the Merry-Go-Round.

Can we go and take a look?

No! Maybe some other time . . .

Why's the water so dirty?

It's not dirty! Don't be so rude! It's just silt from the bottom of the pond.

I can hardly see a thing.

The silt gets all churned up as the river goes through the Boggy Clump.

The Boggy Clump?

Sorry. I mean the mill wheel. My thoughts keep getting mixed up with yours. You're more complicated than a gravestone.

How do you know about the Boggy Clump?

I know all about you now. That's why I need to speak to you. Actually, I need you to wake up, only I haven't figured out how to SCREAM at you yet.

You want to scream at me?

I'll save it up for later. You need to leave the Dormitory.

Why?

I know why you're entering Eisteddfod. Your friends think you'll learn about yourself in the Dragon Fire. They think they'll be able to find out why you Appeared. And stop the Vanishings.

You saw all that?

I didn't really "see" it exactly. It's all in pieces and sudden glimpses. Like being in a tornado and seeing things go whizzing past. I've been busy making sense of it all.

Is it true?

Which bit?

They told me the first story you hear in the Dragon Fire is your own. You learn the truth about yourself.

Yes, that's what you have to do in the competition. A Dragon Hunter takes you into the Deep Woods to find a Dragon, and makes it breathe fire over you. You only survive if you can accept the truth about yourself. Then you become a Dragon Hunter.

It doesn't sound so difficult.

Hardly anyone can accept the truth about themselves. That's why I want to speak to you. You have another idea. Don't you?

You saw that, too? About my Forever Parents?

Yes. I can help you find them, Max. I think they're here some-where, in the Woods.

Why do you think that?

They flew in a Balloon, didn't they?

In my dreams, they did. Why would I dream they did, if they didn't?

Balloons go all over the Beginning Woods. That's how people get around when they have a long journey. It's safer than the Paths. Maybe they work on the Balloons.

Can you show me?

Yes. But first, you have to take me home.

What? Now?

It's only about a day's journey. It's easy to find.

I don't know. I should speak to Boris and Mrs. Jeffers.

What if they don't believe you? Then you'll never find out about your Forever Parents. Not if you get roasted in the Dragon Fire. You should try all the other things first.

They said Eisteddfod was in Paris in a few days. Will we have time to get there if I take you home?

Yes! But if you do Eisteddfod before taking me home, it'll be too late for me.

Because I might die in the Dragon Fire, right?

Well. Yes.

I suppose it does make sense. To do your task first, I mean . . .

So come on! We have to go now! The sun will be up soon.

I've only just gotten into bed!

We're not all lazy sleepy-heads like you are in the World. We get up at dawn.

Why?

Because there's so much to do! Milking the cows. Lighting the fire. Chopping the wood. Cleaning the floor. That's all before breakfast!

We just brush our teeth and go.

Well, it's not like that here!

I'm not sure this is a good idea.

I'm ordering you, then!

Ordering me?

Yes. I'm the Queen. You're the Knight. Let's go.

I didn't know we were still playing that game . . .

It doesn't stop. Move it!

Okay, okay.

What are you waiting for?

I'm still sleeping! How do I wake up?

I don't know! Try swimming up to the surface.

Okay.

Call me when you do. I'll come out and help.

I tried that before and it didn't work.

I was finding my way around in here. I think it will be easier now.

All right. I'm going.

Max—wait.

What?

It's nice of you, being my gravestone, I mean. You're a bit strange. But it's nice.

What do you mean I'm strange?

I've never been inside a person before. I don't know. Maybe we're all like this deep down.

Like what?

Confused.

He opened his eyes.

The dream hung in his head, every detail clear and sharp. So it hadn't been a dream.

He sat up. The Dormitory was filled with the sounds of sleep, with snores, lip-smacking, and dream-filled muttering. Most of the lanterns and candles had burned low. The Dream Harvesters had finished their work and dispersed up the chimney.

He looked at his finger and gave it a shake.

COME OUT THEN! I'M UP! IT'S REALLY EARLY!

He felt a draining sensation in his mind, and a tingle in his finger, and then she was there, cross-legged on the end of the bed just as before.

"Stop shouting!" she whispered. "Next time, make it quieter!"

"I thought you wouldn't hear me." He shivered as his breath puffed in the air. "Are we really going outside? It's so cold!"

"You'll feel better when you're moving."

"What about breakfast? I'm starving."

"I'll find you something. Get changed!"

Her light, gray body darted off, bending down now and again to pillage the bundles tucked under the beds. He threw back the covers and swung his legs out of the bed, wincing as his toes brushed the icy flagstones. By the time she returned, he had struggled into the clothes Father Furthingale had left—a leather jerkin lined with wool, a woolen undershirt and leggings, trousers of thick wool, knitted socks, and short leather boots.

"We have to hurry," Martha said. "We should get into the trees before they all wake up. What are you looking for?"

Max was rummaging in the pockets of his World clothes.

"I can't just disappear. Do you have any paper or anything?"

"What do you need paper for?"

"I'm going to write them a letter."

"Not about me! You can't tell them where we're going. They might send someone after us."

"I won't. I'll just tell them I'm going to . . . try something else before the Dragon Fire."

"There's a guestbook," she said, after a quick think. "It's by the door. Wait a moment."

Off she went again, her bare feet pattering quietly on the flagstones. When she came back, she handed him a torn sheet of paper, an ink pot, and a peacock feather.

"What am I supposed to do with that?"

"With what?"

"The giant feather."

"It's a pen! Don't you have pens in the World?"

"Not like that. I'll need a surface."

"A surface? Why?"

"I need something to lean on."

"Knights don't go around looking for surfaces! Just use the floor!"

"Okay. Hold the lantern near so I can see."

He knelt by the bed and began writing, the peacock feather jiggling while Martha held the lantern over his head.

Hello, it's me I'm NOT running away because I'm scared of the Dragon I'm going to find my Forever Parents they're called the Panthalassas and they work on the Balloons it's a much better idea than trying to hear a story in the Dragon Fire

"Look at your handwriting. It's *so awful.*"

"I haven't used one of these things before."

"Can't you write any faster?"

"Neat or fast? What do you want? You can't have both."

"I can't have either by the look of it."

"Stop distracting me!"

and my Forever Parents are bound to
know about the Appearance and how
it all got started so then I'll come back
here and tell you all about it and we can
stop the Vanishings just like you want.
                    MAX
                     ~

P.S. and if that doesn't work then of
course we can do the Dragon thing.

"What's that stupid squiggle under your name?"

"That's a flourish. It's how people sign when they write with feathers."

"Oh, good grief! Can we go please? Father Furthingale will be up any minute."

He folded the message and stuck it in one of his sneakers under the bed.

It occurred to him that there was no escape from the Dark Man, that someone who had *always* been there would manage to *continue being there*. But he shook the worry off. The Dark Man had turned out to be a scientist named Boris Peshkov. He didn't have any strange powers. He was just a man.

"I'm ready," he muttered, slinging the bag of food over his shoulder. "Let's go."

———

They stopped for a moment on the Dormitory steps. To the east, the sky was beginning to brighten, giving just enough light to make out the curve of the road.

"I'll have to go back under your fingernail in a moment," Martha said, her eyes on the horizon. "Come on!"

Holding hands, they ran across the courtyard. They had only gone a short distance up the road when the Dormitory bell rang out behind them. Max felt a tingle rush up his arm, then a surge of emotion as Martha was back inside him.

Don't stop. The road takes us straight into the Woods, then it becomes a Path. Just keep going after that, there's a while to go before the first turn.

Okay.

The road continued parallel to the forest's edge at first, then slowly drifted inward. In the dim light of dawn, it seemed to Max that the Woods were inching closer to the road, creeping up on it a moment at a time. And then they were under the eaves of the forest. The road was squeezed into a narrow Path, and the air came alive with sounds—crackles of movement, shivering sighs, and groans. Trees lined the Path in haphazard order, hunched and wizened as trolls, old and unmoving. He slowed to a walk, then stopped.

What are you doing? Keep going!

I need to have breakfast, even if you don't!

He sat on a fallen trunk that lay mossy and cold beside the Path.

Sausage. Bread. Cheese.

No cereal?

No what?

Kidding. This is nice. Thanks.

Just hurry.

As he ate he glanced around, uneasily at first, then with curiosity and interest. In the wintry stillness, the movements that came were magnified and startling. A batter of wings overhead as a crow settled on a branch. A scuttle of movement as a woodland creature darted across the Path. Now and again, he glanced up at the strange web of branches that formed the canopy, but this time there were no words or images to be seen. Instead, his ear became attuned to the rustle of the branches as they scraped against each other.

He stopped chewing so he could hear it better. Something was *being said.*

Max, be careful!

I'm trying to listen.

But—

Shhh!

The trees weren't sleeping at all.

Stories . . .

They were telling stories.

They circled teasingly around his head, inches beyond understanding. He stood up, his head cocked to one side. The sound crystallized into a voice whispering clear and close, and the story carried him away in its currents. It was a soft story, a gentle story, a slumbery story—a story about a boy falling asleep in the Woods, filled with the scents of pine and sleep, filled with the scent and sound of dreams, dreams of being a boy asleep in the Woods, of being a boy asleep in the dreams, dreams of being dreams and nothing else but dreams . . . a dream in the dream in the dream . . .

And then—pain. Sharp. The dreams fled. Something had him. He screamed. Something huge and powerful and hairy had him in its teeth, biting down on his neck.

Something all fur and snarls. It shook him, hard. Then let go.

He fell forward, gasping at the shock of it. Face down on the Path, he looked up just in time to see a huge shape bounding into the trees.

He lay there a moment, stunned. Felt his neck. It was wet with saliva. He hadn't been hurt. But some animal had attacked him and then fled.

What WAS that? Did you see?

He got to his feet, looking around warily. Realized she hadn't answered.

He tried again.

Did you see it? It was like . . . a monster!

No response, no voice, not even the flare of her emotions. All he sensed was himself. His own feelings, his own thoughts.

She just hadn't heard him, that was all. The water was deep. She was distracted by the Merry-Go-Round.

Martha?

His voice was nothing more than a hollow echo in his mind.

MARTHA! ARE YOU THERE!

Nothing.

He couldn't feel her inside him anymore. And suddenly he wondered: how long had he been under the spell of the trees? He glanced up at the sky. With a cold shock, he saw the sun had changed position. Completely.

It must have been hours!

He squeezed his eyes shut and imagined himself standing on the edge of the millpond. Took a deep breath. Dived in. Directed his whole being downward.

Martha! Wait! I'm coming!

Kicking hard, he swam into the darkness, past where the shafts of sunlight weakened and broke apart, into the murk and the cold. And there he found her, drifting among the weeds and the frogs, her body a curl in an underwater current.

Max . . .

I'm here!

Reaching out, he caught hold of her limp hand and pulled her toward him. She rose and was with him once more, her voice a freezing whisper as he fell to his knees on the Path.

Don't let me go, my Knight. Don't let me die.

And he promised he would not.

And swore he would not.

And gave his oath to his Queen he would not.

The Wildness

So where now?

We need to be going north. There should be a Northmark somewhere near. Use it to check the direction.

The Path had faded to a smudge on the forest floor, barely a foot wide. Another Path had appeared out of the undergrowth, melting into the first, then splitting off again.

What's it look like, this thing?

A small boulder, about the size of your head. It should be painted white, but the Woods might have sent some moss to cover it up. It doesn't like Northmarks.

After hunting around and pulling at twists of bramble, he found the Northmark at the foot of a tree. An arrow had been chiseled into the surface, pointing along one of the Paths.

That's it. Just follow the arrow. It'll take us in the right direction.

Wait a moment.

What is it?

Instead of continuing on his way, Max moved forward and knelt next to the boulder. On the ground beside it was a dead rabbit.

Oh, the poor thing!

Max looked around at the forest more closely. Everything looked like . . . forest.

But maybe only a trained eye could spot the signs . . .

How do you think it died?

Maybe it was that big scary monster you imagined.

That wasn't a dream. It was real.

It's hard to tell the difference when the trees have gotten you.
It doesn't look like it's been bitten.

Don't you have winter in the World? Maybe it got lost and
froze in the cold. There's nothing to eat.

I think it got lost, all right. Up a Dragon's nose.

You think it got killed by a Dragon?

Maybe.

Don't you know anything? This isn't the Deep Woods.

So?

Dragons don't come out of the Deep Woods. They only eat
Briarbacks, and Briarbacks only grow in the Deep Woods.

I'm going to have a look on the other side of this thicket.

No! You mustn't EVER leave the Paths. That's the worst
thing you can do in the Woods.

Why?

You'll get gotten by the Wildness and that'll be it.

He stopped. She really did sound frightened, and whenever a strong emotion gripped her, he felt it, too.

What's the Wildness?

It happens to people who spend too long in the trees, or get lost
in the Deep Woods. Don't you know about that either?

No.

And you were going to enter Eisteddfod! Most of the contestants get gotten by the Wildness before they get anywhere near a Dragon. And that's with a Dragon Hunter to guide them!

What happens when you get gotten?

First you stop caring how you look, and your hair goes Wild. Then you stop caring what you say, and your words go Wild. Then you stop caring what you eat, and your teeth go Wild. Last of all, right at the end, you stop caring what you see, and your eyes go Wild. When that happens, you're finished and there's no going back—you become a Wild One. You'll forget about ever becoming a Dragon Hunter or finding your Forever Parents. The Deep Woods are full of Wild Ones.

How do you know so much about it?

Every village loses people to the Wildness. We had one not long ago. His name was Little Noah. He was in my class at school. One day he went into the Woods to gather blackberries for his Mother, and he didn't come back. By evening the whole village was out looking for him. They found his basket lying next to a bramble bush. The Woods had used it to tempt him off the Path, and the Wildness had gotten him! He was only nine!

How do you know it was the Wildness?

We saw him now and again. He would come back to the village for a sniff around. Me and my Father saw him once on New Year's Eve. We were walking home from the market, and everyone was baking cinnamon loaves—you could smell them all over the place. We were passing Little Noah's house, and

Dad stopped and pointed, and I looked, and it was him, Little Noah, up on the roof. He was dancing around the chimney, sniffing at it. We could see his Mother through the windows— she was just getting on with her baking. She had no idea he was up there spinning around.

What was he doing?

We thought about that for ages. I guess he thought the chimney was made of cinnamon loaves. Because of the smell coming out of it. He'd forgotten what chimneys were.

The Wildness had gotten him . . .

It really had. He wasn't even a boy anymore. He was all twigs and bristles and teeth. When we tried to get closer, he saw us and leapt down and went off across the fields, all rolling and turning cartwheels!

And he kept coming back?

For a bit. A few months later, that spring, the village started losing lambs. We thought it was Wolves, because we have a lot of problems with Wolves. Usually, the farmers just leave the dogs unchained at night, and that puts a stop to it. But it wasn't the Wolves. It was Little Noah. And the dogs got him and . . . that was it. Dogs don't like the Wild Ones.

Oh.

He was a nice boy. Sometimes he loaned me his penknife. But he never listened to the teacher. Don't leave the Paths! It's the first rule we learn.

Max put his hand against the cold trunk of the tree and looked back at the Path. It was only a few feet away. He would just have to get beyond the thicket to see what was on the other side. It wouldn't be that far.

It'll only be a moment. If I start to go all hairy and gnash my teeth and stuff, then I'll go back.

He began to push himself through the brambles, but all at once, the ground gave way under his feet. He fell, sliding and slipping, his hands flailing as he tried to grab at something solid. It was only a short drop—he hit the bottom with a jolt, and rolled forward in a shower of leaves and debris.

Spitting out grit, he got to his feet.

He'd fallen into a trench. It was wide as a highway, and stretched far into the forest.

Well, at least the trees won't be causing you any trouble.

No, I guess not.

It was like a huge machine had ripped the forest apart. Entire trees had been flung aside, their bodies torn open and the white, husky wood inside laid bare. Deep wounds scored the bark of those still standing—rents like talon marks, or the slipping of enormous teeth as they sought to grip and tear.

Still think it wasn't a Dragon?

It can't have been. Those aren't even Briarbacks. Why would it try to eat normal trees?

Then what was it?

I don't know. Just go back to the Path, Max. I don't like this. Shh!

Stop telling me to shush!

No . . . listen. Listen! Can you hear that?

Hear what?

He scrambled up the side of the hole. A faint rustling had begun in the distance, like Wind stirring leaves. He couldn't tell where it was coming from. But something was moving, out there in the forest. Every moment getting closer.

Not just one thing. A great many things.

What is that?

I don't know, Max. I've never heard anything like it.

He felt her confusion and mounting panic mingling with his own.

I'm getting back to the Path.

Quick, Max. Go!

It was too late. The rustling became a bird-like chirping. Shadows flitted along the forest floor, too fast to follow— then suddenly they were all around, dozens on every side, swarming up trunks and along branches, their saucer-like eyes opening and closing with soft clicks.

What are THEY doing here? They shouldn't BE here!

What are they?

Shredders! Shredders! Shredders!

Max stumbled back to the very edge of the trench, as far from the trees as he could get. A hundred eyes followed him. Rows of teeth gleamed inside wide mouths. Claws, elongated and sharp, curled around branches.

Shredders. He did know about them, from the Storybooks. They were scavengers—they ate the trees the Dragons left behind.

I've never heard of Shredders out of the Deep Woods! Never!
They don't eat people, do they?
They'll eat anything if they're hungry.
Ugh! Keep back!

Several of the closest Shredders made sniffing darts toward him. Their investigations seemed to confirm something, and set off a frenzy that spread rapidly. Suddenly, the forest was alive with howls. Trees shook as the Shredders hurled themselves from branch to branch.

STOP MAKING FACES AT THEM!
I'm not making faces!
Then why are they getting so angry?
How should I know? Why are YOU getting angry?
TRY AND MAKE FRIENDS WITH THEM!
I'm no good at making friends!
Great! Just my luck I get trapped inside some sort of social outcast!
TELL ME WHAT TO DO!
I told you already. Don't leave the Path!
I mean NOW! What do I do NOW?
Kill them!
ALL of them?
You're a KNIGHT, aren't you? It's your JOB to be outnumbered! Oh! Lookoutlookoutlookout!

He twisted to one side. A blurry shape flew past and tumbled into the trench. He snatched up a branch, trying to look in every direction at once. The other Shredders were throwing themselves from side to side, screeching and slapping the ground with their paws.

Why aren't the others attacking?

The one that just went past. It must be their leader! It's like a challenge!

He threw a look over his shoulder—the Shredder that had gone into the trench was already scrambling back up. He swung the branch, catching its head just as it reached the top. The Shredder went sailing backward into the pit.

Got it!

You DID, my Knight! Get it again! Smash it!

A rush of excitement overtook him, and he slid into the trench in a shower of pebbles. The moment he reached the bottom, the Shredder sprang at him, catching him off-balance. And then it was on him, a whirl of claws and teeth.

MAX!

He lost his grip on the branch, and they rolled across the ground, the Shredder's hot snout snuffling at his throat. He got his hands on its head and struggled to force it back.

SNAP

The Shredder's face was inches from his own.

SNAPSNAPSNAP

The teeth grazed his neck.

SNAPSNAPSNAPSNAPSNAPSNAP

Martha screamed.

Fury exploded inside him. He yanked the Shredder's head down. Twisted it. Got its ear right where he wanted it.

SNAP

The Shredder squealed. He clenched his teeth. Pulled back his head. Hard as he could.

The ear stretched.

RRRRRRRRIP!

Joy!

Howling, the Shredder thrashed free and rolled away, kicking up a spray of earth and leaves.

Max spat the rubbery flap of flesh from his mouth and jumped to his feet.

A frenzy had come over him.

He was going to kill it.

He was going to tear it to pieces and EAT IT.

Max! It's the Wildness! It's taking over!

The words came from beyond a thundering horizon, and he barely heard them or understood—but they distracted him. Seizing its chance, the Shredder launched itself at his face, claws swiping down in a death stroke.

It never arrived.

A monstrous gray form flew between them. There was a sickening crunch of snapping bone. Hot blood spattered Max's face, shocking him out of his trance.

Martha screamed again.

A Wolf was there.

And what a Wolf!

A Wolf as tall as he was, its shaggy mane glittering with frost. It had the Shredder in its jaws and was whipping it from side to side. With a toss of its head, it gulped the shrieking beast to the back of its maw and bit down, finishing it off in one savage bite.

CRUNCH!

The limp body dropped to the ground.

The Wolf moved backward to where Max stood, its head held low, its golden eyes gazing up at the trees. The Shredders watched. Silent.

One dropped from the trees.

Then another.

And another.

They're coming!

Five. Six. Loping down the slope on their knuckles.

The Wolf met them, teeth flashing, tossing the first two aside. The others leapt on its back. Snarling viciously, it went down in a flurry of limbs.

They'll tear it apart!

Who cares? Get out of here!

The Wolf is trying to protect me! I can't just run!

It's not a Wolf, it's a Wild One! Go!

It's too late. We're surrounded.

The Wolf had driven back its attackers, but it made no difference. More Shredders were closing in. The Wolf backed toward Max again, its nose wrinkled in a snarl. Strands of bloody saliva hung from its muzzle.

Max bent to pick up a rock.

When he looked back, a second Wolf was there.

Wait—where did that one come from?

I don't know, do I?

You weren't watching.

But Max was watching now, and saw it happen.

The first Wolf bent its head and gave itself a peculiar shake, all along its body, from head to toe. Its outline blurred momentarily, and another Wolf detached itself from the blur, stepping out of it.

Now there were three.

You didn't say the Wild Ones had POWERS!

Well, I'm SORRY I didn't give you every piece of information about everything that has ever happened in the history of EVERYWHERE!

Again and again the Wolf shook itself, and each time another Wolf appeared. Four. Five. Six. Soon there was a pack. A dozen. Each exactly the same as the others.

The Wolves fanned out in a circle. The Shredders leapt and howled. Some darted forward, testing the Wolves, and were ripped apart. By now the noise of their whoops and screams was deafening.

Still the Wolves held firm.

And then, without warning, the scene erupted. Either the Shredders lost patience, or the Wolves did, Max wasn't sure. The creatures flung themselves on one another—and it was over in a second. The Wolves tore through the Shredders, and they scattered, hurtling into the trees. The Wolves drove them off, their bodies bucking powerfully as they climbed the side of the trench. In moments, the scene was quiet.

Nothing stirred. The stillness of the forest returned.

Max stayed exactly where he was, not moving an inch.

The first Wolf had remained behind. It was facing him, its golden eyes unblinking. There was something about that stare Max found reassuring—even familiar.

Don't move.

Am I moving? Do you see me moving?

I can feel you're about to. Don't.

Are you sure it's Wild? It doesn't seem very Wild . . .

Don't. You. Dare! You're daring! Stop daring!

He dropped his rock, and moved slowly toward the huge creature. It stood and loped toward him. They met in the middle of the pit, and the massive head swung low to sniff at his feet. He lifted his hand.

WHAT ARE YOU DOING? KEEP ME AWAY FROM THAT THING!

Reaching out, slowly, carefully, he placed his hand on the Wolf's neck. For a magic moment, waxy fur bristled up through his fingers. Then it turned away and lowered itself. After a moment, it looked back at him.

It wants me to get on.

Get ON? It wants you to get IN, that's what it wants. Get in its big fat STOMACH.

No. I can ride it. Like a horse.

It EATS horses. This thing EATS HORSES WITH ONE SNAP!

If it went Wild, doesn't that mean it used to be a person?

Yes. USED to be.

So it's not a real Wolf.

It's pretending to itself it's a real Wolf. When you go Wild, the things you imagine can become real. That's part of the Wildness.

What if it wants to help? Maybe some part of it's still a person. Like Little Noah. Why did he keep coming back to the chimney at his home? Some part of him must have remembered.

The Wild Ones don't remember who they used to be. That's a horrible idea!

How do you know? Have you asked them?

No. But you go ahead. Ask away. Don't let me stop you.

Laugh all you like. I'm fed up with walking and these boots are giving me massive blisters.

If you get on this Wolf, I will never speak to you ever again.

Deal.

He moved his hand to its neck, grabbed a fistful of fur, and threw a leg over its back.

The Wolf suddenly stood, lifting him with it. "Wooah!" he said, nearly falling off. He found his balance and sat tall, looking around with a startling sensation of height.

See? We're okay. We're okay!

It's just a trick.

I thought you were never going to speak to me again.

I thought you didn't know how to make friends with anyone.

I only know how to make friends with Wolves.

It's not a Wolf, it's a—HOLD ON!

Just in time, he closed his fists on the Wolf's fur. With two mighty bounds they were out of the trench and racing through the trees. But almost at once, the Wolf stopped. They were back on the Path, at the Northmark.

Um . . . what now?

This is your big adventure. You figure it out.

I think it needs directions.

Tell it then.

How?

Talk to it. You're the one going on about asking Wild Ones questions.

I'm going to pull its ear.

Of course. Pull its ear. That'll work.

Its right ear. We have to go right, right?

Reaching forward, Max pulled the Wolf's right ear.

And the Wolf went right.

4

THE ROAD TO GILEAD

It was strange having a ghost in your finger, Max reflected as the Wolf carried them north. Or a girl in your mind.

When she was down at the Merry-Go-Round, like now, it was like she was hardly inside him at all. But when he called her away from the Lions and Scorpions, their feelings swirled together, and it was hard to separate them. Everything he felt, she felt, too. When she was happy or sad, he was happy or sad. Only a ghost, she'd come in through a hole the size of a pinprick—and everything had changed.

What would she have been like to know, really, as a person, he wondered.

Feeling her absence, he called to her. He got anxious if she spent too long away.

What is it? Are we there yet?

No, I was just . . . you know back with the Shredders, when I bit its ear, you said it was the Wildness?

Yes. That was the Wildness, for sure.

I didn't expect it to feel so good.

That's why it's so dangerous. It wouldn't be tempting if it felt bad, would it?

I wonder who the Wolf was, before he got gotten.

Well, it could be someone from the World.

I thought Wild Ones were all Forest Folk.

Not all, no. Forest Folk know not to leave the Paths, so the Wildness doesn't get them so much. But World Ones cross over by accident and don't know anything. They're just suddenly in the middle of the Woods. If they're lucky, they find a Path or a village quickly, but mostly they don't and get gotten by the Wildness. It doesn't happen so much nowadays because of all that electricity you've got in the World. Now, there are hardly ever accidental Cross-Overs. When people in the World carried Old Light it used to happen all the time.

Do you think my Forever Parents crossed over accidentally?

I don't know. Maybe.

I hope they didn't become Wild Ones.

You'll never find them if they did.

What about your parents? Tell me about them.

Why?

I don't know. Just . . . I want to know about you. About your home.

You'll see when we get there. It's just a normal village. Called Gilead. I used to think it was boring, but I miss it now.

She'd grown up there, she said, with her parents (who made pillows and cushions with goose feathers) and her little brother Jake (who told lies). One day, she'd been playing with Jake near the border of the village where the Woods began. They'd found a wasps' nest and started throwing stones at it. The Woods hadn't liked that at all: it had made the nest fall to the ground and the angry wasps had swarmed after them. Jake had run into the cowshed and Martha had jumped into the millpond. First, the current had sucked her down, then the weeds had snared her ankles. Trapped between the weeds and the wasps, the water had been the only way to go.

Lying flat on his front with his arms around the Wolf's neck, Max was so engrossed in her story he did not notice the deepening of shadows as dusk fell. Then a tense anxiety gripped his mind.

What's wrong?

We're nearly here. It's just up ahead. Another mile or so.

I guess we can't go too close with the Wolf.

I've thought of that. Just follow this Path. When the Wolf gets near the edge of the trees, it needs to stay out of sight. Make it follow the tree line to the right. That'll take us up a hill. We can look out over the village from there.

Okay.

She went quiet, but he could sense intense bursts of feeling as he looked around. She was recognizing places she used to know. They brought out flashes of joy and sadness, memories he could not quite read. Under it all, though, she was scared. What were they about to discover? Why hadn't her parents visited her all this time? What if something had happened to them?

Are you sure you still want to do this?

Stop spying on me! Yes, I'm sure. This is where we turn. Just follow the slope up.

The trees are pretty thin here. Won't anyone see us?

Nobody stays out on the fields at this time. It'll be dark soon. Everyone will be heading back to the village. Just stay under the eaves and you'll be fine.

He guided the Wolf as she'd said, up the hillside, keeping to the very edge of where the trees met the farmland.

This is far enough. Over to the left there's a rocky sort of ledge. We'll be able to see the village from there.

Just here?

Yes, this is good.

That's your village?

Yes. And that's Mount Gilead behind it.

Max slid off the Wolf's back and stretched. The village was on the other side of a swath of open farmland. A river ran through it, splitting it in two, then snaking across the fields almost parallel to the road. Lights shined in all the windows and bobbed along paths as the Forest Folk hurried home before nightfall.

Do you see the millwheel?

Yes.

And the little cottage just past the pond?

Yes.

That's my house.

There are lights in the window. That's good, isn't it?

I don't know. I suppose.

So I should just follow the road?

Yes. There's a hedge you can sneak along behind.

Why do I have to sneak?

I don't think you should let anyone see you.

Why not?

Just . . . it doesn't matter. It's not important. I'm probably just nervous.

No. Tell me what's wrong.

Do you promise you'll still go into the village?

Of course!

On the way in here. When you were looking around. When we were getting close.

What?

I saw tree stumps.

So? I saw those, too.

They'd been cutting trees.

They don't cut trees in the Woods?

Of course we do. But there are limits. Boundaries. We're not supposed to go over them. Nobody is. It's one of the laws that nobody ever breaks. And on the way in here . . .

You saw they'd gone over the boundaries?

Yes. Just here and there. Like . . . trying to do it in secret.

Are you sure? Maybe something just changed when you were away. Lots of things have probably changed.

The boundaries never change.

Okay. So . . . you don't want me to talk to anyone then?

Try not to. And if anyone stops you, don't let on you're a World One. Villagers can be funny about World Ones these days. They think you'll bring the Vanishings with you.

So what should I say?

Just tell them you're from Rosethorn village and you got lost. It's at the other end of the valley, about a day away. I'll be listening as well so I can help.

Okay. Look, I should go before it gets too dark.

No. No, there's something else.

What?

We just have to wait a bit.

What for?

You'll see. Actually, I think I hear it now.

Max turned around. Behind him, beyond the crest of the hill, stars were appearing in the darkening sky. The Wolf had turned, too, and was sitting on its haunches, panting slightly, its large triangular ears pointed forward. It whined suddenly. Then barked. Spun around. Then sat and barked again.

I can't hear anything.

You don't know what to listen for. It's right on time. You should probably grab hold of something.

Why?

It's about to get really windy.

How do you know?

Suit yourself.

WHOOOOOSH!

A terrific blast knocked him off his feet and sent him tumbling across the ground. The sky exploded with a burst of orange flame. A huge shadow swept over his head, its belly lit up by fire.

A DRAGON! A REAL ACTUAL DRAGON!

No, it's not a Dragon, silly!

She was right. The Wind had blinded him a second with leaves and grit. He scrambled to his feet, bracing himself against the hurricane, shielding his eyes as he tried to take in all of the magnificent sight.

It was even better than a Dragon. It was a Hot-Air Balloon. And what a Balloon!

It's only a medium-sized one. The five o'clock Balloon to Oslo.

You knew this was coming?

Yes. I used to sit right in this spot with Jake and wait for the Wind to roll us over. It would bring us presents. Funny-shaped leaves. Hats it had carried all the way from London. That sort of thing. You're . . . not listening, are you?

Max was staring upward in wonder. The Balloon was so big it reminded him of pictures of Noah's Ark. Beneath it hung a structure the size of a small house. Soft, golden lights glowed within; he could hear voices, laughter, the clink of cutlery, music. It surged out over the village and into the distance, the Wind sweeping it up and away.

My Forever Parents might be on it. The Balloon in my dream was just like it.

He watched the beautiful sphere grow smaller and disappear among the stars. It was drifting away, sure. But for the first time in a long time, he felt like his Forever Parents were getting closer again.

I'm glad you like the Balloon. Really I am. But we should go. There are lots more in London.

I know.

Sorry.

Okay. I'm going.

He started off down the hill, then stopped and turned back. The Wolf was sitting there, watching him.

"You're still going to be here, aren't you?" he asked.

The Wolf simply licked its lips, then gave a gigantic yawn, its mouth snapping shut.

It's not a person anymore. It can't understand you.

It understands. I know it does.

If you know so much, then why is it helping us?

I don't know. I just . . . it just feels . . . better.

Better, how?

Having it there. And maybe the Wolf was lonely. Maybe it feels better, too.

Why doesn't it bring out all its friends, then?

I think it's difficult for it to do that, or it would have done it much sooner with the Shredders. It only did it because it had to.

He turned to go down the hill. Sure enough, the Wolf stayed behind, watching him from the outcrop of stone. But the steady golden gaze was beginning to make him feel uncomfortable.

The Wolf seemed more intent on watching than on anything else.

And didn't that remind him of someone?

THE RAILING

Down the hill in the darkness, across the fields, and through the hedge.

Down into the ditch, footfalls crunching lightly on frosty grass.

Standing, looking left and right along the road.

Keeping out of sight.

The village, forgotten for now.

There was something else.

They'd seen it as they came across the field, a dark silhouette, glinting in the moonlight.

Can you get closer?

Not without going up onto the road.

Just go.

Max clambered up the side of the ditch and moved closer to the peculiar structure. He circled it, touching its cold metal shell with his fingertips.

I was right. I thought you didn't have electricity in the Woods.

We don't.

Well—you do now.

Just tell me what it is!

It's a street lamp.

What's it for?

They light up roads. They come on at night.

You mean it's a New Light thing?

Yes. It's electric.

It can't be.

Well, that's what it is.

What's it doing here?

You tell me. It's your village.

There's no light coming out of it.

It hasn't been connected yet. It's like they've just built it.

The side panel was loosely fastened—inside, the wires dangled unattached. On the other side of the road, another was lying on its side. A furrow of earth ran along the road toward the village. Farther in the distance stood another street lamp. Then another. Spaced at regular intervals.

It must be something else. Find out what it really is.

Trust me. It's a street lamp. Looks like they're going to light up this whole road.

You don't understand. Electric light is deadly for Forest Folk.

It's not deadly for Mrs. Jeffers. She met me in the World. Electric light is all over the place in the World.

Forest Folk do go to the World sometimes. They have to be careful though. Did she ever get a light shining on her?

But Max was already remembering the umbrella and how the old woman shielded herself as she ran through London. The Book House, too. No lights there, except in his cupboard under the stairs.

Okay . . . I get it. No. She had an umbrella. So what happens if you get hit by electric light?

We call it New Light. We just shrivel into nothing. It's horrible. Have you ever thrown hair onto a fire?

Right.

That's what happens to us. So you see. It's totally impossible for anyone to be building street lamps in the Woods. Even if they wanted to, New Light doesn't work here.

I don't think the Woods and the World are the same these days. The World never had the Vanishings before, and they broke all the rules when they came along. And Mrs. Jeffers did this weird thing with Old Light that she said should have been impossible—

Stop DISAGREEING with me! I'm the QUEEN! You're the KNIGHT! You're not SUPPOSED to have a BRAIN!

I'm just saying—

You shouldn't be SAYING THINGS! You're supposed to DO things, not talk and be CLEVER. You're not supposed to be all, "Oh, the Woods and the World are different" and "Mrs. Jeffers did something impossible with light" and "The Vanishings broke the rules"! I DON'T CARE ABOUT THE STUPID RULES! Just get on with it!

She dropped down to the Merry-Go-Round and snapped herself shut.

Hello?

No answer.

He'd kind of expected it. He'd felt her fear and confusion building. Now, she'd closed herself off.

He stood there a moment, wondering if he should continue on. Well, he had to. He was here now and he just had to. It would be better for her if she found out what had happened, even if it was bad. He would want the same thing.

Still, electricity in the Woods . . .

That was like magic becoming possible in the World. When he got back to Marylebone, he had to tell the Dark Man as soon as possible.

He crawled back under the hedgerow and followed it into the village. There was a large barn on the outskirts—he circled around it, keeping to the shadows.

Hearing a noise, he stopped for a moment, then watched two young girls, four or five years old, emerge from a hut with jars of pickles held before them. They ran across his path and pattered up the porch of a cottage.

Moving on, he passed two big-bellied men on a bench, arguing so heatedly about the price of a cow they did not notice the shadow flitting through their garden.

Creeping through an orchard, he was nearly spotted by a woman who banged out of her house and stood with hands on hips, muttering angrily about whoever she'd left inside.

Whatever the street lamps were for, life in Gilead seemed to be continuing.

The village was small, and he soon reached the cottage Martha had pointed out. Dozens of geese huddled out back in a large run. Smoke curled from the chimney, and curtains hung in the windows. It was a solemn, quiet house, wrapped all the way around with a wooden veranda. Everything looked well.

What now?

She made no reply, and he didn't try too hard to call her. Her silence was too fragile, too tense—he could almost see her hunched before the Merry-Go-Round, legs pulled into her chest, chin on her knees. All he had to do was get a look at her parents and brother. At least she would know they were alive.

He crept closer. Within the house a knife was snicking softly, like someone was chopping vegetables. Then a chair scraped and a shadow slung itself across the curtains. As the person moved, the snick of the knife continued.

Two people at least were inside.

But who?

He waited an age for movement or voices. Nothing.

Snick snick snick went the knife.

There was a small gap in the curtains. He had to get to it. He took a chance and darted right up to the porch. Then padded lightly up the steps.

creeeeeeak

He winced and froze, expecting the door to open at any moment. Instead, there was another noise, a scampering sound directly under his feet. Looking down, he saw a small hole in the steps where the wood had rotted away.

shuffle scuffle

There was something under the porch. Some kind of animal was trapped, and was rushing back and forth.

shuffle scuffle

He bent closer to peer into the hole. Eyes glittered out of the darkness.

A hand shot out. Thin fingers seized him by the ankle.

"The weeds have got you!" intoned a hollow voice. "Now you're dead, too!"

Yelling in fright, Max yanked his foot free and fell backward, landing with a jolt on his bottom. In a flash, the front door opened and a stout woman was on the porch. She was carrying a knife, and her hands and apron were covered in blood and feathers. Behind her came a small, timid-looking man with no hair. He was holding a piece of cloth that trailed long tangles of thread, and he had a number of pins in his mouth, held between his lips.

When they saw Max at the bottom of the steps they relaxed slightly, but only slightly.

"Jacob?" the woman said. "Come out from under there."

A wooden slat in the side of the veranda banged outward and a boy appeared on his knees, holding a squirming kitten against his chest.

"I was getting Pippi."

"Have you got her now?"

"Yes."

"Then come in and finish stuffing the cushions. No buts!"

With a sly smile at Max, the boy flung the kitten back under the porch. "She's escaped!"

He disappeared in a flurry of limbs, but the woman didn't seem to care. Her eyes never left Max's for a second.

"You're not from these parts," she said after a moment. "Who are you? Where are you from?"

Max got to his feet and brushed himself down.

"I'm Ma-Matthew. Mark. Matthew Mark. Panthalassa."

What was that village called? Rose-something? HEY!

The woman raised an eyebrow. "Panthalassa? What kind of a name is that? Where are you from?"

"I'm from . . . Rosethorn?"

"Rosethorn?"

"Rosethorn, yes. I got lost on the Paths."

"There are no Panthalassas in Rosethorn."

"We moved there. The other day. That's how I got lost. Because I don't know the area."

"The area?" She took a step toward him, lifting the knife a little, as if to remind him it was there. "Where did you move from?"

"From London."

Tell her. Tell her the truth.

You're listening? Are they your parents?

Yes, this is them. But they're different somehow.

Okay, I'll tell her.

"I . . . eh . . . I've got a message from Martha," he said. "She wants to know why you haven't been to see her. In the grave-yard. In Marylebone."

The woman's face didn't change or even flicker. After a long silence the man turned and disappeared into the house, leaving Max and the woman alone.

She came down the steps towards him, stopping at the bottom.

"Martha's dead," she said.

"No she isn't, not yet, she's still—"

"Martha's dead. She died three years ago."

Max felt a shock go through him—from Martha.

What's going on? Doesn't she know about the gravestone and the messages?

But Martha didn't answer. He caught a strange glimpse of her sinking into dark water.

"She's been waiting for you," he got out, but that was all he managed to say. Something was happening in his chest. A kind of tightness. It was getting hard to breathe.

The woman smiled bitterly. "You don't believe that old nonsense, do you? When people die, that's it. There's noth-ing you can do except get on with life."

Jake's voice piped up from under the porch. "Why should we think about her when she doesn't think about us?"

The woman's face went still. "Jacob. Go in and help your Father."

The boy recognized the danger and came out from under the porch, the kitten mewling in his grip. The woman waited until he was through the door before she went on.

"I don't know who you are. I don't know who you've been speaking to. But Martha died three years ago. We don't want to hear another word about her."

"But you can't . . . you don't really think that . . ." Max gasped. He had to force each word out. There was a horrible shrinking inside him—a vacuum sucking everything inward.

Martha, is this you doing this? Martha, please . . . I can't breathe!

"It doesn't matter what I think," the woman said then. "It doesn't matter what I want, what I believe, what I hope, what I need. All that matters is what is. And Martha is dead. She drowned in the millpond, and now there's a railing. That's what is." She took a step toward him. "I've answered your questions. Now you're going to answer mine. Who else knows you're here? Who sent you? Was it the Coven?"

Max backed away from the house, hardly hearing. He had to get Martha out of the village. She was drowning all over again. And she was taking him with her.

"It's too late," the woman said. "You can't get away. You'll not last a second in the Woods at night." She smiled suddenly. "Why don't you come in and rest, and we'll talk about it? I'm making soup."

He turned and ran, disappearing into the shadows of the houses.

But now every breath was a painful effort. Something was swelling inside him. A pressure was building that squeezed the air from his lungs.

He'd never make it out of the village. He had to find somewhere to hide. Fast.

Martha, please . . . help me.

And then a bell was clanging out behind him. Doors all around him banged open. People rushed outside as the alarm was raised.

"Who is it? What's going on?"

"There's an intruder!"

He staggered into the narrow space between two buildings. His ribs had locked in place, like they were paralyzed.

He coughed. Water gurgled from his mouth and poured down his front.

Martha, please I'm drowning, too. Martha, stop!

Her voice, faint and far-off, came back at him for only a moment.

Leave me alone! I want to die! You'll die, too, if you try to stop me!

And then she was gone, swimming down into the very bottom of the millpond, into whatever lay beyond.

Gone!

He dropped to his knees, choking, his back arching, his ribs cracking. A torrent of water gushed from his lips.

Martha! Martha, wait! Don't go!

He dived after her.

The moment he plunged into the millpond, there was a strange kind of peace, and it all stopped hurting.

If he knew anything, it was this, he thought, as he swam downward into the murk—how to long for what was out of reach, for far-off lands, for what floated in the beyond. Somehow, he'd lost his Forever Parents to that invisible world, and he'd spent his whole life trying to find them again.

He was not going to lose Martha, too.

He kicked himself down, deep as deep could go, past the Merry-Go-Round, past the Minotaurs and Unicorns and the lights and the music, beyond the bottom of the millpond, which had been only pretend, only make-believe, an imaginary layer. So he sank deeper still, into a depthless darkness that went on and on and on.

And there he found her.

Max, it's all right. You don't have to. This is where I'm meant to be. There's nothing for me up there anymore.

He put his arms around her.

There's me . . .

And then she was beside him, called so strongly she'd come out of his finger into the night, and he was squeezing her thin, sobbing body to him. Together, they lay in the darkness, soaked and muddy and helpless. Seeing them there, the Woods took pity, and sent out its minions to protect them. The moon hid behind a cloud, drawing over them a veil of secrecy, and a flurry of shadows came skittering out of the trees, taking on the form of running boys to lead the villagers on a chase, here, there, and everywhere, before melting away, or falling flat and long against the ground, *ha-ha*!

But now—what was this?

Something stranger than strange. Beams of light, flashing out into the darkness.

Flashlights.

New Light in the Woods.

Forest Folk holding it. Controlling it. Using it. Pointing it between houses. Driving away shadows.

Do what it could, the Woods would always be driven away by volts and amps, and in the village of Gilead, its influence was already weakened by buried power cables, by stores of batteries, by circuit diagrams chalked out on blackboards, by the greasy generator that hulked in oily secrecy under the mill. So when those long beams of New Light swung back and forth, the invisible fingers of the Woods were snipped like ribbons, one by one. And its influence withdrew.

In moments, three men were within earshot of the hiding place, and getting nearer.

Martha blinked back under Max's fingernail, and he held himself as still as his shivering body allowed.

"What is it this time? A Wild One?"

"It's a boy. Said he was from Rosethorn."

"On his own? Up here?"

"Not likely. Must be someone with him."

"Think the Coven sent him? Maybe they got Wind of what's going on."

"Let them come. That's the idea. Not much they can do anyhow."

"I'll fetch the dogs. You two have a look around the back of Murdew's place."

The men moved off. Max got to his feet and peered out from his hiding place, pressing himself flat against the wooden walls of the building. Whatever was going on in Gilead, the villagers wanted to keep it secret. They were on every corner and marching along every path—the moment he left his hiding place he'd be spotted.

Please get me out of here. I don't want to ever come back.

I can't. I'm soaking wet. I'll freeze to death in the Woods like this.

You've got to get to the Wolf. It can take you to Rosethorn.

Isn't it too far?

Maybe.

Can't I hide somewhere? Isn't there anyone you trust?

Not here. Not anymore. But there's a barn. We passed it when you came in.

I remember.

You can hide in the hay loft. It's warm.

They're looking in all the buildings. Won't they check?

There's no other choice. It's high up, you'll be safe from the dogs at least.

Okay. Let's try.

He was about to make a break for it when a solitary howl came down from the hills. The eerie sound floated over their heads.

Every last one of the Forest Folk froze on the spot.

Then: "WOOOOOLVES!"

The cry went up around the village. The search parties scattered as parents raced to find their children. Those carrying flashlights moved toward the outskirts of the village, their faces grim, but unafraid.

Max watched from his hiding place. What was going on?

Was the Wild One attacking the village?

A woman herding a group of children went past. He slipped out of his hiding place to join them, but he'd only gone a few steps when his collar snapped tight against his neck, and a powerful hand yanked him around. Light blinded him—electric light, bright and hot, held up close. Behind it he could just make out a broad, grinning face.

"Would you look at this? A World One. Not a Coven spy at all."

Dazzled, he squirmed and kicked. The man bonked him on the head with the flashlight.

"Hold still, World One. Ho, Bingham! Look what's sniffing around behind your smokehouse!"

Someone else ran up. A hand took Max under his chin and tilted his head back.

"Must be a Cross-Over. Why's he all wet?"

"Who knows? Landed in the pond?"

"That'd be a first. What'll we do with him?"

"Let's lock him in the mill."

"Good idea. I don't want to go up against Wolves, even with New Light on our side."

"Very wise," snarled a voice.

Suddenly and without warning, a plank came whistling out of nowhere and slammed into the man's face with a sickening crunch. He fell backward, the flashlight spinning over his shoulder. The other man barely had time to cry out before the plank came down on his head with a CRACK! He turned, a look of stupid astonishment on his face. The plank caught him under the chin with such force it lifted him clean off the ground—he dropped like a stone.

Max turned this way and that in utter confusion. The plank clattered past his feet, and a shadowy figure exploded out of the darkness. The next thing he knew, he was being carried through the village, stretched over a man's broad shoulders. The man ran low and hard, using the shadows so skillfully, nobody caught sight of them. They were almost at the fields when they came upon a group of villagers gathered around the doors of the barn. The man slowed, then stopped, waiting for a chance to sneak past.

"We've got one trapped!"

"You sure?"

"Listen to that growl! It's a Wolf all right."

"Over here, boys! Over here!"

The man spat and set Max down. For the first time, he saw his rescuer's face, furious and bleak.

"Ready with the flashlights!"

"It'll be mad when it's out! It'll be frisky!"

"NOW!"

"Pull!"

The doors slid apart. "THERE! THERE!"

The crowd jumped back. The doors slammed together. Caught in the cross-beams of a dozen flashlights, the shadow of a Wolf sprang up against the barn, curved and huge.

"They're not working!"

"It's a World One! Must have gone Wild!"

"Don't let it get away!"

"AT IT! AT IT!"

Rakes and shovels rose and fell. There was a terrible yelping.

Something flipped in the air—then another piece.

A half-human, half-animal howl stopped them. A blood-curdling cry of pain.

Astonished, the villagers turned as one at the sound.

Lights raced across the grass.

The Dark Man was too fast. With a fluid movement, he ducked his shoulder and scooped up Max—and then he was on the Wolf once more, racing over the fields and into the trees, away from the village and its cruel, electrical lights.

5

LONDON

Max lay next to Martha in a mound of Wolves, the processes of animal biology, the blood and fur, livers and cells, keeping him warm against the midnight chill of the Woods.

The only cold part of him was the hand Martha held. He knew if he took it away, she would fail and die, so he held on long after his became stiff with cold. He was not afraid of falling asleep; he would remember her in his dreams.

But he did not want to sleep.

He just wanted to hold onto her. This was better than any dream.

They had not gone far from Gilead. As they went, other Wolves had caught up with them, their loping forms visible now and again through the trees. It was Max that had stopped the Wolf—he would have fallen off if the ride had gone on a minute longer. Frozen and shivering, he collapsed at the foot of a tree, and Martha, to his surprise, had come out without his calling. She wordlessly lay next to him, put her thin arms around his neck, and squeezed him as she sobbed and cried for her parents, lost forever.

From a distance, the Wolf had watched. Max had watched back, unashamed—because the Dark Man knew everything about him already, and always would. And then the other Wolves had come out of the trees, and curled themselves around them. Warmth. And softness. Manes and tails. Great ribcages swelling and sinking, rocking him on every side.

He did not want to sleep—he just wanted to hold her. But sleep he did.

The last thing he saw was the Wolf flickering under the trees. Now Wolf. Now Man. Black eyes watching over him. Golden eyes. Black eyes.

The spark of Wildness in both.

"How does she speak to you?"

"With words. It's just like talking, really. Except faster."

"And you hear her in your mind?"

"Yes. But it's strange. It's way down deep inside."

"Is she speaking to you now?"

"No. She's upset about what happened. I think she's watching the Merry-Go-Round."

Boris nodded. "You must take care of her," he said. "If what you say is true, you are bound to each other forever. I wonder if you know what that means."

Max had woken to find the Wolves gone and the Dark Man holding his hands over a crackling fire. They had spent the morning talking quietly. Boris had questioned him closely about everything that had happened, especially in Gilead. Max had waited for the chance to ask his own questions: now he took it.

"She says you're a Wild One. Are you really?"

"Yes. Or I used to be."

"She told me the Wildness is dangerous."

"And you must listen to what she says," Boris warned. "The Wildness is not to be tangled with."

"How did you get gotten then?"

"The same way as everyone else—I left the Paths and got lost in the Woods. What makes me unique is that I found my way back." He rubbed his large hands slowly together, then sat back from the fire. "Maybe I am the only one to escape the Wildness. But it is still within me. Mine takes the form of Wolves. Mrs. Jeffers calls me the Dozen Wolf. I like the name, but after last night, it has lost its . . . numerical accuracy."

"So that Wolf they killed—it was part of you?"

"Not part of. One of."

Max stared at him. "There's . . . more than one of you?"

Boris smiled faintly. "How else do you think I kept an eye on you all those years, day and night? I could not do it alone. That's why Mrs. Jeffers came to me for help. A scientist studying the Vanishings. One who knew the Woods and could set a watch on you like no other. I was the perfect candidate. Of course, I should never have been able to unleash the Wildness in the World, just as Mrs. Jeffers should not be able to manipulate Old Light. But as we know, the World is no longer what it was."

"Wait a moment," Max said. "So last night . . . are you saying one of you died?"

"One of me, yes, you could say so. But what happens to me is not important," Boris said emphatically. "Only one thing matters: stopping the Vanishings."

"But—"

"So you must decide what you are going to do," Boris said, interrupting him. "If you wish, you can search for your Forever Parents on the Balloons. There is still time to enter Eisteddfod, of course. We must leave tonight, however."

The offer of a choice surprised Max. He'd expected to be taken straight back to London. Then he remembered it was the Dark Man who had brought them to Gilead in the first place. "Why did you let me run away? You could have stopped me."

Boris shrugged. "I may not be a Seeker, but I am still a scientist. And most science is based on good, old-fashioned observational discovery." He waved a finger between his eyes.

"Watching what happens, in other words. And look what I have learned by doing nothing! Old Light in the World, and New Light in the Woods. A pattern is emerging, and where there is a pattern, there is a governing principle to be discovered. We are making progress."

Max looked away. What he was about to say was so hard after what the Dark Man had sacrificed at the village. "I'm sorry I ran away," he said. "But I just don't think I can do it. Go after a Dragon, I mean. I'm not brave like you."

"You are braver than you realize. I felt it, when you fought the Shredders. And I have good reason—we have good reason—to believe you will stand in front of the Dragon Fire and survive."

"How do you know?" Max asked, a bit suspiciously.

"I will leave that to the expert to explain. We were scheduled to meet him this afternoon, and we still have time to make our appointment." He gave Max an amused look. "Besides, if you are interested in Balloons, then for sure the best place to start is a Wind Giant."

Max clung onto the Dozen Wolf's fur and leaned between its ears as it loped toward London.

He felt calmer back with the Dark Man. The threat of the Dragon Fire still hung over him, but the news that he might have some special chance of success made it seem less terrifying.

You won't be able to cheat during Eisteddfod. The Dragon Hunters will find out.

He never said it would be cheating. He just said I would be okay. Anyway, he's going to give me a chance to find my Forever Parents first.

You might be surprised when you find them. They might not be who you think they are.

Why not?

I knew my parents for years, and I still didn't know them. You don't know yours at all.

I do so.

No, you don't. You've just had dreams about them.

My dreams aren't regular dreams. They come true.

Just because some did doesn't mean they all will. With that she dropped away from him.

Okay, fine. Go. I was more interested in the scenery. I've never been in the Woods, and it's super interesting to look at.

Glancing around, he sighed. Actually—it wasn't so interesting. Fields. Fields. Fields.

Hedge.

Field. Field. Ditch.

Cow.

Sometimes, the Dozen Wolf had to perform a special maneuver, like bounding over a stream, but mostly it was all featureless farmland.

Then the road was widening, changing from packed earth to paved stone. Human life began to bustle around them.

Building sites replaced the farms. On either side of the road, swarms of workers were digging trenches and laying foundations. One after another, they passed the timber frames of townhouses, each more complete than the last. Farther along, the wooden skeletons were being filled in with bricks and windows and topped off with tiles and chimneys. Finally, new townhouses stood shoulder to shoulder, covered with ropes and pulleys, tarpaulins and scaffolds, as painters and decorators added their finishing touches.

Not one of the workers noticed the Wolf. They were, themselves, passengers on a beast of much greater size, caught up in the frenzy of the city's growth as it uncurled a fresh tentacle toward the trees.

At last, the new road gave way to established rows of townhouses, shops, and markets. Here the city was fully alive, the road jammed with tradesmen pushing barrows, shepherds herding livestock, and darting children. Horses were everywhere, stallions tacked to carriages and shaggy nags hauling wagons—the clatter of wheels and hoofs on cobblestones was deafening. Most of all there was mud, spattering the shop-boards, soaking the hems of dresses, and spoiling the polished boots of well-to-do gentlemen.

Through the city, the Dozen Wolf ran, an intruder from the trees. Horses shied and dogs flattened themselves—but not one of the Forest Folk turned their heads in its direction. Like the builders, their attention was elsewhere. On themselves. On business. On clocks and shops. Only a troop of battling schoolboys dropped their fists and raced after them, their eyes wide, their socks slipping around their ankles . . .

The day the Wolf ran by!

The Peacock Feather Con

The journey ended somewhere near Charing Cross.

It was difficult to tell where exactly in this Woods version of London, because the Dozen Wolf began moving through back streets, loping down one alleyway after another. When it finally stopped, they were in a deserted passage shadowed from the sky by the close-leaning buildings.

It trotted past two small establishments, a pie-maker's and a feather-merchant (both with Closed for Eisteddfod signs on the door), and stopped outside a large window. Under a thin crust of frost, Max could just make out the black letters etched into the glass:

BRIARBACK BOOKS
PURVEYORS OF
FOREST FOLK BIOGRAPHIES
CATALOGS OF WITCH AND WIZARD PATENTS
FESTIVAL ALMANACS
RARE INKS
LUXURY PAPER
&
FINEST IMITATION STORYBOOKS

He slid off the Wolf's back and it immediately loped away. Max felt Martha stir within him, but it was a dim, faint voice he heard.

Where's he going?

He'll be back. He wants to tell Mrs. Jeffers about Gilead.

Why?

Because of the electricity. He says the Coven need to be informed as soon as possible.

Oh.

She sank away from him, pale and lifeless, more like a ghost than ever.

But he couldn't worry about her right now. The Dark Man had told him the owner of this bookshop had important information about the Dragon Fire. And if anyone knew about the Hot-Air Balloons, this was the man.

Except he wasn't really a man, of course. He was a Wind Giant.

Before going in, Max flattened a gloved hand against the glass and scraped at the frosty pane. Peering through, he saw a display of beautiful books with polished covers. The golden thread of lettering glittered prettily as a lantern hanging from a chain cast its light over the mosaic of spines.

The centerpiece of the display was a Storybook, lying open on a stand. He saw the handwriting with a jolt of recognition.

Porterholse . . .

Could it be that Porterholse was the Wind Giant he had come to meet?

That unusual face he'd seen at the window of the Book House . . . he thought he'd imagined it. Had it been the face of a Wind Giant? Hiding upstairs, away from New Light?

Max moved quickly toward the door.

Wind Giant or not, at last he would meet the creator of the Storybooks!

A bell jangled, and then he was pushing through a musty curtain into a spacious, book-lined room. Candles guttered in the rushing exchange of warm air for cold, and he quickly reached back to close the door behind him. As he unbuttoned his coat and removed his gloves, his nostrils filled with the delicious smell of gingerbread, tea, and burning logs, and the acidic stink of chemicals.

It was a large, comfortable room, snugly furnished, with something curious in every corner. Apart from the shelves, which groaned under the weight of their books, rolls of parchment tied with ribbons were stacked neatly in pigeon-holes along the walls. Between them, hand-drawn maps hung in wooden frames, and a heavy desk covered in papers, quills, and inkpots stood imposingly in one corner. Around the crackling fire three armchairs waited complete with cushions, footstools, and woolen rugs, lacking only people to sit in them. A silver tea service was positioned beside each armchair, loaded with sandwiches, cakes and cookies, cutlery, and china. And there, on the mantelpiece above the hearth, stood the sole survivor of the Book House—the iron pig, its butchery regions scorched from the flames.

"Oh-ho!" said a voice. "You must be Max. Welcome to Briarback Books! You're right on time!"

It took him a moment to locate the speaker, as only half his head was visible, poked around one of the doors on the far side of the room. When Max did, he felt a moment of disappointment. This was not the face he'd seen at the window of the Book House. It was much thinner, to begin with, and very weather-beaten, like its owner had done a lot of exploring. All his hair seemed to have been frazzled away by the sun, apart from his eyebrows, which were bushy and white.

"Endymion Rees, map-maker and ink-mixer, at your service," the half-a-head announced. "At your service, at least, the moment I've finished straining these tea leaves. Lunch is nearly ready. No doubt you'll be famished—I know what Furthingale's breakfasts are like. Frugal doesn't even begin to describe them!" The half-a-head looked past Max and around the room. "But where are Mrs. Jeffers and Doctor Peshkov?"

"It's just me," Max said. "He dropped me off." He hesitated. "The Wolf did."

"The Wolf?" said Endymion, seeming startled. "The Dozen Wolf was here? In the city? Whatever for?"

"We were . . . in a bit of a rush."

"But why didn't you just take the carriage from the Dormitory? I sent one this morning. Didn't it arrive?"

"We didn't come from Marylebone. We were at Gilead."

"*Gilead?* What in the Woods were you doing up there? No, don't answer. Wait a moment."

The head twisted upwards, quartering itself to nothing more than a chin, and roared at the ceiling. "GUSTAV! STOP BLOWING AROUND UP THERE AND COME DOWN!"

In the rooms above, a window slid down with a crash and a voice cannoned back: "BLOWING AROUND? WHOOOSH! HOLD YOUR NOISE, YOU DOG!"

Footsteps boomed across the ceiling and down some stairs, and with a CRASH that shook the shelves, a door on the far side of the room was flung open and a man of immense stature appeared, something like a cross between a Professor, Saturn, and a Plastic Bag.

It was him.

The man at the window. Porterholse, the Wind Giant.

It was no wonder he had hidden himself away. His appearance would have caused mass panic in the World. His skin was alabaster-white with a slight translucence, like marble or quartz, and his black, neatly combed hair was so thin it seemed scribbled in ink across his scalp. Every thread and button of his clothes strained under the massive internal pressure of a body that had swollen far beyond its natural dimensions, and was swelling still.

"HOW many times do I have to tell you, Endymion Rees?" he roared, each word a clap of thunder. "When I'm sending out the Wind I'm not to be disturbed. WHOOSH! What will the windmills do? And the kites and the clouds? HUFF-PUFF! And the birds that like to soar and glide? They will PLUMMET TO THE GROUND!"

"But our *guest* is here, you great idiot, you useless, lazy, bag of nothing!" howled Endymion, turning purple and flapping his tea-strainer at Max.

"Wh-what? Ah-ha!" cried Porterholse, all his anger vanishing as he noticed Max for the first time. His features broke into a smile, and he advanced, hands outstretched. "Hello at last, dear boy! Oh my, what a day! HUFF-PUFF! Welcome to the Woods! WHOO-O-O-OSH!"

Max leaned forward to stop from being swept off his feet by the gale-force greeting. With every WHOOSH and HUFF-PUFF gusts of Wind swirled through the room, disturbing sheets of paper, rattling the shelves, and fluttering the pages of books.

"STOP it—WILL you stop it!" screamed Endymion, hopping from one foot to the other and holding his head in despair. "For pity's sake, can't you STOP with that damnable hurricane-ing?"

It was remarkable to watch. As the air huffed out of him Porterholse deflated and his clothes slowly sagged with relief, becoming loose and baggy.

"You know I can't help it," he snapped, tightening his belt seven or eight notches and tucking his shirt tails back in. "The Wind Within gets agitated whenever I do. It's the way the Wizards made me."

"Well . . . learn a bit of self-control," Endymion grumbled. "Go to a psychomotherapractologisteopath! Anything!"

Porterholse ignored him and pumped Max's hand enthusiastically.

"Welcome to our little bookshop, welcome! Sit by the fire, you must be frozen! Lunch is ready, just as requested!" He looked around, frowning suddenly. "But where are Mrs. Jeffers and Doctor Peshkov? They've not gone for victuals, have they? I gave them strict instructions to do no such thing. The shops are closed in any case."

"They're not here *at all*," Endymion said. "For some reason, this one's been up at Gilead."

"He's been *where*?" Porterholse asked indignantly.

"Gilead," said Endymion. "It's an isolated little village, about a day out of London. He came here on the Dozen Wolf."

"What in the Woods are you doing loping around on that Great Golloper?" Porterholse asked, turning to Max. "We sent a perfectly good carriage to collect—"

"I TOLD HIM THAT ALREADY! Aren't you listening? He hasn't come from Marylebone! And take a look at him! He's filthy! If anyone has been in the Woods, this one has!"

Porterholse looked at Max as if seeing him for the first time.

"My dear boy," he whispered, "is everything all right? Sit down, sit down, and tell us all about it!"

By the time the last cakes had been demolished and the teapot drained, Porterholse and Endymion knew it all from start to finish. What shocked them most of all was that New Light had come to Gilead.

"I told you so!" Porterholse said. "Didn't I tell you? WHOOSH! Something is happening in the Woods. HUFF-PUFF! The Winds bring strange tidings every day."

"Pooh! Those Winds of yours are the worst gossip-mongers and storytellers of the lot!"

"This is different. You've heard the rumors."

Endymion flapped his hand. "They're not about electricity. They're about—eh"—he hesitated and glanced at Max—"they're about the . . . *Arboghast draconium*."

"Indeed, they are! And what's he just told us? A Dragon only a few miles north of Marylebone?"

"It's nearly time for their annual migration. The Dragons all head south during migration."

"Not until the Full Moon, they don't!"

"You know how stupid Dragons are. Maybe they're . . . lost."

"Lost?" Porterholse exclaimed. "LOST?"

"Or hiding from this electricity."

"We can't have Dragons coming near villages—it would be a disaster! Who knows what would happen? One breath from a Dragon and you're—"

Endymion coughed loudly and glared at Porterholse.

"Ahahaha! WHOOSH! But not dangerous for YOU, dear boy!" the Wind Giant added hastily. "NO! HUFF-PUFF! You, of course, have nothing to fear from the Dragon Fire. Nothing at all!"

Max leaned forward in his chair. This was what he'd really wanted to get to. "Boris thinks so, too. He says he's sure."

"We are all sure," said Porterholse, nodding. "Fairly sure."

"Quite sure," nodded Endymion.

"How, though?" Max asked.

Porterholse stared at him. "But—don't you know?" He glared at Endymion. "Has nobody told him about the Soul Searcher?"

"THAT'S WHAT THIS ENTIRE LUNCH WAS SUPPOSED TO BE ABOUT!" Endymion burst out in exasperation. "You insisted YOURSELF on telling him. Because the whole thing was YOUR IDEA! And you wanted to COVER yourself in glory!"

"What nonsense!" Porterholse retorted. "I insisted on no such thing." He seemed mightily upset by the suggestion and took a moment to collect himself.

"Wait for it . . ." muttered Endymion.

"The situation being what it is, however," Porterholse continued, folding his hands across his stomach.

"Here it comes . . ."

"I can see it falls to me to explain our plan. To remedy any confusion."

"How convenient," Endymion said. "Just keep it short, will you?"

Porterholse turned to Max, smiling fondly.

"All of us, dear boy, Mrs. Jeffers and I, Doctor Peshkov and Endymion Rees here, have long pondered the question of how to draw back the veil of mystery that shrouds your beginning. Our first idea, for which I claim no personal credit, even though I thought of it, was to ask the Soul Searchers for assistance. They work for the Dragon Hunters, but they live in the World. They are odd folk. Half of the Woods. Half of the World. Truly at ease in neither. Perhaps this is what makes them so good at what they do."

"What do they do?" Max asked.

"That," Porterholse said, "is a secret so secret I couldn't put it in the Storybooks, and it's so terribly important it remains secret that I must ask you to take an oath before all you hold sacred—"

"Cut the drama!" Endymion howled. "It's a secret! Enough! Good Heaven's above get on with it you big Wind Bag!"

"Very well," said Porterholse stiffly. "Max, I will give you an example. There is a little Indian woman, an old thing shriveled up like a walnut, sitting outside a Tottenham Court Road Tube station in London. She sells peacock feathers. Most people pass her by without noticing her. But now and again, someone sees her and decides to buy one of her feathers, if only to fall into conversation with this interesting character. 'How much for a feather, please?' they ask, and they wait for some piece of wisdom to drop from her lips, a word of ancient knowledge passed down through generations. 'A buck and a half!' she snarls, really sticking it to them with the half. Worse, she starts to complain, just some moaning nonsense about the weather or her bones or the noise of traffic. She snatches their money and produces, from a hidden location among the beautiful feathers, the thinnest, mangiest feather imaginable, and they carry on their way, bitterly disappointed. What they don't see is that the little Indian woman is no longer sitting down with her bundle. No, she's writing something in a notebook she keeps tied to her wrist with an old bootlace."

Porterholse stopped suddenly, beaming and blinking.

"You have to ask him what she's writing," Endymion muttered, clasping his forehead.

"What's she writing?" Max asked.

"She's making notes about their soul," Porterholse said. "While they stand there listening to her complaints, she takes a good, long look into the depths of their being. She's able to tell what sort of stories their soul is crying out for. When her notebook is full, off she goes to the Beginning Woods, to report to the Tuileries, the headquarters of the Dragon Hunters. And they see from the Soul Searcher's notes what kinds of stories are needed in the World."

"And then they make the Storybooks?"

"Yes. In great secrecy. We don't know where, and nobody knows what happens to the Storybooks afterward. But every story ends up in the World, where it begins to do its work."

"And you sent a Soul Searcher to look into my soul?"

"We did. At the opening of the Book House."

Max remembered the pale, brown-eyed man who had spoken to him as he sat on the windowsill.

"What did he see? Did he see where I came from?"

"No. He saw something in the other direction, as it were. Where you were going. A prophecy. A great and terrible prophecy!"

"Of what?" Max asked.

"He saw you facing a terrible monster with gleaming teeth. He said you would do something so brave it would change the World forever."

"And when I faced this danger, I would survive?" Max asked intently.

"Yes. He said that part of it was very clear. Not only would you survive, but your survival would be a kind of miracle."

"He didn't see anything about my Forever Parents?" Max asked quickly. "Or about Balloons?"

"Oh Lord," Endymion groaned. "Please don't ask him about Balloons."

"No, do!" Porterholse beamed. "I love Balloons! I love to huff and puff them across the land! Nothing is better to gust at than a big colorful Balloon! WHOOSH!"

Max quickly explained about his dream—about the Hot-Air Balloon, his Forever Parents, and the Panthalassa Ocean. Porterholse and Endymion listened closely. When he'd finished, they glanced at each other.

"I've never heard of anyone called Panthalassa," Porterholse said. "What do you think, Endymion?"

"I'll tell you straight off what I think," said the map-maker, looking directly at Max with a serious gaze. "If the

Panthalassa Ocean is your other avenue of investigation, I'd take your chances in the Dragon Fire."

"Why?" Max asked. "Is it dangerous?"

"Not especially. From your point of view, it's something worse: it's enormous."

Endymion lifted one of the framed maps off the wall and passed it to Max. It was just like the Pangaea map he'd seen in the school geography textbook. At the top, in beautiful scrolled letters was the title: *The Beginning Woods*. Underneath, was a single continent, divided only by thin passages of water. Leaning over him, Endymion drew a finger around the gigantic continent.

"This," he said, "is the coastline you'd have to search. It took hundreds of explorers decades to chart these waters. Unless you know where to start, and it sounds like you don't, you could spend a whole lifetime searching and not even cover a tenth of it."

Max saw at once that Endymion was right. The territory was too vast to cover.

"I disagree," said Porterholse suddenly.

"You do?" asked Endymion.

"Yes," said the Wind Giant confidently. "I do."

He set aside his teacup, brushed the cookie crumbs from his waistcoat, and stood up. "In fact, I know how he can complete his search, in a matter of hours, without ever setting foot out of London!"

WHERE THE WIND COMES FROM

"The Giants . . . were made by . . . the Wizards. We were . . . inventions. Patent . . . Eight Nine Zero . . . something I forget . . . something . . ."

Max sat on the 357th step of the spiral staircase of King's Cross Wind Control Tower and waited for Porterholse to catch up.

"So all the Winds come from the Giants?" he called down.

"Almost all." Porterholse's voice echoed up from below. "There are some left from the Olden Days. Most dwindled down to a breeze . . . a long time ago. Some were stored underground. I believe they're still there, gusting about."

"So Winds were around before the Giants?"

Porterholse came into view, his huge body sagging with exhaustion. He collapsed on the steps and mopped his brow with a red polka-dot handkerchief.

"Oh, yes! Giants were one of the early modifications Wizards made to Winds, so Winds came first. Witches and Wizards never get anything right first time. That's what evolution is—the ongoing tampering of Witches and Wizards with creation. If they love anything more than *creating*, these Witches and Wizards, the Devil take their hides, it's *modifying*. According to the records, which are rather incomplete, the Wizards made Air first. That was back in the Dabbling Days, the early era of the Woods when they were coming up with Fundamentals, Essences, Universals, and so on. They knew Air was going to be important and nobody would be able to do without it, so they made it Still and Quiet and Narcissistic, so it would sit in one place contemplating itself and not suddenly disappear off on an adventure. But that meant the Clouds had to be moved around with sticks and grappling hooks, which was an awful bother. So they took half the Air and gave it Tirelessness, Enthusiasm, and Curiosity, to encourage it to travel and not stay in one place. It all looked good on paper, but when the Patent was activated it was a disaster."

"Something went wrong?"

"Everything went wrong. The Winds became over-excited and started tearing around all over the place. The destruction was catastrophic. Eventually, another Wizard came up with the idea of containing the Winds in bags, so they could be dispersed gradually, as and when required. He called the bags Giants."

"And that's what you do?"

"Yes. I and the other Wind Giants let out our Winds at regular intervals, according to various timed schematics. Naturally, we are in great demand by the Balloon companies, who provide us with a monthly stipend for our services."

He got to his feet and leaned for a moment on the banister, dabbing his perspiring forehead with his handkerchief.

"Okay!" said Max. "Come on! Are you ready for more?"

Porterholse nodded, and they continued up the steps. In only four hours, the last Balloon for Paris before Eisteddfod would depart, and they were climbing the Tower to interrogate the Winds. If any Wind had blown any Balloon out over the Panthalassa Ocean, Porterholse would soon learn of it.

They had already visited the King's Cross launching area. Max had stood by the workers as they loaded the travelers' trunks into the baggage compartment, wondering if his Forever Parents were among them. He must have looked at every last passenger, ticket-collector, and street-seller, desperate for the glinting spectacles or flash of auburn hair that would save him from the Dragon Fire.

Nothing.

Worse, Porterholse had shown him a map of all the flight routes, landing areas, and Wind Towers in the Beginning Woods. Some towers stood in cities, some in isolated outposts in the Woods. Each was serviced by a team of Giants, who took it in turns to emit their Winds at the scheduled moment. There were more than 30,000 Hot-Air Balloons operating in the Woods at any one time, Porterholse had told him. Even if he forgot about searching the Ocean and just checked the Balloons, the chances of finding his Forever Parents were almost nonexistent.

The Winds were his only hope.

At last they reached the top of the Tower and emerged into the bright sunshine. Pigeons exploded up around them in a clatter of wings then dropped down toward the city, disappearing among the rooftops. Max scrabbled up onto the stone balustrade, flopped over on his belly, and peered directly down at the U-shaped courtyard below, where the fabric of the Balloon was lying flat out and wrinkled.

"They're starting to fill it," he called back. The Wind Giant had sat on a small wooden bench, and for some reason was unlacing his shoes.

"Plenty of time," Porterholse replied. "I'll send out part of my Wind to make some inquiries. While we wait for it to return, I'll see if these other Winds know anything."

Max nodded, but his thoughts were turning to Martha again.

She was silent and faint, barely there inside him.

I know you're really upset about what happened. But I helped you. And you promised to help me back.

No answer.

I'm going to have to go to Paris if these Winds don't know anything. You might want to find another gravestone, if you don't want to get all burned up, that is.

She remained silent.

Sighing, he scratched a spot of lichen off the balustrade and crumbled it between his fingers. A Wind caught the flakes and held them in the air, examining them for a moment before flinging them down into the streets of London.

"You should be more careful what you throw into the Wind," Porterholse cautioned. "You never know where it will end up."

"Something that small isn't going to make any difference to anyone," Max muttered.

"Ah! HUFF-PUFF! But what started the Vanishings? A tiny baby, popping up out of nowhere onto a bookshelf! And the whole World is changed!"

The Wind Giant came to stand next to him. He had undressed down to his shirt and trousers, and left his scarf, coat, and waistcoat neatly folded on the bench. He'd even taken off his socks, Max noticed, and was flexing his bare toes on the cold stone. "I have this Wind in me," he went on. "Sometimes, I let part of it escape, and off it goes into the Woods: WHOOSH! Goodbye! HUFF-PUFF! Whatever it does, I am responsible. It is ME out there, moving through the Woods, doing all that the Wind does. It is the same with you."

"No, it isn't," Max said. "I can't blow a gigantic Wind that goes whizzing off everywhere."

"Your actions, what you do and say—those are your Winds. You send them out all the time without even realizing it—HUFF-PUFF!"

He unbuttoned his shirt and handed it to Max. Then, with a snap of leather, he whipped off his belt and stepped out of his trousers. His white body gleamed like a pearl in the afternoon light. Flapping his arms in the crisp air, he shivered and let out a great WHOO-OOOSH! of pleasure.

"Take your crumb of lichen. Off it goes—HUFF-PUFF— off through London, down streets and up alleyways, in and out of windows, shooed away by feather dusters and sucked up by chimneys, until finally it lodges in some fellow's eye.

WHOO-OOSH! Blinking, he ducks into a doorway. The door opens and a woman steps out. He is about to turn away, embarrassed—she will think he is crying. But what's this? Her eyes are red and moist, as well! She's been weeping over something, a tragic story, a broken promise. Each suffers and sees the other's suffering! It's love! They marry and have children. Their children have children. Their children's children have children. WHOOOSH! A countless series of lives, all thanks to that little flake you flung into the World without a thought!"

As he spoke, he completed his undressing. Entirely naked, his arms held wide, his face rapt with pleasure, he stood inflating as the Winds swirled around him, gathering excitedly to welcome one of their brothers.

"The greatest illusion in life," Porterholse cried, "is that I go from the tips of my toes to the ends of my fingers and no farther! This body, this bag, is only my BEGINNING. The rest of me is OUT THERE! HUFF-PUFF! In the EVER AFTER! WHOOOO-OOOOOSH!"

His skin stretching until he was an immense, partially translucent orb, he rolled backward against the wall of the spire and unleashed his Wind with an almighty shout:

IN LIFE!

For some time afterward, Porterholse stood on the balcony interrogating the Winds, shooing some away, beckoning others to him, while waiting for his own to return.

But the minutes passed, and the Balloon below got bigger, and its departure drew nearer, and not one of the Winds had heard a whisper of a rumor about Forever Parents or Panthalassas. Each time a new Wind arrived, Max looked at Porterholse hopefully, and each time the Wind Giant only sadly shook his head.

By the time evening fell, he was boarding the Balloon to Paris.

The Accursed Questions

So that was it.

Dragon Fire.

Why, Max wondered, did the only way to find his Forever Parents have to be *not* a way? Talk of Soul Searchers and prophecies was all very well. But he still had to stand there, in the fire. What was more certain than the fact that fire was dangerous? Nothing! Was there anything more painful than fire? No! And now he had to stand in a fire rumored to be so hot it could melt stone, just because some old man with a notebook had taken a peep into his soul (and made an insulting remark about reading).

As he shuffled up the ramp with Boris and Mrs. Jeffers, caught in the mass of people boarding the Balloon, the gas-powered burner roared above their heads, and flickering shadows chased each other up the brickwork of King's Cross station. The vast silken girth of the Balloon glowed orange from within.

The fire-filled belly of a Dragon probably looked like that, he realized. A lot of fire could fit in a belly that big. Enough to burn down a house, let alone a boy.

But it was too late. The press of people pushed him forward, into the Balloon, like they knew he wanted to turn and go back. Step by step, inch by inch, they were forcing him toward the Dragon. Somewhere in the Woods, it was waiting for him.

There was no escape.

Inside the Balloon, passengers squeezed past each other in narrow corridors. Mrs. Jeffers went one way, and Boris and Max went another, holding their bags over their heads. Their berth was a snug cabin in a corner. Instead of bunks or seats, there were two rolled-up mattresses, a stack of cushions, and blankets. Orbs filled with glowing amber liquid rolled around on the thick carpet, giving off a gentle light and heat.

Moving awkwardly around each other, Boris began gathering cushions and arranging the mattresses, while Max picked up one of the orbs. His chilled fingers tingled with warmth.

"It's leftovers from an early version of Old Light," Boris explained. "Mind your back, I'll open the window. There's a good view as we go up."

He removed two wooden pegs from their fastenings on the wall and folded down a panel to reveal the evening sky.

Outside, whistles were blasting and ropes were hissing through iron hoops. There were several thuds, one after the other, and a sudden lurch as a team of horses began to haul the Balloon clear of the building. They were already rising, so slowly Max had hardly noticed. Popping his head out, he saw King's Cross dropping away below.

"Grab hold!" said Boris, pointing to a leather strap attached to the wall. Max slid his hand through the loop just as the Balloon was caught in a mighty gust. The cabin swung violently, and Max caught a brief glimpse of the stark-naked Porterholse on the balcony of the Wind Tower, his arms held high, waving delightedly. From other cabins came screams and shouts of laughter. But the disturbance soon settled, and Max hung his arms out of the window to watch the view. Solitary clouds were scudding across the moon. London shimmered far below.

Don't you want to see this?

He waited, and after a moment asked again, but Martha made no reply. He trailed his hand in the air, staring at the fingertip where she had taken up her strange residence.

Did you hear me before? It looks like I'm going to be entering Eisteddfod. So it's the Dragon Fire after all.

She didn't seem to hear, and after a few minutes he gave his finger an irritated flick. If she wasn't going to bother with him, he wasn't going to bother with her.

He turned away from the view and watched Boris instead.

The Dark Man was lying opposite the window, lighting a cigarette. He was close enough to touch—but the thought of the Dark Man being touchable still seemed like a bizarre contradiction.

"How did you find out about the Beginning Woods?" he asked. "Did you cross over by mistake and go Wild?"

"No," Boris said after a moment. "Actually, my Father brought me here."

"How did he know about it?"

"He was a storyteller. All storytellers know about the Woods one way or another. Even if they don't know they know, they know."

"That was his job? Telling stories?"

"He wouldn't have called it a job. It was just what he did."

"Who did he tell them to?"

"Anyone who would listen. He loved telling stories."

"Will you tell me about him?" Max asked.

"You want to know about my Father?"

"Yes. You've been following me since forever. You know all about me. And I hardly know anything about you."

Boris seemed to think about this for a moment, then nodded slowly. "Very well," he said. "I suppose . . . I never thought about that."

He crawled across to the window to sit beside Max. Drawing his blanket around his shoulders, he looked out at the darkening sky.

"My parents traveled around the World performing in all sorts of places," he said. "Village halls. Palaces. Theaters. Living rooms. Papa would tell the stories and Mama would accompany him on a guitar. She could make any sound with her instrument, create any atmosphere. She was a magnificent Russian. They both were."

Max gathered one of the orbs of leftover Old Light into his chest. He didn't feel at all sleepy.

"He was an intense, quiet man, my Father," Boris continued. "It was like this between us: we would be walking somewhere, side by side, and I would want to ask him something, and I would turn to him and say, 'Papa?' And I would have to say it two or three times to get his attention. He had the look of one concerned with the *proklyatye voprosy*, the Accursed Questions. We had learned about them at school. Who am I? Where do I come from? Why am I here? What is the best way to live? I began to wonder which question was troubling Papa. When I asked him, he told me he never thought about the Accursed Questions. We had each other, he said, and as long as we did, we wouldn't get gotten by the Questions. They only got people who'd been struck a blow in life, a damaging blow they'd never recovered from, that made them forget what was most important. When I asked him what was most important he only smiled and said: 'That is one of the Questions.'

"Shortly after my twelfth birthday my parents were invited to Moscow for a season of evening performances in a theater on Old Arbat. I enrolled at the local school, the same one we always used when we returned to the capital. On my first day back, the teacher gave me a test 'to see what my travels had taught me.' In those days, exams were conducted differently. Each student was called up to the teacher's desk and asked questions. I had missed all my classes, so I began making up the answers, and my teacher's face darkened as he listened to my fantasies. The other boys began laughing at me, and the teacher began to shout, to maintain order. But then we became aware of another, much louder, commotion going on in the corridors, the furious yelling of a great many people, getting rapidly nearer. It was so surprising we all went quiet. The teacher indicated that I was to return to my seat, and I did so, feeling very fortunate. The teacher moved toward the door to investigate, but right at that moment Papa burst into the classroom, followed by a group of men who were struggling to hold him back. Among them were some other teachers, the headmaster himself, and a man in a long black coat I did not recognize.

"When he saw me, Papa stood frozen, unable to speak. The other men let him go and stood back with solemn expressions. And suddenly everyone was staring at me—even the other boys—as if they expected something from me. Then my teacher walked up to my desk and said words which I will never forget: 'There are no more questions. Go with your Father.' He had realized the truth, or perhaps the headmaster had given him a signal, but I only stared at Papa, who was standing still as a statue. Then, to everyone's astonishment, he simply turned and walked rapidly out of the classroom.

"It was the man in the long black coat who took me to the school infirmary. He sat me on a bed and took the school nurse into the very farthest corner of the room. As he whispered in her ear, her face went white with shock. I could not understand why I was there. I vaguely remembered a story about a plum stone. If you ate a plum stone, you died. Maybe Papa thought I had eaten a plum stone. But I'd had oatmeal for breakfast. When the man in the black coat returned, I told him: 'I only ate oatmeal!'

"He sternly told me oatmeal had nothing to do with it. His name was Andreyev, he said. He was a doctor. And what he said next was a thousand times more unbelievable than any plum stone. I told him he was lying. Doctors never lie, he replied. He'd made the 'final pronouncement' himself. I kept asking where Papa was, but the doctor avoided my questions and I became angry. I ran out of the infirmary and made my way home, beside myself with panic.

"I found our apartment full of people—neighbors, our landlord, and many I did not recognize. They were horrified to see me. When I arrived, shouting for Mama, they all drew back, and I made it as far as my parents' bedroom before anyone stopped me. Papa was sleeping, they said, and wouldn't wake up until tomorrow.

"So I discovered it was all true. Or, at least, things began to happen just as if it was true, but for a long time I did not accept any of it. Some part of my brain knew and understood right from the start, of course—the part that dealt with facts and figures and calculations. But the rest of me did not know, wanted nothing to do with it, and went on for a long time as if nothing had happened. That part of me still expected to see Mama at any moment, to be embraced by her, to feel her fingers on my neck as she straightened my collar, to hear her tuning her guitar in the evening. Even on days long afterward, when Papa was kneeling before me, holding both my hands, saying things he'd said a thousand times before, I still felt it couldn't be true, he meant something else, somewhere a mistake had been made. Then one night, I heard him crying through the walls—he was trying to do it quietly—and then I realized with my whole being it was true, and I felt so sorry for Papa. I rushed into his room and we lay in bed together crying and hugging each other."

Boris paused a moment—his cigarette had gone out. He lit another before continuing.

"She dropped dead on the underground, 'as if someone had clicked their fingers'—I overheard a guest say that at the funeral. One minute she'd been talking to Papa, she'd been living, breathing. The next, she was lying on the platform and her life was over.

"Up until that moment, my world had been a happy one. The worst that could happen had been a bad mark in an exam, a cut knee, or a fight with another boy. But now I understood what kind of things the world had to offer.

"For the first time, the Accursed Questions appeared in my mind.

"Why had this happened?

"Was there a reason?

"Who was responsible?

"I kept the Questions secret at first. But the Accursed Questions don't like that. They want to spread around. And over the months I began to ask other people. I soon noticed something strange.

"Those who had been close to Mama could not answer the Accursed Questions and admitted they could not. They treated me kindly. They poured tea and listened to what I had to say, and they shared stories of their own. They gave no *answers*, but I always left them feeling a little better. Only those people who had nothing to do with Mama thought they knew why she had died. Their answers were of two sorts; I divided them into Doctors and Priests.

"The Doctors repeated what Andreyev had told me. Mama had been born with a thinness in the wall of an artery in her brain. The thinness had become tired and had given way. This could have happened at any time, they said, so she was lucky to have lived so long. When I asked why she had been born with this thinness when other people hadn't, the Doctors told me there was an anomaly in her genes that had caused the thinness. So I asked why she had to have this anomaly. They told me they could not be sure. Either it was because of a mutation, or it was passed on through her parents. This meant they did not understand the question. They kept telling me how the thinness had appeared. I wanted to know why. I was full of emotion, and I expected the answer to be the same. I needed an idea bigger than my Mother's death. Something that would dwarf the question, an answer of greater mass.

"So I turned to the Priests. With their cathedrals and sacred music, their cupolas and icons, they seemed to have hold of something eternal and unstoppable. But I was soon disappointed. They told me something so strange I could not understand it no matter how hard I tried. Everything that happened was God's will, they said. And because it was God's will, it was good.

"As far as I could see, this meant God had killed Mama, and I was meant to be glad. No, they told me. That wasn't the right way to think about it. God had a secret plan only He could understand, and because of this plan everything that happened was wonderful. We had to trust God.

"This seemed very difficult to me. Because there was not only my Mother. There was the blind girl on the corner outside our school who never had enough to eat and had to sit on a bucket all winter in forty degrees of frost and try to sell fish that her brother brought her in a washing tub. People would steal the fish from her and when her brother came back he would beat her. I couldn't understand how this was good, no matter what God had in store to make up for it. And there was a lot more besides—you only had to pick up a newspaper or a history book. But the Priests kept saying if we understood God's plan we would realize how wonderful the world was and how much He loved us.

"'So it's wonderful that Mama died?' I asked them.

"'She is with God,' they said, 'and that is wonderful.'

"*But she isn't with me*, I thought. And that wasn't wonderful at all. And what about the blind girl? She wasn't with God, either, and in the meantime, the boys run up to her and pinch her cheeks. Why did there have to be a meantime? I couldn't understand the Priests at all. Their answer just produced new questions. An answer had to perform the duties of an answer. It had to dispel the question, so the question could be forgotten.

"The Doctors and Priests, I realized, were nothing more than ambassadors of larger schemes of belief. Science and churches were like model boats inside bottles. They'd been constructed outside of life, then brought in and expanded to make it look as if that was where they had always been— inside the bottle, inside life. When in fact, neither science nor churches have anything to do with life, anything at all. Their answers had nothing to do with my Mother or me or my Why.

"Two years after Mama's funeral Papa moved us to Berlin, where his Father taught at Humboldt University. We stayed in my grandfather's house near the Tiergarten, a park in the center of Berlin. One night, Father woke me and told me to get dressed. We were going on a journey, he said. I had not seen him so animated for a long time. His eyes had a strange gleam that frightened me, but I got up and followed his instructions. Now I think it was the first spark of Wildness in his eyes, reaching into him all the way from the Woods. He took a lantern, and we went through the streets to the park. There, among the trees, he guided me for the first time into the Beginning Woods. He'd been coming for years, he told me. And it was time I learned about it, too.

"My Father did not want answers. What he wanted was forgetfulness, to get gotten by the Wildness. We spent many weeks exploring the Woods. One day, we came to a junction in the Path. He told me he was unsure of the direction and instructed me to follow the western fork, while he took the other. I did so and soon came to a village, so I went back to let him know. When I reached the Northmark, I found his clothes lying there by the stone: he'd walked naked into the trees.

"I left the Path at once. Without clothes, I knew, the Wildness would get him more swiftly. And it must have. Because I could not find him. I became lost and frantic. The Wildness was beginning to send its fingers into me, too, to pull me apart. I began to see shapes in the trees. Shadows in the form of Wolves. I ran from them. And then . . . it was like the development of a dream. I was a boy running from Wolves in the Woods. *How can I hide? How can I hide?* The only way was to become a Wolf myself, and run with them. But it was all a trick of the Wildness. The Wolves pursuing me were the Accursed Questions that had taken up residence deep in my own being. I thought I was running from

Wolves—I was running from my own Selves."

"But you learned to control it?" Max asked.

"Not at first. For some time I must have been a fully-fledged Wild One. Of course, I remember none of it. Only how it ended."

"What happened?"

"One day, I came out of the Deep Woods into a graveyard that had long been abandoned, all of its ghosts forgotten. I saw something there that reminded me of who I was, and where I came from. A message from a Mother, written on one of the gravestones:

I

CARRIED

YOU

UNDER

MY

HEART

"Those six words drove the Wildness from me, and I became, once more, a boy. But the Accursed Questions are still part of my being. I have never escaped them. They pursue me through life. Wolf or Man, they break me apart when I summon them. But I only need to remember that inscription, that reminder of my Mother's love, to become whole.

"After I escaped the Wildness, there was only one place I could go—back to my grandfather in Berlin. He knew nothing of the Woods and had been unsurprised by our disappearance after my Mother's funeral, assuming my Father had returned to his travels. All I had to do was add a conclusion to the story he had made up for himself: Papa had decided it was time I settled down, I told him, in a home, with friends and family, and he'd sent me back to Berlin. My grandfather had never approved of my itinerant life and welcomed me back into his household.

"As for me, I needed to keep the Wildness at bay. I feared the Woods now, and feared their lure. I moved in the opposite direction and took up mathematics and science. Grandfather, not knowing my innermost thoughts, helped me with pleasure. He was an engineer, and it was he who instructed me in the principles of algebra, geometry, calculus, the laws of motion, and thermodynamics. The more I studied, the more the world of science fascinated me. Engineering I could understand. In engineering, there are no thin artery walls or secret plans, and the answers always dispel the questions. I built up strong barriers against the Wildness and buried all memory of the Woods deep within me. When the Vanishings started I moved to Paris to join the Symposium. I became one of the chief Seekers under Courtz. But our opinions differed. I did not believe the Vanishings were a question of How. To me, they were one of the Why questions, dreadful, accursed, unanswerable perhaps. I think I knew it all along: the Vanishings were the work of the Woods."

Max looked away from Boris. During the story, night had fallen. Even the moon and the stars seemed to be listening.

"Why do people Vanish?" he asked. "Is it really because they're dreamers?"

Boris regarded him seriously. "I don't believe so. But I don't think the Vanishings are random, either. Certain people Vanish. Others do not. There must be a reason."

"So why, then?" Max asked, putting his head on a cushion and watching the Dark Man closely. For a long time, Boris was silent, and only gazed out at the glittering constellations.

"At the core of life," he said in a whisper, "is an unknown region that nobody can penetrate except in momentary glimpses. This region decides the fate of every man, woman, and child. The Vanishings are an illness of that region."

Max felt his eyelids growing heavy. "What kind of illness, though?"

The Dark Man gestured out at the stars. "All cosmic bodies in the universe are drifting apart. The galaxies are separating and growing more distant from one another. Maybe in some kind of sympathy with the expansion of the cosmos, people themselves are drifting farther and farther apart. The forces that hold them together are getting weaker and the forces that drive them apart are growing stronger."

"So what do we do?" Max asked.

"We have to hold on," said Boris. "To each other. More tightly than ever."

He stood up and covered the window, then looked down at Max. "Now get some sleep," he said quietly. "You'll need it."

"Okay," said Max. "Good night, Boris."

"Good night."

Max lay there, rocked in the gentle swaying of the Balloon, the orbs of Old Light rolling slowly across the floor, the Dark Man's words rolling slowly across his mind, back and forth, back and forth . . .

People were drifting farther apart . . .

Like we did . . .

Like what happened . . . to the Mulgans and me . . .

FIRE

When he woke, Boris was back at the window, smoking another cigarette. Flexing his aching neck, Max joined him and looked out.

They seemed not to have moved—the Woods slid below just as it had the evening before. The only difference was a building rising out of the trees, a tall structure like a light-house with a balcony running around the top. A naked figure was there facing them—another of the Wind Giants. The distant clanging of a bell rang out and the Giant began to swell.

WHOOSH!

A Wind came around them, moving the Balloon in a new direction. Slowly, the trees rotated and a city edged into view.

"The Eiffel Tower . . ." Max murmured. "It's here, too."

"It wouldn't be Paris without it," said Boris. "In the Woods, it's the main Wind Control Tower for the region."

The loops of the Seine sparkled in the morning light as they drew nearer. Soon they were drifting over the rooftops, sinking lower. Like London, the streets were bustling with people. None of them paid much attention to the gigantic Balloon sweeping down upon them.

"Paris is a headquarters for various factions in the Beginning Woods," Boris said. He leaned out of the window and pointed down. "The Trocadéro, what we know as the ISPCV, is occupied in the Woods by Witches and Wizards—the Coven. That's where they keep the Patents for all their inventions, in the Archives."

Max had seen the ISPCV many times on the news, but this building was different. It looked less modern, more like a cathedral with two tall towers on either side.

"It's not the same as the one in the World."

"The Trocadéro in the World was demolished and rebuilt in 1937," Boris explained. "The one you can see here is the original."

"How come the World and the Woods are so similar?"

"Nobody knows," said Boris. "It's always been like this. They are like reflections of each other."

"What's that building there?" Max pointed to one of the many grand old buildings below. They seemed to be headed right for it.

"That's where we're landing, the courtyard of the Louvre. The palace you can see on the western edge is the Palais des

Tuileries. It was burned to the ground in the World by the Paris Commune in the nineteenth century."

"But it's okay here?"

"Oh, yes. In fact, it's the headquarters of the Dragon Hunters. They'll all be there now getting ready for Eisteddfod with the Chief Dragon Hunter, Roland Danann. It's the only time in the year when they gather in one place. Otherwise, they roam the Woods alone."

The Balloon sank toward the courtyard, guided by the gentle nudges of the Wind. Sandbags lowered on long ropes were caught by a group of workers. They attached the ropes to a cart, then whipped at teams of horses, which slowly dragged the Balloon toward its docking station.

Once the Balloon was secured and the ramp lowered, the passengers disembarked. Max and Boris rejoined Mrs. Jeffers outside. The old Wizard was in a foul mood, and had been since the news about the electricity at Gilead.

"Sleep well?" she asked curtly. "Let's get some breakfast. I know a café that does excellent crêpes. It's a bit of a walk, but I like to stretch my legs after a Balloon!"

They came out of the courtyard into a wide boulevard teeming with activity. A tremendous thundering rose around them as cartwheels and hooves rattled over the frozen ground—but the noise from the throngs of people crowding the pavement was even greater.

"They're on their way to the Eisteddfod opening ceremony," Mrs. Jeffers said. "I have no idea why, as it's a total bore. There's a tedious procession and some interminable speeches from the city guilds. We'll go along later for the important part—when the Dragon Hunters register the entrants. But that's not until this afternoon."

Elbows raised, she forged a way through the crowd, and after a tight squeeze they popped out onto the road. Without stopping for a moment, she dodged around the wagons, carts, and horses. On the other side, the going was easier, the streets almost deserted. After a short walk, they reached a steep hill that rose from the north bank of the river.

The café was on a pleasant corner about halfway up. The solitary waiter, glad of the business, bustled them inside with sweeping movements of his arms and proudly seated them by tall windows that gave a grand view of Paris. In moments, he had brought coffee and hot chocolate, lemons and sugar, and then he set about producing a rapid succession of crêpes from a tableside stove on wheels, sliding them straight from the pan, hot and crisp, onto their plates.

As they ate, Boris and Mrs. Jeffers argued about the electricity at Gilead and what that meant. Only half-listening, Max stared out of the windows at the cityscape. The Eiffel Tower stood in the middle of it all like a strange metal plant. Near its base, he could just make out the crowds moving up to the headquarters of the Dragon Hunters. In the distance, a Hot-Air Balloon floated toward the horizon, peaceful and still. Even farther off, but coming steadily nearer, there was a kind of black cloud, something like a dense flock of birds.

Geese maybe, Max thought. *How funny—just like my dream . . .*

He sipped his hot chocolate and waited for the cloud to collide with the Balloon, which it really looked like doing at any moment. But soon he saw they couldn't be geese, or any kind of bird. They were much too large. And now, they were spreading out in a kind of fan. One of the dark shapes split off from the others and glided nearer the Hot-Air Balloon. A speck of red engulfed the Balloon, and it disappeared, leaving a tiny curl of black smoke in the bright blue sky.

Max stood up.

Boris and Mrs. Jeffers stared at him in surprise, and followed his gaze. Then they stood up, too.

The waiter left the café and stood on the pavement, looking out over the city, shielding his eyes with a menu.

Now, the black dots were swooping low over the city. Red blobs appeared on the rooftops behind them. Columns of smoke began trickling into the air. There was not a sound and the dots seemed to be moving very slowly.

Outside, a sudden rush of air swept down the street. The waiter staggered sideways, trying to keep his balance. The menu was snatched out of his hand and went spinning away. A shadow settled over everything, like a cloud was blocking the sun.

The waiter spun around, looking up at the rooftops.

And then it was snowing—great big black flakes of snow. One slapped against the glass.

Rotting leaves . . .

A rattling hail of pebbles and stones . . .

Boris flung the table against the window and yanked Mrs. Jeffers and Max down behind it.

Everything exploded.

Max blinked and moaned.

He was lying face-down on the floor.

Something heavy was squashing him flat, pressing down on him, making it hard to breathe. He couldn't see anything except a cloudy kind of whiteness. It was a tablecloth, he realized. Covering his head.

"Get off . . ." he mumbled.

He pressed his palms into the floor and pushed up against the weight. A table crashed to one side, and he woozily got to his feet, fighting free of the tablecloth, then coughing as his lungs filled with smoke.

The café looked as if someone had tipped a bonfire in through the window. Tables and chairs were toppled at crazy angles. Napkins lay smoldering and burning. Red-hot embers were scattered across the floor. He pressed his sleeve against his mouth, and looked around, his eyes watering.

There!

Boris was slumped on his side against a wall, his clothes spotted with glowing splinters. He'd been knocked out. Max staggered over. Swiped away the embers. Tried to wake him.

The Dark Man did not respond.

Max glanced around. The fires inside the café were spreading. He had to get Boris outside.

He grabbed him under the arms and tried to haul him toward the door. He managed only a few feet, then collapsed. He remembered Mrs. Jeffers and called out for her. His voice rasped painfully, barely more than a hoarse whisper. There was too much smoke to see.

He tried moving the Dark Man again, dragging him across the floor, kicking chairs out of the way. He got almost as far as the door.

Just then, an ear-splitting roar shook the building.

It's still outside.

I know.

Are you going to do it?

Do what?

You know what.

I have to make sure Boris is okay.

Gasping with effort, he hauled Boris through the doorway and onto the steps. Smoke was curling out the top part of the door, but low down the air was clean.

He'll be fine here. What about Mrs. Jeffers?

I couldn't see her.

Maybe she got out.

Max didn't see her outside, either.

All he saw was a street scorched black with soot, and drifts of burning embers piled up in doorways. Shop awnings hung in charred skeletons, and fires were blazing in every window.

And above them . . .

On the rooftops . . .

It looked like a forest at first, like it had all just grown there among the chimneypots.

Then the Dragon moved.

Its long body was still encrusted in its earthen mantle. As it crawled along the roof, a deluge of mud, leaves, bricks, and tiles rained down. Only the head had shaken free of its crust. Its eyes were mad with fury, and glowing splinters were tumbling from its crocodile jaws.

Max, you can do it now! This is your chance!

But you're still inside. What if it doesn't work?

Don't worry about me. Just go!

He hesitated in the doorway. The Dragon hadn't seen him. But . . . she was right. He could find out everything he wanted. He could find out the truth. He just had to run into the middle of the street—the Dragon would do the rest. Four steps. That would be enough.

Four steps and it would all be over.

He stepped back.

Max, I know you're scared. But I know you really want to do this, too! And I'm sure Porterholse was right! I'm sure you can stand in the Dragon Fire!

It isn't possible! Look at the street! Look at what it did! Nobody could survive that!

You can, Max. YOU can.

Then order me to.

What?

Order me. Let's . . . play the game. Like it's a game. Like it's just pretend.

I order you to, brave Knight!

Yes . . . my Queen.

You have nothing to fear!

I have nothing to fear . . .

Knights always win against Dragons!

That was true! They did!

He took one step out from the doorway.

Then another.

When he took the third, the Dragon saw him.

Down it came off the rooftops, moving headfirst like a lizard on a wall.

The Dragon comes, my Knight!

I will keep you safe, my Queen.

Then charge!

He held his breath, and mounted his horse, and lowered his lance, and rode out into the street.

The Dragon roared and threw back its head.

Its mouth fell open, fire dripping from its jaws.

Goodbye, Max!

Goodbye! Wait—what? What do you mean goodbye?

You know. Just in case.

JUST IN CASE?? You weren't very "just in case" a second ago!

BONK!

A cobblestone bounced off the Dragon's head.

"HEY!"

Another stone hit the Dragon, hard. Its mouth snapped shut. It swung sharply to one side.

The Dark Man was there, standing right in the middle of the street.

What's he DOING?

I don't know!

Is he crazy? He's going to get himself killed!

Now Boris was pulling off his jacket. He began sweeping it over his head, back and forth, with big movements.

He's trying to distract it!

From what?

From you?

No—look!

Mrs. Jeffers!

The tiny, shrunken old Wizard was creeping through the broken window of the café. As the Dragon surged past her, she reached up and drew the long silver bodkin from her hair.

What's she going to do with that thing?

But whatever it was, the old woman was too slow.

There was a deep groaning sound.

The Dragon's body gave a great convulsion all along its length.

The Dark Man turned his back and flung his jacket over his head—then disappeared in a blast of black smoke and red sparks.

"BORIS!" Max screamed. "NO!"

The smoke billowed outward, filling the street with its choking fumes. Max ran at once straight into it, but the ferocious heat drove him back.

Then Mrs. Jeffers was moving.

Leaping in front of the Dragon, she sent her bodkin spinning upward with a snap of her wrist. Up it went, up into the sky, where it met the cold brightness of a winter sunbeam, and threw off a glancing scythe of Old Light that turned and flashed down in a shimmering bolt.

CRUNCH!

With shocking suddenness, the Dragon's head was pinned to the road. Its long body spasmed and thrashed, slamming into buildings. Its claws gouged furrows in the cobbles. Then the creature shuddered and went still.

Silence.

And then Boris was there, staggering out of the smoke, his clothes scorched from top to bottom, and his face black with soot.

"WHAT TOOK YOU SO LONG?" he roared, spinning toward Mrs. Jeffers.

"Revenge for the chandelier, Doctor Peshkov," she shot back. "Besides, I saw the Dragon had used up all its fire. You were never in any real danger."

She broke off suddenly and glanced sharply at the Dragon, her eyes narrowing. Boris turned toward it as well.

It was definitely dead, there was no doubt about it. So . . . why was it making that strange noise?

click click click click click click

whirrrrrrrrrrr

click click click

It sounded like some sort of machine.

Boris moved closer to the creature's enormous head and bent down to listen.

"It's coming from its mouth," he said. "Max, help me here!"

Boris squatted down, and got his shoulder under the heavy fold of the Dragon's upper lip. Max took hold of it, too. Together, they forced the slimy flap upward.

click click click click click click

whirrrrrrrrrrr

click click click

"What in the Woods!" Mrs. Jeffers exclaimed, her face turning white with outrage.

A metal scaffolding covered the Dragon's gums. Razor-sharp needles were darting in and out of the pink flesh, pricking it over and over again.

click click click click click click

whirrrrrrrrrrrr

click click click

"Boris," Max said faintly. "Mrs. Jeffers."

"What is it?" the Dark Man asked.

He pointed.

In the distance, a flight of Dragons circled a roiling cloud of smoke near the Eiffel Tower. Now and again, one swooped into the black cloud, which glowed red from within as the Dragon unleashed its fiery deluge.

"That's impossible!" whispered Boris. "They're working together. They're intelligent. But the smoke . . . I can't see which . . ."

"It's the Palais des Tuileries," Mrs. Jeffers muttered darkly.

"The Dragons are going after the Dragon Hunters!"

6

Corporation Cooperation

The dissecting table in the main lecture hall of the Coven was a slab of granite that had long ago lost its original coloring and was stained iodine-brown and acid-white. Trickles of blood and other ichorous liquids were draining from the many arteries and tubes that dangled loosely from the Dragon's severed head, which lay like a hunting trophy on the table. The precious fluids ran along chiseled indentations in the table surface, dripping into dangling copper pots that were periodically unhooked and carried away by attendants for study in the Coven laboratories. Still, some managed to get onto the tiled floor and was washed toward a drain by a sullen man operating a hand-pump.

The Dragon's mouth was held open to its fullest extent by a series of hooks and cranes. Its eyes glared vengefully at the audience of Witches and Wizards, as though it might at any moment disgorge the blazing rubble of its stomach, even though they had all just come from viewing the body, which was in the adjacent chamber undergoing a simultaneous dissection. This effect of the Dragon still being alive was enhanced by the machine in its mouth, which was still clicking and whirring a full day after the attack on the Tuileries.

Boris and the Chief Patent Officer of the Coven were in the process of detaching the apparatus from the Dragon's jaw. They soon located two large pins at the back of the Dragon's mouth, drilled into sockets made vacant by the removal of a molar from each side. Once these pins were removed, the mechanism came free in one piece. Grunting slightly, Boris placed it on the floor in front of the audience. A murmur of fascination rippled through the auditorium, as all the Witches and Wizards craned their necks to get a better look.

"Never seen anything like it!"

"It's from the World, it has to be."

"It's not electrical, though?"

"Some kind of clockwork by the looks of it."

Boris slid his hands into the machine and tweaked something—the clicking stopped. A sigh of relief went around the chamber, as though a bomb had just been defused. Several hands were raised, and there was a request for Boris to give his opinion.

"It's not good," he said. "Not good at all. As you've probably guessed, the material is some kind of lightweight steel alloy not found in the Woods. The terraces of pins are driven continuously into the Dragon's gums, putting it into a permanent state of rage. It should be obvious that this mechanism is designed to closely mimic the gum torture of the Dragon Hunters, and it seems beyond doubt all the Dragons involved in yesterday's attacks were fitted with identical machines. This hardly accounts for their behavior, which was coordinated and deliberate—most un-Dragon-like. My first reaction was that they had acquired intelligence. This seems unlikely—the first act of an intelligent Dragon might be vengeance, but would not be self-torture. In any case, they could certainly not have constructed these machines, and I now believe they were under the control of the agency who did. Let me be clear: this was a deliberate attack, planned and carried out by an intelligence that has not yet presented itself."

There was a shocked silence. Then, up and down the chamber, from floor to ceiling, everyone stood up and began talking at once.

It had been confirmed that morning: the Dragon Hunters had been wiped out. Trapped inside the Palais des Tuileries, they had died not in the Dragon Fire but in the inferno of the building itself. Only the Chief Dragon Hunter, Roland Danann, had survived, and few expected him to live long.

It was up to the Coven to determine a course of action. The Chief Wizard, Professor Theodore Mommsen, hammered on the arm of his chair to quiet the excited voices, and when this had been achieved, he stood up and moved forward. He was a hunched, skinny old fellow. His face and hands were pitted and stained with chemical burns, with the drip of alkali and acid, and his long fingernails were cracked and brown as his teeth, which showed easily behind his thin lips. He looked as though he'd spent every year of his long existence flinging chemicals into jars, overseeing detonations, and greedily inhaling noxious fumes through his nose.

Max had learned all about the careers of the main Witches and Wizards from Mrs. Jeffers. Mommsen had invented many things to do with Water, and though it had been years since his last Patent he was still revered for altering Water to expand when it froze, thereby floating on its own liquid, sparing the lives of the fish that had hitherto been crushed under descending ceilings of ice each winter, and altering at a stroke the occupation of fishermen, whose original job had been to rescue as many fish as possible and store them in great tanks until warmer days returned.

He was joined by the High Witch, Doctor Ulla Andromeda, a small, clever-looking woman in scruffy World clothes—jeans, a cardigan, and sneakers—which signified, Mrs. Jeffers had whispered to Max, her contempt for those afraid of the World. She did not look much older than a teenager, and she fiddled constantly with the hem of her cardigan, which reached almost down to her knees. Her narrow, pinched face watched the Chief Wizard with a slightly mocking expression.

"In the Great History of All That Is," Mommsen began, "there have been times when the difference between the Woods and the World was hard to make out. In those Mingling Days, men and women from the World made their way happily through the Woods, thinking they were in the World, and those of us in the Woods could now and again find ourselves in the World, without noticing much change.

"Since the Rise of Science, those days have ended. The World and the Woods have drifted apart. How can we forget the nineteenth century and the minds that completed the long process of separation? Those mighty Tinkers—Tesla, Edison, Faraday, and a hundred others, our great counterparts—banished the Forest Folk and the Woods forever to the outer regions of thought, and set the World off along its own Path, with New Light in their lanterns. I must confess, dear colleagues, I long wondered if it was all up with the Woods and the World. We in the Woods would be forgotten, I told myself, needed no more nor wanted, become nothing more than the dreams that children have, while the World went on, ever more practical, ever more industrial, ever more technological, ever more World-ish than ever. Happily ever after. Electronically ever after. Robotically ever after. Scientifically ever after. Without stories, without whimsy or dream, only Knowledge and Reason and *click click whirr*! So

I thought it would be. But then, dear colleagues, just when I thought the last tiny threads linking the Woods and the World had been severed: BANG!"

He brought his hand down on the surface of the dissecting table with a crash, and everyone jumped.

"BANG!" he said again. "The Vanishings! Whimsical, paradoxical, and poetical—scientifically IMPOSSIBLE! Here, I thought, is something that does not click and whirr. Here, I thought, is something of the Woods—in the World. And now we find a mystery from the World—in the Woods. A mechanical mystery that clicks and whirrs, while in Gilead Forest Folk meddle with electrical light without fear of Bio-Photonic Disintegration.

"There can be no doubt about it: the Woods and the World have drifted close again. Not in the proper fashion, which is gradually, over the centuries, allowing us to grow accustomed to the change, and indeed, barely notice it. No—this time the Woods and the World came together in an instant. In a single moment. And it happened, esteemed colleagues, in a place where the Woods still had one last outpost." His voice sank to a whisper. "It happened in a bookshop."

Max found himself at the end of Mommsen's finger.

"This boy Appeared out of nowhere. And from that day on, the Woods and the World have been thrown together with disastrous consequences. Thrown together, so that instead of influencing each other, instead of communicating in the unconscious manner of twins, they are becoming confused, they are intermingling and corrupting, they are struggling, perhaps, for supremacy. The Woods and the World are tangled and must be pulled apart. But how? That is the challenge now facing us."

He left his audience with that question unresolved, and returned to his chair. Looking up and around, Max saw many troubled faces. This news that the Woods and the World had suddenly crashed together with such violence had clearly shaken the Coven.

It was the High Witch's turn to speak. According to Mrs. Jeffers, she'd been responsible for introducing Bad Habits to the Woods. She'd started with Nose Picking, and had gone on to Knuckle Cracking, Neck Snapping, Nail Biting, Scab Nibbling, Throat Clearing, Booger Rolling, Leg Jiggling, Pimple Popping, Toe Clicking, Mouth Breathing, and Teeth Clenching. Despite being in the grip of all these habits himself, Mommsen touched her elbow fondly and whispered something in her ear as she took the stage.

"What's, then, to be done?" she began in a quiet voice, standing still and thoughtful, speaking in a plain tone just as if she were thinking aloud.

"To answer this question, we must first be clear about Who We Are. For humans that has always been a vexed question. For Witches and Wizards there is no such difficulty. We had no childhood and no parents. We came into being complete and fully developed. We do not change over the years. We are the inert gases of the Woods that do not alter in the presence of other elements. We are fixed, because our job is fixed. And what is our job?

"We add ingredients to the potion.

"We invent the good, we invent the bad.

"And we mix it in.

"We create compounds, not elements. Mixtures, not essences. We are making a potion, and what is a potion except something that bubbles and boils—a brew that is partially alive? That life, that bubbling and boiling, is what we seek to maintain. But the only way for the bubbling to take place is to introduce ingredients that antagonize each other.

"Hence the good.

"Hence the bad.

"That is our sole responsibility. We know who we are and we know what we must do. We are fortunate it is so clear. There are those for whom the answer is more difficult to make out."

Her eyes were expressionless as she looked at Max. He stiffened—he already sensed what she was about to say.

"A boy Appears, and the Woods and the World are brought together. To untangle them, the process that caused the Appearance must be understood, and if possible, reversed. The boy planned to enter Eisteddfod and confront a Dragon to learn his story. This confrontation must still take place.

"The boy must find out who he is, and where he came from.

"The boy must be brought before the Dragon Hunter."

The Truth and the Tooth

Are you still scared?

A little. Actually . . . I'm more annoyed.

You did it back then, though! I mean, the Dragon didn't have any fire left, but you couldn't have known that. It'll be easier next time.

That's why I'm annoyed. There's a next time. I did it once. Now I have to do it again.

The first time is the hardest time!

I'm not so sure.

Why not?

It was all so sudden. It just happened. Now I have to find a Dragon and make it angry. Maybe I'll be okay in the fire. But okay if it tries to bite me in half? Or rolls over me? I don't think the 'prophecy' said anything about being squashed. How am I even going to find one? There aren't any Dragon Hunters left.

There's this one.

He's no use. Weren't you listening?

Just because I'm inside you, doesn't mean I'm permanently focused on every tiny detail of your life.

He can't help. He's too badly injured.

What about Boris? Can he go with you?

I hope so! I'll ask him when he gets back from Paris.

We're in Paris.

I mean Paris in the World. He's gone back to do some nosing around. Anyway, it's still me that has to stand in the fire.

You don't believe what the Soul Searcher saw, do you?

I don't know. But I was thinking about that. The Soul Searchers look inside people, right?

Yes. That's what Porterholse said, at least.

So can't you have a poke around in there? See if you can find something about it, too?

I don't know, Max. I don't think it works like that. Everything in here is . . . actually, I don't know how to describe it. Messy.

Messy? How am I messy?

Don't get all offended. I'll see what I can find.

Okay. Thanks.

"Max! This is it. We're here."

He blinked and focused outward. "Sorry Mrs. Jeffers, I was . . . thinking about something."

"This isn't the time for dreaming. You need to listen to this man. He's the last Dragon Hunter we've got left."

Max glanced apprehensively at the large wooden door Mrs. Jeffers was opening. Behind it was a *dying man*. He'd never seen a *dying man* before.

"You're not coming in with me?"

"No. He insisted on meeting you alone."

"Alone? Why?"

"He's a Dragon Hunter," Mrs. Jeffers said. "They don't like large groups."

"Three is a large group?"

"Just quit stalling and get in there. I'll wait for you out-side, in the main courtyard. Come down when you're done."

"Okay."

"In you go, then." She placed a hand on his shoulder, and gave him a little shove. The door closed at his back.

You are SUCH a scaredy-cat.

I'm going in, I'm going!

Yes. An inch at a time.

Aren't you supposed to be busy with something?

For a moment he stood still, allowing his eyes to adjust to the gloom.

They were high up in a tower of the Trocadéro, and it was nighttime. Globes of Old Light, shining dimly, hung from the ceiling like moons. A gowned attendant was stooped over a table nearby, washing her fingers in a bowl. Without looking around, she shook free the water drops and dried her hands on a towel, then quietly left by another door.

A tapestry on the wall.

Heavy curtains with satin folds.

Max studied all this as long as possible, trying to look at IT last—the bed at the far end of the room, where the dying Dragon Hunter lay. He was propped up in a sitting position, one arm in a sling, his legs little more than a bony ripple beneath the sheet. Slowly, Max moved toward him. Once he'd looked at the Dragon Hunter's face, he couldn't look away. It gleamed where ointment had been applied to his burns. A bandage covered his eyes, but when Max sat in the chair by the bed, the Dragon Hunter turned his head toward him.

"So," he said in a soft whisper. "It's YOU!" And he began to chuckle quietly.

What does he mean by that?

Don't ask me. And stop eavesdropping!

"You're the one . . . who started the Vanishings," the Dragon Hunter went on, his voice little more than a dry rustle. "Come on. Tell me. How'd you do it?"

Max bent closer. Even in the slight whisper, the Dragon Hunter's American accent was unmistakable.

"I don't know," he said. "That's what I'm trying to find out."

"You sure you want to be a Dragon Hunter? Sounds more like you ought to be a Wizard or a goddamn Witch, making up stuff like that."

Max wondered if Mrs. Jeffers had explained things properly to the old man.

"I don't want to be a Dragon Hunter," he said. "I just want to find out who I am. They think they can untangle the Woods and the World if I do. And then the Vanishings will stop."

"Who's going to gather stories, if you don't?" The old man frowned, wincing as it cracked his reddened skin. "When something comes along that nobody else can do—and believe me, that doesn't happen every day—when that happens, it's a defining moment in life. Yes, let's call it that. A defining moment. You should—*ackhack*—grab it. With both hands."

He coughed and had to stop a moment. His free hand twisted the bedsheets in pain.

"Listen, kid. I don't have time to do any persuading here. Maybe I can leave that to the Dragon Fire. If you're not going to carry on our work, that's your call. But if you are, you'll need to know a few trade secrets. Things you wouldn't normally know, seeing as you're not even an Apprentice. Some I'll tell you now, so you can go meet your Lizard. The rest I'll tell you when you return. And you got to return, if you survive. Understand?"

"What do you mean, if I survive?" Max asked quickly. "They said I would be safe!"

"No, kid. There's no defense against the Dragon Fire."

"The Soul Searcher . . . He saw . . ."

"They told me that," the Dragon Hunter said. "They're not trying to trick you. They believe it's true. Trust me, it isn't."

"But—"

"Kid, nobody gets a free pass in front of a Dragon. You stand in the fire, you take the same risk as anyone else. Whatever the Soul Searcher saw, it didn't have nothing to do with Dragons. You just got to be brave."

"But . . . it must hurt!"

"Yes, it hurts. It hurts like all getout."

"How did you survive?"

"I don't know . . . nobody knows. I was just like you. I ran away, too. From home. We all do. All the Hunters. We're all—*ackhack*—children from the World. Just kids on the run." He coughed again, his breath tearing in his chest. "Like me, my real name's Joseph Markovitch, I'm from New York. My old man was a construction worker. He was Polish. He had a hand building most of the old city. And my mom was a lot of things. She did whatever she could, but she ran off with some guy when I was only a kid, because my Dad, he had big hands, all day they pounded away, and they didn't stop pounding when they got home. That's why I came here, to the Woods. I don't even remember how I crossed over. It must've been through Central Park. I was always mooching around there. A whole lot of stuff I've forgotten, but listen . . . I still remember what that old Dragon had to say about ME."

He reached out and without even feeling around, he grabbed Max's wrist. Max gasped—the old man's grip was solid as a rock. He was pulled forward off the chair so fast he almost fell across the bed.

"When that fire hits you, it hits you like a freight train. It rips you up and scatters you to the Winds. You'll never be the same. You'll stand there holding onto your toothpick, and sooner or later that Lizard of yours will quit his bucking and rolling and puke up that fire of his the way you want him to. And then—*ackhack*—then you'll see . . . then you'll find out . . . who you really are . . . and it'll be worse than your worst nightmare, by God and all that's Holy it will."

He let go, fell back, and again his whole body contorted in a fit of coughing, his legs twisting under the sheets.

"But you've . . . you've got to—*ackhack*—you've got to see it through. The Dragon Hunters have to keep going. We have to keep yanking those stories out the flames. The World needs them, more than you think. And I'll show you when you're ready, when you're done with your task, what the Storybooks really do, what they're for. Because it's got to be you. You got to take over. You're the next one, the last Dragon Hunter, the one that puts us all back on our feet—and maybe you'll stop the Vanishings, too. Wouldn't that be something? Listen to me now."

Max bent closer. The old man's voice was barely audible.

"First thing's first: you got to find yourself a Lizard. And you got to do it quick. Dragons, see, they're ancient, they're from the earliest days of the Woods, before even the Dabbling Days. That's why they're so precious—there's a fixed number of them. None are born. And none die, except if they're killed. What they do is migrate, back to where they spawned, to Ethiopia, the Danakil Depression, the hottest damn place in the Woods, where life got started. They bury themselves. The force of life . . . the heat . . . it's still there, in the ground. It rejuvenates them. Their migration begins the last Full Moon before the winter solstice. That's seven days from now. After that, they'll all be gone. And it'll be too late."

"Why? What's going to happen?"

"This machine they found in that Dragon's mouth. Someone's out there putting these things in the Dragons. Nobody here can do that, they don't have the know-how. It's someone from the World, and he must be . . . trying to destroy the Woods."

"Destroy the Woods?"

"He's going about it right, that's for sure. It's like . . . he knows us. Knows Dragons. And this New Light. That must be him. He's behind it all. It's all part of the same . . . the same plan. Whatever he's doing, he's already started!"

He gripped Max's arm again and his lips compressed into a hard line. "You'll find this Tinker at Gilead, that's where to look for him. And when you find the Tinker—you'll find a Dragon!"

"And what then?"

"Then you get your story. You find out who you are. How you Appeared. You untangle the Woods and the World! And—*ackhack*—stop the Tinker!"

Max stared at him. "Stop the Tinker?" he whispered.

"I've got something for him," the Dragon Hunter said then. Opening his mouth as wide as possible, he reached in and took hold of one of his teeth. Saliva ran down his chin. He began to work the tooth around, rotating it slowly—it was rotting and dark.

He pulled sharply.

The saliva ran pink.

He dropped the blackened tooth on the blanket, and rolled it around to dry it. Then held it out between finger and thumb.

"This here's for the Tinker. He's so interested in teeth he can have one of mine. Go on, take it!"

Max took the tooth, and put it at once into his pocket. "You want me to give it to the Tinker?"

"Don't call it a giving. Put it in his food. Mix it in with his soup. Stuff it in his bread, the way you give a dog a pill."

"But why?"

"Why? Because he killed my friends. Because I'm too old to get him myself. That's why."

"I can't do this," Max whispered. "It's—"

"You got to do it, kid. You got to! It won't kill him, don't worry about that. It'll lodge in his throat and he'll fall asleep. And then he'll dream. He'll have dreams you don't want to know about. You do that for me, you get me my revenge. Then come back to me, and I'll tell you the rest of what you need to know. But you got to do it quick. Seven days before the Dragons leave. Seven days, I reckon, before I leave, too. Remember, I'm a World One just like you. When we go, we go for good, no hanging around in graveyards for us. So listen, you go fast. Don't you spend time wondering about Whys or Hows. Come back before the Full Moon. Tell me the Tinker's dreaming. Tell me what your Lizard had to say. Then I'll tell you about the Books and the Light—and I'll know I'm not the last of the Dragon Hunters."

PART THREE

THE DRAGON HUNTER

What exactly are the Vanishings?

Some say they are death.

Some say they are mass abductions by the CIA.

I believe they are the last echo of music in the cathedral. A diminuendo. A slowly walked journey to nowhere.

Doctor Boris Peshkov,
Reflections on the Vanishings

1

THE MRS. JEFFERSES

When Max found his way outside Mrs. Jeffers was sitting with the Dark Man on a stone bench at the far side of the courtyard, where steps led down into the boulevards of Paris.

He drew back into an alcove.

He was surprised to see Boris back from the World so soon. Still with his lantern, he was hurriedly explaining something to Mrs. Jeffers, who was staring at him in bewilderment. Max had never seen the Dark Man so agitated.

Why are you spying on your friends?

I'm not spying.

You're crouching in the shadows in a shadowy corner. That's what spies do.

Listen to me a second.

Why should I? You never listen to me.

What? I do so!

You do not. You're not interested in me. You're only interested in yourself.

Like how?

You only care about Hot-Air Balloons and dreams and things. Gravestones aren't meant to get distracted by dreams. They're meant to be all solid and gray and not go charging off all over the place.

Make up your mind. Am I a gravestone or a Knight?

That's another thing. What kind of Knight is scared of Dragons? Knights are supposed to be brave.

Queens are supposed to be kind.

No, they're supposed to be cold as ice so the Knight suffers as much as possible and then, at the last second, they melt and the Knight takes control.

When's the last second going to come?

At the very, very end. Really it will be the absolute end.

Before or after he gets burned alive?

See, you ARE scared!

I'm not scared, I'm just taking the safe option.

What safe option? What do you mean?

Didn't you hear him? The Soul Searcher thing is just a big mistake.

So wait. You're not going to face the Dragon?

No, I'm NOT going to Gilead. I'm NOT facing the Dragon. I'm NOT tracking down a Tinker and messing with his crazy, metal-mouth Dragons! I'm going to the Ocean instead.

You're NOT!

I'm going to the Panthalassa Ocean and I'm going to find my Forever Parents and I need help. You said you would help and I'm asking you to help.

You're going to the SEASIDE, are you CRAZY? What are you going to do? PADDLE and BUILD SANDCASTLES?

It's better than getting buried under three tons of burning SAWDUST!

It's not going to work. You heard the Dragon Hunter. Nobody gets a free pass.

I thought I had a free pass! What happened to my free pass?!

Max—

No! I'm going to follow my dreams. And my dreams tell me my Forever Parents are connected to the Panthalassa Ocean. So that's where I'm going!

I don't understand this "Forever Parents" thing. What does it mean? Where did you get it from?

They're my real parents. The ones I dreamed about.

But that's what I don't understand. How can DREAM parents be REAL parents? Weren't the Mulgans your real parents?

No. They weren't. They were pretend. They hated me and I hated them. Okay?

Everyone has Scorpions and Minotaurs, you know. A Scorpion or two—that's completely normal. It doesn't mean they weren't your parents. I mean, obviously it's best if the Scorpions don't outnumber the Butterflies. That would be bad. But—

How your parents were at Gilead, for five minutes, that's how mine were ALL THE TIME. For YEARS. Imagine what that would be like. I'm glad they've Vanished.

You're GLAD they Vanished?

Yes.

You're actually glad? As in happy glad?

Yes! And THEY probably are, TOO!

But he suddenly wondered at what he had just said.

He *was* glad the Mulgans had Vanished. He'd never said that before. He'd never even thought it, at least not with those exact words.

Once, he'd watched a TV documentary about the Vanishings. The host had been interviewing someone whose brother had Vanished. They were in the man's living room, and as the man talked about his brother and said how much he missed him, he kept glancing down to his left. At the end of the interview the man stood up to show the host around his house, and the camera zoomed out momentarily to reveal what had been distracting him: a slice of Victoria sponge on the coffee table. Forbes had been watching the program, too, and he'd found this hilarious, that the man had been saying how much he missed his Vanished brother and all the while he'd been wanting to get at the rest of his cake.

But Max hadn't found it funny.

Maybe everyone was like that man, he'd thought. They were all talking about how much they missed the Vanished people, but actually, they didn't miss them that much, not really. They still ate Victoria sponge and changed the channel and went out for milk and got angry if someone was being slow in the line at the supermarket, and nothing changed, not really. Everything just continued. And he'd thought that was awful, that you could Vanish and everything would just continue like that. Maybe people cared at first, sure. But there would always come a time when Vanished brothers were less important than half-eaten slices of Victoria sponge. Because, at the end of the day, if the Victoria sponge was there and the brother was not there, then the Victoria sponge would win every time.

But at least the man hadn't been glad his brother had Vanished.

Being glad that someone had Vanished was a hundred times more awful than just eventually preferring the Victoria sponge. And he was very glad the Mulgans had Vanished. Even now, if there was a button he could press that would bring the Mulgans back—he wouldn't press it.

When he thought about it like that he could see that something was wrong somewhere. He should press the button. But he was one hundred percent sure he wouldn't.

I think you probably would.

I'm not sure . . .

You would. You'd probably press it then run away very quickly. But you'd press it.

What makes you so sure?

Well, mostly it's dark down here in the pond. I mean, there's light from the Merry-Go-Round. But mostly it's dark. Just now and again, this sunbeam comes down. I can hold out my hand, and the water is warmer there.

Where does it come from?

You. There's lots of daylight in you. Except it's in boxes. Sooner or later you're going to get tired of holding them shut.

"He's HERE? In the WOODS?"

It was Mrs. Jeffers, her voice snapping out in surprise.

He peeped out from the alcove. She was on her feet, and Boris was talking urgently, one hand on her elbow. Before he was able to finish, she pulled free and strode back toward the entrance. Max drew back into the shadows.

"What about that light?" Mrs. Jeffers asked as they went past. "The one in the window."

"It was just a ruse," said Boris. "He was never up there."

"The fiend!"

They disappeared into the building. Perfect.

The way was clear.

He stepped out from the alcove and headed for the street. He took only a few steps, and then stopped dead.

Mrs. Jeffers was coming up the steps toward him.

Twice.

There were two of her. Walking side by side. Coming right for him. The one on the left even smiled and waved.

He took an uncertain step backward.

Are you doing something to my brain?

Trust me, if I could take control of you, I'd have done it a long time ago. Maybe Boris taught her his separating trick.

I don't think it's something you can teach . . .

He looked from Mrs. Jeffers to Mrs. Jeffers, expecting one to vanish, to be a trick of the light, a momentary hallucination. But they both persisted through that instant of astonishment and came out the other end intact. And then they were standing in front of him, smiling as if there was nothing impossible about their complete impossibility.

"Good evening," said one.

"Good evening," said the other.

The tower of silver hair, the embroidered gown—it was all exactly the same as the Mrs. Jeffers he had seen a moment ago. The only difference was a canvas sack held by the Mrs. Jeffers on the left. "O'LEARY IRISH POTATOES—Spuds You Can Trust," read the logo. She was lifting and opening it at the same time, as if she was about to pull it down over someone's head.

"We're very sorry," said one Mrs. Jeffers.

"We don't mean to do it," said the other Mrs. Jeffers. "Mother told us to."

"Angry Mummies, upset tummies."

"Wha—" Max managed to get out, but no sooner had he opened his mouth than an O'Leary Irish Potato was placed between his teeth. A second later, the world disappeared. His head went down, his feet went up, and he tumbled to the bottom of a hot, scratchy, airless hole. With his face pressed up against the sack's crudely-woven fabric, he saw the pavement flashing past as his captors made off with their prize.

"You said I could do the potato!"

"You were too slow."

"You're the slow one! Get a move on!"

"It keeps banging my ankles!"

"You're not lifting!"

"I am!"

"Then turn! You go first!"

"What?"

"Backwards! Carry it backwards!"

"How's that going to help?"

"Someone's seen us! RUN!"

"They haven't!"

"Why are you stopping?"

"I can't remember where we parked."

"Over there! The corner! Not THAT one the OTHER—"

"Calm down, we're nearly there."

"Get him up! Higher!"

"Open the door first!"

"Ready?"

"Ready!"

"One-two-three-HEAVE!"

Max was dumped on a hard surface and given a shove.

"About time, you chumps!" a woman's voice barked. "Now DRIVE!"

A door slammed. With a whoop of breath, he expelled the O'Leary and roared with all his might:

"Kidnap! Murder! Mayday! S.O.S.!"

The darkness promptly opened.

THWACK!

A hand crashed into the side of his head, stunning him into abrupt silence. He found himself staring down the finger of a grim-faced woman.

"That's for being a tattletale! Now get up off the floor. It's covered in germs."

He was in the cabin of a stagecoach. His head ringing, he slid up onto the cushioned bench opposite the woman—but immediately fell forward as the carriage leapt into motion.

THWACK!

"Stop jumping around and sit still!"

Scowling furiously, he jammed himself into the corner, bracing himself as the carriage pitched from side to side. He couldn't see out—both windows were covered in curtains fastened top and bottom on brass rails.

Door?

He grabbed the handle and shook it.

"Locked," the woman said. "Can you pick locks, Mr. Clever Clogs?" She parted the curtains a crack and peeked out, looking behind.

And then . . . he began to stare at her.

To really look at her closely.

There was something familiar about her. Though she wasn't very old, she gave the impression of *always having been old*, exactly as old as she was now. Definitely she'd never been young, not for a second, not for a single game of hide 'n seek or an afternoon's bike ride. Her black hair was pulled back in a bun so tight it stretched out the skin on her forehead, and her head was spherical but slightly squished, like a bluebottle's, giving a slight bulge to her eyes. She wore a polo-neck sweater with the sleeves rolled up, trousers, and shoes with chunky heels—all of them black. For a coat, she had on one of those green fisherman's vests with many pockets and compartments for hooks and flies and spinners and line.

"I suppose you could always unlatch the windows," she speculated. "But at this speed . . . if you jumped you'd break your neck. SNAP!"

As she spoke, she took a short length of wire from one of her pockets and began twisting it into some kind of miniature structure with Origami Master precision. Mostly, she used her long, clever fingers and teeth, but at one point, she took a tiny pair of pliers out of a pocket and gave the wire an extra-sharp twist.

When it was finished, she raised a fist to her mouth, cleared her throat, and hocked a fat, green bullet of phlegm into her palm. She rolled the gooey slime between her fingers until it hardened into a rubbery pellet, which she used as a kind of booger-clay to flesh out the skeleton. Then she began going through her pockets. From one, she took a Dandelion Head, from another a Black Bead, from another an Inch of Black Wool, from another a Nettle Leaf. All these components, she worked onto the skeleton. Finally, she popped the whole thing into her mouth, rolled it around like a gobstopper, and spat. A thing a little larger than a Wasp buzzed out into the air.

"Go on! Shoo!" she instructed. "See if we're being followed!"

She opened a window and the newly manufactured insect flew off.

Max squeezed himself deeper into the corner.

He knew who it was all right.

It was the Wasp Witch. He'd fallen into her clutches.

The Wasp Witch? You mean she made Wasps?

And lots of other things . . .

She's the one that killed me!

"See what you've stirred up, snooping around Gilead?" the Witch said. "Someone ought to slice your nose off before it gets too long, Mr. Nosey-Parker. I'll do it when we get to my workshop if you like—hey! Quit staring! What's the matter with you?"

"The Woodcutter chopped you up . . ." Max whispered. "Into little bits . . ."

The Witch scowled. "Tittle-tattle! You'd think the Winds had better things to talk about!" She leaned across and jabbed his knee. "You think you can do away with a Witch just by chopping her up? Some Apprentice you are! We're not alive like Parakeets or Hogweed. We're not dead like the Dragon Hunters. We're non-living like Rubies and Iron and Hailstones. We exist. And then we stop existing. We don't have to put up with all that Being Born and Dying hogwash."

"Into little bits though . . ." Max muttered, still hypnotized by this figure from the Storybooks.

The Witch scoffed. "Little bits, big bits, who cares? You keep saying that like it means something. It doesn't mean diddly-squat. If you really want to know, my children, my darlings Kaspar and Hauser, got all my 'little bits,' all my fleshy chunks, slopped them into a tray, and left the tray in the cellar away from the light, where it was nice and warm and moldy . . . and that was all it took! Haha! A bit of warmth and a bit of darkness works wonders on fleshy chunks, you should see what grows!" She burst into a loud guffaw. "And you know what I did to that Woodcutter? You know what I went and did, naughty old me? Bet you don't, Mr. Know-It-All, Mr. Smart-Aleck Big-Brain Hot-Shot Nosey-Parker."

"I don't want to know."

"Yes, you do, all that's nasty and horrid about you wants to know. So I'll tell you. I sent a Weevil to his house. Just one, nothing wrong with that! Weevils have to live, too! And when he was asleep, when his fat old head was lying on the pillow, that Weevil wriggled in through his ear and started nibbling. By morning, he was deaf as a post, and boy oh boy, you should've seen his face when he couldn't hear that Bluebird sing. I was peering in at the window—you should have seen his features drop. And the Weevil didn't stop. It kept right on going, until it got to the good stuff, the juiciness. It's there to this day, plump and happy, nibbling away deeper and deeper and farther and farther and around and around and around. Haha! Nibble nibble nibble! HA HA HA! How's THAT for revenge? Haha!"

The carriage took a corner so fast it tilted dangerously. Max braced himself like the Witch by putting his feet up on the opposite seat.

"That's what gave the World One his idea," she went on. "He heard about my Weevil in The Brain trick and tracked me down. 'I want to control a Dragon,' he said. 'Can it be done?' 'Impossible,' I told him straight off. 'They're too stupid. They're just a bundle of reflexes and instincts.' 'But what if you built something that went in its brain?' he said. 'The Coven wouldn't license it,' I said. 'They don't need to know,' he said. 'It'd be risky,' I said. 'Name your price,' he said. And I did, and he didn't like it, not one little bit did he like it. But he came around in the end. So I went to the market, bought myself the biggest cow I could find, and commenced my experiments. Haha!"

It was her? She sent the Dragons to attack the Dragon Hunters?

She's working for someone. Let me listen!

"These Dragons, he told me, would be spitting full of madness and anger. That was the hardest thing. You try saying to a docile Dragon, 'Go left!' and see what happens. It's not so dramatic! Telling an *angry* Dragon what to do is like giving directions to a thunderstorm. I had to come up with a whole new class of invertebrates: Arachnids! I

went through hundreds before I hit gold. *Trigonotarbida?*
Forget it! *Phalangiotarbida?* Almost! *Phalangium opilio?*
Perfect! The breakthrough was Barleycorn Bristles for legs.
Only Barleycorn Bristles were long enough to slide into the
Dragon's brain. I put a hook from a Burdock Seed on each
leg, so it can give a good, hard yank on the brainy softness at
the right moment. Clever, eh? Dragon or no Dragon, angry
or not, a good hard YANK on the brain won't go unnoticed!
Even then, there were a few runaways, a few that got a little
bit, eh, out of control."

She must mean that Dragon near Marylebone.

I told you they never come out of the Deep Woods!

"Just as well the World One didn't need many! But it was
worth it in the end. The Dragon Hunters—wiped out, or
soon to be! Eisteddfod—cancelled! Only YOU weren't put
off," she said, slapping Max on the knee in a friendly way.
"You're a brave one, I must say. And you're clever, you must
be if you started the Vanishings. I was at the Coven, I heard
it all. How'd you do it, eh? You can tell me, haha!"

Max said nothing and only stared at her. She wasn't going
to get a word out of him. Not a single word.

"Ah!" the Witch went on. "It's a secret! Hoo-hoo! Children
always have dirty little secrets. Well, the World One's going
to be very interested in you. He'll be happier than a Maggot
in an eyeball I snatched you away so quickly."

Who's this World One she keeps going on about?

She must mean the Tinker.

Suddenly, the Witch jumped up and whipped back a communication hatch. Cold air blasted in and Max caught a glimpse of the Mrs. Jefferses, high up on a driver's bench.

"Hey there! Lazybones!" the Witch shouted through. "What's the big delay?"

One of them turned.

"We needed to get a straight piece of road!"

"Get GOING! Full speed ahead! We've got to be in Gilead by morning."

Gilead? She'll never get there in this old thing.

How long will it take?

Four, maybe five days.

But then the Witch sat back and gripped a leather strap hanging down from just above the door.

"HOLD ONTO YOUR HATS!" she roared.

The carriage lurched upward. Bounced. Lurched again.

Max seized the strap above the other door.

His stomach dropped.

A force pressed him back into his seat.

His body felt lighter.

That's . . . gravity!

The rattling of wheels and the clattering of hooves—it all stopped and everything went still. The carriage swayed from side to side, creaking quietly.

"Go on, take a look!" the Witch said. "Jump if you like!"

Glancing at the Witch mistrustfully, Max pulled back the curtain.

Sure enough, they were flying.

The road was already far beneath them, the outskirts of Paris dropping away as they whooshed up into the sky. Pressing his face against the glass, he could just make out the front of the carriage, and the long curl of the whip as it flickered out over the backs of the horses.

Or what used to be horses.

Their legs hanging motionless, they buzzed upward on gigantic insect wings.

"I call it a Horsefly," the Witch drawled complacently. "The *elytra* were the trickiest parts. I had to get the amount of calcium carbonate just right . . ."

Max hardly listened as she boasted about her bio-mechanical skills. Soon they were high above the trees, heading north once more.

He leaned his head against the window and closed his eyes.

He'd thought, when he got to the Woods, it would be simple to catch hold of his dreams. But it was the same as before. They were just out of reach, beyond his fingertips.

Only one thing was different.

Now, there was a Dragon in the way.

MATH

The flight ended with a jerk that sent him crashing into the other side of the stagecoach.

"HeeHAW," brayed the Witch as they rocked wildly from side to side. "Brace yourself, we're coming in for landing! Oh, too late! I was going to wake you, but you looked so ANGELIC!"

Max struggled back to his window. It was morning on an overcast and chilly day. Isolated flakes of snow were drifting down from the sky. They were driving through open fields: that meant a village or town was nearby.

Is this . . . ?

It's Gilead. We're close.

Sure enough, they trundled by a street lamp, a man bent beside it. Work had progressed. Now the bulbs were flickering with a faint pink light.

The Witch whipped the curtain across. "Nothing you haven't seen already, Mr. Stick-Your-Nose-in-Where-It's-Going-To-Get-Chopped-Off."

The carriage rattled to a halt soon afterward. The door opened and the Witch leapt out, locking the door behind her, but not before Max caught a glimpse of a crowd of villagers gathered at the millpond. Some kind of meeting was about to take place.

He waited a moment, then carefully opened the hatch and peeped out. The Witch was clambering onto the driver's bench to deliver a speech to the villagers, who shuffled closer to listen. From his position, he could only make out a few faces. If Martha's parents were there, he couldn't see them.

Are you okay being back here?

No. But thanks for asking.

"Stage One is complete!" the Witch bellowed, thrusting a finger into the air. "The attack was a rip-roaring success! The Dragon Hunters have been wiped out! Their leader is near-as-can-be a goner! In a few days, he'll pop his clogs without a replacement and that'll be the sorry end of the whole sorry lot of them! A distinguished line extinguished. Haha! Best of all: they're onto us, thanks to that snooping snitcher you let escape. The Coven will be on their way in due course."

The villagers muttered among themselves, but did not seem too surprised. Several nodded quietly. Some even seemed pleased that it was all, at long last, about to begin.

"But when they come, we'll be ready. You know our story. You know what to say when they accuse us of meddling with their precious Dragons. They've been terrorizing our valley for months! We had no choice! We had to use New Light to protect ourselves! The World One showed us how—you should listen to him. He knows a thing or two. He's got a plan for those Dragons. You'll see."

"And you're sure they'll be against it?" someone called out.

"It's a one hundred percent certainty! The Coven will never permit New Light in the Woods. And what will the Forest Folk think about that, with Dragons on the rampage? They'll turn against the Coven!"

"Nobody turns against the Coven."

"Oh, I think they will! When they hear what the World One has to say, they'll be with us all the way. You know how persuasive he can be! Then YOU'LL be the Dragon Hunters. Only this time, you'll not be gathering stories—you'll be frying those Lizards with heavy-duty flashlights! And when the normal Dragons come back from migration you'll be able to fry them, too, before anyone notices they're just good old dumb-as-a-doorstop Lizards. Once the Dragons are gone, you can take your axes to as many trees as you like. You'll be able to cut and chop to your heart's content. And wait till you see what happens THEN! When you can build as many mills as you like! As many houses, as many boats, as many barges, as many factories and chimneys and cars and roads and bridges and towns and cities and motorways and quarries and mines and furnaces and forges and power plants! Wait till you see how good life gets! You'll LOVE IT. You can bet your JACKSNAPPERS you'll LOVE IT! But FIRST YOU'VE GOT TO DISPOSE OF THE DRAGONS!"

"Are the other Forest Folk really going to want to kill the Dragons?" asked an old woman near the front. "They don't do anything but burrow around and eat Briarbacks."

"NOT ANYMORE THEY DON'T!" screamed the Witch. "Dragons are *killers*! Dragons are slavering, destroying demon beasts with maiming fangs and a howling intelligence of sinister evil bent on total WARFARE. They destroyed half of Paris! And tonight, we've one lined up for Rosethorn! A Dragon attack at midnight! To catch them in their beds!"

A wave of shock passed through the crowd.

"Rosethorn?"

"Why?"

"They're our neighbors!"

"Come on!" the Witch snapped. "You turned your back on them two harvests ago!"

"But . . . you can't!"

"It's too much!"

"TOUGH! We need proof you've been living in harm's way. *The same thing will happen to you if you don't follow the World One!* That's the line we'll take."

"But more people will die!" called out a woman near the back of the crowd. "It's been enough already!"

The Witch went still. "Enough?" she whispered, so quietly even Max could hardly hear. "Let me tell you this—we're nowhere *near* enough. We're not even close. We're a thousand miles from enough."

"We got to enough when we wiped out the Dragon Hunters," the woman shot back. A few of the villagers nodded in agreement.

"Then let me ask you a little question, dearie: How many children have you had? Eh?"

"I've had six. What of it?"

"Six! Six beautiful little angels! And how many of your most precious little loved ones did you lose?"

Every single face seemed to freeze at this question.

"Two," the woman said.

"How about the rest of you? How many have you all lost? All you poor Mothers? How many darling little angels came and went without even saying 'Mama'?"

Nobody answered. Finally, an old woman said: "Five this year. Nine the year before."

"Just here? Just in this little corner of the Woods? And how many died OVERALL? In the entire Woods, how many? In all the villages here and there, how many do you think? In the cities and towns how many?"

The crowd of villagers shuffled their feet and remained silent. "How many sweet-faced innocents died of disease? How many of infected wounds? How many died of the Bloody Flux and St. Anthony's Fire, Lepry, the Ague, and Measles, of Childbed Fever and Cholera? How many had the Red Plague ten years ago? How many died of Typhoid? How many got lost in the Woods and were never seen again?"

"Too many," the old woman sighed, shaking her head. "Dear bless them, the little angels!"

"Let's do away with the Dear Bless Thems!" snapped the Witch. "Dear Bless Thems never helped anyone! You've lost too many to count! And forgetting for a second about the little angels—as if that were even possible, as if they weren't an ache in your hearts forever—think about YOURSELVES! How many of YOU lead a life of suffering and labor, of back-breaking slog in the fields, a slave to the elements, eating or starving on a whim of the clouds, relying on the meager patch of land the Dragon Hunters have allowed you to take from the trees?"

"Every one of us."

"And NOW you're talking about ENOUGH?" the Witch exploded. "You should be saying enough, all right. YOU SHOULD WELL BE SAYING ENOUGH! Enough to the Dragon Hunters with their wild stories, who stop you chopping the wood you need, or taking the land when it's there to be had! Enough to the Coven who oversee this morass of stupidity! Enough to the suffering and death and horror every year for years and years until THE COWS COME HOME because the World Ones need a BEDTIME STORY for their aching little souls! And how to get out of it? How to get clear of this disgusting rut? A few deaths, a hundred, two hundred, sure—Boo-hoo!—and then you have improvement and progress, comfort and cure. You have control of creation! You'll ALL be World Ones then. You tell me that's not better! You tell me someone who refuses to kill a hundred to save a million isn't a MURDERER who should be locked up in a dungeon infested with RATS and COCKROACHES and FLESH-GUZZLING MAGGOTS! Morality has NOTHING to do with it," she finished. "It's math! Math, math, math!"

This final argument seemed to win over the villagers.

"Well I'm no murderer, so she must be right."

"We've come this far. May as well finish the job."

"We've just got to remember the numbers."

"Plough the soil, then sow the seed!"

The Witch sprang down from the bench and Max slid the hatch shut. Outside, the Witch gave one last flurry of commands.

"I want to see this place lit up like Christmas by nightfall! Prepare the torches. Fire up the generators. Now, hop to it!"

The carriage was moving again almost before she'd climbed back in. Max sat staring straight ahead, pretending to have heard nothing.

I know what you're thinking. But I can't.

You have to try. You can't just let them all die. They're families, Max!

Even if I could escape, how do I have any chance of stopping a Dragon?

You can warn them, at least!

It's too far. You said it was a day's travel, and the attack's at midnight.

You're not even going to TRY?

If I escape now, I might not find the Tinker. She's going to take me to him. Then I can give him the tooth.

So you're going to do the only part that's EASY and avoid everything else?

No, I'm going to do this FIRST, and then the OTHER THING.

By then it'll be too late!

Maybe if we stay with her, we can stop her. She must be the one who controls the Dragons.

Maybe MAYBE! You're just SCARED! You're not a KNIGHT at all.

That's right, I'm not. I'm just a boy! They must have lots of boys in that Rosethorn place. There's probably a gang. Let the gang deal with the Dragon.

You're just a COWARD and I HATE YOU!

Oh, go and stare at your Scorpions. Or whatever it is you do.

A FAMILY QUARREL

By the time the stagecoach rattled to a halt, the fighting had been replaced by tense, inner whispering.

We're on Mount Gilead somewhere.

How do you know?

We've been going up, and the air is colder. What time is it?

I guess about noon.

The Witch clambered out, the Mrs. Jefferses clambered in, and Max was reinserted ("There! There!" "Now! Now!") into the sack.

"Come on!" the Witch ordered. "We'll lock him in the workshop!"

"We never did the potato!"

"It's my turn!"

"You're no good at it!"

THWACK!

THWACK!

"Forget the potato. We're miles from anywhere. Now, hop to it!"

Max felt himself being carried again. Footsteps crunched on snow and voices hissed at each other.

"That was your fault."

"You said about the potato."

"We won't get dinner now!"

"You're not lifting again!"

"I am so!"

"You have to turn! We can't get him in sideways."

"Then you have to go backwards!"

"Why should I go backwards? You go backwards!"

"I went backwards last time."

"I can't hold him. He's slipping!"

"The corner! Into the corner!"

"Hold him down!" the Witch instructed. "I'll fasten the chain."

Max was pinned against the floor. A hand reached into the sack, seized his ankle, and locked something heavy around it.

"Got him!"

The hands let go. The sack came off. Max sat red-faced and furious. A chain had been padlocked to his ankle. The other end was welded to the leg of a pot-bellied stove.

You should have escaped when you had the chance! Now you'll never get out.

He looked around. Where was he now?

In the Witch's workshop.

The hub of her manufacturing operations.

A chipped stone table stood in the center of the room, with bunches of tools hanging from its edges on hooks—hammers, tongs, pliers, saws, files, drills, screwdrivers, and knives. All the tools were tiny, as if they had been magically shrunk to a fraction of their normal size. In another corner was a crate with a hinged lid, something like a toy box, with a few ragged blankets folded over the sides. But the most unusual feature of the workshop was the enormous collection of jars. They were stacked floor to ceiling against every wall, each meticulously labelled.

CHITIN
ARTICULATED CLAWS
HOCKED SNOT
PIPE CLEANERS
SPLINTERS
GANGLIONS
RANCID BUTTER
SAWDUST
GLASS BEADS
MANDIBLES
TURPENTINE
MALPIGHIAN TUBULES
GOLD
ELEPHANT VOMIT

All these shelves and jars were festooned in cobwebs. Here and there spiders could be seen trickling down on gossamer threads.

"Get this cleaned up," the Witch snarled. "I don't want a single WHICH ONE'S WHICH until the whole place is spic-and-span."

"What about him?"

"Isn't he going to help?"

"No. He's a Vanishing Mastermind. There's no telling what he could do. Now, get to it. I'm going to take a nap. It's going to be a busy night!" With that, the Witch disappeared through a second door that led, Max guessed, into her cottage.

For the rest of the afternoon the Mrs. Jefferses bent to their task.

First, they snagged the cobwebs down with brooms and laid them out flat on the workbench. Then they retrieved dead flies from the cobwebs, picking the bodies apart with tweezers, salvaging legs and wings and compound eyes for later use, and storing them, along with the cleaned cobwebs, in bottles.

Max made several secret attempts to loosen the chain.

Nothing worked.

He tried to trick the twins into unlocking him. He complained he was hungry. They brought him shriveled apples.

Thirsty?

Some water.

The bathroom?

A bucket in a corner.

The shadows lengthened as the sun set.

There was no sign or word of the Tinker.

Inside, Martha was frantic.

You have to get to Rosethorn! We're running out of time!

HOW? Tell me how and I'll do it!

At long last, the Witch returned—but only to inspect the work.

"Not bad, not bad," she said, running a finger along the surfaces. "Keep an eye on Fish Face while I make dinner."

She left.

Her parting remark delighted the Mrs. Jefferses. Name-calling, cruelty, and bullying—nothing was better! They began prodding Max with broom handles.

"Fish Face FISH FACE!"

"Fish Face FISH FACE!"

"At least I've got my own face!" he growled, whacking them away with his hands. "I don't have to copy anyone else's."

This only delighted them even more. They exchanged sly, cunning glances.

"You've got your own face?"

"Is that right?"

"We'll see about that."

Max stared at them. "Don't you dare!" he whispered.

But they had already started. Joining hands, the Mrs. Jefferses began to dance, capering around and around, throwing their heads back and laughing.

He ran at them, snarling. The chain snapped him back. Around and around they went.

"Who are we?" they sang as they danced. "Who are we?"

Who are we?

Who are we?

Let us see!

Let us see!

You and me!

You and me!

Who are we?

Who are we?

Around and around . . .

And around and around and around and around . . . aroundandaroundandaroundandaroundandandaroundand around . . .

And then they jumped up a gear, disappearing in a blur of color.

FFWWWWWWZZZZZZZZZZZZZZZ . . .

But this moment of maximum velocity lasted only a second.

The spinning slowed. The colors came apart.

Two shapes became distinct.

Two Max-shaped shapes, holding hands, dancing around and around.

This is us!

This is us!

What a fuss!
What a fuss!
One of us!
Two of us!
This is us!
This is us!
Just remember—you're the You with the Me in the finger.
Is that what I look like on the outside?
Yes. Sort of cute in a not-enough-sunlight kind of way.
The Maxes came to a stop.
Unlinked their hands.
Turned to face him.
"What do you say now?"
"Got your own face, have you?"
"That's my Me," Max said. "Get your own You back."
"We can't."
"We don't know who we are."
"Yes," said Max, "you do."
"No, we don't."
"We've never known."
"You know inside. You don't need anyone to tell you."
"Oh?"
"Do you know who you are?"
"No. But that's . . . that's different."
"See—you don't know who you are, either."
"You don't have a Mother. We can tell."

"Only Mothers can tell you who you are."

"There's no use trying to know things on your own."

"Sometimes we think we know without her, it's true."

"When we wake up and the sun is shining."

"And the insects are singing."

"And Mother's still asleep."

"And the box is all warm and cozy."

"Then he says he's Kaspar."

"And he says he's Hauser."

"And it feels right."

"It feels perfect!"

"And we rush to wake up Mother!"

"And we tell her we've finally got it!"

"And she sniffs our breath and tells us we're each other."

"And then she gives us what for."

"Because we woke her up."

"She pretends she knows! She just takes whatever you say and switches it around."

"Why would she do that?"

"She loves us."

"If she did that, she wouldn't love us."

"If she loves you so much, why's she always hitting you and calling you names?"

"Because we're bad."

"We're naughty."

"We pick our noses."

"It's disgusting, but we do it."

"But she's not even your real Mother! It's all a big lie! She stole you from your real parents just after you were born!"

"That's silly."

"She's our Mother. She ate our Father. She told us she'd eat us, too, if we're bad!"

"But you've got another Mother!"

"What's the good of another Mother?"

"Our Mother's right here."

"She's the only Mother we need."

"What do other Mothers do?"

"Do they feed you?"

"Or teach you?"

"Or tuck you in?"

"Or lock the monsters out?"

"Or give you a comfortable box to sleep in?"

"What's it like when other Mothers love you?"

"I . . . I don't know. I never had any parents. I mean, I did—but they weren't my real parents."

"You had parents but they weren't your real parents?"

"Yes . . ."

"That doesn't make sense."

"It does . . . it does make sense."

"You're the one who's confused."

"Our Mother loves us!"

"You can't tell us she doesn't!"

"You're the one who doesn't know who you are."

"You don't know what it's like to be loved!"

"THAT'S WHY I'M TRYING TO FIND MY FOREVER PARENTS!" Max screamed. "Because I DIDN'T! I NEVER KNEW!"

He felt a dizzying surge—then Martha was there, hands on her hips, confronting the astonished twins.

"I know what it's like to be loved!" she said. "My parents loved me when I was alive and now they don't, but they loved me when I was alive, and I remember so I know. And I know they loved me because when I went to bed, I used to be scared of the dark and so Mommy would come in and get into bed with me until I fell asleep, and once when I was sick there was this dream I had that made me scream and I woke up and my Mommy was still there even though she had to get up early the next morning to milk the brown cow. And my Father, he never held my hand, but I know he loved me because I could see it in his eyes even when he shouted at me, and he made these dresses for me that were nicer than all the other dresses in the village and, best of all, he would sew my name into the hem in really beautiful stitching that would take him hours and hours late at night and it was just my name that nobody except me could see. And, one time, there was this time when I was out playing in the fields and I fell asleep under a hedge because it was sunny and the bees were making this noise that made me feel sleepy and dreamy and the whole village came out looking for me because they thought I'd gotten lost in the Woods and when they found me they took me back to the house and my Mom and Dad were there and they were so angry that I knew they loved me so much! So I know what it's like to have parents that love you. I do! And this horrid old Witch, even if she is your Mother, she shouldn't be, because she's HORRID and MEAN! As for you, Mr. Knight-In-Shining-Armor," she rounded on Max, her eyes flashing, "if you DARE ever say you don't know what it's like to be loved, then I—"

There was a clatter of utensils from the kitchen—the Witch was coming. Martha disappeared in a flash. The Maxes leapt at the shelves and began dusting furiously.

"WHAT'S going on in here?" snarled the Witch, throwing open the door. "What's all the hullaballoo?"

The Maxes lowered their heads guiltily. The Witch grinned at their new forms.

"Playing copycats are we, when poor old Mom is slaving over a hot stove? Well, what are you waiting for? Dinner's ready! Wash your hands!"

"He says you're not our Mother," one Max blurted out suddenly, pointing at Max.

"He does, does he?" The Witch came into the room, her eyes gleaming. "And what else has Fish-Face-Nosey-Parker been saying?"

"He says you're always mean to us."

"He says we don't deserve it."

"I'll tell you what you don't deserve!" the Witch snapped. "You don't deserve DINNER! You don't deserve lamb chops and mashed potatoes, apple pie and custard! Not if you listen to a liar who trundled in out of nowhere instead of your own Mother."

The Maxes sulked. They'd only been trying to get Max in trouble, and their plan had backfired.

"We don't even like custard!"

"We hate it."

"We never get food like that, anyway!"

"We just get carrot porridge!"

"You had apple pie the other week, don't you dare tell me you didn't! You had a golden-crusted apple pie that I busted a gut to make and you left nothing for me, not a crumb! As for not liking custard, just have a look in the pantry! Will you see any custard? You won't! Why? Because you polished it off! You had LOADS of the stuff and you kept asking for more!"

"But we don't like custard."

"Custard is what comes out of eggs when they poo."

"Yuck!"

"We hate custard."

"Hate custard?" spluttered the Witch. "Why—why— you've a fine way of showing it, if you hate custard! Straight from the jug! Glug glug glug. That was you last week, jug-gulpers."

"No . . ."

"That can't be right . . ."

"We really DO hate custard."

"Ah!" cried the Witch triumphantly, snapping her fingers together. "But if I never give you that kind of food, how do you know you hate it? Eh? Eh?"

"Because one day we crept into the pantry when we were hungry . . ."

"And we stole some . . ."

"And it was so yuck we were sick . . ."

"Which meant you found out . . ."

"And you punished us . . ."

"That's when you bought the chain and padlock from the blacksmith."

"That chain there."

"Yes, and that padlock."

"Okay okay, you hate custard," the Witch chattered. "I'm old, sometimes I get confused. It's because I'm tired, because I have so much to worry about. Dinner and Anteaters and Dragon Brain and the World One and BADLY BEHAVED UNGRATEFUL SNOTNOSES, so much that I . . . I just can't . . . you ungrateful little horrors, I ought to . . . wait till your Daddy gets home! He'll take the STRAP to you!"

The twins stood bolt upright, their mouths dropping open. "You said you ate Daddy!"

"You said you had to because he never helped with the housework!"

"Did you eat him or didn't you?"

"I didn't. Of course, I didn't. Why would I eat your horrid old fat, hairy Daddy? Eugh!"

"You're a liar!"

"You've been lying to us!"

"None of it's true!"

"None of it!"

"Well, so what?" the Witch said. "Big deal. Who cares?"

The Maxes shrieked. Their faces turned purple. They began stamping their feet and rushing up and down the room.

"You're never to say you're our Mother again!"

"You're NOT our Mother!"

"You're just a MEAN OLD WITCH!"

"WITCH WITCH WITCH!"

"WE HATE YOU!"

"WE HATE YOU. YOU'RE A HORRIBLE OLD WITCH AND YOU SMELL!"

The Witch's face became cold as stone. "So I'm not your BIOLOGICAL Mother. I admit it. Boo-hoo. You think your *real* Mother is any better? What do you suppose happened after I stole you? A few tears, a snotty hankie, sure—everyone loves a drama. But then what? Do you think she's going to snivel and snot all her life? No. Along comes a new little darling, a new sproglet, and Kaspar Hauser is forgotten forever. You should be grateful you've got ME! Because when it comes to Mothers, SOMETHING'S better than NOTHING!"

"You're a fibber."

"We don't believe you."

"Bully for you! Your stomachs will believe me when you go without dinner. Now get in your box and don't come out until morning."

"No!"

"No!"

"What?"

"No . . ."

"No . . ."

"No?"

"NO!"

"NO!"

The Witch narrowed her eyes and lifted a finger. She began to speak in solitary words, each as indestructible as an Ogre's Mountaintop Citadel with Human Skulls on The Battlements.

"IF.

"I.

"HEAR.

"ANY.

"MORE.

"LIP.

"FROMEITHEROFYOU!"

The finger jabbed: "From you, Kaspar."

The finger jabbed again: "Or you, Hauser.

"I'll THRASH you like there's no tomorrow! Now get going! Into your box! HOP IT!"

The twins didn't budge. They didn't even seem to be paying attention to the Witch. Instead, they were staring at each other closely.

"That's wrong," said one.

"She's got it wrong," said the other.

"Wrong?" spluttered the Witch. "What do you mean—wrong?"

They took no notice. Their faces were intent, their breath coming faster and faster.

"You aren't Kaspar. Are you?"

"No."

"But . . . you're not Hauser, either."

"That's right."

"That is right."

"That's why we could never get it."

"That's why we were so confused."

"It's so simple!"

"Why didn't we think of it before?"

They grabbed each other's hands and stared at each other in a rapture.

"You're me!"

"Yes!"

"And I'm you!"

"We're us!"

"We're each other!"

They danced. They sang. They capered wildly, and it didn't matter that the Witch spat and cursed—they were unstoppable. They spun, spun, spun, they sang, sang, sang, they disappeared in a blur of color, and this time, when they broke apart—there was no apart. There was just a single, solitary boy, rolling across the floorboards like a marble, laughing merrily, then sitting up and staring in astonishment at his hands.

"ARRRGGGGGHHHHH!" screamed the Witch. "No no no! No no NO! Go back! Go back! Reverse! Rewind! Undo!"

Kaspar Hauser held up his hand solemnly. "I've got a splinter!" he announced. Then he burst into tears.

"I don't care about your SPLINTER! Good! If you've got a splinter, GOOD!"

"Take it out!" Kaspar wailed. "M-m-mommy m-make it b-better!"

"Take it OUT? I'll do no such thing. I'll take YOU out. YOU'RE the splinter, you good for nothing little NOSE-MINER!"

The Witch seized a broom from the corner and swept the blubbering boy toward the door.

"I've had it with you! Be off! Go on! Shoo! Vamoose! See how long you survive in the Woods WITHOUT YOUR MOTHER TO LOOK AFTER YOU!"

She flicked Kaspar into the cold, wintery night, slammed the door and put her back against it.

"Oh, don't look at me like that, my dear," she said to Max. "There comes a time when every little birdie has to fly the nest. It's cruel on poor old Mom, but still. If you raise them to be confident, brave, and adventurous, you can't expect anything other than heartbreak. They'll set out in the Woods whether you like it or not. Hey-ho!"

"He didn't fly away," Max told her sternly. "You kicked him out."

"Well, all right, I kicked him out. But I wouldn't do anything to hurt YOU, my little munchpot, not on any day of the year." A look of almost unbelievable cunning crossed her face. "And especially not on this day, your Special Day, your Darling Day."

What's she talking about? What special day?

I don't know . . . I don't like the way she's looking at me, that's for sure.

"Don't you remember?" she asked, coming closer. "It's your BIRTHDAY, you great silly-billy. You haven't forgotten your BIRTHDAY, have you?"

"Today isn't my birthday."

"When is it then, diddums?" smiled the Witch. "When is your birthday?"

"Nobody knows. Including you!"

"Do you think your own Mother doesn't know when her Darling Pudding Princeling has his birthday?"

"You're not my Mother."

"Oh, but are you sure of that, too? Are you absolutely one hundred percent bullet-proof sure?"

"You don't have any children. It's all just lies."

The Witch began clicking her fingers and singing.

Happy Birthday to you!

Happy Birthday to you!

Happy Birthday Dear Cut-in-Two-So-He-Can-Help-Out-Around-the-House BOY!

Happy Birthday To You!

"Yes! Oh yes! Out with the old, in with the new! Divide and conquer! Haha!" Shrieking with laughter, she tossed him the broom. "I've got to meet a certain World One now. Get this place extra spic-and-span! We can't have any nasty germs flying around for the Grand Operation! Don't worry if it takes you a while, next time you'll have HELP! Haha! I'll be back in a jiffy! Toodle-oo!"

She hurried out of the workshop. The moment she was gone, Martha tore out of Max with tornado speed and ran to the door. There was a clatter of hooves and the rattle of a carriage.

"She's gone!" Martha spun around. "Quick! We have to get to Rosethorn before the Dragons."

"Go after her! She might not be going far! Get the key to this thing!"

"I can't. If I go too far from you I'll die."

"What? Why?"

"I can't stray from the gravestone. It's just how it works!"

"Then look for a spare key! She's going to cut me in half when she gets back!"

Martha stared at him, her eyes narrowing in fury. "So THAT'S what you're worried about! You don't care about Rosethorn at all!"

"HOW CAN WE GET TO ROSETHORN? You said it was miles away! Even if I could get free, how could I get there in time?"

"You could use the Seven League Boots," said a voice. "A single step. Then—BANG! You're there."

The door to the outside had opened a crack—a small round face was peeking in.

"Kaspar!" Martha ran to him and took his hands pleadingly. "You have to help, Kaspar! We have to get to Rosethorn village!"

"You can go anywhere with the Seven League Boots. But why would you want to go there? It's so-o-o-o-o boring."

"What use are Seven League Boots when I'm chained up?" Max howled. "You think I'm going to jump around with an oven on my leg? The key! Ask about the key!"

"YOUASKHIMHE'SRIGHTHERE!" Martha screamed. Then she turned to Kaspar and said sweetly: "What about the key, Kaspar? Do you have a spare key for the padlock?"

"No."

"Oh."

"That's why I made Gerald."

"Gerald?"

"He's one of my creations. I use him when Mother locks me up and then—because, you know, sometimes she's busy with things—forgets she's locked me up. HEY! LET GO!"

Martha grabbed his arm and hauled him into the workshop, then slammed the door and pinned Kaspar against it.

"You're saying you made an insect that can open the padlock?" she asked intently.

"Y-y-yes," Kaspar stammered. "Any lock. He's a triple-headed rotational tumbler."

"WHERE IS HE?" Max yelled, yanking on the chain to try and get closer to Kaspar. "Where's GERALD?"

"I'm not really sure. I let him out to play before we left for London." Kaspar got down on his hands and knees and began crawling around. "He'll be here somewhere. Ger-ald! Where a-a-a-a-re you?"

Martha immediately dropped onto all fours, too. "How big is he?"

"He's about the size of a large Spider," said Kaspar. "I just hope he hasn't gone outside!"

"Oh my God," Max sank to the floor. "He could be any-where. We'll never find him."

"What does he look like?" Martha asked, searching under the shelves.

"He's shaped like a starfish."

"Really? So pretty!"

"I think so, too! He's basically three Centipedes stitched together in the middle. Oh!" Kaspar stopped suddenly. "There he is!"

"You see him?" Martha spun around. "Where is he?"

"It's probably best . . . if you don't move."

She froze. "Why? Am I going to squash him?"

"No. No, I don't think so. It's just some people panic."

"Why would I panic?"

"Well, he's in your hair, so . . ."

"Kaspar! We don't have time for joking around!"

"No," said Max. "He is in your hair. I see him. Can't you feel him? He's pretty big."

"GETHIMOFF!GETHIMOFF!"

Kaspar quickly lifted "Gerald" from Martha's hair, then held him proudly out in the palm of his hand. The three Centipedes, wriggling and twisting in Kaspar's fingers, were joined in the middle by a delicate series of stitches. Long, curling feelers had been attached to each head.

"Wow, he's . . . really, really ugly," said Max.

"He's BEAUTIFUL, Kaspar," Martha said, giving Max a shove. "Now LET'S GO LET'S GO!"

Kaspar placed Gerald over the padlock. The Centipede heads began to rotate slowly, each set of feelers dipping into the lock, one at a time.

CLICK!

CLICK!

CLICK!

The lock sprang open.

"It worked!" Max gasped. He unclasped the shackle and jumped up, rubbing his ankle.

"Thank you, Kaspar!" Martha exclaimed, throwing her arms around the boy's neck and kissing him. "Thank you, thank you! Now please—get us the Boots!"

He smiled at all the kisses, but when she mentioned the Boots he looked at her blankly. "The Boots?"

"The Seven League Boots! So we can get to Rosethorn!"

"I know. I'll get them when Mother gets back."

"No, Kaspar, we need them now!"

"Why do you need the Boots now?"

"Because . . . because we need to catch up with your Mother. We need to . . . help her! She left us behind by accident!"

Kaspar blinked.

"You need to . . . help Mother?"

"Yes!"

"You've come here to replace me?"

"What? No!"

"Nobody helps Mother but me!"

"Wh-what?"

"I heard what she said. She wants to turn him into me!"

"Kaspar . . . please just give us the Boots! Tell us where they are!"

"You can't have them."

"Why not?"

"They're in the carriage."

"The . . . carriage?"

"That's where we keep them."

He moved toward the shelves. Reaching up, he took down a jar marked FRESH WASPS.

"It's time for you to leave," he said.

"Kaspar," Martha whispered faintly. "Please. Don't. Open. That. Jar."

"This is my workshop! And these are my insects! And that is MY Mother! And if you DON'T LEAVE NOW I'LL—"

Max football-tackled him, and they rolled across the floor. Martha pounced on him, too. In moments, they had confiscated Gerald and padlocked Kaspar to the pot-bellied stove.

Then they were outside in the cold night air, running to the edge of a clearing, where the trees began.

The Witch's cottage stood on a steep slope, surrounded on all sides by the Woods. Over the treetops that dropped sharply away they could see the moonlit valley below.

"Do you know where we are?" Max asked. "Martha?"

She was standing just in front of him, still and quiet.

"It's no use, it's too far . . . they're all going to die . . . and my parents are a part of it!" She sank to the ground, sobbing uncontrollably. "What does THAT become? What does that end up as, on your Merry-Go-Round? It can't be a SCORPION! It can't be a MINOTAUR! I've got those and I never did anything so EVIL! What kind of thing ends up coming around at you AGAIN and AGAIN and AGAIN? Don't they know that's what's going to HAPPEN?"

"Martha." He knelt beside her and held her shaking body close. "Martha, let's try anyway. Let's try."

"We can't, it's TOO FAR! And it's TOO LATE!"

"But I have an idea. Listen. I just . . . I need your help to make it work."

She lifted her tear-streaked face. "W-what? Really? You have an idea?"

"Can you find your way to Rosethorn in the dark?"

"Yes, it's easy. It's down the valley, just straight down. But it's so far! I'm sorry for yelling at you because it really is, you're right, really, it is far."

"Maybe I can do it," Max said. "Maybe I can run there."

She went quiet. "No, Max," she whispered. "Nobody can run that fast."

"I can if I get gotten by the Wildness."

"NO!" she gasped. "If you get gotten you can't come back!"

"The Dark Man does it. He remembers what it was like to lose his Mother and goes Wild. Then he remembers having her. That's how he comes back."

"You never really had your Forever Parents, though. You never lost them, not like he lost his Mother."

"I'm not thinking about my Forever Parents," Max said, looking at her intently. "I'm thinking about someone else. Someone I have nearly lost."

"Who?" Puzzled, she looked back at him. Then her eyes softened. "Oh," she said quietly. "That's . . . so romantic!"

"If I felt like that again, if I thought I was losing you, I could go Wild fast, I know I could."

"That's still not going to work," she said, shaking her head firmly. "If you're Wild why would you go to Rosethorn?"

"Because you'd be inside me," Max said. "You'd be inside me when I was Wild. And you could keep hold of me in the Wildness."

She stood, her gray dress fluttering around her body. Above her, dark, violent clouds tumbled together in the night sky.

"Max, if it doesn't work, if I can't—you'll go Wild. You'll be lost forever."

"And you'll be stuck inside a Wild One," he said. He smiled wanly. "Now it's your turn to keep hold of me."

She bit her lip, her eyes full. Then she nodded quickly. "Take off your clothes, then."

He blinked. "Wait—what?"

"It'll help. The Dark Man said so. Clothes are like armor against the Wildness. It'll get in faster if you're naked."

He nodded. He remembered. "Okay, I'll do it."

He reached into his pocket for the Dragon Hunter's tooth. After thinking for a moment, he pressed it into his earhole until it was wedged securely. Then he began to undress, dropping his clothes one by one into a crumpled heap. Soon he stood shivering violently in the cold air.

"Stop staring."

"Are those what World Ones wear for underpants?" she asked curiously.

"I knew you'd start making fun of me."

"Didn't Father Furthingale give you something proper?"

"They felt itchy."

"Those don't look very warm."

"They're not," he said. "Can we get on with this please?"

She held out her hand. "Come close to me," she whispered, her eyes wide and serious.

He stepped close. They stood for a moment, puffs of breath between them. With a quick, firm movement she pulled his head down and pressed her lips against his mouth.

"That's what I'm like when I'm here," she whispered in his ear. "Now." She drew back a little, and stared at him seriously. "You need to feel like you're losing me?"

"Yes."

"I suppose you could just imagine what it'd be like. To be without me. I know what an imagination you have. But I don't want you to do that. Ever. Not for anything."

"I have to try."

"No," she said softly. "I have a better way."

She pulled her hand out of his. Then, reaching out, she touched his cheek lightly with her fingertips.

"Don't forget me, Max!" she whispered. "I hope you find your parents!"

He frowned and shook his head, because he didn't understand.

Understanding—that she was saying goodbye—came a moment later, when she turned and ran into the Woods.

2

THE DRAGON FIRE

M ARTHA!"

He dived after her. If she got too far ahead, if she got out of the gravestone's reach, the bond holding her to existence would break, and she would disappear forever into the darkness under the millpond.

There! Her gray form flickered ahead, a Will-o'-the-Wisp, uncatchable and slight.

"MARTHA, WAIT!"

He gave chase, an agonizing pain lit up in his heart. His feet slicing open as they slipped on frozen roots and sharp stones—that was nothing. The branches whipping his side and scratching his face—he hardly noticed them. All he felt was the pain of the connection between them, the pain of it stretching, about to snap forever.

It was as if he'd never felt it before.

"Martha!" he gasped out. "I . . . can't!"

She drew farther ahead.

He was losing her.

And that wasn't right. It couldn't be. It wasn't FAIR. It wasn't POSSIBLE. It wasn't the way things were supposed to WORK!

You're NOT GOING TO GET HER! he snarled at the Woods. SHE'S MINE!

She's MINE FOREVER!

And the Wildness found its entrance.

It cracked his soul apart, charging him with a coil of energy. He became a wild dervish, a demon unleashed from a bottle buried a million years underground. His fingers were claws, his teeth were fangs, his hair bristled with hoar frost. A tail flickered out behind him. His eyes sharpened against the dark. He dropped on all fours and he was galloping so fast he caught up with her in three snarling bounds leaping on her back knocking her down and then over her and beyond into the trees into the WildnessintotheWildnesstheWildness—

In a flash, she was back inside him.

Where everything had changed.

Before, she could find safe spaces from the whirlpools and currents. Now the roots of the Woods were coiling through the millpond's waters. They found her the moment she returned. Circled her legs and arms. Pulled her down.

MINE!

I'm not yours or anybody's!

MINE!

The roots snarled around her body as she struggled against them. They tightened and squeezed. She kicked, her arms reaching up, her eyes fixed on the surface.

Bright, astonishing bubbles rose, the last precious moments of life held in watery skins.

It was the weeds again.

The weeds. The Woods. The Roots.

MINE!

They drew her down, down through the bottom of the millpond, into the darkness below. Feet first. Then legs. Body. Neck. Head. Her face gasped up. Her fingers.

Mud slid over her eyes. Mud slid down her throat.

A dim, soft shaft of light, a sunbeam, floated down through the green murk.

Max?

Martha . . . help me!

She ripped herself free. She grew—she could grow to any size. The millpond was a puddle, the weeds ribbons around her wrists. She tore them apart.

You won't get HIM or ME! MAX! Listen to me! GO FAST!

. . . fast, yes.

Fast was good.

It felt good to be fast and free and Wild.

He was a black spark from the Woods, a boy-thing born with a bite, born with the mark of Wildness WilednassWildnsdns.

Faster Max! Faster!

He hurtled into the night. Leaping. Bounding. Ducking. Rolling.

The joy of it!

The joy!

If only the girl would go, the gray girl holding him back. He wanted to feel the final bite, to pass over into the WildnesstheWildnesstheWildnessthenwnsskns.

She wouldn't let him. She was too strong. She had him in an iron grip.

Yanking his ears!

There, there! Turn!

He swerved and leapt, cleared a hummock and a fence with an agile spring and landed on a white, snowy surface that slipped under him. His limbs flailing, he skidded down the slope, and crashed into something narrow and hard.

He felt around it.

Bricks.

Hot.

Smoke and smells!

He knew this thing.

A chimney!

The Wildness dwindled, pushed out of him by something bigger, something that was bigger and kept getting bigger, swelling and expanding, something bright and pulsing and golden . . .

You're here! NOISE! MAKE NOISE!

He jumped up and down, kicking and stamping. He roared down the chimney pot. Startled shouts came up from below. He stood straight and tall, and put his hands to his mouth and screamed, because the gray girl told him to.

Move! KEEP MOVING!

He bounded down from the roof. A door opened, a man was holding a lantern, a cluster of frightened children behind him. A word exploded in his mind, bright and startling, like a firework—the gray girl had set it off.

He flung it in their faces.

DRAGON!

He raced to the next door. Hammering. Shouting. Flinging out fireworks that exploded in the night.

DRAGON!

DRAGON!

Doors and windows clattered open. He went from house to house. His knuckles burst from hammering. His voice cracked from shouting. But still he shouted. Still he hammered.

DRAGON!

DRAGON!

DRAGON!

DRAGON!

Someone caught at him, trying to drag him away. He pulled free. Then, all around him:

DRAGON!

DRAGON!

Other voices. Other voices were shouting it. They were awake.

You did it! You warned them! Max YOU DID IT! Oh Max, THANK YOU!

DRAGON!

DRAGON!

And then the Wildness rushed out of him, all its roots and leaves and branches gathering before him in a vast snaking form.

DRAGON!

The Forest, itself, was before him.

DRAGON!

Its cavernous mouth opened.

DRAGON!

And he saw all the way in, to a bonfire, a bonfire that was rushing toward him—the burning shards of a thousand trees.

Oh Max . . .

And he did not need to decide.

He did not need to be brave or make a choice. The Dragon Fire was all around him.

And he sat down in it.

-d-

-e-

-m-

-e-

-a-

-r-

-r-

-demarer-

-daermer-

-draemer-

Oh . . . Max.
MAX

    MXMXAYUOMAX
YOYUOYUYOUMXAPANERT

DMERREA
PARNTDRAMEEERDERAMERFPARE

NTSPARENTDREAMER
R
D
E
A
M
ED
DRAMEEDDRAMDEDYORUPARENTS

YORUPRAENTSYOUROLNYPARENTS

WERETEHRETREHETHERTHYERE
WEHETANSGMULE
WREHETMULNSGA

WTINGWAITINGWAITINGTHEYWANTEDYOU
TURNEDAWAYAND

VANISHTEHYHD

YOU WREE TEHIR LSATDERAM

THEYHDNOTHERDREAMSS

THYEWNETHTEYLEFTTHEYVANISHEDYOU
TURNEDAWYATHEMANDDREAMEDTADNO
REASONHEYTOREMAINTHEYVANISHED
BECAUSEOFYOUTHEYVANISHEDBECAUSEOF
YOUTHEYVANISHEDBECAUSEOFYOUTHEY
VANISHEDBECAUSEOFYOUTHEYVANISHED
BECAUSEOFYOUTHEYVANISHEDBECAUSE
OFYOUHeykidNOREASONHEY!HEYLISTENUP!Hey
kid listen up. HEY! Remember when Forbes wanted to hold
your hand and you didn't let him? You remember, don't
you? And you said, what did you say, you said you HATED
HIM? How'd you think that made him FEEL? Like his life
wasn't hard enough, standing at that grinder all day, bust-
ing his gut—for what? For dirty looks? And you remember
how Alice took you to the bookshop and you wanted her
to go away in case your Forever Parents showed up? She
knew what you were thinking, don't think she didn't. And
like that wasn't the only time! You never had a word for
her. You've been turning your face away from the World
since day one. You want to know who you are? THAT'S
who you are. You want real people to disappear so they

don't get in the way of your dreams. And now, guess what? They went and Vanished. But hey—that's what you wanted, right? Goodjobkid. And sweet dreams. Sweet dreams, that's what you prefer isn't it, that's WHAT you PREFER YOU PREFERRED THAT your WHOLELIFE YOU YOUPREFERREDTODREAMYOURDREAMPARENTS Kid, your dream parents, those guys in the Balloon, that wasjustanicedreamThat'sallitwasYOURDREAMPAR ENTSNEVEREXISTEDNEVEREXISTEDYOUMADET HEM UPTHEYWEREDREAMSDREAMSNOTHINGBUT DREAMS Not that it wasn't a good story, I'm not saying that but that's allitwasAGOODSTORYAGOODSTROYSOTYR SOTYUOLOSYLSOTYYOULYORSTOSTYROUL STYOULOSTTHEONLYPARENTSYOUEVERHAD THEONLYPARENTSYOUEVERHADYOUHADNO OTHERPARENTSNOOTHERPARENTSYOUHAD NOOTHERPARENTSNOOTHERPARENTSYOU HADNOOTHERPARENTSNOOTHERPARENTSNO OTHERPARENTSNOOTHERPARENTSNOOTHER PARENTSNOOTHERPARENTSNOOTHERPARENTS NOOTHERPARENTSTHEMAWAYYOUIGNORED THEYEHYEAHYEAHyeah!Ifyoucan'tmake itrealit'sworthnothingnothingnothing MANDTHEYVANISHEDANDITSALLYOURFAULTIT SALLYOURFAULTITSALLYOURFAULTTHEY VANISHEDITWASYOURFAULTTHEMULGANSVAN ISHEDYOURFAULTYOURFAULTMAXYOURFAULT

MAXSTOPMAXYOURFAULTSTOPSTOPMAXYOUR
STOPSTOPMAXSTOPRUNNINGMAXSTOP
STOPSTOP
   STOP
     STOP
      STOP MAXIDON'TKNOW
MAX STOP

MAXWHERE

Max!

"Max Max Max . . . stop running stop running Max I don't
know where we are . . ."

He stumbled. The blinding darkness lifted and he saw
his arms, thrust deeply into snow drifted against a boulder.
Martha was kneeling beside him, tears dripping from her
narrow, pinched face. He closed his eyes, wanting the darkness to return, to blot it all out.

"Max, you survived, it's all right. You survived the fire!"

But he hadn't survived.

He understood now.

Nobody survived the Dragon Fire.

It had burned inward, burning up the dreams and lies
that had encased who he was. All that remained was that
voice, the unconscious voice that had whispered inside him
his whole life. The voice he had drowned out with dreams.

Forbes and Alice were his Forever Parents.

He'd always known this and he'd hated them for it. He'd hated them because they were real. He'd hated them because they loved him. He'd turned away from that love, and longed, instead, for a fantasy love, an imaginary love that didn't exist, that had never existed and never could exist. A painting on a wall. A Balloon in the sky. A magical word.

Panthalassa.

A word that meant nothing.

He'd lost the only parents he'd ever had.

That was the truth the Dragon Fire had revealed.

And he'd run from this knowledge, deep into the Woods.

He'd accepted it, but he'd run from it.

He'd lost sight of everything except tree and sky, snow and ice. He began to cry, sobbing and shivering, even though he was warm, so warm. He'd been living inside a dream, but the Dragon Fire had stripped that dream from him and now he had nothing. Only Martha was there, keeping the Wildness at bay. He threw his arms around her, he squeezed her desperately, crushing her, crushing her as tightly as he could.

She pulled herself away and took his head between her hands.

"Max, I can't keep you warm! You're going to freeze to death!"

She stood up and took a few steps into the flurrying snow. "Somebody help us!" she called out. "Help!"

He watched her gray form darting among the trees.

Why was she worried? He was warm, and snug. And it was all so quiet and white.

He lay back in the snow.

He was warm and in bed and at home, and it was good to lie here in bed at home . . . his Queen smoothing his hair and whispering, her words full of love.

"My Knight! I'll tell you a story and . . . it'll be easier. It'll be easier when you sleep."

"Yes, my Queen," he murmured. "Tell me a story!"

"There was a girl lost in the Woods, my Knight! She'd been put there by her parents, who didn't want her. She got so cold she sat under a tree and began to freeze, and then Father Moroz came, who comes to everyone who freezes in the Woods. He came down through the trees, bringing the frost, his fingers snapping, his breath crackling. 'Are you cold, little girl?' he asked. And she shivered and froze like never before because Father Moroz was so close, but smiled and said through chattering teeth, 'No, dear Father, not cold at all. I'm quite warm, thank you. How are you?' And Father Moroz was pleased with her politeness, and took her to his cave, made her warm, and gave her gifts. My Knight, my King—when Father Moroz comes and asks, tell him you're warm, and he will bring you to his cave and give you gifts. When you hear his fingers snapping . . . you're to tell him, 'I'm warm!' . . . and I'll be waiting for you when you wake . . . I'll be here . . . and I'll be yours forever . . ."

And he was warm.

A thousand feathers were drifting down out of the sky. He was lying in a bed of them.

The deeper they were, the warmer he became.

Reaching up, he pulled the goose feather quilt over him.

Then Father Moroz was there, coming down through the trees, his fingers snapping.

And his beard was frost. And his eyes were ice.

THE WORLD ONE

"I'm warm," he said loudly. And he was—too warm.

The fingers crackled and snapped and he moaned at them to stop, because it was the fingers making him hot. He tossed and turned, trying to escape the heat, and discovered his legs were bound together and he couldn't separate them.

So he sank.

Back down into darkness, where the girl was waiting.

She took his hand and he understood. Together, they swam through the murk. Their passage disturbed toads that slipped up from the muddy silt and propelled themselves in bursts toward the dingy light above. Tiny beetles floated past attached to sacs of air, swallowed now and again by the gulping mouths of sticklebacks.

In the deepest, coldest part of the pond the girl stopped and began sifting through a Boggy Clump of decaying junk. There were beheaded dolls, castles with shattered walls, and bent magician's wands, but she didn't want them, she was looking for something else. A cloud of silt grew around her and he paddled close at her side, digging, too, digging through the mud and the slime until they uncovered what she was looking for in the pile of sunken toys.

It was a Merry-Go-Round.

It's yours.

How do I make it turn?

It only turns when you're Cold.

But I'm Warm.

You were Warm once. Now you're Cold, like me.

They pulled it out, heaving together, causing the slow collapse of the Boggy Clump. And then the pond drained away from them and they were sitting in a darkness so deep he thought he'd be able to reach out and stroke it.

In front of them he sensed the Merry-Go-Round, massive now, massive and dark and unlit.

Then the lights blazed out.

And the Merry-Go-Round turned. And there were Centipedes.

And Scorpions.

And Worms.

CLUNK CLUNK

Shuddering, he opened his eyes. He was lying on his back.

Above him, a red glow flickered against a craggy ceiling that glistened with moisture.

CLUNK CLUNK

He turned his head weakly from side to side. He was in a cave, and someone was here with him. He pushed himself up and looked toward the sound.

A fire was burning at the mouth of the cave. Next to it, stood an old man. A weather-beaten face. A shaggy beard. A mouth set in a hard, straight line. He had a long pair of tongs in his hands. He was using them to turn large stones resting above the fire on a griddle.

The iron tongs clacked.

The stones clunked.

The effort of sitting up was too much. He collapsed back, noticing for the first time that a circle of the charred stones surrounded him, giving off a deep, throbbing heat. His bed was some kind of pallet that raised him off the ground. Animal fur bristled under his fingers, and he discovered why he hadn't been able to move his legs—he was encased in a fluorescent-yellow sleeping bag. As soon as he spotted its HiTECH Iso-pore™ label, he knew this person, this cave-dweller, was a World One.

The Witch's World One?

The Tinker?

He saw a familiar sheepskin coat folded over the end of the bed. His fingers plucked at his shirt.

They were his clothes.

The Witch must have brought them.

There was an odd feeling in his ear—the Dragon Hunter's tooth, he realized. He'd forgotten all about that.

Are you still there, too?

Yes.

Where am I? What happened?

He rescued you. He brought you here, to his cave. You nearly died and he saved your life. You've had a fever.

How long?

Two days I think.

Do you know where we are?

I'm not sure. I think it's Mount Gilead, near the top. He must have been near Rosethorn for the Dragon attack. The Witch brought us here in the carriage. Don't you remember? You were talking a lot. I thought you were awake.

I don't remember . . . I just remember the Dragon Fire . . .

You saved them, Max. The villagers.

I don't care.

Max . . .

Leave me alone.

He closed his eyes.

No. He didn't care about the villagers.

He didn't care the Appearance was still a mystery.

He didn't care about the Vanishings.

Or the Woods and the World.

He couldn't think about any of that.

All he could think about was Alice at the kitchen table. "Don't look around until we tell you." That was the last thing she'd said, and now he could not get those words out of his head. They were carved into his mind, like messages left by the Cold Ones.

DON'T
LOOK AROUND
UNTIL WE
TELL YOU

What she'd wanted, more than anything else, was for him to look at her. To see her. To be with her properly. Every day she'd wanted that. And that was all. Maybe, watching from the kitchen when he came and went, she'd just been waiting for a turn of the head, a smile, something small.

He hadn't given her a single one.

How must that have made her feel?

Even at the last moment, when she had her last chance, she didn't ask him to look. She chose to protect him instead. "Don't look around until we tell you."

She didn't want him to see it happen.

And maybe if he had looked around, if he had turned around and looked at them both properly, like he was meant to . . . if he'd held onto them like he was supposed to . . . tightly . . . then he would have stopped the Vanishing.

He hadn't even realized that, until now.

CLUNK CLUNK

The Tinker lifted a stone off the griddle and brought it over. The moist ground sizzled as he placed the hot rock in the circle.

Seeing him up close, Max stared, then looked away quickly.

One of the Tinker's eyes was completely transparent, like a glass orb.

The other shined with a blue light, like the glowing, robotic eye of a machine.

Saying nothing, the Tinker removed a glove, held a hand over each of the stones in turn, selected one, and returned to the fire, where he placed it on the griddle above the flames.

Max watched every movement. It looked as if the Tinker had been living here for months, maybe years. His clothes—expensive survival gear from the World—were old and faded. Many storage chests and boxes of all sizes were stacked neatly against the walls, and shelving had been put up for tools and equipment.

The Tinker hung the tongs from a hook on the wall, tended briefly to the fire, then turned and stood gazing out of the cave.

He was looking at something, out there in the darkness.

Max unzipped his sleeping bag and got up, his legs shaking with weakness. He found his shoes, hung his coat around his shoulders, and made his way to the mouth of the cave.

Standing beside the old man, he looked out over the Woods. The Woods below them had been hacked back from the cave—the shadowy form of tree stumps were dotted around in the darkness. Farther down still, in the basin of the valley, the sodium-orange lamps of Gilead glowed like a patch of radiation, a meteorite crater, its brightness foreign to the landscape.

"Let there be light!" the Tinker said, almost to himself, and he looked down at Max, his seeing eye glowing with that electric blueness that almost beamed out of his skull.

"Were you ever, when you were small, afraid of the dark?" he asked then.

Max shook his head, and the Tinker looked back at the New Light of Gilead.

"I was afraid of the dark," he admitted quietly. "I had good reason. If I did badly at school, my Father locked me in the cellar and turned off the lights. One day, my Mother tried to comfort me by whispering fairy tales through the keyhole. She didn't understand how terrifying it was, to hear those stories, down there in the dark. In the dark, you can't see there's no Goblin in the corner. You can't be sure. There's always a tiny doubt in your mind, but that doubt always has the loudest voice. What if the Goblin really is there? What if he's watching me? What is he thinking about, there in his corner? Are those his eyes I can see, or some little part of light? Yes, I was scared of the dark when I was a child." He nodded to himself for a good while. "But not anymore. No, not anymore."

"Why did you bring me here?" Max asked. "Are you going to let me go?"

The question seemed to surprise the Tinker. "I brought you here because you were cold. You are free to leave at any time." He smiled ironically. "But perhaps you should remain for the night at least."

"Yes," Max said. Then he added: "Thank you for saving me."

"You're welcome!" The Tinker looked at him, considering something. "So. You wished to become a Dragon Hunter?"

Max shook his head. "I don't care about that."

"Hm," the Tinker said, nodding. Then: "I know something about you, I admit."

"What do you know?"

"I will tell you," said the Tinker. "And then you should say what you know about me. Do you agree?"

"I agree," Max said after a moment.

"You Appeared out of nowhere in a bookshop," the Tinker said. "And you remember nothing of where you came from. You were supposed to find out from the Dragon Fire."

Max kept quiet. But there was something gentle about the questions, and the Tinker's voice.

"Even though you do not know where you come from," the Tinker went on, "you have always felt that you . . . came from somewhere else. Is that right?"

Max gave a small nod.

The Tinker closed his eyes and lifted his head back, like he was trying to sense something invisible. "And all your life, you have been plagued by strange dreams. Dreams you cannot explain. That seem . . . more than real."

"Yes," Max said quietly.

"And when you ran away from home," the Tinker went on, "you ran away to get to the Woods."

Max glanced at him. "How do you know I ran away from home?"

"Oh, all the Apprentices run away from home," the Tinker said. "All the Dragon Hunters are from the World. They run away and come to the Woods. They're dreamers, all of them. Or used to be," he added in a low voice. His forehead creased slightly. "So. Why did you run away from home?"

Max felt the Dragon Fire stir inside him, reminding him.

"My parents didn't know who I was," he whispered. "They couldn't tell me. I had to find out."

"Why did you expect them to know?"

"Because they were my parents."

The Tinker shook his head. "It's precisely because they were your parents that they didn't know, and could never know."

"Parents know their children."

"Your own experience tells you otherwise."

"They should. They're meant to."

"Should and Meant To are simply descriptions of What Is Not. They are dreams. Parents see only the hopes they have for their children, or the fears. You cannot expect such people to see you clearly."

The Tinker's voice was hypnotic, his speech measured and slow. Max felt the dim stirring of a memory. Hadn't he heard this voice before?

"We see one another through lenses of our own devising," the Tinker went on. "You look at me now, and you think you see me. But you do not. You only see an idea you have of me. Perhaps, a bad idea. You see a person you have created, that has nothing to do with me, nothing at all. You see a story.

Just as your parents, looking at you, saw a story."

"I didn't see them, either," Max whispered. "When I looked at them . . . I saw something else."

"You are not to blame," said the Tinker. "It is our habit. It is the way we function, the way we have always functioned. The World is all around us, waiting to be seen, but all we see is the Woods. Why? Because we prefer it."

The old man's voice rose and fell in persuasive cadences, and Max suddenly remembered where he'd heard it before.

"Now," said the Tinker, "tell me what you know about me."

"You're Professor Courtz," Max said. "You're the Chief Seeker."

"True. What else?"

"You changed the Dragons."

"Some of them. What else?"

"You started the Censorship."

"Good. But why?"

"You want to bring science to the Woods."

"No," said Courtz. "No. I want to bring it to the World."

"The World?" Max stared at him, confused. "But . . . it's already there."

"It is there. This is true. But we have never taken it absolutely into our hearts. We use it. We employ it. We buy it and sell it. It is a tool. But it does not define who we are. Instead, we are defined by our dreams. To this very day, we prefer not to see, and until there are no dreams, this will never change. Now," he said, "what else do you know about me?"

"You don't like dreams."

Courtz laughed, a rich, welcoming sound. "And what do you think I'm going to do about it?"

"I don't know."

"Then I will show you. It has already begun. When I am finished, there will be no more dreams. Ever again." He pointed out over the Woods. "Watch the trees now. These are the Deep Woods, you see. They are coming."

The sky was turning gray with the first light of dawn. From horizon to horizon, tiny curls of green lifted up from the trees, like buds of new life sprouting from soil.

It was the Dragons.

The migration to Ethiopia was beginning.

"I will not keep you here," Courtz went on. "You can return to Paris to become the last of the Dragon Hunters. You can hunt for stories and poison the World with fantasies. Or you can stay here, with me. You can be my Apprentice. Together we can free the World from the influence of the Woods. It is your choice. But before you decide, ask yourself: what have dreams done for you? Are your dreams with you, giving you strength and life? Or have they left you empty? Have they deceived you? What have they brought you? Something? Or nothing?"

With that, he turned and walked back into the cave, leaving Max where he was, paralyzed, unable to move.

He had no defense against Courtz's arguments.

Not after the Dragon Fire.

So he stood there and watched. Flying low over the trees, the Dragons came closer, calling to each other with sonorous booms like whale song. Soon, the first were passing overhead, scattering a rainfall of seeds, trailing a dispersal of new life. These Dragons were pure, untouched by Witch's spiders or Tinker's tools—it was like the last Denizens of the Woods were departing, fleeing from the influence of the New Light at Gilead. Watching them go, he felt a wrench, as if something was leaving him, too, some belief he had long lived under, a hope of something magical.

"For too long, the World has been misguided and tricked by fantasy," Courtz spoke behind him. "The Age of Dreams has run its course. And now the Age of Science will truly begin."

There was a loud, metallic CLICK-CLACK—then an almighty crash split the air.

Max jerked and ducked, covering his ears.

Courtz was standing with one foot on a rock, his blue eye gazing along a rifle at the sky. He waited a moment, then lowered it with a nod of satisfaction. One of the Dragons peeled away from the flock and fell, spiraling slowly, into the forest.

The other Dragons continued on their way, unaware of what had happened—unaware of what awaited them on their return.

SNAP

White Styrofoam balls cascaded onto the floor of the cave as Courtz heaved out a clanking piece of metal from one of the crates. Grunting, he set it down on a canvas tarpaulin and began inspecting every coil and pin of its workings.

Max watched as he stirred their porridge over the fire. The scientist was assembling a set of mechanical jaws like the one Boris had cut out of the Dragon's head at the Coven. It had many separate parts, taken from different crates. All the equipment. All the gear and tools and boxes. Courtz couldn't have got it here on his own. The Symposium had to be helping him. There had to be other Seekers who shared his beliefs. Maybe they'd even driven Boris out. They'd wanted him gone.

Boris.

He wondered what the Dark Man would have said to Courtz.

He'd have disagreed. He'd have had arguments.

But what were those arguments?

He couldn't think of any.

Not a single one.

Everything that Courtz had said seemed true.

The Dragon Hunter's tooth was still in his ear. Courtz had his back turned. He could easily drop it into his bowl. Put the Tinker to sleep and get back to Paris. He could complete the mission. There was still time before the seventh day.

He could do it.

He really could.

There was just one thing stopping him.

He didn't want to.

This man had created the Censorship. He'd told the World that dreams were dangerous, that it was better to focus on what was real. Max had thought that was wrong.

The Dragon Fire had told him it was true.

It was stories that had taken away what he wanted. If it hadn't been for dreams about his Forever Parents, his life with the Mulgans could have been better. They wouldn't have drifted so far apart. Things would have just worked.

So maybe Courtz was right about science. Maybe it was time to stop dreaming and see the World clearly.

By DESTROYING the Woods?

He doesn't mean DESTROY, as in literally. He means make the Woods the same as the World. With science. He just needs to clear out all the story-ish stuff. There's no point having a Censorship if people are still going around dreaming their heads off.

Look. I know you need time to think. But I'm NOT going to sit here quietly and let you THINK if it means you AGREE with him! He's killed people. He's a murderer.

Yes. He has. And that is terrible. But remember what the Witch said?

The WITCH??

The Woods has killed more, Martha. What about Little Noah? He got gotten by the Wildness. And he got torn apart by dogs! Dogs!

That doesn't make this right. What he's doing is wrong.

I think it's wrong, too, Martha. I feel it's wrong. But I can't figure out why. Maybe the Dark Man would be able to tell me, if he was here. But he isn't.

You should listen to your heart.

No, Martha! I shouldn't! That's EXACTLY what Courtz is talking about. "Listen to your heart." "Follow your dreams." Those are just stupid things people say so they can avoid what's real. What do they even mean? My heart—it doesn't have a voice! They just mean listen to some vague thing going on in your head that could come from anywhere, that's what they mean. Instead of saying, "Listen to your heart!" they should just be honest and say, "Don't bother thinking carefully, just go ahead!" There is no "Listening to your heart"! There is no "Following your dreams"! It's all just stories! And I'm tired of stories. I don't want any more.

You're turning into my parents! This is what happened to them!

No—

You're going to stop believing in me, too, like they did. Aren't you?

How can I? You're a voice in my head.

So that's all I am now? A VOICE in your HEAD?

No, that's not what I meant. You know it's not.

Soon I'll be nothing more than a memory. Then I'll be even less than that.

She sank sadly down to the Merry-Go-Round.

Max spooned out the porridge with angry splats.

"It wasn't stories that started the Vanishings, you know," he said, wanting to do something to test the scientist. "You were wrong about that."

Courtz took his bowl and glanced at Max with an amused smile. "I wasn't wrong because I never believed that to be true," he said.

"Yes, you did. You started the Censorship to stop the Vanishings, and all those books got burned."

"I didn't know what started the Vanishings—I never did," Courtz said. "The Vanishings were simply an opportunity, and I took it."

"It was my Appearance—"

"Yes, yes," Courtz said, cutting him off. "In the bookshop, I know. Your Appearance brought the Woods and the World too closely together, and the Vanishings became possible. How this all happened may be a matter of personal curiosity for you. But I am sure you will agree: the Vanishings must be stopped."

"Yes," Max said. "They must."

"So we agree on this. Well, that is something. But let us think through what this little fact means. Because facts are handy, and can be used to discover other facts. Shall we do that?"

"All right," Max said cautiously.

"Well, then. Are the Vanishings of the Woods or of the World?"

"They're of the Woods."

"And the Vanishings are only possible because the Woods and the World have been brought together. Is that correct?"

"Yes."

"So none of this is disputed, and we are on solid ground. Now tell me: if this is the case, as we have shown it to be, how are the Vanishings to be stopped? I would like to know."

"The Woods and the World must be separated."

"For a short while, or permanently?"

"Permanently."

"Then all that remains is to decide how a permanent separation between two things can be brought about. I will describe the ways, and you can tell me if I have missed any. Let's call these two things A and B. The complete destruction of either A or B would ensure a permanent separation, would it not?"

"Yes."

"So that is, in theory, a solution. But it is not practically possible. Are we still in agreement?"

"Yes."

"Then there is only one other option: A must entirely lose the qualities that make it A, and assume those of B. Or vice versa."

"Yes."

"So the Woods must become the World, or the World must become the Woods. Have I missed any ways?"

"I . . . don't think so."

"The choice, then, is this: Science or Stories. Which would you prefer?"

Max looked away; Courtz had gotten him again.

The scientist picked up a spoon and hunkered down near the fire.

"I am glad we are in agreement," he said. "Now, eat. We only have a few hours before the tranquilizer wears off."

They hiked down the slope toward the part of the Woods where the Dragon had fallen. From the mountainside, they could see the gash in the trees ripped open by the impact, about a mile into the forest.

The metal jaws were strapped to Courtz's back on a leather harness. Spanners, wrenches, pliers, and knives jangled from his belt. As he strode along, the apparatus and the tools clanked and rattled, like the scientist was, in fact, a robot driven by pistons and engines.

Courtz seemed to know every inch of the mountain— when they reached the trees, it was at the very spot a Path began.

As they went he continued to talk. He seemed to be glad of Max's company, and glad of the chance to describe his thoughts.

"In the World, I had to teach people to hate what they loved, to fear it," he said. "If they hadn't been afraid of dreams, the Censorship would have been impossible. Here, it is the same. The Forest Folk must learn to hate what they love. So we must violate what is sacred to them—the old ways, the Dragons. Only then will they embrace science. Then we will reach the final era, the ending, when confusion can be set aside and we can finally progress."

"What's the final era?" Max asked.

Courtz glanced at him. "You have read a great many stories, I am sure. Did you ever come across the tale of the Lindworm Prince? When I was your age, it was my favorite."

Max shook his head, surprised to hear the architect of the Censorship mention stories. He realized Courtz was still trying to persuade him. Probably he thought a story would help.

"A Princess goes to marry a Lindworm," Courtz said. "She has no choice, she has to, even though the wicked serpent has already married and gobbled up all her sisters. But she takes the advice of a wise old woman, and on their wedding night, she goes before the Lindworm in seven dresses. Each time it asks her to remove a dress, she asks the Lindworm to shed a skin. Finally, she is naked, and the Lindworm, well, it is a pink lump of flesh! Following the old woman's instructions, the Princess puts the Lindworm in a bath of milk, rolls up her sleeves, and scrubs it, hard. She scrubs and scrubs, and slowly the Lindworm's true form emerges. It becomes a handsome Prince.

"In that story, you have the entire history of our World. For thousands of years, its true form has been hidden, obscured by seven skins. With painful effort, we have stripped them off. Now, at last, the true flesh is about to emerge. For the first time in our history, we are going to see ourselves as we truly are. But we must roll up our sleeves, and scrub, and scrub hard!"

With those words, he left the Path and strode into the trees.

"Come!" he said, when Max hesitated. "There is no need to worry about the Wildness. You are beginning to think, I can tell. The Wildness has no power against people who think. You will see!"

Max stepped off the Path, into that space where the Wildness snarled in the air. And it was true. He couldn't feel it anymore. The trees were just trees, and the Woods was just a forest.

Already, the Woods was becoming the World.

Courtz found the Dragon's crash site with no trouble at all, marching straight up to it like he could smell it.

It looked like a landslide, a jumble of rocks and branches. Though it was sleeping, the bonfire in its belly was still burning, and the heat rose off it in waves, melting the snow.

When they reached the Dragon's head, Courtz unfastened the harness and set down the apparatus. He stretched himself, then leaned in and plucked a nodule from above one of the Dragon's closed eyes. He tossed it to Max. The muddy crust crumbled away between his fingers, revealing a tiny acorn.

"If you're wondering what Dragons are, that's it," Courtz said as he laid out his belt of tools on the forest floor.

"An acorn?"

"Dragons seeded the Beginning Woods. Where they sleep underground, they emit warmth to awaken dormant seeds, and scatter them when they travel. They are nothing more than engines of fertilization. Machines of growth. They are not fantastic. They are not wonderful. They have a purpose, which we are about to modify. That is all."

Selecting a large pair of pliers, he clambered onto the Dragon's lower lip and put one arm over its neck to support himself. Clacking the pliers to loosen them, he gripped the slimy top lip and hauled it up to reveal white molars, big as wedding cakes. "See the upper back teeth? They must come out so we can anchor the apparatus." He jumped down and took up two short rods with braces at each end. "We'll do this side first."

Max hesitated, looking at the tools with their angles and cutting blades, then at the Dragon and its mossy lips.

It was sleeping, he reasoned, and wouldn't feel anything. It was like . . . being at the dentist's. Courtz was carrying on as if it was all a slightly boring chore. He'd handled the Dragon's lip the way a blacksmith hammered nails into a horse's hoof. That was probably the best way to think about it—as if it was an operation, no more gruesome than anything a vet might do.

Together, they heaved the fearsome mouth wide, and propped it open with the short metal rods. Then Max watched as Courtz pinned up the top lip with a series of butcher's hooks. The lip was heavy, and Courtz grunted as he hauled it away from the gum, as if he were dragging heavy fish out of water.

I can't watch this. And I can't watch you watching it.

Okay.

Max replied almost absently, hardly noticing the sadness in her voice. A feeling of detachment was coming over him, the opposite of the Wildness, coming from Courtz and the business-like way he operated on the Dragon.

And the detachment soon became fascination.

Now that the lip was pinned up, how was he going to remove the tooth? It was tucked away in an awkward spot in the back corner of the mouth. He watched as Courtz unclipped a metal spatula from the belt. Almost before he knew what was happening, Courtz had slid it under the gum, and with three sharp movements—up and along, up and along, up and along—levered it until the gum ripped free from the tooth and hung in a loose, bloody flap.

Max moved into a better position so he could see what Courtz was doing.

Next it was a hammer and chisel.

CRACK!

With a sharp blow of the hammer, Courtz drove the chisel between the molar and the adjacent tooth. They came apart slightly, and he struck the chisel again, driving it deeper, widening the gap further.

"That should do it," he muttered. "Now, for the hard part." He took a crowbar and pushed it into the space. He pressed with all his strength, using the other tooth as a fulcrum. The first three times his struggle had no effect. His face turned purple with the strain, then his breath exploded and he swore and wiped his forehead. But the fourth time there was a small movement from the molar. He tried again, bending all his weight down until a long groan escaped his lips—under the crowbar's pressure the tooth began to lean out of position.

"Come . . . on!"

He yanked the crowbar back and forth, back and forth. The molar shifted in its socket more freely, until Courtz was able to take it in both hands and wiggle it himself.

"Stand back," he said, panting slightly. Max stepped away, bloody snow squishing under his feet. But it hardly troubled him. Courtz had picked up his pliers again, and with careful, precise movements was adjusting a screw on them so he could open them wider. With a rough *clunk* he got a solid grip on the tooth, put a foot on the Dragon's lower jaw, and pulled. The tooth came out a short distance, then stopped. Courtz unexpectedly reversed direction, driving the tooth into its socket, hard—then threw all his strength into a sudden, powerful yank. With a deep slurp of blood, he flew backward. The huge tooth bounced across the forest floor and landed at Max's feet, its long roots reaching up toward him.

Courtz retrieved the tooth, turning it in his hands, then drove it into the forest floor with heavy strikes of his hammer.

"Sit!" he said, pointing at the strange mushroom.

So Max sat, and watched Courtz continue his work. After removing the other tooth came the fitting of the apparatus. Estimating the size by eye, Courtz made several adjustments by sliding bars and tweaking screws, then slid the machine into position. When it was secure, he screwed the apparatus in place, then beckoned to Max.

He was going to "turn it on."

Max went to stand at his shoulder. He watched as Courtz reached up and under the front teeth to the back part of the mechanism, where he began to tighten a coil with sharp twists of a key.

click click whirrrrrr

The needles began to flicker in and out of the gums.

click click whirrrrrr

click click whirrrrrr

The Dragon's eyelids flickered.

"It's moving," Max said uneasily.

"And it'll keep moving for months," Courtz replied, still turning the key. "Just as long as nobody interferes with the mechanism."

"No," said Max. "I mean the Dragon's moving."

"Just a reflex," said Courtz.

And then the Dragon's jaws widened a tiny amount, and the metal rods holding them open tumbled out of position.

The mouth snapped shut.

Max jumped back at the sudden CLANG. Courtz didn't move or make a sound. He just knelt there, completely still. The Dragon's head rolled to one side and the scientist leaned over, following the Dragon's movement as if he was trying to peer up its nose.

Even then Max didn't realize what had happened—that the mouth had closed on Courtz's hand, and the rolling turn of the Dragon was twisting it off.

Then Courtz fell backward, clutching the mangled end of his arm, and he knew.

His first thought was that this was all inevitable. Some part of him had even known it was going to happen. Nothing could have prevented it.

It was written.

It had all happened before.

The second thought, which drove out the first, was that Courtz mustn't go into SHOCK, because if he went into SHOCK he would die. Forbes had told him many times about the day the grinder had snapped off his hand. The big danger, he'd said, was this SHOCK.

Two things made SHOCK worse.

Losing blood.

Being cold.

Courtz seemed to know this, too. He was sitting cross-legged, gripping his upper arm to shut down the blood supply. His face was ashen-white, but calm. Turning at the waist and leaning forward, he pulled the belt of tools toward him, shook off the spanners and pliers, and strapped it around his arm, tight.

Then he looked at Max. "Get me back to the cave," he said in a strangely normal tone of voice.

He stood, as if it was all going to be easy—but his legs buckled at once and he sank to his knees. Max darted forward and helped him up. With Courtz leaning on him heavily, they staggered from the clearing. Behind them, branches were already beginning to snap as the Dragon stirred.

Hurry, Max. It's waking up!

I can't go any faster.

Why are you helping him? Just leave him!

He ignored her.

They soon reached the Path. But Courtz had used up all his strength to get there. Exhausted, he fell forward and knelt in the snow, one arm planted down as a support. He did not speak. He seemed unaware of where he was, or what was happening.

Suddenly, there was a strange pulse through the ground.

Snow fell off the branches of the trees around them.

It's coming, Max!

How does it know where we are?

It's the Woods. The Woods is sending it after you! Because of WHAT YOU DID!

"Come on!" Max begged, tugging Courtz under his shoulder. "We have to keep going!"

He heaved Courtz to his feet, pulled the scientist's good arm around his shoulders, and staggered along the Path. But the weight was unbearable. Unable to support himself, his feet dragging, the scientist was far too heavy. They could only go a few steps at a time.

Leave him! This is all his fault. Let him deal with it.

I can't!

Courtz's feet began to weave. The pulses went through the ground again and again and again. Every few yards, a tremor knocked them off their feet, and each time it took Courtz longer to get up.

Then the winter sun was glancing off snow, dazzling his eyes. He stopped, blinking. They had made it out of the trees.

But now what?

How could they ever get up the mountain?

The steep slope. The narrow, stony trail.

It was too far.

He tried anyway, dragging the scientist across the broken ground. He managed only to reach the first tree stump. With the last of his strength, he helped Courtz lie against it, then collapsed beside him, unable to move an inch farther.

GET UP! KEEP GOING!

He didn't have the strength to answer, even with a thought. He'd climbed just high enough to see over the top of the trees. And there it was—the Dragon on its way. Amazing how it came! Like a whale, hurling itself out of the water! Trees and earth exploded upward with each surge of its body, and a shrieking roar filled the air.

"I'm sorry," he whispered to the Dragon. "I didn't mean to."

MOVE MAX! HIDE!

But there were no places to hide. Courtz had cut down the trees.

He got to his feet anyway. Why, he did not know.

Tried, for some reason, to drag Courtz around the other side of the tree stump.

They were thrown from each other when the Dragon burst out of the trees and hit the mountainside. It tore up a mouthful of earth and flung it in the air. Then again. Then again, as though trying to wreck the machine that was torturing it on the rocks and stones.

Fallen onto his side, Max watched, hypnotized. The Dragon's teeth flashed. Flashed. Flashed.

Dragon teeth.

Grinder teeth.

Shark teeth.

Teeth absolutely everywhere.

The tooth! MAX! THE TOOTH!

Martha's voice snapped him back to where he was, and what was happening.

The tooth?

The Dragon Hunter's tooth! Give it to the Dragon!

He rolled onto his knees and tugged off his gloves. His frozen fingers jabbed the tooth farther into his earhole.

Stuck!

The Dragon surged up the mountain.

Run, Max! RUN!

He didn't move. There was no point. He couldn't escape the Dragon.

The tooth was their only chance.

He used his pinkie. Jiggled it, like he'd gotten water in his ear. Then whacked the other side of his head again and again and again.

It popped out.

He fumbled it.

Bounced it off one palm onto the other.

Dropped it.

It vanished into the snow.

The Dragon came down with a rush and a roar—he threw himself to one side. Scooping up another mouthful of earth, it tossed its head back. Under the rattling hail of pebbles, leaves, and branches he curled into a ball and covered his head. The mountainside was sliding out from under him. He tumbled past the Dragon's thrashing body, dragged by the breaking earth. He clawed at the ground, but everything he grabbed was moving, too. He couldn't breathe. He could hardly see. Lost in a roar of rocks and snow, he gave up struggling and let it take him.

A hand came out of nowhere.

Courtz!

Grunting, the scientist hauled him into the shelter of the tree stump as the landslide thundered around them. The noise passed down the mountain, rumbling and echoing, subsiding into an eerie silence in which nothing moved.

Slowly, he twisted his head out from under Courtz's arm.

The Dragon was only a short distance away, already looking in the twilight gloom like a mound of rubble.

Did it work?

It worked! The tooth worked!

He wriggled out from under Courtz. The scientist's body
was heavy and limp, his breath faint and shallow.

I told you. And you never believed me.

What did you tell me?

Knights always win against Dragons!

Max tried a smile—it trembled apart on his face. He
could not stand, let alone help Courtz stand. Battered, freezing, exhausted—he simply lay there, barely able to breathe,
watching Courtz, watching the scientist move.

He was getting himself up.

Why?

After a minute or so, he was kneeling.

What for? It would be better to just let night come. Night,
and the cold.

Courtz raised his head, his whole body trembling with
the effort.

Looked at Max.

Deep within the scientist's bright blue eye, a tiny spark
was burning furiously. It was the unconquerable spark of life,
of the desire to live and be alive.

It was the spark that had died out in the Mulgans.

Max got to his feet.

He got Courtz to his feet.

Together, they started up the mountain.

He wasn't going to see that spark die out again. Not in anyone.

Four hours later, bedraggled, bloody, and half-dead, they reached the cave.

The Seven League Boots

The Witch's carriage was outside the cave entrance. She was there with Kaspar Hauser, sitting by the fire.

Kaspar was toasting marshmallows. He glared at Max shiftily, and popped them all into his mouth, one by one, until his cheeks bulged.

The Witch was playing a ukulele and singing a lullaby. As Max guided Courtz toward the fire, a single step at a time, she followed him with her eyes.

> *Be snuggle be dapple*
> *Be drowsy be deep*
>
> *Be fallow be willow*
> *Be Little Bo Peep*
>
> *Be lithesome be mighty*
> *Be soul shall thou keep*
>
> *Be Tickle Toe Tommy*
> *Be tinkle be sleep.*

They collapsed just as the Witch strummed her final chord. With a final effort, Max rolled Courtz onto his back. He lay absolutely still, his skin clammy and cold.

The Witch set her ukulele aside and peered over his shoulder.

She read the entire story from start to finish in a glance.

"Kaspar?"

"Yes, Mother?"

"Go to the workshop and get my toolbox, two sheaves of Chitin, half a pound of Cobweb, four pairs of Socks, and a Hacksaw."

"Tools, Chitin, Cobweb, Socks, Hacksaw," repeated Kaspar, holding one finger to the side of his head. "Anything else?"

"If I wanted anything else I'd ask for it! Take the Seven League Boots."

"Say please!"

"I'll do no such thing!"

"Say it!"

"Who are YOU all of a sudden?"

"Mother. We talked about this. It's just a word. But it has a nice effect."

"So's WHIPPING! WHIPPING is just a word! AND it has a nice effect."

"Mother!"

"A man's dying, and you're fiddling around with etiquette! What kind of monster have I raised?"

"MOTHER!"

"Please. Now SCRAM!"

Kaspar disappeared into the carriage, then sat on its running board, pulling on a pair of knee-length boots. He walked clear of the cave, stopped, drew back a leg, and kicked an invisible soccer ball.

BANG!

He rocketed into the sky, reduced to a distant speck in a moment.

Max watched with a dull sense of astonishment, then shifted away from the Witch as she explored the oozing stump of Courtz's arm with her fingertips.

"It didn't work, you know, your little midnight alarm," she muttered. "So you saved a few villagers—big deal! By the time the normal Dragons return, the Forest Folk will be ready for them. Flashlights and laser beams! We'll cook those Lizards like marshmallows!"

He just stared at the fire. "Is he going to be okay?" he whispered.

"I've seen worse," the Witch shrugged. "He could do with a few Snot Maggots, I suppose."

She snorted, hocked a blob of phlegm into her hand, rolled it between her palms, added some Ashes and a couple of Swear Words, then began pinching off little balls, which became— after a brief incubation under her tongue—yellow, wriggling Maggots. One by one, she spat them onto the stump of Courtz's arm. They seemed happy there and began chewing around.

"Their saliva numbs pain and fights infection," she explained. "So even though they're guzzling away, you don't feel a thing! Terrifically effective against horses. Mind out!"

BANG!

A divot of earth flew up, and Kaspar landed beside them with a picnic basket under his arm. He took off the boots and left them at the cave entrance.

"Here're the things. Came as fast as I could!"

"You think I was born yesterday?" growled the Witch. "You dillied and dallied! Now look sharp and lend a hand. Hoo-hoo! Lend a hand! Haha! Clear a space, you!"

Max moved away and sat with his back to them, looking out of the cave over the Woods. They lay beneath him, seeming to snarl up at the cave, furious at his escape.

Maybe they knew what was about to happen. Maybe they could feel it coming.

The Forest Folk would wipe out the Dragons with New Light. The Coven would try to stop it, and the Forest Folk would turn on them, too. Once the Dragon Hunters, the Dragons, and the Coven were gone, the Woods would be cleared, bulldozed, and built over.

The Woods would become like the World.

And the worst thing of all: he didn't know if it was good or bad.

Dreams had left him with nobody. No parents. No home.

Dreams were thieves.

Dreams didn't add things to life. They stole them away. Down with dreams!

So what are you going to do? Sit here in this cave?

What else can I do?

You can go!

Go where?

Where you've always wanted to go. The Panthalassa Ocean.

I don't want to go there anymore.

Are you sure? It's one last dream you can check. Maybe it will come true.

It won't. It's all nonsense.

Then take me there. I would like to see it.

Even if I wanted to, it's too far. I saw the map.

Not when Kaspar has left you the Boots . . .

Max lifted his head. The Seven League Boots were only a short distance away.

He left them on purpose?

He still thinks you're after his Mother.

I don't have a Mother . . .

Neither do I, Max. But we've got each other. Let's go and look at the Ocean!

He glanced back at the Witch again. Kaspar caught his eye and made a secret signal, jabbing a finger at the Boots.

See! Go Max! Go!

Max scooted over and pulled them on. They came up to his knees, and fit perfectly, even though they had seemed much smaller on Kaspar.

He got to his feet. Took a cautious step. Nothing happened.

"Hold it!" snapped the Witch. "Where do you think you're going, Mr. Vanishings?"

She jumped up and ran toward them, hacksaw glinting.

"KICK THE BALL!" yelled Kaspar. "KICK THE BALL!"

He kicked the ball.

BANG!

Trailing a scream, he flew in a soaring arc over the trees—then he was falling, his feet peddling wildly, and the Woods were rushing up. He hit the ground with a jolt, staggered forward, and—BANG! The stagger was transformed into an explosive bound that rocketed him up into the atmosphere, far over the lights of Gilead and into the beyond.

BANG! By the third leap he'd managed to stop screaming.

BANG! By the fourth, he'd gotten his arms and legs under control.

BANG! By the fifth, he'd mastered the boots, and could choose his direction by making a quick pivot of his hips as he landed.

Okay, I think I've got the hang of it. Which way's the Ocean?

Go in any direction. It surrounds us. You'll get there eventually.

He swung his legs toward the moon, seven leagues to a stride. BANGBANGBANG! Soon he saw a mountain range on the horizon.

It'll be on the other side.

He used the mountains like stepping stones, jumping from one to the other, higher and higher until he stood on the highest summit and could see what lay beyond.

That's it!

There was no more forest. Instead, a rippling darkness, the Panthalassa Ocean, stretched as far as the eye could see. The moon lay broken across its surface, as though it had fallen and smashed apart into glittering shards.

It's beautiful . . .

Yes. But it's not anything else on top of that.

What do you mean?

It's like my Forever Parents. Just something nice to look at once in a while.

Martha came out of his finger and stood beside him. "Max," she said. "It's all right for things to be beautiful." Then she smiled at him. "I want to show you something!"

She looked around carefully, then ran a short distance away, stretched up, and pressed her hand against the night sky. It gave slightly like sand, and she left a handprint there, which was carried off by the slow turning of the heavens.

"See!" she said. "Mountains were made so the Wizards could reach the sky. But you have to get to the very highest part."

Wonderingly, Max joined her on the highest part and reached up to touch a star. It worked! The star came away on his fingertip and glowed there, a tiny, beautiful part of light.

He collected one on each fingertip until he had ten, then placed them one by one in Martha's hair.

"A crown for my Queen," he said.

She watched him shyly. As the Three-Quarter Moon passed on the revolving Stuff of Night, she lifted it down and handed it to him.

"A shield for my Knight," she said.

He turned it awkwardly, because there was no handle on the moon. So he held it against his chest and looked out again at the Panthalassa Ocean.

"Do you think it's true what the Dark Man said?" he asked.

"What did he say?"

"The stars are drifting apart, and people are doing the same. The forces holding us together are getting weaker."

She thought about it for a moment. "Didn't he also say we have to hold onto each other as best we can?"

"Yes. But that's just what I'm not good at."

"Then we'll start with each other," she said, with a determined nod. "And work the rest out later."

Her tiny hand crept into his. They stood there watching the sky turn and the Ocean gleam.

"Can you dance?" she asked then. "I've been wanting to ask you for ages."

"D-dance?"

"Yes. You know." She looked at him with serious intention, and his heart began to pound. "Dance."

"I don't think so. I never tried."

"Why not?"

"Nobody ever asked me."

"You're supposed to do the asking, silly."

"Why me?"

"I don't know. It's one of the rules."

"I thought you didn't care about rules."

"You're right. That rule is silly." She turned to face him. "Will you dance with me?"

He swallowed. "Here?"

She nodded in a business-like way. "It's romantic. I'm a Queen and you're a Knight. We should dance. You'll have to put the moon down. You need your hands free. I get to keep the stars."

Max turned to put the moon down.

"Stay like that," she whispered then. "There's something I need to say and I can't say it when you're looking at me. Only turn around when I tell you to."

The words sent a shock through him, and he remembered again how he'd stood at the kitchen sink, Alice and Forbes at the table behind him. This was how it had always been—if he turned his back on something, it disappeared. But Martha had given him an order, and he had to obey.

"Do you remember you asked me when the end was going to come? When I was going to stop being the Queen and become yours forever?"

"I remember," Max whispered. He knew what she was going to say, and he didn't want her to say it.

"The end is coming for us," Martha said. "I can feel it. It's coming like the sun comes, bringing color to the trees, melting away the grayness. I'm going to melt away, too, because that's what the sun does to cold things. And I'm beginning to think . . . maybe it's good. I'm gray now, but I used to have colors! I had red hair and my eyes were green. I like to think of you seeing me like that. If I went away I'd be in the place where all the color comes back, the place where I get to become a dream. Your dream."

Max didn't want to hear any more. "That's all just a story. You wouldn't know about it. You'd be dead. The place where people go and become dreams, it's a nowhere place, it's nothing. You wouldn't know I'm dreaming about you."

"I know that, and I can't explain it," she said, "but when the sun is coming up and you're melting away it doesn't feel like that's so bad. As long as you know someone is going to be dreaming of you, it doesn't seem so bad to become the dream. Now turn around and look at me."

Max turned, afraid she was going to vanish the moment he laid eyes on her, to disappear into nothing the way everything else had.

But she didn't.

She stepped into his arms.

"I've never danced with anyone," she whispered in his ear. "I'd like to dance with you. I think this is a good place."

"There's no music."

"The stars are making music."

"I can't hear it."

"I can. It's going Dum-Da-Da-Dum, Da-Da-Dum."

"Stars don't go Dum."

"How do you know if you can't hear it?"

"I don't think I believe in it . . ."

"Then listen to your heart." She placed her hand against his chest. "It sounds like the stars. Dum-da-dum-da-dum."

"Dum-da-dum?"

"Da-DUM." She smiled and pressed her cheek against his. "Now do what I do, and don't let go."

3

The Homecoming

They tore out handfuls of sky to make a hole, then crept into the soft darkness and covered it with the moon. Through its silvery transparency, they looked down on the Woods. The revolving dome bore them up and away, away from the Ocean, and back over the trees.

Martha soon fell asleep beside him. But Max could not sleep. Neither of them knew the Wizards had crafted the spongy darkness from Despair and Loss of Hope, trying to remove as much as possible from the Woods. Under their influence, his thoughts turned to those questions that could never be answered.

Who am I?

Where do I come from?

The Accursed Questions.

In Russian it really had sounded like a magic spell cast by a Witch over a cradle.

Pro-klyAT-ee-yeh-vo-PROSS-ee!

The questions were like curses in fairy tales. Under their influence, it was impossible to live like other people. You had to wander, driven by the curse until a cure was found.

But there was no cure.

And now Martha was going to disappear as well, like everyone else. What would he do then? He would go into the Woods and let the Wildness get him, like Boris's Father. That's what he would do.

But that wouldn't work, either. Every time he saw the moon, he would remember this night and Martha, and the Wildness would be driven from him. Just like when Boris remembered his Mother, the moon would bring him back.

The moon would be his gravestone.

The moon . . .

He blinked suddenly.

"Martha," he whispered. "Martha, wake up!"

She stirred beside him, blinking sleepily. "What is it? What's wrong?"

"What was it the Dragon Hunter said? If I came back before the Full Moon, he would tell us about the Books and the Light. That was it, wasn't it?"

She frowned, then nodded. "Yes. Yes, he said that."

"You're sure?"

"Yes."

"Do you know what he meant?"

"No. I just thought it had something to do with the Dragon Hunters. One of the things an Apprentice would need to know to take over. Why?"

"Maybe it's a clue. Everything is about Light: Old Light. New Light. And the Books? He must have meant the Storybooks. Boris said a pattern was emerging. What if the Storybooks and Light are connected somehow?"

"But you didn't do what he asked, Max. He won't tell you any of the secrets."

"He has to. It's like he said. If I don't become a Dragon Hunter, who will? We have to get back to Paris."

"We don't know the way. The sky's been moving all this time. I don't even know where we are."

"We can ask for directions."

"Ask who?"

"Just come on!"

They opened the moon and dropped down from the night. Max ran with a BANG BANG BANG until he found the day.

Then he bounded around with a BANG BANG BANG until he saw what he was looking for: one of the Wind Towers, rising out of the trees.

The Wind Giant on duty was reclining in a deckchair with a handkerchief over his face.

BANG!

The Wind Giant toppled backward.

Paris?

He was miles off!

This was the Canadian Yukon!

But that was easily fixed—the Giant let out a Wind and ordered it to Paris.

BANG!

Max followed the stirring of the treetops as the Wind raced ahead.

By the time the Eiffel Tower appeared on the horizon evening was falling, and it was raining heavily. BANG! Soaked and shivering, Max made one final leap to the city boundaries, and hitched a ride into the center on a pumpkin cart.

The wagoner was a small, wiry man with a long, pointed nose that twitched as he spoke—and he spoke almost constantly. It was a lonely ride in from the fields, he said, and it was nice to have company, even if it was a runaway ragamuffin who ought to know better. It wasn't safe wandering around in the Woods, after all, now that the Dragons had gone bad. Not that the Woods had ever been safe, but still, you knew how to deal with certain troubles, and there wasn't much you could do against trouble in the form of a hundred-ton, fire-breathing monster, was there? Especially now that the Dragon Hunters were gone.

"There's still the Chief Dragon Hunter," Max said, interrupting the man's chatter.

"Died yesterday. Haven't you heard? I wasn't going to bother coming in. Don't suppose there'll be much business, what with all the doom and gloom. But what's better in weather like this than a hot drop of pumpkin soup or a slice of pumpkin pie!"

Max huddled under the cloak the man had pulled over them. Rain dripped off the end of his nose. A dull shudder went through his body.

So that was it.

The last chance. Gone.

Even the people in the street seemed to know it. They were going around with heavy frowns. Now and again, they glared at him angrily, and he could read their thoughts plain as daylight.

If you'd just dropped that tooth in the porridge like you were supposed to, you'd have gotten back in time. You'd have stopped the Tinker, you'd have learned the secret, and who knows— found out about the Appearance. Now what have you got? A wagon of pumpkins and that's it.

"Don't look so glum, lad!" the wagoner chuckled. "It isn't that bad. Me—I'm turning Woodcutter. That's where the work is these days! And where there's work, there's money! Say—I'll be looking for an Apprentice. Maybe you and I, we could work together?"

"I'll get off here," Max managed to croak out. "Thanks."

"Suit yourself—hey, you want a pumpkin? You look like you could use one!"

Max jumped down and walked away, huddled against the rain. But he soon regretted not taking one. It was a long walk through the city, and he would have eaten one raw, he was so hungry.

Pumpkins. They always reminded him of Halloween. Candy apples. Chocolate.

Witches.

The Better Chocolate.

Pumpkins.

Hollowed out the head, he muttered, again and again. What was that about?

Pumpkins.

Halloween.

Hollowed out the head.

Jack-O-Lanterns. Old Light.

His head was hollowed out. Hollowed out and dead.

Hollowed out the head.

By the time he reached the Trocadéro, he was burning with fever. Somehow, he made it up the steps. A Witch was arguing with a Wizard in the Grand Entrance. They threw up their hands when he came squelching through the entrance—they'd been at the Dragon Head dissection and recognized him at once. Doctor Peshkov? He'd been hunting high and low for him!

Stay there! Don't move!

They rushed off in different directions.

He stayed. He stood, stood, under the vaulted roof, a pool of water forming on the marble floor around his feet. He couldn't move, no, not another inch. Even when the door boomed open at the end of the hall and Boris appeared, half-running, he only stood and watched—not understanding how anyone could be so glad to see him, such a selfish dreamer, back from the dead, returned from the Woods.

And when the Dark Man lifted him off his feet and hugged him, he dissolved like the Squonk in a pool of bubbles and tears, helpless in the bottom of the Hunter's bag.

The fever tore him apart.

The Dragon Fire came over him again and again, burning him, burning him, and following the fire came thousands of Imps with dark eyes. They tortured him, like a Dragon Hunter tweaking him where it hurt most. He was a Dragon, thrashing in front of a thousand Imps who were jabbing him with long metal spikes.

He was a Dragon.

He was a shark.

He was a grinder.

And there were a thousand boys with spikes . . .

And then he sat up, and there was only one boy, and it was him. He was in a four-poster bed, the kind Queens slept in. Curtains all around him.

He crawled across the blankets, and peeked through the curtains. The room was crammed full of forest. Trees. Branches. Brambles. Thorns. Not a chink of space was left.

Then a Dragon's head was pushing its way through the thicket. It floated forward and hovered at the end of the bed.

"Well, kid, this is it," the Dragon's head said. "You got to start over."

"Do I have to?" he asked.

"It's the only way," said the Dragon.

"Well, all right then."

"Are you ready?"

"Yes."

"You're not afraid?"

"I did it once. It's just annoying having to do it again."

The Dragon's mouth began to open and close with the mechanical precision of a machine.

CLANG

CLANG

He crawled toward it.

CLANG

CLANG

He rolled into the flashing teeth.

CLANG

CLANG

Half of him went one way.

CLANG

Half went the other.

CLANG

CLANG

CLANG

CLANG
CLANG
CLANG
CLANG
CLANG
CLANG
CLANG
CLANG

Bells were ringing. CLANG CLANG CLANG—dull, iron bells sullen with disappointment. A funeral procession was moving through the city to the final resting place of the Dragon Hunters. There were only the Chief Wizard Theodore Mommsen, the High Witch Ulla Andromeda, Mrs. Jeffers, Max, Boris, and Porterholse, arrived that morning from London. Two Witches and two Wizards walked ahead with Roland Danann's body, stumbling now and again on the slippery cobbles.

As they passed, Forest Folk stopped going about their business to watch, their faces showing little sympathy. It was common knowledge now. Before their migration, Dragons had gone on the rampage all over the Woods, not just in Paris. Some had even remained behind, attacking towns and villages. What defense could be raised against such mighty beasts?

What defense?

Well might you ask!

Rumor had it a Tinker in the north had harnessed the power of electricity. The people of Gilead had become immune to Bio-Photonic Disintegration, and were keeping the Dragons at bay with New Light.

The power of New Light, here in the Woods?

That was an interesting development!

The cities were getting rather large, after all. If the Deep Woods could be cleared, the Wild Ones, not killed off (nobody was suggesting that!) but driven back—they could use the space. They could use the land for farms. A few more towns and roads. Why not? There were an awful lot of trees, after all. Did there need to be quite so many? A balance had to be struck. That was reasonable.

So no, they weren't going to bother much about that Dragon Hunter's funeral. He was a strange old fish. Kept himself apart. Never joined in. Had a good life, no doubt. Told some interesting tales, but now . . . well, bless him and all that, but it's time for something new.

None of this surprised Max—it was exactly what Courtz had planned. On that first morning after his fever broke, Boris and Porterholse had sat with him to hear his story while Mrs. Jeffers made preparations for the funeral. He told them about the Witch in her carriage, and the twins in the cottage. He told them about Courtz in his cave, and the escape with the Seven League Boots.

He didn't say a word about the Dragon Fire.

He simply glided from the Witch's cottage to the Tinker's cave without mentioning Rosethorn. He just couldn't bring himself to tell Boris he'd been in the Dragon Fire and still knew nothing about the Appearance.

The Dark Man had devoted his life to stopping the Vanishings.

If he found out the only way was to help Courtz destroy the Woods, Max feared it would tear him apart. Again.

Boris's suspicions had fallen on Courtz from the moment he learned about electricity in the Woods. Symposium expenditure was a matter of public record. On his short trip back to the World, he'd come across regular payments to a company that supplied and maintained street lamps—a company set up by Courtz, himself.

After the funeral, Boris planned to find the cave on Mount Gilead and confront his old rival.

Max wasn't sure what the point was. It was too late to stop Courtz. The plan was already in motion.

And maybe it was for the best.

Maybe it really was time for the Era of Science to begin, for the Lindworm to take on its final, true form.

But he kept quiet about these doubts. All he cared about now was holding onto Martha for as long as possible.

She was fading away inside him. The pond was getting deeper, every hour adding a new fathom, making it harder for her to swim up to the surface.

And instead of sitting in a corner of Paris, in a quiet park under a tree, where he would be able to think himself down to her—he had to bury a Dragon Hunter.

The long march through Paris ended at Montparnasse Cemetery, the burial ground of the Dragon Hunters.

A high stone wall enclosed the graveyard, and they walked at least two miles along its length before they came to the only entrance—an iron door set deep in the crumbling masonry. The door was locked, but the Dragon Hunter had given Mrs. Jeffers all the necessary instructions for his burial, along with a set of keys.

They waited in a silent huddle while she found the correct one. Despite the solemnity of the occasion, Porterholse was excited. Nobody except the Dragon Hunters had ever entered this door, he'd told Max several times. Nobody knew what they'd find behind it.

The cemetery, though, was just like any other. There were tombstones, statues, and sepulchers, hundreds of them, all crowded closely together. Following the customs of the Woods, these too bore messages instead of names and dates, but it appeared these had never once been refreshed. The tombstones were old, the letters worn and faded:

I AM
NOT SORRY

I NEVER
RETURNED

IF YOU MISS
ME LIKE I
MISS YOU
YOU MISS ME

WHY DID
YOU DO
WHAT YOU
DID?

The words floated around them, half-obscured by lichen, shattered by cracks, soaked by rain. It seemed to Max the dead Dragon Hunters were whispering to him as he went by, and he saw behind their simple words deep sadness and long regret. All the Dragon Hunters ran away from home, Courtz had told him. He glanced over at the Chief Dragon Hunter on his litter of Briarback branches, remembering the sad story he had told of his childhood in New York. Though his body was wrapped in white cloth, the scarred face was still visible.

Do World Ones always smile like that when they're dead?
No.
So why's he smiling?
I don't know . . .

The Dragon Hunter seemed to smile more with each step, until Max could have sworn he was positively grinning.

"What words did he choose for his gravestone?" he asked Mrs. Jeffers.

"None," she replied. "According to his instructions, Chief Dragon Hunters do not get buried in the main cemetery. They are interred in a special crypt." She pointed to a squat circular tower in the center of the graveyard. "That thing there, apparently."

"I was wondering what that was," Porterholse said. "It looks more like a windmill than anything else. With the sails removed."

"Exactly as he described it!" said Mrs. Jeffers.

When they reached the door, she unlocked it and they all peered inside. Beyond was nothing more than a narrow space and a trapdoor. A supply of lanterns hung from hooks on the walls, some dusty, some showing signs of recent use.

"This doesn't look like much of a crypt," said Boris. "Are you sure this is the place?"

"Very sure," Mrs. Jeffers replied. "He said we'd have to go down through a trapdoor, and then there would be a door, and then everything would be made clear."

Boris glanced at her. "Everything would be made clear? Those were his exact words?"

"That's what the man said."

"It's an unusual choice of words, don't you think?"

"He was an unusual man."

Opening the trapdoor revealed a set of stone stairs that curled down into darkness.

Mrs. Jeffers thought for a moment. "I think we'd better leave him up here until we find out what's what. Stay with him until we send word," she instructed the Witches and Wizards.

They set flames to the Argand burners and made their way down the steps single-file, Mrs. Jeffers in front, then Porterholse, then Boris and Max, and finally Ulla Andromeda and Theodore Mommsen. At first, the steps were quite dry, but quickly they became slick with underground moisture and the slimy trails of snails and worms.

"Why couldn't they have one of those nice little crypts on the surface?" Mrs. Jeffers muttered, holding her lantern before her and lifting the hem of her gown. "We must be below the level of the sewers already."

"I'm not sure this is a place for burying bodies," Boris replied.

"Indeed," Mommsen muttered. "The only thing you bury this deep are secrets."

In the stillness of the tunnel, their voices sounded echoey and strange. The steps showed no sign of ending, and twisted deeper and deeper into the earth. Porterholse was emitting anxious gusts of Wind that made the lanterns flicker.

This is horrible down here.

It's going to be even worse climbing back up.

They had grown so used to the never-ending steps uncoiling out of the darkness below them that the door, when it came,

came as a shock. It was a solid thing and completely round, a cross-section of a gigantic tree trunk, the ever-decreasing circles of its life still clear in the dark wood.

It was cut from a Briarback tree.

None of them spoke. For some peculiar reason, they had all stopped to listen, holding their breath as if they expected to hear something, even this far underground.

But of course, there was nothing.

They huddled behind Mrs. Jeffers while she bent over the lock.

In that moment before the door opened, Max felt a very strong urge to jump forward and stop her. It was as though he knew that once THIS door was opened, nothing would be the same ever again. It would be better to just return to the streets, and sit somewhere in sunlight among lots of people—and above all, never, ever think of the door, ever again.

But he didn't jump forward, and Mrs. Jeffers unlocked the door and threw it wide, without even opening it a crack to peek through.

Because of the silence, which really had been complete, nobody was prepared for the sudden surge of noise, the clamping, stamping, and hammering, that burst over them.

Neither was anyone prepared for the flood of light, for the enormous size of the cavern, or for the bewildering number of small people within it, every last one of them naked, filthy, and without a stitch of clothing.

Most of all, most of all, by FAR most of all, nobody was prepared for the fact that every one of these little people—of which there had to be hundreds—with their pale faces and large, black eyes, their spindly limbs and their gleaming teeth, was the dead and spitting image of Max Mulgan himself.

Nobody moved.

Nobody said a thing.

A minute passed—still they just stood there and watched all the Maxes running around.

Some kind of industry was going on, a coordinated activity in which every Max knew his place and his job. Some of the Maxes were turning mounds of leaves over with pitchforks, drying them under lanterns that dangled from long lines.

Others stood at workbenches, rasping away at sheets of dark, burnished wood with sandpaper. A few stood beside long, narrow troughs that lined the walls, scooping handfuls of mud into their mouths and chatting quietly as they ate. But most of the Maxes were sitting at writing desks in the center of the room, peacock-feather quills jiggling in the air as they scribbled away.

"By the Winds, they're making Storybooks," Porterholse said in hushed tones. "Genuine, bona fide, one hundred percent original Storybooks."

The Maxes were so involved in their work that almost a minute passed before they noticed the small group standing in the entrance. When they did, silence spread through the chamber. The bookbinders stopped carving and polishing. The writers looked up and set down their quills. Even the mud-eating Maxes wiped their lips and looked around. All the Maxes put down their work, and all of them to a Max stared at Max. And then a ripple went through them, an excited whispering that spread throughout the room.

"He's back."

"It's him."

"The One Who Cleans the Teeth the Best!"

"He's the same age!"

"He hasn't been gotten by the Getting Older!"

"Do you think he found our parents?"

"Oh my heavens," croaked the Chief Wizard, turning pale. "It's the Kobolds!"

4

THE KOBOLDS

Let's keep our hats on here," said Mrs. Jeffers. "Let's not get the heebie-jeebies. Theodore, you'd better tell us about the Kobolds. Then we'll find out what these Maxes know about . . . Max."

The group had gathered among the writing desks. Boris was rubbing his black hair so violently it stood up like a forest. Porterholse was furtively inspecting a Storybook. Ulla Andromeda had picked up one of the tools and was examining it curiously. Mommsen was blinking and hiccupping.

Strangely, Max did not feel strange at all.

He wasn't confused. He wasn't amazed or astonished. He felt as though he was about to understand it all, and he had always understood. The pieces of the puzzle were turning and rotating. He couldn't make sense of it right now. But it was like a Rubik's cube—at any moment, it would all fall into place. The Maxes had gathered in parliament at the far end of the cavern. They knew nothing about the recent events in what they called "the Above." From their agitated whispering, it was obvious they worked closely with the Dragon Hunters and were shocked to learn of their fate.

"Who's going to bring us the stories?"

"We've got enough to last a few months."

"And what then?"

"We'll have to get them ourselves."

"Won't we get gotten by the Getting Older if we go into the Above?"

"The One Who Cleans the Teeth the Best didn't get gotten."

"What about if we make up our own stories? Is that allowed?"

Several Maxes had scurried down a hole in the center of the room to spread the news to other areas of what they called "the Warrens." Now a constant stream of Maxes were coming out of the Warrens, to see The One Who Cleans the Teeth the Best for themselves.

Mrs. Jeffers had collared one to interrogate, but he seemed barely able to understand the situation.

"*Dragons* killed the Dragon Hunters?" he kept asking. "*All* of them?"

Theodore Mommsen was almost as astonished, himself. "I simply don't believe it. I thought the Kobolds had been scrapped. They were little more than prototypes."

"Prototypes of what?" Ulla asked. "I've never heard of them."

"Kobolds were precursors to children," Mommsen replied.

He turned to the Kobold. "How long have you been down here?" he asked.

"A few years."

"How many exactly?"

"I don't know. Ten?"

"Ten?" Mommsen screwed up his eyes suspiciously. "Or thousands?"

"Something like that."

"Millions?"

"Yes," said the Max. "Somewhere between ten and a thousand million. Not long."

"And you've never gone out?"

"We can't. The Dragon Hunters told us we'd get old and die if we went outside."

"They're Kobolds all right," Mommsen said, nodding in fascination. "Credulity was one of their defining qualities. And they've no concept of time."

"Just tell us what you know, Theodore," Mrs. Jeffers suggested impatiently. "None of us have heard of the Kobolds."

"It was long before I came into existence. Long before the Olden Days and long before the Coven was formed."

"In the Dabbling Days?"

"That's right." Mommsen turned to the others. "The Dabbling Days were a bad old time when Witches and

Wizards first began to alter Creation. Patents were written down and slotted into the Archive with little thought for the consequences, and there were many disasters. The biggest was when one of the Wizards invented the Passage of Time in order to enable the Seasons, and everything started to Get Old. Nobody understood the Getting Older at all. Different Wizards reacted in different ways. One noticed that the oldest people were too weak to look after themselves and came up with the Kobolds to act as servants. There was no need to differentiate between them, so he made them all the same, and of course, they were immune to the new Getting Old. Best of all, they didn't need any looking after: the Wizard gave them sharp teeth so they could eat the ground on which they stood, and wonderful imaginations so they wouldn't get bored as they went about their work.

"But then the very oldest Forest Folk began to die. If Getting Old had been strange, this Being Dead business was stranger still. Nobody could make head nor tail of it. Why didn't they move? Why didn't they breathe? Were they sleeping? They didn't respond to prods and pokes, loud noises, shakes, caresses, tears, songs, chanting, being rolled down slopes, swung on a string, or the smell of their favorite foods. Dead Forest Folk tossed into lakes made no effort to save themselves and sank without a trace. Some were left outside to recover in the fresh air and sunlight—'It's the best thing for them!'—with consequences that were terrible to behold. Whatever force had held them together, given them motion and life, had departed, and soon the flesh was departing, too, dwindling down, piece by piece, particle by particle, atom by atom, dissolving into the ground. This ghastly process caused hitherto unknown questions to appear. Would everyone suffer this terrible disintegration? Was it universal? The Forest Folk practically tore their hair out in despair. They started to bury the dead Forest Folk before the disintegration took hold, so they did not have to watch it. They marked the places where the Forest Folk lay with stones, and left hammers and chisels so they could leave messages if they returned, which their spirits did, summoned back by the power of remembering—until the day when the disintegration had progressed not only through their bodies, but through the minds of those who had known them, until nothing at all was left, not even a particle of a memory, and they sank into oblivion, becoming in the end nothing more nor less than atoms in the glorious mixture that is Creation. Dust, but Dust that had danced!

"The Wizards saw all this and realized a two-fold solution was needed. Most urgent was the practical matter of replacing the dead Forest Folk before they ran out. But they also knew something inspiring had to come into being, to remind people about life in its full force—an idea of equal weight to match the dreadful new fact of dying, that would provide hope for the future. They took the idea of Kobolds and adapted it, coming up with their most beautiful Patent, the most delightful of all their creations: Children. These new creatures retained some Koboldish features, such as the desire to interact with mud, the monstrous gullibility, and the powerful imaginations—but this time they were not immune to the new Getting Old, so they grew up to replace the dying adults."

"I knew about the Passage of Time and Dying," Mrs. Jeffers said. "But I've never heard about the Kobolds, and I've read the Patent Lists as thoroughly as anyone. I thought the Wizards just went straight to Children from scratch."

"An idea as wonderful as Children can only be created from something already partly formed: it cannot come out of nothing," Mommsen replied. "Sometimes, the imperfect needs only the smallest twist to be transformed into a miracle. The Kobolds were that imperfection." He looked at Max, he coughed, and blushed red. "They were regarded as a rather embarrassing piece of craftsmanship, I have to say. They did not suit their original purpose at all well."

"What was the problem?" Ulla Andromeda asked bluntly.

"Well, the Wizard in question, whoever it was, made their imaginations too powerful. Instead of being companions for the old Forest Folk, they spent most of their time daydreaming, staring out of windows, and so on. Anyway, the Kobolds were discontinued and the whole affair was hushed up."

"How do you suppose the Kobolds got here?" Boris asked.

"In the Dabbling Days, faulty prototypes and experiments were simply released into the Deep Woods. The Dragon Hunters must have rescued some of them."

"Some of them?"

"Well, naturally most of the Kobolds got gotten by the Wildness," said Mommsen. "Eventually, they became the Shredders."

"Are you saying these Kobolds have been stuck here since the Dabbling Days?" Mrs. Jeffers asked. "That's thousands of years!"

"He went out!" the Kobold suddenly said, pointing at Max.

"This one?" said Mrs. Jeffers. "That's impossible."

"He did. The Dragon Hunters didn't want him to go. They said he had to stay here. This was his home, they told him. But he wouldn't listen. He wanted to find his parents."

"Kobolds have Patents, not parents," said Mommsen.

"The Dragon Hunters kept telling us that, too," nodded the Kobold. "But the One Who Cleans the Teeth the Best wouldn't listen. He dreamed about finding them, about Being Tucked In, and Birthday Cakes, and Cuddles From Mother. Then, one day, he just disappeared. We all thought he'd gone to find them."

"How long ago was that?" Mrs. Jeffers asked. Then she held up a hand. "Actually, never mind."

"Did he have any idea where to look for his parents?" Boris asked.

"Oh, yes," said the Kobold. "He was sure they were some-where in the World. But why are you asking me all this? He's standing there himself! Why don't you ask him?"

"He doesn't remember," Boris said.

"Why do you keep calling me The One Who Cleans the Teeth the Best?" Max asked, surprising them all, because he'd been silent up until that moment.

"You really don't remember?" the Kobold asked skeptically.

"No," Max said, frowning—because it wasn't really true. Remembering and not remembering. He was still somewhere in-between.

"The Dragon Hunters named us. I'm the One Who Carries the Buckets Too Slowly." He pointed across the room to a Kobold that had just appeared from the hole. "That's the One Who Spills the Ink All the Time. That one with him is the One Who It's Best Not to Sleep Beside. That one over there—"

"No," Max said. "I mean, which teeth did I clean the best?"

"Oh! They're in the Warrens." The One Who Carries the Buckets Too Slowly pointed toward the hole. "Would you like to inspect them? You'll need to take the Chief Dragon Hunter down there anyway."

"You go," Mrs. Jeffers said to Boris. "I'll deal with the Dragon Hunter." She glanced at Porterholse, who was gazing longingly at the bookbinding tables. "And I think one of us would like to have a poke around the Storybooks. Mommsen and Ulla, perhaps you could stay here. Find out more about these Kobolds."

The Chief Wizard and the Head Witch nodded and strolled over to the Kobold conference in the corner.

"This way! This way!" said the One Who Carries the Buckets Too Slowly, beckoning cheerfully to Max.

Max glanced at the Dark Man. Boris gave his shoulder a squeeze of encouragement. Together, they followed the Kobold into the Warrens.

Are you all right?

I'm fine. I feel fine.

That's what I'm worried about. It should be all earthquakes and tornadoes in here. But you seem really calm.

I am calm. I think the Dragon Hunter did this deliberately. I wasn't supposed to come back in time to speak to him. I was meant to come to the funeral. To see this. He knew I was one of the Kobolds all along. He recognized me, right from the moment I sat down next to him on that chair.

So why didn't he just tell you?

He wanted someone to stop the Tinker. He wanted revenge.

But you can't have been one of the Kobolds. You grew up in the World. You started out as a baby.

I know. I don't understand that either. But I think we're about to.

There were no stairs in the passageway, just a burrow curling down into the earth. Around and down it went, down and around, lit like the first room by globes of Old Light ensconced in the wall. The Maxes they met on the way were all astonished to see him—but he passed them by with barely a glance.

There was something bigger, down in the Warrens.

Something waiting for him.

The Kobolds were only the beginning.

After a few curling loops they came to a plain wooden door, which the Kobold ignored.

THE SKELETONS

"What was in there?" asked Boris, glancing back as they went by.

"Bones!" said the Kobold. "That's where we bury the Chief Dragon Hunters. Come! Come!"

They continued on their way, and soon came to another door.

THE ARBORETUM

"An Arboretum?" asked Boris. "Underground?"

The Kobold stopped. "Where do you think we get wood for the Storybooks? And leaves to make paper?"

"They come from Briarback trees, don't they?"

"Yes," said the Kobold. "That's what's good about Briarbacks: they're grow-in-the-dark. Would you like to see?"

I want to see! Tell him yes!

"Yes, please," said Max, and the Kobold threw open the door.

On the other side was a great underground cavern, lit up by the luminous tendrils of mossy plants that dripped off the walls and hung in huge fronds from the roof. Globes of Old Light sat on stalks of wood like weird mushrooms. The whole cavern was full of Briarback trees, a forest of the black-leaved giants. Here and there, Kobolds were planting saplings in the sandy floor. Nearby, one Briarback tree was lying on its side, and the Kobolds were swarming over it, stripping it of branches—they did, actually, look quite like Shredders.

"Who else knows about this place?" Boris asked curiously.

"Nobody," the Kobold said. "Not a soul."

"Not even the Soul Searchers?"

"Oh, no. The Dragon Hunters meet them somewhere in the Above. You are the very first guests! You are seeing things that nobody has ever seen before! Nobody except the Dragon Hunters, of course."

They left the Arboretum.

Around and down.

Down and around.

Then, another door. This one had no sign. Keeping his head down, the Kobold hurried by. "This is a bad door," he muttered.

"Hold on," said Boris, examining the door. "What's in here? There's no handle. Or keyhole."

The Kobold came back. "Only doors you want to open have handles and keys."

"Why have a door at all, in that case?"

"Because when you don't want to ever let something out, you have to have a place to never let it out from," said the

Kobold.

"Never let what out?" asked Max.

"Well," said the Kobold, his eyes glowing. "You know how, in many stories, there's a door, or a box, that must never be opened, not under any circumstances? And then it gets opened? And it's the biggest disaster ever?"

Boris stepped back. "This is that door?"

"The original version."

"So what's in there? Something bad?"

"Bad, yes. Dangerous, too," the Kobold whispered. "The Unthinkable Idea."

Boris frowned. "An idea? You can't lock an idea in a room."

"Not these days you can't—but this door has been closed since the Dabbling Days. Ideas were different then. They came in all shapes and sizes. Some Ideas would fly into your mind, make a tiny adjustment, then escape before you even noticed they were there. Other Ideas would lumber about squashing minds. The Unthinkable Idea was the worst of them all."

"What was it?" asked Boris.

"It was the Idea that you, alone, possessed the Truth. If this Idea got into your head, it turned your mind to stone. Some people's minds turned into nice stones, like Diamonds or Pearls or Pebbles on the Beach. But many ended up with Lumps of Coal for a mind, or Granite, or strange formations of Quartz. The Unthinkable Idea turned thousands of minds to stones, before a brave Wizard tracked it down, bottled it, and gave it to the Dragon Hunters for safe-keeping. But many minds were still stuck as stones. So the Wizards created a new Patent as a cure. This Patent was designed to shatter your mind. Break it apart. Smash it into pieces."

Boris stared at the Kobold, his eyes widening. "That Patent—it's where the Wildness comes from!"

"Yes," said the Kobold. "And it's the only cure. So you see—it's best not to open this door!"

They went on, and soon came to a third door.

THE PAPER ROOM

The One Who Carries the Buckets Too Slowly stopped here. "This is it," he said. "This is where you Cleaned the Teeth the Best."

He flung open the door with a dramatic flourish.

SLAM

SLAM

SLAM

Max left Boris and the Kobold, and walked toward the other end of the room, where a huge machine was vibrating and juddering, its pistons clanking, emitting jets of steam and loud metallic shrieks.

SLAM

SLAM

SLAM

It was a Grinder.

Of course it was a Grinder.

Kobolds were swarming over the hulking machine, adjusting dials, spinning wheels, and shoveling coal, whipping it into an ever greater frenzy, until with a roar and a tremor, it released a blast of steam, shuddered violently, and began the whole cycle again. While all this went on, baskets of Briarback leaves were being tipped into a mouth of pounding teeth. Out of the other end came a stream of pulp, which was immediately pressed flat between two sizzling-hot plates. The enormous paper pancake was then whipped off and taken to another part of the room, where it was sliced into smaller sheets. The Kobolds carried on their work even in their astonishment at seeing newcomers.

Standing right up close to the Grinder's teeth on a metal platform was a Kobold with a long pole and a hook. Now and again he quickly leaned forward and hooked something out, twirling his pole skillfully, and dropped the something into a bucket by his side.

That's what Forbes did . . . at the slaughterhouse.

Forbes did that?

Just with meat, not leaves. Hooked things out.

What does that mean? It can't be a coincidence.

No . . . it's a pattern. I'm beginning to see them.

Patterns?

Yes. Lots of them. Like, it's also what the Dragon Hunters did with their toothpicks. Forbes and the Grinder. Hunters and Dragons. Kobolds and the . . . the Leafgobble! That's its name!

You remember?

Yes!

And sure enough, right then, the One Who Carries the Buckets Too Slowly spread his arms importantly—this was the Leafgobble 5000, one of a kind, an upgrade from the Leafnibble 300, which had only managed six cubic feet of leaf a minute, as opposed to the . . .

He trailed off as Max walked straight past him. By now he'd seen the mural.

Another pattern!

It was on the back wall of the cavern, behind the Grinder, a slapdash mess of gaudy color. There was a spaceship circling a moon. A town bustling with shoppers. A farmyard of mooing cows. A pyramid and a sphinx. A Great Wall of China stretching across a mountainside. A Niagara Falls sending up a white spume and a rainbow. A Stonehenge in a misty dawn. A tribesman in a jungle squatting by a river. A factory churning out cars. A classroom where children sat in examination rows. A fairground where they bought cotton candy. A beach where tourists basked on their backs. And many more.

"It's the World," Boris murmured. "Who painted this?"

"The One Who Cleans the Teeth the Best," said the One Who Carries the Buckets Too Slowly.

Max nodded. "I wasn't painting the World, though," he said, pointing. "I was painting *them*."

They were in every part of the mural—ten times, a hundred times. Playing hook-a-duck at the fairground.

Sunbathing on the beach. Wandering around Stonehenge. Peering through the classroom window. Driving off in one of the new cars . . .

His Forever Parents.

His Forever Father with his glinting spectacles.

His Forever Mother with her auburn hair.

He'd found them at last. And still—they were nothing more than paintings on a wall.

"How could he have known about the World?" Boris asked. "Did the Dragon Hunters tell him?"

"Partly," said the Kobold. "But mostly it's from what the Light shows us. We can look around the World whenever we—"

He stopped and stared at Boris. "Actually," he said slowly. "I'm not sure we're allowed to talk about that with guests. We've never had any visitors before."

The Light, Max. That must be it. What the Dragon Hunter wanted you to see.

"The Light—it's farther down in the Warrens, isn't it?" Max asked. Then, a sudden flash of understanding: "It's where you keep the Storybooks."

The One Who Carries the Buckets Too Slowly leaned in close and whispered.

"That's a secret place. Only Kobolds and the Chief Dragon Hunter are allowed in there."

"I'm a Kobold. You can show me."

"Well, of course *you* can see it. You've seen it a million times already. Not him, though," the Kobold nodded at Boris. "He's not allowed."

"You go, I'll wait here," Boris said. He moved again toward the mural. "There may be clues in these paintings about how you went from working at a Grinder in the Woods . . . to Appearing on a bookshelf in the World."

So Max went on with the Kobold, deeper into the earth. He felt hypnotized. It was all so familiar. Every step of the way.

The tunnel ended abruptly at a final door.

THE LUMINORIUM

He watched as the Kobold pushed the door open. Light swelled out, blinding him, and he edged forward, shielding his eyes.

It took him a moment to get used to it.

Ooooh. It's . . . a library forever!

The cavern widened around them like the yawn of a giant, and continued to widen as they moved away from the door, craning their necks.

Books.

Billions.

Terraces of rickety shelves zigzagged in higgledy-piggledy rows up to the cavern roof hundreds of feet above. Kobolds clambered around on these shelves like bees on a honeycomb, slotting Storybooks into the gaps. Here and there sections of shelves collapsed in a tumbling shower, sending Kobolds screaming to the ground—but they only leapt up, gathered the Storybooks, and began rebuilding. More shelves were under construction, and the cavern rang with the noise of banging and sawing. Everywhere sat stacks of Storybooks, backlogs in the operation, thousands of stories waiting to be added to the vast collection.

But most astonishing of all was the Light.

All of the Storybooks were lit up from within like lanterns. The Light filled them and flowed around them. Something was going on in that Light, too, some kind of process. It wasn't a lazy sunbeam sort of Light. It was flickering excitedly, flaring out now and again from some Storybooks, dimming in others, but always changing.

The Kobold was watching Max closely. "You don't remember this, do you?" he asked.

Max shook his head. He didn't remember. But he knew that somewhere inside his mind he did know, only he couldn't retrieve the memory. It was like those fairground machines with the lowering claw that never quite managed to grasp the stuffed toy.

"Tell me what you meant," he said, "about looking around the World."

"Oh, that's tremendous fun!" the Kobold replied. "I'll show you."

They walked across the cavern floor to the shelves, where the Storybooks were immersed in the Light.

"Just hold your hand near the Books," said the Kobold. "Let the Light come near."

Max tentatively reached out and placed his hand on the spine of a Storybook. The Light flickered toward his hand and enveloped it in a glowing nimbus.

And then he saw it.

The World.

Just as though he was dreaming, images flowed through his mind, clear as photographs. A man sitting at a desk in an empty room, chewing on the end of a pencil. A girl hanging upside down from a jungle gym, her face soft with a thought. An old woman creeping through a No Zone with a bucket of paint. A couple wandering through a park, hand in hand, not talking. A boy peering through a telescope at the moon.

Thousands upon thousands of people, all lost in thought as something entered their minds—a dream, an idea, a notion, a fear, a hope, an unexplained emotion, the soulful pulse of something deep within them.

Still dreaming, despite all the efforts of the Censorship to stop them.

Max slowly withdrew his hand and looked up at all the millions of Storybooks on all the thousands of shelves.

So that was the World?

Yes.

What were all those people doing?

They were dreaming . . . This is where dreams come from. From the Storybooks. The Light puts the dreams into the World.

Show me again!

We should probably go. I need to speak to Boris.

Just a bit more? I've never seen the World. It's the only chance I'll get!

So Max reached his hand into the Light once more, and let the World fill his mind.

The Yule Log

And then the World was gone—Max was yanked back from the shelves, the contact with the Light broken. The One Who Carries the Buckets Too Slowly had spun him around.

"What have you done?" he demanded, his dark eyes glinting. "Who did you bring?"

Two more Kobolds were with him. They looked alarmed. Scared.

Max shook himself free. "What are you talking about? I haven't brought anyone."

"There are OTHERS."

"I know. They're my friends."

"Your friends have New Light!" snarled one of the other Kobolds. "They're invading the Warrens!"

"What?"

Max looked at the door just in time to see a Kobold come tumbling in backward, followed by a red-faced man carrying a cudgel and a bright yellow, rubberized flashlight—the extra-powerful kind used by deep-sea divers and emergency workers.

I know him! That's Farmer Wilberforce!

He's from Gilead?

Yes!

What's he doing here?

HOW SHOULD I KNOW?

But the man wasn't alone. Right after him came the Wasp Witch. Followed by Kaspar. Followed by more Forest Folk with more flashlights. Followed by Professor Courtz, his injured arm heavily bandaged and strapped to his chest.

Max ducked behind a stack of Storybooks.

"Well, well!" he heard the Witch say. "Just like the Archives! Exactly as you described."

Moving it slowly and carefully, Max pulled one of the Storybooks from the stack and peered through the gap.

The Witch also had one of the flashlights, but she was holding it carefully away from her body like a kettle of boiling water. Kaspar was tightly clutching a small wooden box, and gazing around in wide-eyed wonderment. Courtz seemed smaller than before. His face had lost its robust strength and sagged ashen gray.

They must have gotten Mrs. Jeffers and the others.

Not Boris. They won't have gotten Boris.

But then came a second group of Forest Folk. They had the Dark Man prisoner. His arms were pinned behind his back by two burly villagers. His face was beaten and bleeding.

Oh no . . .

Don't move. You can't help him right now.

I've got to do something!

Just wait. The Kobolds will stop them.

Kobolds were already swarming down off the shelves and advancing on the intruders, their dark eyes glinting. One rushed toward Courtz and the Witch, waving them backward and shaking his head.

"You can't come in here! It's forbidden! You must leave, at once, at once I—"

click

Light lanced out.

The Kobold vanished in a puff of ash.

The other Kobolds stopped dead.

Did she just? Is he—!

Oh my God.

Don't look! I don't want to see!

click

Another Kobold exploded in smoke.

Martha screamed. The Kobolds edged backward.

The Witch cocked her flashlight, letting the New Light dance across the ground in front of them.

"Who's next? You? Or you? Well . . . what's the difference?"

Cackling, she flicked the flashlight at the Kobolds—they leapt away from the deadly disc of light. The other Forest Folk marched forward, driving the Kobolds back. Soon a large area was cleared.

Courtz came farther into the cavern, looking up at the terraces of shelves.

"You see, old friend?" he said, turning to Boris. "The heart of the Beginning Woods! Isn't it beautiful? It operates on the same principle as the Archives. There the Coven write the Patents, and put them in the Light, and they become part of the Woods. Here the Dragon Hunters take their stories, put them in the Light, and they become part of the World. Dreams and ideas, floating around, ready to be sucked up by fantasists too feeble to confront reality. But not for much longer. Shut this place down, and nobody will even know what stories are. That space in their minds where stories enter will lie empty. It will be blank. Cleaned out. *Tabula rasa.*"

He's coming! Get down!

Max got down as low as possible. Courtz was wandering over. He stopped just on the other side of the stack of Storybooks.

"If you destroy this library," Max heard Boris say, "you destroy the World as it is."

"But I do not value the World as it is," Courtz replied. "We live in a World where any idea is possible, in which any feeling, or fancy, or dream, can invade the mind. We are divided into believers in one idea, fanatics of another. You must admit this is hard to manage and creates certain problems. Wouldn't it be better if there was one external source of fact we could rely on and refer to? A single idea?"

"You mean science, I suppose?" Boris asked.

"Of course."

Boris began to laugh.

"You find it amusing?" Courtz asked. "You know, my friend, I respect you and would like to be in agreement with you. But you must offer more than laughter."

"Then I will offer you a story."

"We have no time for stories."

"This will be the last story ever told. Even you cannot resist such a delicacy."

"I can."

"And you wish to stop the Vanishings. I know you do."

"That is true."

"My story will explain why your solution will not work. Why science cannot stop the Vanishings."

There was a short pause.

"Very well," Courtz said. "Let us hear it."

He leaned back onto the stack of Storybooks, and there was a scuffle as Boris was released. Max listened breathlessly, trying to identify every sound.

Max . . .

Not now!

How did Courtz know about—

But before she could finish the thought, Boris started talking.

"When I was a boy, my parents traveled from place to place, telling stories. You know this, Eric."

"Yes, I know it."

"They could not afford to give me my own bedroom, so I would sleep in the living rooms of rented apartments. Early each morning, my Mother would enter to build the fire. I would pretend to be asleep, so I could watch her as she worked. First, she placed the kindling. Then the strips of bark. Soon, I would hear the crackling of flames. Finally, she would send a shovel of coals sliding into the grate. The coals would make a pleasant sound as they slid off the shovel. That was how I woke each morning: to see my Mother build a fire so warmth would come."

"Lazy wretch," muttered the Witch. "Letting your Mother slave like a dog!"

"Do not interrupt him," warned Courtz. "Let him finish his story. There will be no other after it."

"When my Mother was a girl," Boris went on, "building a fire was another matter altogether. She grew up in the forests of Siberia, where to be warm you had to go into the woods and chop down a tree. There was no other way. Her Father—my grandfather—made hundreds of such trips, and my Mother joined him. It took great effort to fell a pine, to strip it of branches, and cut it into logs, all in the middle of a vast, untamed wilderness. Hard work, you say? Hard work that made them strong! Knowing they'd done it themselves, with their own hands and tools, well, they knew why they put food in their mouths—they had no doubt why!

"Each year on New Year's Day, her Father went into the forest alone to search for a log to be burned the following Christmas. This search was a great mystery to my Mother. She would wait outside the house listening for the sound of returning horses. The log her Father brought back was so large it took them both to carry it into the woodshed, where it lived in a basket, wrapped in a blanket. For a whole year my Mother would go out in the early morning to fetch wood for the fire, and each time she would lift the blanket, and peer at the log, thrilling to see it lie there, hard and drying. She would watch the life scuttling around it—the spiders that covered it with their cobwebs, the roaches that laid eggs in the cracks beneath the bark. And when Christmas came they would bore holes in it and fill the holes with scented oils, before burning it in their hearth. What did this Yule Log mean to her, at the time of her childhood, and for years afterward, throughout her life? It cannot be described in words. Unless, of course, you are describing it scientifically. In which case, it was a piece of wood in a hut.

"That was long ago now.

"But let us go further back. Deeper in the past, life was even harder and more mysterious. Our ancestors gathered around fires in the open air, or in the mouths of caves. Those fires burned for many days, and were not allowed to go out. They hadn't been brought to life by matches or tinderboxes. They hadn't been struck from flint and steel. They'd been torn from the sky! In those ancient times fire had to be hunted like an animal and brought back to the tribe. This bringing of fire was so momentous, whenever a man arrived with a flame in his hand, it was as though he'd stolen it from the gods themselves!

"But nowadays, nobody appears before their tribe like a god. Nobody wonders at the Yule Log. No boy lies awake as his Mother builds a fire. Those moments of wonderment have been removed from life. And now . . . we Vanish. We Vanish because we do not live. We simply consume, and operate, and press buttons, and turn dials. We want to eat, but we don't want to hunt. We want to be warm, but we don't want to build fires. We don't realize that being warm isn't important—it is the struggle to be warm that matters most. It's the building of fires that gives life its purpose, not the enjoyment of them. Yet all the energy of science is directed toward making things easier, toward eradicating the very thing that life comes from: struggle. The proper use of our bodies and minds. All your science has given us, Eric, is absolutely nothing to do. Under these circumstances, what difference does it make if people Vanish? And is it any wonder that they do?"

Max heard Boris moving closer to Courtz, until he stopped directly in front of him.

"You believe in science, Eric. You believe in a new Era. You glory in your ingenuity, when it is this very ingenuity that has destroyed our greatest treasure: the sensation of Life. Take away that sensation of Life, as you have done, and no number of hospitals or schools, no technological advancement, no increase in ease or comfort, no mountain of gold and food can replace it. Your Era will be one of emptiness and laziness, one of listlessness and apathy. The children of our time ask why Life has no meaning, not realizing it is their lives, not Life, which is to blame. That is your gift to them. Emptiness. Meaninglessness. Is it any wonder that the rise of those horrors has been simultaneous with your ascendancy?"

For a long time, Courtz did not speak. The silence became almost unbearable. Everyone was waiting for the scientist to react.

When he finally spoke, his voice was flat and implacable.

"Take him to the Grinder."

"The Grinder?" one of the Forest Folk repeated.

"I was hoping we might be able to change his mind. I see now this is impossible. If he loves stories so much—let him join them!"

"Do what he says!" the Witch snarled. "Hop to it!"

"The rest of you, find the Apprentice and dispose of the Kobolds," Courtz instructed. "Release the *Collembolla* before you come back up."

He glanced around at the Luminorium, then shrugged and moved away from the stack of Storybooks.

Max, they're not REALLY going to throw Boris into the Grinder?

I think they will. Courtz will do anything if he thinks it's necessary.

What are you going to do?

I . . . I don't know. There's so many of them.

He peeped through the gap in the Storybooks, just in time to see two of the Forest Folk pushing the Dark Man through the door, followed a moment later by Courtz. The remaining Forest Folk formed a vanguard, facing into the Luminorium with the Witch in the middle.

"Right boys!" she cried. "Let's get to work. If you zap one that doesn't frazzle, it's the Apprentice. And mind you don't hit me!"

By now, many of the Kobolds had taken to the shelves, thinking themselves out of danger. But a contingent had still remained behind, watching and listening. They glanced at one another uneasily and started to back away.

"Where do you think YOU'RE going?" laughed the Witch. "Sneaky little NOSE-MINERS! AT 'EM LADS!"

The flashlights blazed outward.

Entire rows of Kobolds were incinerated in an instant.

Then there was chaos. Kobolds throwing their arms in the air. Screaming. Fleeing. Falling over Storybooks. Tripping over themselves. Scrabbling up the shelves, before falling back in puffs of ash.

Max! I don't want to see it. Don't watch!

I have to! I might get the chance to sneak out.

He saw it all. Kobolds leaping. Storybooks tumbling. Shelves crashing.

New Light.

Burning bright.

The Witch strode toward the shelves, picking the Kobolds off one by one.

"Yoo-hoo! Mr. Apprentice? Are you up there?"

POOF!

"Not you!"

POOF!

"Not you!"

POOF!

POOF!

POOF!

POOF!

"Not you! Not you! Not you! Not you!"

Max! Maybe they'll stop if she sees you!

He hesitated, torn. Forest Folk guarded the doorway, making sure no Kobolds could escape. There would be no way past.

"Not you! Not you! Not you! Hahaha! Which one's which? WHICH ONE'S WHICH? Haha!"

POOF!

POOFPOOFPOOFPOOF!

MAX PLEASE MAKE HER STOP!

"Stop!" he yelled. He jumped out from his hiding place and ran toward the Witch. "I'm here! I'm here!"

She swung around—three beams of New Light from other Forest Folk converged on the same spot. He stopped in the spotlights, blinking, unharmed. The Witch's face gleamed with triumph—she'd gotten him!—then her eyes widened with horror.

"NOT YOU!" she shrieked, falling to her knees. "NOOOOO! NOT YOU! NOT MY LITTLE CHOOKUMS!"

Max looked down.

Beside him was a pile of ash and a small pair of hands still clutching the wooden box.

He jumped back, and Martha squealed.

YEEK!

The Witch had incinerated Kaspar Hauser.

"You KILLED him!" she howled, rushing forward.

"I . . . I didn't kill him . . . it was you!" Max stammered.

"You KILLED my little Kaspar! My baby! My little snookums!" She fell on the box, sobbing and wailing. Strangely, though, as she sobbed and wailed, she was at the same time checking the box was intact—and then trying to get it open. "My POOR BABY! My POOR DARLING . . . my little . . . my little . . . GrraaaGHHHG! What's the MATTER with this thing?" She stopped suddenly and stood up, glaring at Kaspar's tiny hands and his pathetically small pile of ashy remains. "Didn't you think of your POOR OLD MOM when you BUILT this hunk of junk? You SELFISH LITTLE NOSE-MINER! ALWAYS screwing the lids on the jars too tightly as well! Don't think I didn't know what you were up to! Don't think I didn't!"

"Um . . ." said one of the Forest Folk. "Would you like me to try?"

"WHAT TOOK YOU SO LONG? Letting an old, arthritic woman struggle! Shame on you!"

She handed the villager the box. It sprung open at once in his hands.

"You had to slide the catch, not press it. See, like this."

"WHO ASKED YOU Mr. Smartypants? Keep hold of the Apprentice while I deal with this."

The Witch snatched the box off him and strode over to a stack of Storybooks. She opened the one on top and upended the box over its pages. Mud, twigs, and leaves tumbled out—nothing more.

"Wake up my little darlings!" said the Witch, stirring it a little with her finger. "Time for din-dins!"

The villager holding Max edged closer to get a better look, so he saw it, too. Slowly, the pile of leaves shifted a little, then began sinking into the pages, like acid into metal. Something was eating away at the paper. Within a couple of minutes, all the pages were gone, and only an empty wooden cover remained: a Storybook with nothing in it.

"Eugh!" the villager muttered. "What are they? Giant lice?" Hundreds of bugs were skittering around, looking for more. They soon located the Storybooks below and swarmed down.

"*Collembolla*," the Witch announced. "They're detriti-vores. This means, Mr. Walnut Brain, they eat dead leaves. And guess what Storybooks are made of?"

"Stories? No. Books!"

"Dead leaves, you bumpkin! I made a few adjustments, of course. Principally, to their reproductive cycle. Every two minutes, their number doubles. In a few hours, this place will be infested. By the time they're done, there won't be enough paper down here for a postage stamp."

Sure enough, the entire stack of Storybooks was begin-ning to sag and collapse. She picked up a handful of the dirt and blew it toward the shelves like a sprinkling of fairy dust.

"Now, let's go! I don't want to miss Mr. Yule Log going into the Grinder!" She reached forward and tweaked Max's cheek. "And I'm sure you don't, either, Mr. Apprentice! CHOMP CHOMP CHOMP! Haha!"

Outside, the tunnel was bustling with activity. Forest Folk were uncoiling lengths of cable and hammering light fix-tures into the walls.

What are they doing?

Installing lights. I don't know.

Max, I don't understand. How did Courtz know to bring all these things? Like these funny long pieces of string.

Wires.

Wires. How did he know there was a big tunnel down here? How did he know about the Luminorium?

Maybe the Witch told him about it.

No. He told her. When she saw the Light she said, "Just as you described."

He can't have gotten in here. There are too many Kobolds. They would have spotted anyone sneaking in. And nobody knew there was anything under the Cemetery. Not even the Coven. Only the Dragon Hunters knew.

So how did HE know?

They stopped at the door to the Paper Room, but before they went in, the Witch grabbed a villager passing with a box of tools.

"Hey! How's it going up there?"

"We'll be able to start the generators in an hour or so," he reported.

"Don't turn them on until I've left. And what about those rooms? Cleared them out yet?"

"That's not my side of things," the man said. "Look, I've got a schedule to stick to."

"I was up there a minute ago," said another villager. "They finished the Skeletons, but they're still working on the Arboretum."

"What's the delay?"

"These Kobolds are tricky little Devils. And that World One is giving them problems. The one with the heavy fists."

"No, they caught him. He'll be in the Grinder in a minute."

"They did? Well, the Kobolds are at home in the Briarbacks, that's for sure. We could send for some Woodcutters. Clear the trees out."

"NO WOODCUTTERS!"

"Oh, and we got that other door open. The funny one with no keyhole. Had to use sledgehammers. Took some doing."

"He told us not to bother with that."

"We thought the Apprentice might be hiding in there."

"Well, he wasn't. But fair enough. Find anything?"

"An empty bottle."

"That's it?"

"Place was just a cupboard."

"Right," said the Witch. "Let's go, you."

An EMPTY bottle?

Okay! Who cares about that? They're going to throw Boris into the Grinder!

THWACK!

"STOP DAWDLING!"

The Witch dealt him one of her blows and he staggered into the Paper Room.

The room was oddly quiet. With no Kobolds to operate it, the Grinder had fallen silent; a group of Forest Folk were investigating its workings. Boris was standing on the platform with his back to the room, looking down into the open mouth of the Grinder.

We're not too late! He's still here!

But what are you going to do? They're just trying to start the thing up.

Mrs. Jeffers, Ulla, and Mommsen were huddled near the Grinder, as well, circled by Forest Folk with flashlights. Porterholse had his own bodyguard. Evidently, they knew what the Giant was capable of and had him under close surveillance, ready to incinerate him at the very first sign of inflation.

When Courtz saw Max with the Witch, he beckoned them over.

"So you found your way back here at last?" he said. "How does it feel to be home?"

Max peered at him. There was a strange glint of amusement in Courtz's eye. "What do you mean?"

"I recognized you at once, of course," Courtz said. "I did wonder, when I came back here, whether or not the Kobolds would recognize me. But it's been so long. I was a younger man. The beard helps. Do you know, I'm very sure not one of these Kobolds remembers me."

"Why would they?" Max asked slowly.

"Because I remember them. And I remember you. Of course, I knew you by another name in those days." He smiled, and said each word very clearly: "The. One. Who. Cleans. The. Teeth. The. Best."

Then, right then, at exactly the same moment, both Max and Martha understood.

HhEe'Ss Aa DdRrAaGgOoNn HhUuNnTtEeRr!

"You knew who I was all along?" Max whispered. "You knew I was a Kobold?"

Courtz nodded.

"You knew . . . this is where I came from?"

Courtz nodded again. "What matters now is that you have the chance to begin again. You can become my Apprentice, as I promised. Remember what the Dragon Fire taught you. Remember how your dreams betrayed you."

Max's mind was racing. He looked at Boris on the platform. The villagers surrounding his friends. Then back at Courtz.

"I agree with you," he said. "You're right. You were right about everything. I lost everything to my dreams. But I want to talk to Boris. I think I can change his mind."

"Out of the question. It's too late for him."

"You said I have the chance to start again. If that's a rule, it has to apply to everyone and everything. That's how science works."

Courtz pressed his lips together in irritation. "Go," he said shortly. "I'll give you a couple of minutes."

Max quickly climbed the Grinder steps to join Boris on the platform. The Dark Man had both hands on the railing and was looking down into the jaws, which gaped up at him. When Max came near he turned and gave him a faint smile.

"He wants me to go into that machinery. If I don't, he'll incinerate our friends." He frowned, seeming perplexed. "What a violent end!"

Max looked down at the Forest Folk working on the machine.

They were out of earshot, if he whispered. "Listen," he said. "Courtz is a Dragon Hunter."

Boris stared at him. "That's impossible," he said flatly.

"He just admitted it!"

"I don't believe it. It must be a trick."

"It isn't. He knew how the Luminorium works. He explained it right away."

Boris frowned. "Did he? When?"

"When he brought you down there! Didn't you hear?"

"I . . . wasn't really paying attention," said Boris. "I was concentrating on something else."

"And he's brought all this equipment for lighting the place. And the Witch has just let these insect things out to destroy the Storybooks. How did they know the Storybooks were down here? We didn't. We thought it was just a crypt!"

Boris was shaking his head. "There has to be some other explanation."

"There isn't! Courtz knew about the Luminorium before any of us. And he survived all that time in the Woods, on his own—just like a Dragon Hunter could. He tracked down Dragons—just like a Dragon Hunter could. He told me all the Apprentices ran away from home when they were small— and it sounds like he did, too, just like a Dragon Hunter!"

"No," said Boris. "He's a scientist. He was always a scientist."

"Are you sure? Did you know him when he was a young man?"

"No, but—"

"*You* went to the Woods before you became a scientist. *You* went Wild before you became a scientist. Why couldn't he have become an Apprentice, then a Dragon Hunter, then turned to science?"

"Why would he turn to science? What made him change?"

"I think we just found out."

"What?"

"The Forest Folk opened that door. With the Unthinkable Idea. And there was nothing there."

"Nothing?"

"Just an empty bottle."

"Empty?"

"Yes. Boris, what if Courtz opened the door when he was a Dragon Hunter? And now he's got it. The Unthinkable Idea. And his mind turned to stone. And he's doing all this. And the Unthinkable Idea has spread to the others. The Forest Folk. The villagers. They're all in the grip of it. Martha's Mother and Father, too."

Max, you don't need to make up excuses for them.

I'm NOT making up excuses! How could they do that to you? It doesn't make sense. It's like something took them over. It's him. Or IT. The Unthinkable Idea. And Courtz is spreading it around.

The Dark Man was staring at Max, nodding slowly. "Maybe you're right," he muttered. "It fits together."

"We have to stop him!"

"I know," Boris said. "I know we do." He glanced furtively toward Courtz. "If only we had . . . just a little more time."

But there was no more time.

The Forest Folk had fixed the Grinder. They began to operate the levers. A shudder went through the machine, and below them the jaws began to move, slowly at first, then faster.

SLAM!

SLAM!

SLAM!

"BORIS!" shouted Courtz. "IT'S TIME!"

"What were you dreaming about last night?" Boris asked quickly. "I meant to ask you."

"What?" Max thought he hadn't heard him properly above the noise. "What did I dream about?"

"I was there. Beside you. You kept calling out in your sleep. *I don't want to! I don't want to!*"

Max had completely forgotten the dream. But why was the Dark Man bothering about that now?

"There was a Dragon," he explained hastily. "I had to crawl into its mouth. But it was strange, it kept saying I had to do it again. Like it had happened before."

"It had happened before?" Boris frowned. He seemed mesmerized by the flashing teeth.

"YOU HAVE UNTIL THE COUNT OF THREE!"

"I don't know! It was just a dream."

"ONE!"

The Forest Folk lifted their flashlights. Max screamed down above the noise.

"Don't HURT THEM! He's GOING TO JOIN US!"

"TWO!"

"Max!" Boris said behind him. "Max, look at me!"

Max spun around. "Just pretend! Just pretend you agree with him!" And even as he said it, he knew it was hopeless, that this was a story Boris could never tell.

"THREE!"

"Max," the Dark Man said, in a voice that he would never forget. "Listen to your dreams."

And then he leaned backward and went over the railing, into the Grinder, into the ocean—where sharks were circling, arguing about who was to get what.

SLAM, CHOMP, PLOP

Listen to your dreams . . .

Max stared at the space where the Dark Man had been, that was now and would forever be empty.

How could something that had always been there, so solid and sure, *suddenly not be there?*

Everything just stopped.

He knew the Grinder was still going because he could feel the shake of its SLAM SLAM SLAM. But still, everything stopped. He couldn't hear it. He couldn't hear Martha, either. All he could hear was the Dark Man's final words, repeating themselves over and over in his mind.

Listen to your dreams . . .

When was the last time someone had told him to do that?

It was all so strange . . .

Courtz and the Dragon.

Forbes and the Grinder.

His Forever Parents and the sharks.

And now this.

Boris and the Leafgobble 5000.

Listen to your dreams . . .

So he did.

"Well, kid, this is it," the Dragon's head had said. "You got to start over."

"Okay."

"Are you ready?"

"Yes."

"You're not afraid?"

"I did it once already."

Done what once already?

Gone into the Dragon?

When?

He looked down through the platform at the Grinder's flashing teeth.

And then he noticed. The platform. It was made of a metal grill.

A grill of tiny hexagons.

Hexagons . . .

And then he knew. He understood it all.

Patterns. Everywhere.

The mural around the Grinder.

Just like the mural in his bedroom.

The Wolf that Boris turned into when he got gotten.

Just like the Wolf in the mural.

The Balloon in his dreams.

The Balloons in the Woods.

Forbes at his Grinder.

Max at his Grinder.

And teeth!

Teeth everywhere!

Biting. Chewing. Chomping. Hands gone. Bodies gone. People gone. Everything chewed up in bits and swallowed. Tangled and together and around and around and around.

All the bits of him from the Woods—sent into the World.

That's how I Appeared . . .

Yes! It must be!

I fell into the Grinder . . .

And the Kobolds made you into a Storybook.

And I went into the Light.

And the Light put you in the World.

Along with all the little bits of me . . . All the bits of my story . . .

And the Woods and the World had been pulled together.

Because that was a part of him, too: as a Kobold he'd wished the Woods was like the World. As Max he'd wished the World was like the Woods.

But not anymore. He knew now they needed to be separate.

I need to go in again . . . That's how to reverse the Appearance. It's the only way to make things right!

You can't! You need to stop Courtz first! Otherwise, who'd make the Storybook?

He stopped with his hand on the railing.

She was right.

He turned.

Mrs. Jeffers, Porterholse, Ulla, and Mommsen were still surrounded by Forest Folk. They gazed up at him, horror-struck by the Dark Man's disappearance into the Grinder.

"Deal with them!" Courtz said, pointing at Mrs. Jeffers and the others. "They're dreamers, too. All of them."

"You LIED!" Max howled.

He raced down the steps, but was immediately caught and held by one of the villagers. Kicking and screaming, he watched as the Forest Folk lifted their flashlights.

Mrs. Jeffers.

Mommsen.

Ulla.

Porterholse.

They all squeezed their eyes shut. And then—

BOOM!

On the other side of the room.

The door burst open. Three Forest Folk were flung backward.

The Dark Man was in the doorway. Eyes blazing. A Storybook in each hand.

HE'S ALIVE!

He . . . it's the Wildness . . . oh my God I'm going to GET HIM!

A villager leapt at him. The Dark Man clubbed him to the ground with a Storybook. Behind him came three more Dark Men, holding branches ripped from Briarback trees. Outside, the tunnel was a chaos of bodies locked in combat, flying objects, rocks, stones, and most of all, leaping Kobolds.

The Forest Folk raced for the door, flashlights blazing.

Faster than fast, the Borises with branches whirled through them, unharmed. Knocked the flashlights out of their hands. The Boris with Books roared into the corridor.

"NOW!!"

And then Kobolds were pouring into the Paper Room. Gnawing. Tearing. Biting.

SNAPSNAPSNAPSNAPSNAP

The Forest Folk fell back under the onslaught—but only for a moment. The villagers operating the Grinder raced into the fray, snatching up the fallen flashlights. The first ranks of Kobolds began to burn. More followed after, but had to come through the door, and it was easy for the Forest Folk to pick them off.

One Dark Man went down, buried under three Forest Folk. Another was pinned against a wall.

More flashlights were retrieved.

The Forest Folk marched toward the door to secure it. The Dark Men lay snarling on the floor. The last few Kobolds hopped around, leaping between the lancing beams of New Light.

"GET THEM!" the Witch screamed, hopping from foot to foot. "GET THE LITTLE MONSTERS!"

But in all this chaos, in the sudden ferocity of the attack, in their surprise and in their shock, and even in their victory, the Forest Folk had forgotten the most important thing, forgotten the most important thing by far: To Keep An Eye On The Wind Giant.

The attack had only had that purpose. And now, he had no flashlights on him.

His buttons popped.

His trousers burst.

His shoes exploded.

"FOR THE WOODS!" Porterholse boomed. "FOR THE WOOOOOOO

OOO OSH!"

Wind slammed across the chamber, knocking everyone off their feet. The villager holding Max toppled backward. The wooden vats near the Grinder were tossed over, and the air swirled with a blinding blizzard of Briarback leaves. Flashlights went slamming into the walls, breaking apart in showers of glass.

Max kicked himself free and rushed to Mrs. Jeffers and the others, forcing his way through the gale. She was helping Mommsen to his feet. Ulla Andromeda was crouched low, her eyes flashing.

"Courtz?" she yelled as Max ran up. "Where is he? He mustn't get away!"

Through the storm and the confusion of bodies, he saw the scientist staggering toward the door. But before any of them could give chase, the Wasp Witch appeared.

"Well, well," she snarled. "The Chief Wizard and the High Witch. You miserable bureaucrats!"

She hefted her flashlight and slid her thumb across the button.

click

The light flickered and died.

She scowled and shook the flashlight.

clickclickclickclick

"What's the good of a light that runs on batteries?" Mommsen muttered. "Mrs. Jeffers? Would you be so kind?"

"Certainly, Theo."

Old Light scythed through the air.

"Missed!" growled the Witch. "You old has-been!"

Theodore Mommsen stepped forward. "PLOP!" he said, jabbing the Witch in the face with his cane.

Her head toppled backward and bounced across the floor.

The rest of the Witch dropped the flashlight, crouched, and began feeling around for her stray head. Ulla Andromeda got to it first, trapping it underfoot.

"You second-rate hacks!" the Witch's head snarled up. "You call yourselves a Coven? I'VE MADE MORE PATENTS THAN THE LOT OF YOU PUT TOGE—"

click

POOF!

"Works for me," Ulla muttered. Shrugging, she tossed the flashlight aside.

"You have the knack for this World gadgetry," Mommsen said. "Now, where's that Tinker got to? Lower the Wind, Porterholse!" The Wind Giant sagged back against the wall, and the storm subsided. Courtz, though, was nowhere to be seen. Kobolds were swarming into the room by the dozen. The Forest Folk, badly outnumbered and stripped of their flashlights, were backing against the wall.

THERE HE IS!

He was being dragged back into the Paper Room. One of the Dark Men had him in his grip. His face twisted with fury, he hauled Courtz across the floor with one hand.

What's he going to do?

He's going to throw him in the Grinder!

No . . . no, he won't do that.

But the Dark Man was already dragging Courtz up the steps to the platform.

You sure?

Max ran after him.

"NO!" he shouted. "Boris! Don't!"

The Dark Man had his hands around Courtz's throat and was slowly forcing him backward over the railing.

Max hauled on his arm. "Listen to me! Boris! It's not him that needs to go in! It's me! It's me!"

The Dark Man stood there, panting, his shoulders trembling. Then he pulled Courtz back and threw him onto the platform.

"I know you do," he said. "I know." He nodded wearily. "I guess . . . it's your turn . . . to follow me."

5

An Industrial Accident

Max stood on the platform of the Grinder and looked down at his friends.

It was time to say goodbye.

First came Ulla and Mommsen.

"Once you go, you will never be able to return," the Chief Wizard said solemnly. "If what you say is true, the Woods and the World will be pushed far apart. Farther apart than they have ever been, perhaps."

"I know," Max said. "But . . . it's the only way to stop the Vanishings."

"On that we're all agreed," Ulla said, nodding. She leaned forward and kissed Max lightly on the cheek. "You would have made a wonderful Dragon Hunter!" she whispered.

Mommsen winked at Max, shook his hand, and followed her down the steps.

Porterholse came after.

The Wind Giant was strangely subdued.

"Do you remember when you would sit on the hill in Newton Fields and look at the trees swaying in the Wind?" he asked quietly, his moist eyes gazing fondly at Max. "Do you remember?"

Max nodded. "That was you, wasn't it?"

Porterholse nodded back. "It will always be me!"

With that, the Wind Giant burst into tears, and was led away, before he caused an incident.

Then came Mrs. Jeffers. She was holding one of Porterholse's handkerchiefs.

"Just in case you cry," she said, handing it to him. "I'm not going to. Well, I might. Later on, when nobody can see."

"I'm not going to remember you, am I?" Max asked. "I'm not going to remember any of this."

"No," she said. "No, dear boy. You won't remember a thing. Oh dear!"

"What's wrong?"

She smiled at him, her eyes glittering. "It's later on already!" Shuffling forward, her arms out, she took him in a hug stronger than any he'd ever known. "When you light a candle, dear boy, then you'll remember us!" she whispered hoarsely. "At least, the general idea of us. That's what Old Light is good at!"

Squeezing him one last time, she, too, went down the steps.

And then it was the Dark Man, and they simply looked at each other.

"I'm not sure who I'll be, when you meet me," Boris said. "But you'll meet me. I've gone ahead, after all. Or one of me has. They'll put us in the same Storybook—so we'll be together in the World."

"I know," Max said. "But what about you? Are you going to be okay in the Woods? They said you won't be able to get back to the World."

Boris smiled. "I'll tell you something strange," he said after a moment. "When I was hiding from the Forest Folk in the Arboretum, just before I brought the Wildness, I decided something important."

"What?"

"I decided this would be the last time. That I didn't want to see them anymore."

"The Accursed Questions?"

"Yes. I made a decision." He smiled again, and shook his head in amazement at himself. "I never knew I could just decide."

"So what are you going to do now?"

"Now?" Boris breathed out, his eyes wide. "Now, I want to sleep, and enjoy life, the way that other people sleep and enjoy life. It's time for me to be happy." He nodded thoughtfully. "The Woods are a good place to grow a garden. Maybe I will do that. Grow potatoes and cherry trees. Every year—have a Yule Log!" He stopped, struggling a little. "Max, goodbye!"

For a while, Max disappeared inside the hug. Then the Dark Man stepped back. Their eyes filled with tears, and each one that trickled down their cheeks said everything they had left to say. And a lot was said—maybe everything.

So Boris turned and went.

And then it was just him, and Martha, and the Grinder.

Well, this is it.

Yes, Max. Try to think of it as a portal to another World . . .

He curled his fingers around the metal bar and climbed over so he was hanging from the other side. Below them, the Kobolds set the Grinder in motion.

Now all you have to do is let go. Easy!

SLAM

SLAM

SLAM

He was ready.

The Luminorium was being repaired, the infested Storybooks removed and burned.

Courtz was in the custody of the Coven, and the Forest Folk had surrendered.

Now a stack of leaves was ready to go into the Grinder. It was time to go home.

A ride to the World through the Light on a Book.

But still . . . he had to jump. And there was one thing he needed to be sure of first.

When you said you'd be mine forever, did you mean it?

Yes . . . my Knight . . . yes, I did.

Do you promise? I don't want to go on my own.

I'm here. Don't be scared!

Will you be there, though?

I think I will. I think it's whatever you want, Max. However you want the World to be, that's how it will be. That's how it must work.

I want it all to begin again . . . but be better.

Then that's how it will be.

He opened his eyes.

SLAM

SLAM

SLAM

Don't start imagining it! You'll never do it if you start imagining!

But how could he not imagine? What would it be like to go into those smashing jaws? Would it be painful? Maybe only for a second—but what a second!

You did it before. You can do it again!

Maybe it was an accident before. Maybe I just . . . fell in somehow.

He felt the eyes of those watching. They would not blame him if he did not jump. They would understand. Maybe they would even be glad.

Max—remember what the Soul Searcher saw?

Yes. I remember. Why?

He said you would do something incredibly brave that would change the World forever. It wasn't about facing the Dragon. It was about this. It was about going into the Grinder.

Yes. But I can't. I just can't!

He looked away from the Grinder. He lifted his head and saw the mural—just as he'd always done as he cleaned the Grinder's teeth.

And there they were.

High up in the far corner of the painting, a Hot-Air Balloon was drifting above the World, floating through the blue. His Forever Parents were in the basket, faces smiling, hands raised in a wave, waving at him!

He reached for them one last time, stretching out his fingertips.

Leaned an inch too far.

Lost his balance.

Put out a hand to steady himself.

SNAP

His hand was gone—Martha with it.

He jumped after her.

EPILOGUE

There was a time, not so long ago, when a mysterious phenomenon swept the world, baffling scientists and defying explanation.

It had nothing to do with gravity or electricity.

It altered no weather patterns, sea levels, or average temperatures.

The migration of beasts across the globe did not change, and plants continued to grow, bloom, and die in their proper seasons.

Even the biochemical reactions that sustain life went on with unceasing vigor, as they had for millions of years, propelling organisms down myriad paths of development, just as the continents drifted apart, moved by the massive forces generated in the bowels of the earth.

Almost the entirety of creation was ignored by the new phenomenon, which concerned itself with one thing alone.

Us.

The phenomenon took place in every country. It was compared to a plague that knew no boundaries, or a fire that ravaged a forest. But scientists were able to cure the plague, and the secret of putting out fires had been discovered long ago.

They were powerless to stop the Vanishings.

It is strange, then, that no record of the Vanishings exists in history books, or in the minds of the people they once threatened.

Some changes made to the World are far-reaching and comprehensive in their scope.

Some Patents are only minor adjustments, nothing more than tweaks to the workings of the universe.

And others mean building it all again from the ground up.

Worlds remade. Histories expunged. Stories rubbed out and written again.

The Vanishings never happened.

The Vanishings Vanished.

There was also a time, not so long ago, when travel from the World to the Woods was free and easy, when all it took to take you was a candle, a tree, and a little bit of night.

That time, too, has gone.

But life goes on in the Woods, just as it does in the World. Perhaps there is yet traffic between them, traffic of a kind; the passage of ideas and impressions, glimpses of ghosts; stories picked up from goodness knows where by writers hunched over desks, pen in hand.

Pen in mouth.

Pen in hand . . .

And life goes on!

Under hearts, under hands, lives grow and swell in the ancient way. Some lives are whole and move from beginning to end on a straight Path. Others are dealt a blow from which there is no recovery. They can only stagger around in the trees, becoming Wild. Seeing what only the Wild can see. Hearing what only the Wild can hear.

And so it was, and is, for us all.

Even Max.

Every year at Christmas, Forbes tells the story of how he was found in the back of a garbage truck, and if he hadn't been there, if Forbes hadn't been there on the early shift to hear the baby's crying and snatch him from the crushing jaws—who knows what would have happened! A baby thrown in a trash can! Who'd have thought of it? Such a precious thing to throw away!

And there is nothing more precious, Forbes would say, raising his glass.

And Alice would smile, her eyes shining, and this Forbes, this big, blustering Hero of Life, who had hooked the last of his dreams from the Grinder—he would rock with laughter, and cut the turkey, and pass the plates.

And the boy went on, half in this world, half in another— making friends, curious to meet people, staring at every face in the street, as if looking for someone in particular, not finding them but enjoying the search all the same. The world he lived in was without that person, but a world with that person was waiting somewhere—if he could only find it, that other world, how good it would be! He had to wait—oh, he had to wait!—for that other world to begin.

But it never did.

And he began to wonder if it ever would.

Then one day, a day when he was older, when he was a student of Who Knows What with a head full of Goodness Knows and a pocketful of Nothing At All, when he was hurrying to Peshkov's Bookshop before it closed, he glanced up at the clock of King's Cross, and receiving a speck in the eye for his trouble—a crumb of lichen brought from afar by a mischievous Wind, a reminder sent by distant friends—he moved into a doorway, blinking away the tears.

Just as she stepped out.